TALES OF MA̲̲̲̲̲̲̲̲̲̲̲̲̲̲̲̲ AND HIS VALIANT LIEUTENANTS

Tales of Magistrate Bao and His Valiant Lieutenants

Selections from *Sanxia wuyi*

Susan Blader

The Chinese University Press

ISBN 962–201–775–4

THE CHINESE UNIVERSITY PRESS
The Chinese University of Hong Kong
SHATIN, N. T., HONG KONG
Fax: +852 2603 6692
+852 2603 7355
E-mail: cup@cuhk.edu.hk
Web-site: http://www.cuhk.edu.hk/cupress/w1.htm

Printed in Hong Kong

For Dorothy and Rubin Blader
and
All my heroes:
Teachers, Students, and Friends

ṽ

Contents

Preface

These translations of the most exciting crime and courtroom episodes from *Sanxia wuyi* 三俠五義 have become far more a part of my life than I could ever have expected. In 1971 when I first happened upon this novel in a bookstore in downtown Taipei, I had little reason to suspect that I would be spending so significant an amount of time in the company of the heroes and gallants who people the narrative, or that it would lead me eventually to the fascinating world of storytelling and the performing arts. Perhaps I should have known that, as with other fictional characters who become part of our lives, Magistrate Bao and his helpers would become inextricably tied to mine. No matter how often I read *Sanxia wuyi*, I find myself, in every instance, moved to laughter and tears as though it were the first time. The "iron-faced and impartial" Magistrate Bao, whose smile is "rarer than clear waters in the Yellow River," who has the good sense to heed his wife's sage advice, who does virtually nothing, but around whom all revolves; the adorable, brave, and decidedly alcoholic Little Hero, Ai Hu; Jiang Ping, the "swimmer" gallant whose selfless compassion for others and shrewd intelligence quietly save many a day; and the dashing, arrogant, loveable, infuriating, and tragic Bai Yutang — all are unforgettably depicted in this narrative of murder, mystery, and mayhem.

Even before I understood what it meant to say that *Sanxia wuyi* was derived from the oral tradition, it was clear that the vivid language, the colourful characters, the poignant human relationships, and the humourous narrative style that characterized the novel made it a compelling and markedly distinct piece of literature in the larger Chinese context. Once I began to delve into its origins in the world of oral, performed storytelling, I would never look at "literature" in the same way again. The new directions in which *Sanxia wuyi* has led me have changed both my research and my life.

I owe one great debt to the publishers of *Sanxia wuyi* for opening up to me an enormously rich and abundant treasure house of art works for which nothing in my experience up to that moment had prepared me. My other great debt, and I sincerely hope it will become yours, too, as readers of what follows, is to The Chinese University Press of Hong Kong for waiting so patiently for me to make this delightful Chinese narrative accessible to an English-educated audience.

❦

Acknowledgements

A project that has spanned so many years has incurred debts to more people than I can remember here. The following people can never be repaid for help they gave along the way: Roger Yue, who first put Chinese into my head in his inimitably expert fashion; the late Adele Rickett, Derk Bodde, and W. Allyn Rickett, who have been mentors and dear friends since I began my Chinese studies; Barbara Ruch, who introduced me to the world of oral literature and my current research; R. L. Green, my ELC; Shelby Grantham, my American editor without whose felicitous touch my translation would have remained unbearably literal; Gail Vernazza, who typed this manuscript, with unruffled patience and precision, twice; John Deeney, who first introduced this project to The Chinese University Press; Mr. T. L. Tsim, former director of The Chinese University Press, who encouraged me gracefully from the early stages; Tse Wai-keung, who edited the final manuscript with care and speed; Ivy Siu, who helped proofreading and J. R. Yao, who kept me going happily for years.

For their friendship and support at important junctures, I wish to thank Kate Stevens, Galia Speshnev Bodde, Pamela Crossley, David Keenan, Peter Rushton, Zou Shining, Marysa Navarro, Judy Goldberg, Leo Lee, Ehud Benor, Wang Jingshou, Xiang Jingjie, Cai Yuanli, Bao Chengjie, Nancy Davies, Otmar Foelsche, Susan Bibeau, Beverly Boucher, Rosalyn Gershell, Judith Ginsberg, Galia Bodde, and Edward and Antoinette Shapiro. My family, Jay, Linda,

Brian, and Jonathan Blader, have provided the continuity of love and loyalty that all people should enjoy. From Jin Shengbo and Sun Shujun I learned how to live in stories.

My work was funded throughout by grants from Dartmouth College. The National Academy of Sciences' Committee on Scholarly Communication with China made possible my first two stays in China, which immeasurably enriched my understanding of *Sanxia wuyi*.

❦

Introduction

The novel *Sanxia wuyi* 三俠五義 (Three Heroes and Five Gallants[1]) is a remarkably successful synthesis of three diverse genres of fiction: the historical narrative; the detective story; chivalric literature. In addition, it derives from the extraordinarily rich oral tradition of China, in which it is still being performed before live audiences today. These factors are no doubt responsible for its continuing popularity as written fiction as well as television and radio drama.

The excerpts from *Sanxia wuyi* that follow are, to my mind, translations of the best and most representative episodes in the lengthy narrative. They were selected precisely because they demonstrate the happy synthesis of the three fictional genres that Shi Yukun 石玉崑, the storyteller to whom the narrative is attributed, performed for the delight of his audiences. We can never know how much of the credit for combining the three genres goes to Shi, himself, since the issue of authorship is not recognized in the oral tradition. We can only assume, with reliability, that it was because Shi's version was so compellingly performed that it was preserved in writing for posterity.

Readers less interested in the textual evolution of the novel can go directly to the story and leave the introduction for later

---

[1] For the title, I have used Lu Xun's translation, *Three Heroes and Five Gallants*. See his *A Short History of Chinese Fiction* (Beijing: Foreign Languages Press, 1964), pp. 359–71. All other translations that follow in this introduction are my own, unless otherwise noted.

perusal. Issues of historical background, provenance in the oral tradition, attribution to the storyteller Shi Yukun, and the definition, in cultural context, of *xia* and *yi* that are primarily of concern to the specialist may be found in this Introduction.

Historical and Cultural Background of the Narrative

Sanxia wuyi is a masterfully told story of Magistrate Bao 包拯 (999–1072) and the heroes and gallants who come to his aid in protecting the imperial government from a rebellious and treacherous prince. Any attempt to understand the novel must take into account both the historical period in which it came into being as well as the period in which it is set. The *Longtu gongan* 龍圖公案 (The Criminal Cases of the Lord of the Imperial Sketch, i.e., Magistrate Bao) was created as an oral narrative and flourished, we can say with certainty, no later than the 1870s. Revised twice to become *Three Heroes*, this narrative was published in 1879,[2] a mere fifteen years after the end of the worst internal conflict China has ever experienced — the Taiping Rebellion of 1851–1864.[3] It is no coincidence that a narrative extolling the virtues of an incorruptible magistrate, serving the empire with fearless impartiality and aided by heroes, gallants, and braves committed to quelling an incipient rebellion should have been performed by storytellers and published at this time.

Chinese history of the end of the second half of the twentieth century is filled with the political chaos of the disintegrating Qing empire (1644–1911) that collapsed finally in 1911. During the lifetime of Shi Yukun (*c.* 1810–1871), China was ravaged by the Opium War (1839–1844) and the Taiping Rebellion, "the world's most destructive civil war and the bloodiest armed conflict

---

[2] For more details on the editions, see "Textual History," pp. xvi–xxiv.

[3] Pamela Crossley, *Orphan Warriors* (Princeton: Princeton University Press, 1990), p. 125.

before the twentieth century" (thirty million dead).[4] At the time, there were other major rebellions in the Northwest (Nian rebels of Anhui) and Moslem uprisings in Yunnan.[5] In 1870, tensions between foreigners, mostly French, and Chinese over religious activities finally resulted in the Tianjin Massacre, in which two French officials, seven foreign residents, and a number of Catholic fathers and sisters, not to mention Chinese converts, were killed.[6] While reformers continuously tried to reestablish a strong government, foreigners relentlessly attempted to gain footholds in all areas of Chinese life, from education to economics. The conflict between foreigners and Chinese erupted once again in 1898 in the Boxer Rebellion, which, by 1900, most seriously affected the Manchu garrisons in Beijing, adding to their poverty and misery.[7] It would be hard to imagine a time of greater chaos and destruction than the period in which Shi Yukun lived and told his romantic and arguably naive stories of heroes and gallants who joined up with Magistrate Bao to quell an incipient rebellion during a dynasty eight centuries earlier. Furthermore, the evidence that *Fengbo Pavilion* 風波亭 , the narrative about Yue Fei 岳飛 (1103–1141), one of the best-known loyalists to an imperial government in Chinese history, was also one of Shi Yukun's performed narratives, further strengthens the case for Shi's support of order in a time of great chaos.

Shi Yukun's tale was narrated in a style that modified the earlier *zidi shu* 子弟書 genre created and sung by Manchu bannermen (see pages xxiv–xxv of Introduction). Whether or not Shi, himself, was a Manchu, we still have no conclusive

---

[4] Ibid., p. 125.

[5] Robert Scalapino and George T. Yu, *Modern Chinese and Its Revolutionary Process, Recurrent Challenges to the Traditional Order*, 1850–1920 (Berkeley: University of California Press, 1985), p. 42.

[6] Ibid., p. 47.

[7] Crossley, Ibid., pp. 174–76.

evidence.[8] We can, however, understand Shi's narrative in an
historical context without such evidence. It would be quite natural for a Manchu to tell stories of allegiance and service to a
previous imperial government of Han China at a time when the
Qing empire of the Manchus was being attacked from all sides. It
is, in fact, a literary tradition in China to point to one thing while
alluding to another, done in most cases to avoid the wrath of the
person or parties at whom one is really pointing the literary
finger. In other words, if Shi were actually a Manchu, he could
easily have popularized this narrative for its moral of loyalty and
devotion to the imperial government, which in this case was
under Manchu control. It would not be much different from the
Qing court's promotion of "the cult of Yue Fei," the Song loyalist
depicted in *Fengbo Pavilion*. Yue Fei was executed by the Southern Song court for refusing to go along with the ceding of North
China to the Jurchens, ancestors of the Manchus, because "it had
decided to emphasize the absolute value of loyalty over the
relative value of cultural enmity."[9] If Shi were not Manchu, then
he could be understood to be promoting a return to Han Chinese
control, as in the days of the glorious Song. However, since it
was precisely the introduction of the incipient rebellion into the
Magistrate Bao narrative that may be attributed to Shi and since
such a rebellion could be seen to parallel the rebellions against
Manchu rule occurring during Shi's lifetime, there is every reason
to think that Shi was, in fact, anxious to have order restored
under Manchu rule.

Textual History of *Sanxia wuyi*

The late nineteenth-century novel *Sanxia wuyi* 三俠五義 (here-
after referred to as *Three Heroes*) is a one-hundred and twenty

---

[8] See pp. xxiv–xxvii for more information on Shi Yukun.
[9] Crossley, ibid.

chapter, semi-historical narrative of adventure, crime-detection, and courtroom drama that belongs to the episodic novel genre of traditional Chinese fiction. The historical component of the narrative centres on the famed Song dynasty (960–1278) magistrate, Bao Zheng 包拯, more commonly known as Judge or Magistrate Bao (Bao Gong 包公), who, over the centuries, moved in and out of the world of myth, never departing, however, from his characterization as the quintessential *qingguan* 清官, incorruptible government official.[10] The non-historical component, which represents the creative genius of the storyteller, revolves around a group of heroes and gallants, and, eventually, a new *qingguan*, who is introduced into the narrative in chapter thirty-two and who replaces Magistrate Bao as the functioning *qingguan* by chapter eighty-four.

In 1879 the first published version of this narrative appeared under the title *Zhonglie xiayi zhuan* 忠烈俠義傳 (A Tale of Loyal Heroes and Gallants). Soon thereafter the title was changed to *Sanxia wuyi*. All we know about the person who made these changes is his Taoist priesthood name, "Wenzhu zhuren" 問竹主人 (Master Bamboo Questioner), and this we know from his preface to the narrative in which he claims most of the credit for the work. This preface, for which I provide a translation in the appendix, is considered by some scholars to be an indication that "Wenzhu zhuren" is, in fact, Shi Yukun, himself, who, we have ample evidence, was literate.[11]

The 1879 version, however, is twice removed from what we assume to be an early, perhaps even one of the first extant

---

[10] Y. M. Ma, "The Pao-kung Tradition in Chinese Popular Literature" (Ph.D. Diss., Yale University, 1971), p. 244.

[11] Li Jiarui 李家瑞, "Cong Shi Yukun de *Long tu gongan* shuo dao *Sanxia wuyi* 從石玉崑的龍圖公案說到三俠五義 " (From Shi Yukun's *Longtu gongan* to *Sanxia wuyi*), *Wenxue jikan* (April, 1934), pp. 394–95.

manuscript versions of the narrative, entitled *Longtu gongan*.[12]
One of these early manuscripts exists in the Fu Sinian 傅斯年
Rare Book Library in an incomplete fifty-volume (*ce* 冊 : thin,
hand-written, traditional Chinese volumes of approximately thirty
pages sewn together) version and appears to be a transcription
of an oral performance. There are slips of paper with the words
Shipai shu 石派書 (Shi [Yukun] School of Storytelling) inserted
into many of the volumes, which indicates that this version of the
narrative was artistically, but not necessarily linearly, derived
from Shi Yukun. The manuscript is a *changben* 唱本 (song-
book), which consists of alternating sung and spoken sections
and can be compared to present-day opera libretti. It is extremely long, but, in terms of its content, i.e., here, character
count,[13] represents only one-sixth of the first published 1879
version.

----

[12] Bao was given the name "*Longtu* 龍圖 " because his was the
face of the man sketched by Emperor Renzong 仁宗 after a dream in
Chapter 6. By using this "Imperial Sketch," Minister Wang was able
to locate Bao, who had gone into retirement after mishandling a
case, and bring him back to serve the emperor. This *Longtu gongan*
is not to be confused with the late sixteenth-century Ming dynasty
(1368–1644) collection of short stories, having the same title, revolv-
ing around Magistrate Bao. See "The Textual Tradition of Ming
Kung-an Fiction," by Y. W. Ma, *Harvard Journal of Asiatic Studies*,
35 (1975), pp. 190–220.
[13] Susan Blader, "A Critical Study of *San-hsia wu-yi* and (its)
Relationship to the *Lung-t'u kung-an* Song-Book" (Ph.D. Diss., University of Pennsylvania, 1977), p. 154. There is another song-book
manuscript with the same title and generally the same content housed
in the Beijing Imperial Library, and some fragments of yet another
with the same title possessed by the late Chinese scholar Wu Xiaoling
吳曉玲. I have not studied either of these in depth.

Li Jiarui 李家瑞, who did pioneering work in the field of folklore scholarship, provides us with important information on the probable history of the song-book:[14]

> The *Ping Kun lun* 評崑論 says that Shi Yukun used to sing "The Courtroom Cases of Magistrate Bao 包公案 (i.e., The Courtroom Cases of the Lord of the Imperial Sketch 龍圖公案) in a bazaar. Therefore, Shi Yukun's *Courtroom Cases of Magistrate Bao* must be a song-book. In the preface to the *Catalog of Song-Books* copied and sold by the Leshan Company (Leshan tang 樂山堂) it says: "This publishing house copies and sells . . . the new book by the Shi School, with the sung parts, which were obtained from a famous person who had put it together. . . . This publishing house has, for the past several years, been making detailed inquiries, and has acquired several drafts which, fortunately, concur with the Shi manuscript.
>
>   The last category in the catalog of rhymed and sung stories is the *Longtu gongan*. Below is the commentary which says: "It is copied and sold by sections (episodes), and there is a separate catalog. Those who want one may order it to be copied for them." This catalog is in sections and is no longer available. However, in the Shi Storyteller's Catalog put out by the Baiben Company (百本堂), there is also a sixteen-part section index of the *Cases* manuscript, beginning with "Jiu zhu 救主" (Saving the Master) and ending with "Qing shou 慶壽" (Birthday Celebrations). Luckily we also obtained the fifty-volume cases' manuscript copied and sold by the Baiben Company. Comparing it with the section index, the index shows thirty-four more volumes (than the above sixteen-part one), but it is, nonetheless, complete. We also obtained a copy of "Qi shi 啟事" (The Announcement), which Baiben Company requested from among the Shi Storytelling Manuscripts. We know from comparing it with the catalog that the additional volumes it has were added later, and that Shi Yukun's "Longtu gongan" is not complete.

---

[14] Li Jiarui (see Note 11).

We learn several important facts from Li Jiarui's remarks: publishing houses that were able to obtain manuscript copies of performed oral narratives, which they then recopied and sold (to whom we do not know precisely), most likely, for reading purposes; the so-called "new book (or story) by the Shi School," which the publishing house obtained, contained the sung sections and was gotten from a "famous person who had put it together"; when the house later made inquiries and collected other drafts, they concurred with the "Shi manuscript." This tells us that there was a single version that the publishing house considered "authentic," as the result of having acquired it from a famous person and it was identical to other manuscript copies then in circulation; finally, one of the copies obtained by the publishing house was a fifty-volume version of Cases, which coincided by sections with the version indexed in the Shi Storyteller's Catalog.

However, there is one piece of evidence which casts doubt on the possibility that the song-book housed in Taiwan at Academia Sinica is a transcription of a performance by Shi Yukun himself. This is the "Limao huan Taizi 狸貓換太子" (A [Skinned] Wild Cat Is Exchanged for the Heir-apparent), the story of the Song emperor Renzong 仁宗, the first episode in the song-book, which is interwoven within the first thirty-eight volumes. There are five instances in which the storyteller, in the storyteller's persona, invokes the name of Shi Yukun. For example, after a long preface on the importance of "timeliness," i.e., waiting for the right time to act, the storyteller says:[15]

---

[15] All references to the handwritten manuscript *Baogong an* 包公案 (The Courtroom Cases of Magistrate Bao) housed in the Fu Sinian 傅斯年 Rare Book Library of Academia Sinica (Zhongyang yanjiu yuan 中央研究院) are by volume and page number as I marked them after a close reading and rearrangement of the episodes according to the order of their occurrence in later versions.

. . . The word "timeliness" is really quite formidable. Let's just take Third Master Shi Yukun as an example. No matter what, I cannot outdo him in storytelling. At present, he no longer makes appearances. But, when he would go to that storytelling hall, he would tell three chapters of a story in one day and collect many tens of strings of cash [one thousand cash to the string, ten cash to the ounce]. Now today his name resounds in the nine cities and there is no one who has not heard of him. I, myself, collect only one or two strings of cash a day for my storytelling, and what can they buy these days? This, too, is a result of "timeliness." (Volume 32, pp. 25–26)

Another example of the use of Shi Yukun's name occurs when Bao Xing 包興, Magistrate Bao's faithful, lifetime servant/companion, is urged by the palace lackeys to tell of his master's most recent, great success in Chenzhou 陳州. This occurs while Bao Xing is waiting for Empress Dowager Li (Li Taihou 李太后), who is disguised as Magistrate Bao's mother:

In lofty words, exaggerated,
Bao Xing told of the Chenzhou affair.
Every detail
He spoke for the ears of the palace people.
First he told
Of the "Nine-Heads' Murder Case (*Jiu tou an* 九頭案)" in Three
    Star Village.
In this one case
Was hidden a wealth of injustices.
When the people had listened up to this point
They called out "Marvellous" without stop.
From outside
Entered many other palace attendants,
Laughing all together:
"We, too, want to hear about these strange events."
So speaking,
Everyone was there to press him,
Pressing to hear
Bao Xing tell how the spirit blew out the lamp.

This Bao Xing
Got happier and happier as the listeners increased.
Truth be told it was
More clamorous than ever was the hall of Shi Yukun.
(Volume 32, pp. 31–32)

These and other instances of the invocation of Shi's name indicate that the episode involving the discovery of the exiled Empress Dowager Li, the real mother of Emperor Renzong, was most likely told by someone other than Shi himself (unless this kind of self-referencing was a game played by storytellers). Furthermore, these invocations of Shi occur only in this particular episode and in no other, which leads us to wonder whether the fifty-volume transcribed song-book had multiple storyteller/ "authors."

At some point after the appearance of the song-book versions, the first prose version of *Longtu gongan* appeared under the title *Longtu erlu* 龍圖耳錄 (Aural Record of the Lord of the Imperial Sketch). Although we cannot assume that any one of these song-book manuscripts led directly to the *Longtu erlu*, we do know that this forty-volume prose narrative is considered to be a transcription of some storyteller's — we would like to suppose it was Shi Yukun's — live or command performance for the sole purpose of transcription, of the oral narrative, minus the sung sections, as it had existed in the folk tradition.[16] *Aural Record* is, indeed, considered to be a transcription of the complete narrative written down from memory by someone who heard it performed by Shi Yukun himself.[17] While this supposition cannot

---

[16] Albert Lord, *The Singer of Tales* (New York: Athenium, 1973), p. 125.

[17] The last page of the *Aural Record* manuscript housed in Academia Sinica has the following written remark: "Ci shu yu ci bi yi xi hu hou wen wei neng ting ji zhu gong ru you ting zhe qing ji xu zhi. 此書於此畢矣惜乎後文未能聽記諸公如有聽者請即續之 (That this story ends here is a pity. I was unable to hear and transcribe the rest of it. If anyone among you has heard it, please continue it.)

be verified, it is nonetheless the case that the forty, thin volumes housed in the Rare Book Library of Academia Sinica in Taiwan and the *Longtu erlu*, which was recently published in China, can clearly be seen as the predecessor to *Three Heroes*. The episodes in *Aural Record* correspond exactly to those in *Three Heroes* and *Qixia wuyi* 七俠五義 (Seven Heroes and Five Gallants), the version that was revised from *Three Heroes* according to standards of written literature, shortened by twenty chapters, and published in 1889 by the well-known Qing scholar Yu Yue 俞樾 (1821–1906).[18] A revision of *Three Heroes*, by Zhao Jingshen 趙景深, appeared in the People's Republic of China in 1956. Zhao's revision adhered to ideological guidelines, as opposed to literary principles, and anything in the novel that concerned "cause and effect" and "divine retribution," glorification of the emperor, superstition, and disrespect for the common people was removed. Fortunately, by the fall of 1980, the original *Three Heroes* was republished in China with a long introduction explaining its historical and literary development.[19] Throughout these decades, however, both *Three Heroes* and *Seven Heroes* and its two most popular continuations — *Xiao wuyi* 小五義 (Five Little Heroes) and *Xu xiao wuyi* 續小五義 (Sequel to Five Little Heroes) — continued to be published and read in Taiwan.

In 1988 a two-volume novel entitled *Bai Yutang* 白玉堂 was published in China.[20] This published narrative is attributed to Jin Shengbo 金聲伯, the brilliant Suzhou *pinghua* 平話 (straight narrative) artist, in the same fashion that *Three Heroes* is attributed to Shi Yukun. The version was transcribed by Jin Shengbo's

---

[18] Yu Yue 俞樾 was a famous Qing dynasty scholar/official, philologist, and textual critic who taught and wrote prolifically on the classics and histories. Preface to the revised version of Zhao Jingshen 趙景深, *Sanxia wuyi* (Shanghai: Commercial Press, 1956).

[19] Shi Yukun, *Sanxia wuyi* (Guangdong: People's Publishing House, 1980), Introduction, pp. 1–16.

[20] Jin Shengbo 金聲伯 and Jin Shaobo 金少伯, *Bai Yutang* (Dongbei: Beiyue wenyi Publishing Company, 1988).

son, Jin Shaobo 金少伯, who states in the preface that he made
only minor changes that were absolutely necessary to meet the
demands of transforming what was originally oral into a written
medium.[21] As with all such attempts to preserve an oral performance in writing or print, it does not succeed in capturing the
artistic genius of a live performance by Jin Shengbo.[22]

Shi Yukun 石玉崑

Little is known about the life of Shi Yukun who was active
between 1810 and 1871 and who was born in Tianjin, but spent
most of his life in Beijing performing stories of the *zidi shu*
(Manchu Bannermen[23] stories) genre.[24] Shi was a practitioner of
this exclusively Manchu genre of storytelling and, since he bore
the surname Shi, a common Manchu surname, we should keep
in mind that he very possibly was a Manchu. *Zidi shu* were a
kind of folk ballad that flourished from about 1736–1850 and
began to decline in popularity only at the turn of the twentieth-
century.[25] These ballads had a seven or occasional ten-beat line
in every case, and the materials used by the singers were taken
primarily from fiction contemporary to those times, as well as
from earlier, Yuan times. Composed and performed by Manchus,
who lived in the banners, but were not necessarily noblemen as

[21] Preface to *Bai Yutang*, pp. 1–2.

[22] See S. Blader, "Oral Narrative and Its Transformation into Print:
Bai Yutang 白玉堂," forthcoming in *Yangzhou Oral Narrative Con-
ference Papers*, edited by Vibeke Børdahl. Curzon Press: Surrey,
England, 1997.

[23] See Crossley, ibid, pp. 174–76.

[24] Introduction to 1980, Shanghai Commercial Press reprint of
Sanxia wuyi, p. 1.

[25] Chen Jinzhao 陳錦釗, "*Zidi shu* zhi ticai laiyuan ji qi zonghe
yanjiu 子弟書之題材來源及其綜合研究," (Ph.D. Diss., National
Zhengzhi University, Taipei, 1977), pp. 1–4.

has previously been thought,[26] these *zidi shu* were considered the most elegant and highly-respected form of folk entertainment at that time.

The ballads were divided into two categories, depending on the musical accompaniment: *dongdiao* 東調 (Eastern Modes) and *xidiao* 西調 (Western Modes). Stories sung in Western Modes were mostly love stories, whereas stories sung in Eastern Modes were mainly stories of epic proportions, often semi-historical or legendary. There were set rhyme schemes for the singers to follow, with the regulation that each chapter maintains a consistent rhyme. *Zidi shu* was a genre that so popular for so long that, in spite of its own eventual decline, it influenced a host of other oral genres of folk entertainment, of particular interest to us was the *Shipai shu*, Shi [Yukun] Stories, which may be considered a modified form of *zidi shu*.[27] Whereas the seven or ten-beat line of *zidi shu* derived from an earlier form of drumsong, the alternating three- and seven-beat lines of the Shi School stories are said to derive from the *bianwen* 變文 texts, dating from the Tang dynasty (618–907), which were discovered in Dunhuang 敦煌 at the turn of this century.[28] Shi Yukun's revival of the alternating three- and seven-beat line from *bianwen*[29] and the use of alternating prose and sung sections distinguished him from other storytellers of the late nineteenth-century.

---

[26] Guan Dedong 關德棟 and Zhou Zhongming 周中明 (eds.), *Zidi shu cong chao* 子弟書叢鈔 (Collected Transcriptions of *Zidi* Tales [2 volumes]), (Shanghai: Guji Publishing Company, 1984), Introduction, p. 3.

[27] Ibid.

[28] Blader (see Note 13).

[29] For in-depth studies and translations of *bianwen*, see Victor Mair's *Tun-huang Popular Narratives* (Cambridge, England: Cambridge University Press, 1983) and *T'ang Transformation Texts* (Cambridge, Mass: Harvard University Press, 1989).

Shi Yukun's most popular storycycle from 1871–1875 was the
Baogong an 包公案 (Courtroom Cases of Magistrate Bao), also
known as *Longtu gongan*. We are extremely fortunate to have
two descriptions of Shi's storytelling art, not to mention a number of manuscripts attributed to the Shi School of Storytelling,
both in China and Taiwan. Translated below is one of these
descriptions:[30]

Shi Yukun, styled Zhenzhi 振之 , was from Tianjin. However,
everyone thought that he was from Beijing because he had been
there so long singing his tales. During the Xianfeng 咸豐 reign
(1851–1862), he became very famous for singing to the three-
stringed instrument [*sanxian* 三弦 , samisen or mandolin]. He
used to do "The Courtroom Cases of Magistrate Bao" in a bazaar,
which has now been closed for many years, to an audience of
more than one-thousand each time. The bazaar gave him a lounge,
a wash room, and a snow-white room with silvery flowers in
which to compose and polish his verses. Those social climbing
guests who were vain and ostentatious would prepare mellow
wines, fragrant teas, and delicate tidbits for him. If they were
lucky enough to have their invitations accepted by him, their
eyes danced and their faces shone with pride.

By the time he started to sing, the table was filled with a
gleaming silver kettle brimming with tea, a tea jar from the Nine
Streams Pottery Works, and manny patterned snuff dishes. The
teapot and tea jar were for quenching his thirst. The snuff was for
sniffing.

Behind these utensils was laid out a shining, lacquered
three-stringed instrument. When Shi raised his hands to tune the
instrument, it was as though a military man had sent down an
order —everyone was still. Even the birds and ducks were perfectly silent. He played naturally and nimbly. His voice was loud
and clear. His words were crisp and fresh. He chanted, and every
word was praised, every phrase commended by the audience. It

---

[30] Li Jiarui (see Note 11).

was hard to believe that he was so good with books and poems, editing and collating. Although he sang mostly the unofficial histories, they were all elegantly rhymed.

During this same period, there was a singer of popular songs who was famous for singing "The Water Margin (*Shuihu zhuan* 水滸傳)." His particular style, however, was rustic, whereas Shi Yukun, on the other hand, was renowned for clever tunes and marvellous words.

This description tells us a great deal about Shi and the art of storytelling. In addition, there is now a complete, published version of a *zidi shu* by an anonymous author, entitled "Shi Yukun 石玉崑."[31] As a folk artist in the oral tradition, Shi was believed to have had more than the usual talents and skills. As a famed teller of *zidi shu*, Shi Yukun specialized in the "Baogong an" and left to us the narrative that we now know as *Sanxi wuyi*. "Master Bamboo Questioner," author of the first preface to *Zhonglie xiayi zhuan* and thought, by some, to be Shi, himself, says of the narrative:[32]

Although it belongs to the genre of popular tale, which is shallow in ideas and crude in literary style, the storyteller made all parts fit together without seams. He was also very skilled at using everyday language to tell of world-shaking matters. The actions of the three heroes and five gallants and the other braves were truly spirit-shaking and soul-shattering. What men dared not do, they did. What men could not enact, they enacted. It is for this reason only that they were called "hero and gallant."

The author of the second preface to the same work, Captivated Daoist (*Rumi zhuren* 入迷主人) has this to say:[33]

From the time I was a young man, I cast off scholarship and went into government service. In my liesure time, I loved to open and

---

[31] Guan (see Note 26), Vol. 2, pp. 734–37.

[32] *Sanxia wuyi*, p. 15.

[33] Ibid., p. 16.

read all kinds of books. Whenever I heard about a literary piece which told of the marvellous and reported the strange, I would ask widely and seek all over for it. The detective stories that I have hunted up and dug out these thirty years have filled a trunk to overflowing. My only desire is to have a book in hand in my leisure time — I have no other craving. In the spring of the year *xinwei* 辛未 (1871), I obtained from my friend, Master Bamboo Questioner, this book and read it, loving it so much that I could not put it down. Although it belongs to the genre of popular literature (vernacular literature, not dealing with serious subjects) and is not profound, I love all its details. In telling his story [the storyteller] avoided becoming boring and drawn out. Moreover, it is without obscene language. Even with respect to retribution, it is so clearly displayed that it can especially move people to be good-hearted. It is generally felt that whenever one opens a book it has some beneficial value, especially this book.

Aside from the three prefaces to the first publication of *Zhonglie xiayi zhuan*, all dated 1879, we have the words of Lu Xun in his *Short History of Chinese Fiction*:[34]

The world has just gotten tired of supernatural events and romantic stories, and now prefers the unusual tales of rustic heroes. Among storytelling tales, this one is outstanding. This is also to say that this book has extremely few frivolous, supernatural, and improper elements. This novel of adventure is also different from such collections as *The Criminal Cases of Magistrate Shih* and *The Criminal Cases of Magistrate P'eng* which exclusively propagandize those ruffians who help the feudalist class, such as those whom Magistrates Shih and P'eng deal with. These are concerned only with brigands who came from the marshes, how they "surrendered to the court," how they relied on the official world, how they turned around and repressed the "robbers." The

---

[34] Lu Xun, *A Short History of Chinese Fiction* (Beijing: Foreign Languages Press, 1964), pp. 359–71.

"Tyrant of the Yellow Heavens" in *The Criminal Cases of Magistrate Shih* even considers it his contribution that he represses Tou Erh-tun, who is plotting for the restoration of the Ming house. In *Three Heroes* there is none of this kind of devoted loyalty to a different clan or the despicable behavior of selling friends to buy glory. Magistrate Pao in the novel, ever since the Yuan Dynasty, has been loved for his purity, righteousness, and bravery in the face of brute force. Because of this the stories and plays concerning Magistrate Pao continue to be handed down without decline even up to the present time. Although the gallant heroes described in the book are still all loyal ministers and not peasant heroes rising in rebellion or revolutionaries opposed to the spirit, their acts of opposing violent brigands and beheading evil tyrants, just from the point of view of the history of that time, express somewhat the injustice suffered by the people who were so long cruelly oppressed by the feudal system.

When mentioned in histories of Chinese literature, *Three Heroes* is said to be a superior example of the genre of chivalric-detective fiction. C. T. Hsia praises the language of *Three Heroes*: ". . . *San-hsia wu-i* is assuredly written in a vivid colloquial style that deserves the appellation 'real *pai-hua*'. . . ."[35]

Other *Shipai shu* 石派書

Extant in manuscript form are two other stories attributed to the Shi School of Storytelling: *Fengpo ting* 風波亭 (Fengpo Pavilion) and *Qingshi shan* 青石山 (Black Rock Mountain).[36] *Fengpo Pavilion* is a semi-historical story that takes place after the unjust execution of Yue Fei 岳飛 (1103–1141), his son Yue Yun 岳雲, and his son-in-law Zhang Xian 張憲, for the undying

---

[35] C. T. Hsia, "The Scholar-Novelist and Chinese Culture: A Reappraisal of Ching-Hua Yuan," in *Chinese Narrative*, edited by Andrew Plaks (Princeton: Princeton University Press, 1977), pp. 267–68.

[36] Academia Sinica, Fu Sinian Rare Book Library.

loyalty to the Song dynasty they represented. The bodies of all three are to be exposed outside the prison in which they had been held before the emperor, egged on by the evil minister Qin Hui 秦檜, ordered their execution. Mourners, or anyone trying to bury the bodies, are to be executed on the spot. The story begins here and the remainder of the action is devoted to the attempt by Yue Fei's loyal servants, Zhang Bao 張保 and Shi Quan 施權, in spite of the risk of death and many other obstacles, to bury the corpses.

The moral of the story — retribution is divine and humans should not attempt to take it into their own hands — is conveyed through the person of Hu Di 胡迪, an impoverished Confucian scholar portrayed in a farcical manner. His efforts require a trip to the Underworld and therein unfolds action that is totally dependent on the supernatural and therefore quite different from the narrative. Like *Three Heroes*, however, *Fengpo Pavilion* is a narrative in alternating prose and verse. The only concrete evidence that this story was ever told by Shi Yukun himself or his disciples are those slips of paper that classify the narrative as belonging to the Shi repertoire.

The second and, I believe, more interesting narrative is *Black Rock Mountain*, a story whose plot also depends heavily on the supernatural. A young man named Zhou Xin 周信 and his trusted servants visit the grave of Zhou's father on *Qingming jie* 清明節 (the Grave-Sweeping Holiday). The nine-tailed jade-faced fox-fairy (*jiuwei yumian hu* 九尾玉面狐), who inhabits the mountain and leads a band of fox spirits (the most frequently occurring variety of animal spirit found in Chinese fiction), marvels at Zhou Xin's sincerity and dignity in performing the rites of filial piety. She, therefore, transforms herself into a beautiful woman, Miss Hu 胡／狐 (pun on fox), in order to put Zhou under a spell and later eat him. Eating such a pure-hearted soul like Zhou would increase significantly her degree of self-cultivation, which is a Buddhist goal. The remainder of the narrative involves the discovery, by the young man's loyal servant, that his own son, Yan Shou 嚴壽, has been eaten by the fox-fairy and that his master, Zhou Xin, now weak and sickly, is obviously suffering from demon-possession and is certain to be the next victim. The story unfolds as the old servant tries everything in a brave attempt to save his master from suffering the same fate as his son.

Although *Black Rock Mountain* frequently resorts to the supernatural to resolve narrative tensions, it is surprisingly sophisticated in character depiction. It is, indeed, a very moving and delightful story. The plot derives from several short, farcical eighteenth-century *kunqu* 崑曲, opera originating in Suzhou. Although *Black Rock Mountain* retains a certain farcical tone in its handling of the Daoist religious elements, it is, on the whole, a touching love story told in alternating prose and verse. Below is a short sample from the narrative:

Prose
After the jade-faced fairy had pursuaded Yanshou to come down from under the tree, she waved her sleeve, called out "Ji," and was transformed into her original form, a nine-tailed fox. She rushed toward Yanshou, who uttered only "Aiya" before falling face down on the ground. The real form of Miss Hu was truly hideous!

Verse
He saw a thing
Its form was truly frightening.
Comparing it to
A four-foot being,
Tails there were nine
Black all over
Silvery face
A slippery thing.
Comparing it to
Tigers, deer, jackals, wolves —
Ten-thousand times more clever.
Eyes like lantern beams
A fixed gleam.
Straight and staring
Black and white parts
With evil overflowing.

Savage-looking
In the dark of night, it devours others — so daring,
Its pointed mouth
Blood-red lips
Saw-like incisors
What enters there
Is chewed to powder.
Its pubic region attracts and absorbs sun beams.
Its four claws
Like steel probes
Curved like hooks
Sharp as knives
At all things grasping,
With no chance for escaping.
But most hateful and most obscene —
That foul stinking
Awful to smell.
Ever transforming
With the gods communing,
Always and all others bewitching.
The jade-faced fairy
Its true shape and form now revealing.
So pitiful that
Little Yanshou's life, there was no saving.
To the explanation later, keep on listening.

The "Heroes" and "Gallants" of *Sanxia wuyi*

Although the original title given this narrative by Shi Yukun
was *Sanxia wuyi*, Yu Yue, the southern scholar who revised
Sanxia in 1889, changed the title to *Qixia wuyi* 七俠五義 (Seven
Heroes and Five Gallants).[37] In Yu's estimation, there were, in
actual fact, seven functioning *xia* in the narrative who played
significant roles. It would be difficult to disagree with him,

---

[37] Lu Xun (see Note 34), pp. 359–71.

particularly since the original "three" heroes were actually four, if we count the "twin" heroes as two separate individuals. There is a clear hierarchy among the "heroes" that is not evident from the English terms used to translate the Chinese *xia*, *yi*, and *yongshi*. Below is a list of the men in all three categories, with their names and nicknames and the chapter in which they make their first appearance:

The original Three Heroes (*sanxia* 三俠, which actually refers to four)

Zhan Zhao 展昭, the Southern Hero (Nanxia 南俠), styled Xiongfei 熊飛(Flying Bear). Introduced in chapter 3.

Ouyang Chun 歐陽春, the Northern Hero (Beixia 北俠), styled Ziran bo 紫髯伯 (Purple-whiskered Uncle). Introduced in chapter 59.

Shuangxia 雙俠 (Twin Heroes):

Ding Zhaolan 丁兆蘭 (Elder Ding). Introduced in chapter 30. Ding Zhaohui 丁兆蕙 (Younger Ding). Introduced in chapter 28.

The three additional Heroes included by Yu Yue in his revised title:

Zhi Hua 智化 , styled Heiyaohu 黑妖狐 (Black Fox Demon). Introduced in chapter 72.

Ai Hu 艾虎, the Little Hero (Xiaoxia 小俠). Introduced in chapter 72.

Shen Zhongyuan 沈仲元 , the Secret Hero, styled Little Zhuge (Xiao Zhuge [Liang] 小諸蓋〔亮〕, supreme strategist of *Romance of the Three Kingdoms* [*Sanguozhi yanyi*] 三國志演義). Introduced in chapter 72.

The Five Gallants (*wuyi* 五義)

Lu Fang 盧方 (Eldest Brother), styled *Zuantian shu* 鑽天鼠 (Penetrating-Heaven Rat). Introduced in chapter 31.

Han Zhang 韓章 (Second Brother), styled *Chedi shu* 徹地鼠 (Piercing-Earth Rat). Introduced in chapter 31.

Xu Qing 徐慶 (Third Brother), styled *Chuanshan shu* 穿山鼠 (Boring-Mountain Rat). Introduced in chapter 31.

Jiang Ping 蔣平 (Fourth Brother), styled *Fanjiang shu* 翻江鼠 (Overturning-River Rat), also named Zezhang 澤長 (Master of the Marshes). Introduced in chapter 31.

Bai Yutang 白玉堂 (Fifth Brother), styled *Jinmao shu* 錦毛鼠 (Brocade-Coat Rat). Introduced in chapter 13.

The Four Braves (*si yongshi* 四勇士)

Wang Chao 王朝 (Eldest Brave). Introduced in chapter 6.
Ma Han 馬漢 (Second Brave). Introduced in chapter 6.
Zhang Long 張龍 (Third Brave). Introduced in chapter 6.
Zhao Hu 趙虎 (Fourth Brave). Introduced in chapter 6.

Robert Ruhlmann's discussion of Chinese "heroes" is helpful here.[38] He identifies three categories: "the impetuous, uninhibited, and generous Swordsman, a lovable and explosive 'good fellow'; the Scholar, of outstanding intelligence, resourcefulness, eloquence, and self-control, 'knowing all knowable things and some others,' whose powers of reading minds, of seeing into the future, of influencing the forces of nature have a supernatural cast; and the Prince, holder of Heaven's mandate, who does nothing spectacular himself, but is skilled in judging men and in choosing the Scholars and Swordsmen who will enable him to fulfill his destiny." The heroes, gallants, and braves of *Three Heroes* fit neatly, although some distinctions must be made, into the first category; Magistrate Bao, and later Yan Chasan 顏查散, fit the second. Third is Emperor Renzong, whose very benevolence and wisdom in choosing the right people allow him to "fulfill his destiny," and places him in the "Prince" category. On the other hand, it would not be difficult to consider Magistrate Bao a candidate for the "Prince" category, because of the many parallels between his own and Emperor Renzong's birth and

---

[38] Robert Ruhlmann, "Traditional Heroes in Chinese Popular Fiction," in *The Confucian Pursuasion*, edited by Arthur Wright (Stanford: Stanford University Press, 1960), p. 175.

rise to power, parallels that involve mythical or supernatural elements that, in general, characterize the life of this kind of "hero." Gongsun Ce 公孫策, the quintessential scholar/strategist, fits comfortably in the Scholar category.

To help us refine the "Swordsman" category defined by Ruhlmann, we may turn to *The Chinese Knight-Errant*, in which James J. Y. Liu gives a comprehensive survey of the development of the "knight-errant" in history, poetry, fiction, and drama. "Knight-errant" is Liu's translation of the term *youxia* 游俠 (wandering) or simply *xia*. For *yi* 義, Liu prefers the translation "altruists," although the term *xiayi* or *yixia* often occurs as a single concept and is then translated as "chivalrous" or "chivalrous and altruistic," or even "chivalrous and altruistic knights-errant."[39] When actually discussing *Three Heroes*, he refers to the five *yi* as "altruistic knights-errant," in which case the distinction, if there truly is one, between *xia* and *yi* is completely obliterated. Liu proposes that this group of people, sometimes including women, were not always dependent "on chivalry for a living"; not always were they "professional warriors"; not necessarily famous for "expert swordsmanship or military genius, but for altruism and sense of justice": and, finally, he feels that "it is best to regard the knights-errant not as a social class or a professional group but simply as men of strongly individualistic temperament, who behaved in a certain way based on certain ideals."[40]

Liu also lays out the ideals which form "the basis of knightly behaviour":[41]

1. Altruism, (the *yi* of *xiayi*) toward strangers as well as friends. Feng Yulan's definition of "*yi*," normally thought of as "righteousness," is called up here to show that, with

---

[39] J. Y. Liu, *The Chinese Knight-Errant* (Chicago: University of Chicago Press, 1967), pp. 117–20.

[40] Ibid., p. 4.

[41] Ibid., pp. 4–7.

regard to "knights-errant," "*yi*" has the nuance of "super-moral" behaviour, i.e., doing a good deed and refusing any kind of reward, as the heroes and gallants of *Three Heroes* do regularly.

2. Justice, which supercedes family loyalties. Throughout *Three Heroes*, the men who fall into this category never hesitate to take justice into their own hands when necessary, although they defer cases to Magistrate Bao once they have sworn allegiance to him. Since corruption in government was common throughout Chinese history, these men, more frequently than not, could not depend on officials to carry out justice.

3. Individual freedom, in general, characterizes the knights-errant of Chinese fiction and those in *Three Heroes* until they swear allegiance to Magistrate Bao. Even after committing themselves to Bao, however, although they are "on call" at all times, they still retain a certain element of freedom of movement. Miraculously, of course, they always turn up at Bao's side when needed.

4. Personal loyalty, in all cases except when they are officially attached to governement men, supercedes all other loyalties for the knight-errant.

5. Courage, of an almost superhuman quality, was necessary for all knights-errant. Fulfilling one's loyalty or acting on one's sense of justice was of paramount importance; a hero's physical life is of no consequence in these matters.

6. Truthfulness and mutual faith — these qualities were noted by Sima Qian 司馬遷 (*c.* 145–86 BC), "The Grand Historian of China": "They always meant what they said, always accomplished what they set out to do, and always fulfilled their promises." They would often commit suicide to prove that betrayal after the act was impossible.

7. Honour and fame were not unsought by these men, if only as an indication of their own integrity.

8. Generosity and contempt for wealth — wealth was nothing to them other than a means to carry out altruism and chivalry. *Three Heroes* is full of incidents of altruism and

chivalry, no one more representative than the episode in which Bai Yutang tests Yan Chasan three times.[42]

Liu's analysis of the three main differences between Western knights-errant and Chinese ones is useful : Western knights constituted a social class, for which there were "strict rules of admission," whereas the Chinese knights did not; Western knights had religious affiliation and the requirements that came with it: they "were supposed to defend the faith," whereas the Chinese did not; Western knights later on became associated with "courtly love," but the Chinese did not, influenced as they were "by the popular belief that sexual abstinence would help to preserve one's vitality."

Regarding *Three Heroes*, we need mention here only the obvious: since Magistrate Bao was the supreme Confucian minister and *qingguan*, serving a Confucian emperor in the imperial (Han) China of the Song dynasty, the heroes and gallants who served Bao inevitably adhered to the Confucian code of behaviour. However, Magistrate Bao, himself, was something of an anomaly in being so trusted by the emperor as to have had the power and right to execute first (*xian zhan* 先斬) and memorialize the emperor afterwards (*hou zou* 後奏). In this sense we may think of Magistrate Bao as being supra-Confucian. However, in spite of his fame and power to act, he actually does very little on his own. A careful reading of *Three Heroes* will bring to light the fact that almost all his detective work and divining is carried out or inspired by his wife, servant, and the heroes, gallants, and braves who work with him. He rarely has any ideas on his own.[43]

Let us now return to the difference between the *xia* and *yi* in this narrative. To deepen our understanding of these concepts, we will first turn to the storyteller, himself, who speaks to us

---

[42] For a complete and illuminating discussion of the "ideological affinities and antipathies" of the four major Chinese philosophical schools and chivalric behaviour, see James Liu (see Note 39), pp. 7–13.

[43] Blader (see Note 13), p. 58.

throughout the narrative both in his own voice and through the actions of his characters. *Xia* is clearly a cut above *yi* in the hierarchy of *Three Heroes*, and this can be proven in many ways throughout the text. Zhan Zhao, the Southern Hero, who is the first to appear in the narrative, is a good example. Before Bao has passed the official examination — indeed, on his way to take it — he is saved from disaster twice by Zhan, who is unknown to him at the time. Later, after saving him a third time,[44] Zhan is summoned by the emperor before whom he exhibits his extra-ordinary agility and cat-like prowess, causing the emperor to exclaim spontaneously "Qi zai! Qi zai! Zhe nali shi ge ren, fenming shi zhende yumao yiban" 奇哉！奇哉！這哪裡是個人，分明是朕的御貓一般 (Marvellous! Marvellous! How can this be a human being? He is clearly exactly like my Imperial Cat)[45]

The storyteller, himself, feels compelled to jump out of the story to comment on Zhan's remarkable behaviour the third time he saves Bao's life:[46]

> What a true perpetrator of good deeds and executor of justice! Wherever he goes, he rights whatever wrongs he happens to see. It is not that he absolutely must pull up the tree by its roots. It is just that, once he sees an injustice, he leaves it alone; it is as though it were some personal affair of his own. It is precisely because of this that he does not do shame to the word "hero."

Little Hero, Ai Hu, is also praised by the storyteller on his first appearance:

> Alone and solitary was this little hero, whose will was proud and who had an uncommon air. He was fourteen years old and was

---

[44] Alan Dundes, "The Number Three in American Culture," in *Every Man His Way: Readings in Cultural Antropology*, edited by Alan Dundes (Englewood Cliffs, New Jersey: Prentice-Hall, 1968), pp. 401–24.

[45] *Sanxia wuyi*, Chapter 22.

[46] Ibid., Chapter 13.

named Ai Hu. He served as a boy in the Hall of Summoning Worthies. He had observed that among the many retainers there was only one, Zhi Hua, who was truly heroic and who, in addition, had very extraordinary talents. So, he was cautious at all times, and made note of everything that happened in the household, and aspired, unbeknownst to all, to take Zhi Hua as his master. Zhi Hua was truly moved by him and liked him extremely. That is why he accepted him as a disciple and secretly taught him the martial arts. Who could have guessed that his intelligence was so quick that no sooner was he taught, he mastered it; something need only be pointed out to him and he grasped it! Within less than a year's time, he had acquired a bodyfull of martial arts. He often confidentially told Zhi Hua: "You, Old Sir, should not try to reason with our master [the treacherous Ma Qiang] any more. It is not only a waste of your tongue and lips, because he is unwilling to listen, but, what's worse, it makes all the others complain about you behind your back —they say that you are a coward: 'What's so terrible about raping a few women? they ask. If Zhi Hua is frightened by this, how can he handle more important matters?' You, old sir, should think about this a little — aren't all those people doomed anyhow?"

But, in answer to Ai Hu's cautions, Zhi Hua would only say: "Don't chatter so much! I have my own way of doing things."[47]

Ai Hu is put to the supreme test when sent on a critical mission to Magistrate Bao to "inform" against his master, Ma Qiang. He must accuse him of having in his possession the emperor's crown. This crown was supposed to have been stolen by Ma Chaoxian and given to Ma Qiang for safe keeping until such a time as the rebellious and treacherous Prince of Xiangyang should successfully overthrow the ruling family and come to power.[48] Charged with impertinence by Bao, who suspects that

---

[47] Ibid., Chapter 72.
[48] See Chapters 83–88 of the translation.

he has been sent by someone to slander the Ma family, Ai Hu is
told that his four limbs must be chopped off. Bao orders his men
to bring out imperial torture instrument:[49]

> Both lines of officers called out in response. Wang, Ma, Zhang,
> and Zhao carried the dog-head guillotine into the courtroom and
> placed it in on the floor. They removed the wrapping and the
> cold, shining blade of the guillotine was revealed and placed
> directly in front of Ai Hu. When the Little Hero faced it, he said to
> himself: "Ai Hu, oh, Ai Hu, you have come to save loyal subjects
> and righteous men. Never mind my four limbs — even if they
> were to chop me in half — as long as I get the deed done, I must
> not under any circumstances leak the affair."

Ai Hu braves it out and succeeds in his mission. The traitors
are brought in after the imperial crown is found exactly where Ai
Hu had reported it to have been hidden three years previously —
it had, of course, been planted there only days before by the
heroes and gallants to implicate the treacherous Ma Qiang.

Finally, the storyteller provides us with another moving
monolog about the bravery of heroes who work behind the
scenes acting as double-agents, as it were:[50]

> The actions of all heroes and gallants are not the same. The deeds
> of one such as Shen Zhongyuan are especially difficult [to accom-
> plish]. He himself first took on the reputation of being one who
> follows traitors and aids the wicked. Moreover, he has had to be
> agreeable and amiable in front of that treacherous prince, receive
> guests, and be ingratiating and subservient. How can we per-
> ceive his heroism? One surely cannot tell from a glance that his
> wisdom is superior to others. Yet, he sees through everything
> and, as though he were holding a script in his hands, he goes on
> stage to act out parts. When a hero appears on such a stage as
> this, then he is a true hero. As for those such as Southern Hero,

---

[49] See Chapter 82 of the translation.
[50] *Sanxia wuyi*, Chapter 100.

Northern Hero, the Twin Heroes, and even Little Hero — who all help the distressed and aid those in danger — who is not aware of their heroism and uprightness? It is always apparent and clear heroism, and that, contrary to what you all might think, is easy. Someone like Shen Zhongyuan absolutely cannot be compared with them. He works behind the scenes without letting out the least whisper; he adapts himself to all circumstances, deceiving others in a multitude of ways. And, in the end, when he finds himself counted among the heroes, was that not an extraordinarily difficult thing to accomplish? His clear mind and cleverness do justice to the nickname "Little Zhuge."[51]

Throughout the narrative, there are countless examples, similar to the above, of how the storyteller subtly humanizes the heroes and gallants who might otherwise remain the stereotyped characters we meet at first glance. Furthermore, Shi Yukun is so skilful a storyteller that each and every one of his heroes takes on a truly unique and consistent set of characteristics and behaviour patterns throughout the narrative. Even Bai Yutang, we are led to believe from the beginning — which makes it possible to accept in the end — must suffer from his "tragic flaw": arrogance, and the emotional immaturity that goes along with it.

In conclusion, by using the criteria of physical prowess, intelligence, good sense, and emotional maturity, we can rank the "heroes" of *Three Heroes* in the following order:

The Four Braves: these are loyal and strong men who serve as guards to Magistrate Bao in his yamen. They stay put and do their job well, but they would not be capable of more sophisticated mental or physical tasks.

The Five Gallants: these are five sworn brothers, each of whom has a certain physical talent — hence their nicknames — and who roam around the countryside carrying out altruistic and chivalric deeds. These five men are extremely talented, yet they lack a certain sophistication and heroic elegance. The single

---

[51] "Little Zhuge" refers to famed strategist period. Zhuge Liang of Three Kingdoms.

obvious exception is Jiang Ping, whose intellectual, emotional, and physical prowess compares favourably with that of any of the "heroes."

The Three or Seven Heroes: the *xia* are clearly positioned at the top of the heroic line. They are, with the exception of Ai Hu, the Little Hero who matures before our very eyes, exemplars of everything we recognize as heroic. They are supremely reasonable men and, although they are frequently compelled to kill those who have violated the human rights of others, we find them neither cruel nor savage. Their concept of right and wrong is as well-defined as Magistrate Bao's and they act on it with dispatch whenever and wherever needed. Yet, they understand human psychology and prefer to use reason to resolve issues whenever possible. According to Jin Shengbo 金聲伯, the contemporary Suzhou *pinghua* 平話 (straight narrative) artist whose masterpiece is *Three Heroes*, the *xia* can be most easily distinguished from the *yi* because of the breadth of their bosoms (*xiongchang kuan* 胸腸寬). In other words, a hero's defining characterisitic is the ability to deal courageously and magnanimously with the challenges presented by an unpredictable world.

And, now, the story . . .

• Appendix •

Preface to *Zhonglie xiayi zhuan*

The original name of this book is *Longtu gongan* [The Court-room Cases of the Lord of the Imperial Sketch]. It is also called *Bao Gongan* [The Courtroom Cases of Judge/Magistrate Bao]. The original performance of the cycle lasted for over thirty sessions, and the book was made into sixty volumes. Although it tells of the marvellous and reports the strange, and it is difficult to avoid mentioning supernatural powers and wild spirits, I have now changed the old parts and created new parts, added to the good points and mended the shortcomings. I have removed all heterodox matters and revised it into orthodox literature in order to show esteem for loyal and brave ministers, gallants, and chivalrous knights. However, I could not mention each and every brave and moral woman, loyal servant and maid, the officials and the masses, the priestly and the common man who love to carry out heroism and justice. Therefore I have chosen the title "Loyal and Brave Men," and made it into one-hundred and twenty chapters. Although it belongs to the genre of popular tale which is shallow in ideas and crude in literary style, the storyteller made all parts fit together without seams. He was also very skilled at using everyday language to tell of world-shaking matters. The actions of the three heroes and five gallants and the other braves were truly spirit-shaking and soul-shattering. What men dared not do they did; what men could not enact, they enacted. It was for this reason only that they were called by the two words "hero" and "gallant."

As for good and evil, heterodox and orthodox, each had its distinction in the novel. It was truly that the good received their rich reward and the evil always had disaster descending upon them. The heterodox were doomed to meet with a violent and early demise, while the orthodox always met with good fortune. When the truth was clearly revealed, retribution was sure and direct, giving the reader such happiness that he banged on the table and shouted for joy. No one would ever lay aside this book (in disgust) and sigh. Whether or not these events really happened, emotions and reasons were completely expressed so as to bring delight to men's eyes and joy to their hearts. In this case, the words used must be extremely marvellous and good words.

In the first part of the book, Magistrate Bao is the principal character. The story should start out with Magistrate Bao, so why does it begin by telling of (the emperor) Renzong? There is a reason for this. It is because the affairs of Magistrate Bao are complex and many, whereas the affairs of Renzong are easier to talk about. If we first told how Magistrate Bao was born, how he met with difficulties, how he was harmed by others and then, later, added on the story of Renzong, you would feel, on the contrary, that it was meaningless. So the best thing is to put the ruler first and the minister second. Having clearly told the story of Renzong, to speak, then, in a coherent and connected way of how Magistrate Bao came into the world prevents the literary thread from becoming confused. Then, when we reach the chapter "Meeting the Empress at Grass Bridge," we feel that we need not waste time telling who the empress is. The reader also understands it at a glance.

However, the pages and volumes of this book are excessive in number. Since copying them all would not be easy, we have made use of movable type to print it all in one volume for everyone's enjoyment. But, because the characters speak with rustic, local dialects, I have added explanations to make it easier for the reader to understand it.

Guangxu jimao [1879]

First Month of Summer

by Wenzhu zhuren

[Master Bamboo Questioner]

(Second) Preface to *Zhonglie xiayi zhuan*

From the time that I was a young man I cast off scholarship and went into government service. In my leisure I loved to open and read all kinds of books. Whenever I heard about a literary piece which told of the marvellous and reported the strange, I would ask widely and seek all over for it. The detective stories that I have hunted up and dug out these thirty years have filled a trunk to overflowing. My only desire is to have a book in hand during my leisure time — I have no other craving. In the spring of the year *xinwei* [1871], I obtained from my friend, Master Bamboo Questioner, this book and read it, loving it so much that I could not put it down. Although it belongs to the genre of popular literature (vernacular literature, not dealing with serious subjects) and is not profound, I love all its details. In telling his story, [the storyteller] avoided becoming boring and drawn out. Moreover, it is without obscene language. Even with respect to retribution, it is so clearly displayed that it can especially move people to be good-hearted. It is generally felt that whenever one opens a book is has some beneficial value, especially this book. Therefore I have made a rough copy of it and preserved it carefully. In the year *yihai* [1875], when I was free of my official responsibilities, I looked it over again and copied it into book-form. It took me more than one year, and then I divided it into four sections. Last winter a good family friend, Master of Retiring Thought, craved this book and carried it off. He did not return it for a very long time, so I joked with him about borrowing books and returning them tardily. He was embarrassed to tell me that he had loved it and finally had given it to Juren Publishing House to be printed. I laughed at how much he had loved the book, even more than I had. Therefore I have added this short preface [of his] to it.

Guangxu jimao [1879]

Summer

by Rumi zhuren

[Master of Entering Oblivion]

(Third) Preface to *Zhonglie xiayi zhuan*

It is being said nowadays that there is a new version of the old edition of *Longtu gongan* (Courtroom Cases of the Lord of the Imperial Sketch). This version added many new words to the old and, like clothing made in heaven, there was no trace of a seam.

It was written in a special style like woven-silk, tailored perfectly. One-hundred and twenty chapters all together unite the blood and veins of the work. Can you believe in the righteous gall and brave bosoms of the three heroes and five gallants? The loyalty of Magistrate Bao and his men? The courage of Mr. Jin and others like him? The chivalry of Mr. Ou-yang and the many gallants? And the righteousness of Yutang and the others? That it was called "A Tale of Loyal and Brave Men" was truly appropriate and not inaccurate. The author expended a great deal of effort on it. If the reader can read it, although it is not the classics or the histories, he can still delight in the changing of the old into the new. No matter how frivolous the episodes may be, the words are without profanities and the reader may be moved to do good deeds. He will not remain long in the sentimental and maudlin [if he reads this story].

By nature I have always loved to hear stories of ghosts and spirits. Whenever I run into tales which tell of the marvellous, I am delighted and gather them to read.

In the winter of the year *wuyin* [1878], I obtained this book from the home of the "Captivated Daoist" [Master of Entering Oblivion]. I knew that this book had been added to, divided up, and made into chapters by my friend "Master Bamboo Questioner." I returned home to read it and I loved it so much that I could not put it down. Therefore I discussed it with my two friends and then gave it to a printing house to be printed on movable type so that everyone could benefit from it.

Guangxu jimao [1879]
First Month of Autumn
by Tuisi zhuren
[Master of Retiring Thought]

Bai Yutang (left)
Jiang Ping (right)

Ding Zhaolan (left)
Ding Zhaohui (right)

Ai Hu (left)
Sha Fengxian (right)

Ouyang Chun (left)
Zhan Zhao (right)

Chapter 1

❦

The Exchange of an Heir-apparent; A Hero's Fatal Sacrifice

The time of the Five Dynasties was chaos and confusion
Until the clouds parted and the sky was seen again.
New rain and dew washed the ageless trees and grass;
Rivers and mountains, everything was restored to its original
civilized state.
Streets and alleys filled again with filmy silks,
And stages rose where winds and reeds were heard anew.
Great peace was in the empire, eventless days
When lovely ladies of the street slept long and late.

The story goes that, during the Song Dynasty when the troops mutinied at Chen Bridge and the generals set up Taizu as emperor, the rivers and the mountains were unified and went on being unified under Taizong and Zhenzong as well. Peace was everywhere and people delighted in their work. Winds were harmonious and rains favourable, rulers correct and subjects goodhearted.

But there came a day at morning court when Wen Yanbo, astronomer and western chamber censor, addressed Emperor Zhenzong in the presence of all the civil and military officers.

"I observed the heavens last night and saw signs of deficiency in the Dog Star. It is inauspicious, Imperial Majesty, for your heir-apparent, and I have sketched a chart, which I offer humbly."

The emperor took the sketch and laid it out on his table. When he had looked it over, he said, "I see the signs — but I have no heirs, so how can it be inauspicious for them? Please return to your office, sir; I will deal with these signs." With that, he concluded the morning court and dismissed the imperial servants.

But Emperor Zhenzong returned to the inner palace unhappy and thoughtful. "Ever since the death of my proper wife, her position has remained empty," he mused. "How fortunate that concubines Li and Liu are both pregnant. Can it be that the heavens have sent this sign for them?" He decided to summon the two concubines — but they appeared suddenly beside him before he could send for them. They performed obeisance, knelt, and addressed him.

"Today is the mid-autumn festival. Your wives and concubines have prepared food and drink, and we invite you to the imperial garden to enjoy the moon and spend the night in pleasure."

The concubines led the delighted emperor to the garden, where, though the autumn colours were bleak and desolate, the flowers were fragrant and the wind sighed gently. It was impossible not to feel expansive and cheerful there, and the emperor spent some time in contemplation of the beauty before him. Then he called the concubines Li and Liu to attend him in the Imperial Hall. He took his throne, and the palace maid poured tea.

"Wen Yanbo spoke today of an insufficiency in the Dog Star that bodes ill for my heir. I lack an heir now, but it delights me that you both are pregnant — though we cannot know who will give birth first or whether it will be a boy or a girl. Since the heavens have sent down a sign, however, I will bestow on each of you imperial swaddling cloth to protect against the star.

"Furthermore, I have a pair of golden balls, and in each of them is concealed a priceless pearl given to me by the former emperor. Since my youth, I have worn them always at my waist, but now I shall present them to you. Each of you shall have her name and her palace name engraved on one and wear it at her waist."

Li and Liu thanked the emperor, who took the golden balls off his belt and ordered the eunuch Chen Lin to take them at once to the imperial jeweller for engraving. Then the concubines had wine set out to toast the emperor, the drums began, and a colourful drama unfolded before them, rich and splendid beyond description.

By evening, the moon hung brilliantly over the garden, illuminating it as if by day. Ruler and concubines gave themselves up to the pleasures of the dazzling night, and they drank together raucously while the icy stars wheeled overhead.

The emperor was half drunk when Chen Lin came and knelt before him with the golden balls. The emperor scrutinized them carefully. One read, "Yuzhen Palace, Concubine Li," and the other, "Jinhua Palace, Concubine Liu," and the engraving was delicate and skilful. Highly pleased, the emperor presented them at once to the two concubines.

Li and Liu knelt and attached the golden balls to their waist-bands. Then each one toasted the emperor with three glasses of golden wine. The emperor refused none of them, and before he knew it was thoroughly drunk.

He laughed and cried, "Whichever of you gives birth to a male heir — will become the empress!"

Once again, Li and Liu thanked the emperor, but the significance of his words escaped the drunken man. Who could have guessed that these words would give rise to endless complications? Do you know why?

Concubine Liu was not a good person and had long harboured jealous feelings. No sooner had the emperor spoken the fateful words than Liu became obsessed with the fear that Li would bear an heir and become empress. Returning to her palace, she called Guo Huai, the general manager, to her and conspired with him to destroy Li. But one of Liu's most trusted servants, a palace attendant called Kou Zhu, was too upright and loyal to bear easily the sight of her mistress plotting with Guo Huai.

When Guo Huai received his orders, he sent a trusted servant to fetch an unsavoury old midwife named Mistress Yu. At first she was terrified and asked Guo Huai to appoint her husband as her assistant. When Guo Huai apprised her of Liu's plan, she felt it would be a very difficult task.

"If you can do it successfully, you will have endless wealth and position," Guo Huai told her.

This thought held sway with the old woman, who then creased her brow and came up with a plan, which she outlined in great detail to Guo Huai.

"Marvellous!" cried Guo Huai. "Marvellous. If you can bring

that off when Liu gives birth to an heir, you will go down in history." He urged her to take care and to make no mistakes, and then he presented her with a great many gifts. She left, highly pleased with her bargain, and Guo Huai straightaway reported all this to Liu, who was overjoyed.

Then they had but to wait. Almost before they knew it, March arrived and the emperor had occasion to go to Yuzhen Palace for a visit with Concubine Li. When she greeted him, he waved aside the formalities and began to chat with her. Suddenly it struck him that the following day was the birthday of the imperial uncle at Nanqing Palace.

The emperor called for Manager Chen Lin and sent him to the imperial gardens to arrange for delicacies with which to celebrate the uncle on the morrow. No sooner had Chen Lin departed on his errand, however, than Li's tightly knit brow caught the emperor's attention. He saw that she was in great pain and he knew that it must be time for her delivery. Alarmed, he hurried at once to summon Liu and the midwife to Li. Liu set out immediately to Yuzhen Palace, while Guo Huai rushed to inform Mistress Yu.

Mistress Yu had prepared everything long in advance. She handed a large basin to Guo Huai, and together they went to Yuzhen Palace.

The basin Guo Huai carried was covered, and it looked like a dish of food. But what it really contained was the fruit of their scheming — the skinned carcass of a hairy wild cat, glistening with blood and totally unrecognizable. It was an unbearable sight.

When they arrived, Li was just about to give birth, and she fainted away as the child was born. Guo Huai and Mistress Yu took canny advantage of the hustle and confusion and exchanged the cat's carcass for the heir. The baby they wrapped quickly in the imperial swaddling cloth and deposited in the basin, which they carried straight to Jinhua Palace.

Liu called Kou Zhu and told her to take the wicker basket to Suojin Pavilion. There she was to strangle the newborn with a strap from her petticoat and throw him under Gold Water Bridge.

Kou Zhu dared not refuse, fearing that, if Liu sent someone

else, the consequences would be disastrous. So she carried the wicker basket from the Fengyou Gate to Zhaode Gate and from there headed straight for Suojin Pavilion, where she opened the basket and lifted out the child. Wrapped as he was in imperial swaddling cloth, he rested quietly and without distress. Kou Zhu held the infant in her arms and thought, "The emperor has been without heirs till middle-age. If I kill this child, can heaven be thought benevolent? It was not easy for Concubine Li to have this heir, and now she and I have fallen into the trap of a treacherous woman! Oh, let me be done with it! I shall jump in the river with the child. My loyal heart must die with him."

She was about to leave the pavilion when she became aware of someone approaching. She drew back and watched through the window as he crossed Yinxian Bridge. He was dressed like an older servant of the imperial family, in black boots, and a string of Buddhist worry-pearls. A clothing duster stuck out of the left side of his collar. His skin was very white, and he seemed highly energetic, with eyes full of spirit. He carried an imperially sealed palace box layered with gold threads. Kou Zhu was delighted, and silently she thanked the Buddha. "The heir-apparent is saved!" she thought.

The ever-loyal eunuch Chen Lin — for it was he — was on his way to gather fruits in the imperial garden, as he had been instructed. When he caught sight of Kou Zhu, he approached her and inquired about the infant in her arms. Kou Zhu told him the whole strange story. The imperial swaddling cloth could not be denied, and Chen Lin was alarmed.

They decided to put the heir into the fruit box. The baby just fit, but, as they laid him down in the box, he began to cry. The two servants prayed in silence, and soon the crying stopped. They bowed thanks toward the sky and asked the Buddha to protect the heir and smooth their way. Then they parted, Kou Zhu returning quickly to the palace while Chen Lin, with the box in his hands, turned toward the forbidden gate.

Filled with feelings of loyalty and heedless of his own fate, the eunuch crossed the bridge and walked straight up to the forbidden gate. Just as he reached it, Guo Huai appeared and stopped him, saying that Madame Liu was calling for him. Chen Lin had no choice but to follow Guo Huai into the palace. At the door, Guo Huai stopped and instructed Chen to wait while he announced him.

When he came back, he said, "Madame Liu wants you to enter."

Chen went in and, setting the box aside, knelt before her, saying, "Madame, your humble servant pays respects. I don't know what instructions Madame has for me."

Liu said not a word. She drank slowly from the teacup in her hands. Finally, she spoke.

"Chen Lin, where are you going with that box? It has the imperial seal on it — why?"

"I have imperial orders to go to the imperial garden to pick fruit to present to the eighth prince for his birthday, and it is therefore sealed," answered Chen. "It is not just a whim of my own."

Liu pondered his words, looked hard at him and scrutinized the box.

"Is there something *secreted* inside? Confess! Lie to me and I will punish you beyond your endurance!"

Chen Lin abandoned all thought of life and death, steeled his heart, and replied with utter composure. "There is no secret item in the box. If Madame doubts me, she should remove the imperial seal and see for herself."

As he spoke, he made as if to remove the seal, but Madame Liu stopped him.

"Who dares take such a liberty!" she cried. "Can it be that you have forgotten all that is proper?"

"I shall not dare, I shall not dare." replied Chen Lin, kowtowing deeply.

Liu was thoughtful for quite some time, but the morrow was indeed the birthday of the eighth prince. At long last she dismissed Chen Lin, saying, "So be it! Go!"

Chen Lin rose, picked up his box, and turned to leave, but Liu suddenly called him back. She looked him over carefully, but his face was expressionless and finally she said slowly "Go then!" And Chen Lin finally did leave the palace, his heart beating wildly.

He used the forbidden gate and went straight to Nanqing Palace, where he announced, "The imperial decree has arrived." Once in the inner hall, he held up the box and performed the ritual obeisance toward it. Then Chen Lin, having been sent by the emperor, was allowed to sit, but, when he did, he burst into tears. Prince Baqian, alarmed and suspicious, quizzed him.

"Uncle," demanded Baqian, "what is the reason for this? If you have something to say, say it."

Chen Lin looked about nervously, and the worthy prince understood. He ordered his attendants to withdraw, and, once they were alone, Chen Lin told the prince his story.

"How can you be sure that this child is the heir-apparent?" asked the prince.

"The imperial swaddling cloth is proof."

The prince opened the box and lifted out the infant, who was, indeed, wrapped in the imperial cloth. The baby decided to tell his troubles himself and began to cry lustily. The prince took him at once to the inner room, signalling to Chen Lin to follow.

He greeted Madame Li and told her the whole story. They decided in the end to keep the child in the Nanqing Palace temporarily and wait until things settled a bit before making any further decisions. Chen Lin took his leave and returned to the palace to report to the emperor.

But Liu had been there before him, with the report that Li had given birth to a strange and horrid creature. The news had angered the emperor, who showed his displeasure by ordering that Li be exiled to the lower courtyard of Cold Palace and that Liu be elevated to the rank of Third Imperial Concubine of Yuzhen Palace.

This was a grave injustice, but to whom could the pitiful and defenceless Li appeal? Luck was with her, though, for the master of Cold Palace was Qin Feng, a loyal and honest man. There was no love lost between him and Guo Huai, and he suspected treachery. He could hardly bear seeing Li in her present pitiful condition. He tried to comfort her in myriad ways and commanded the young eunuch Yu Zhong to look after her carefully.

Yu Zhong was a young eunuch with a countenance strikingly

like that of Li herself. Qin Feng and he were teacher and disciple, though their relationship was more like that of father and son. The eunuch had a deep chivalric streak in him, which led him often to sacrifice himself for others, and for this Qin Feng loved him. Seeing Madame Li suffer so terribly, Yu Zhong wished that he could suffer in her place. He tried and tried to think of a plan to save her, but in the end he had to give up.

Liu was delighted with the success of her plan. Secretly, she rewarded Guo Huai and Mistress Yu, and then she appointed Yu to help at her own birthing, which was not far off. After a full ten months, she too gave birth to a boy. The emperor was delighted, and at once Liu was heralded throughout the empire as Empress. Guo Huai was treated as though he had founded the country, Mistress Yu was made manager of the compound, and Kou Zhu became an attendant in the main palace with few duties and much leisure.

But tragedy waited in the wings. After six years, Liu's son sickened and died. The emperor was prostrate with grief and cried out against being middle-aged and again without heir. His heart ached deeply, and he could not hold court for many days.

One day Prince Baqian arrived asking after the emperor. Zhenzong sat the prince down opposite him and asked, "How many sons do you have and how old are they?"

The prince told him of his sons, and, when he mentioned that the third one was the same age as that borne by Li, the emperor was delighted. He summoned the child to his presence, and what he saw pleased him. The strange thing was that the child's countenance and manner were exactly like the emperor's and Zhenzong's grief loosened its hold on him. He made a joyful proclamation that the third prince should inherit the throne, and he was named heir-apparent of Eastern Palace.

Chen Lin was ordered to take the new heir to pay his respects to Liu and then to take him on a tour of all the palaces. When the heir performed the ritual greeting before the empress, she noticed the amazing resemblance between the prince's third child and the emperor. Her suspicions were aroused. Chen Lin explained that the child was next to be taken to all the palaces.

"Well, then, take him," snapped the empress. "But return quickly to me, because I have something to discuss with you."

When Chen Lin took the heir past Cold Palace, he explained, "This is Cold Palace, where Madame Li was exiled because she bore a monster. She is a very virtuous woman."

The heir-apparent did not quite believe the monster story. How could he, being a true-born prince and intelligent beyond his years? Little did he guess that the whole strange story revolved around him. He had just resolved to go in for a look when Qin Feng came out of the palace. Qin Feng, who had been told all about the exchange many years before by Chen Lin, was delighted to see the two. He greeted the heir-apparent ritually and then went back inside to tell Madame Li.

The child was invited into the palace, and Chen Lin went with him. Seeing the woman, the child burst into uncontrollable tears, an effect of the natural affinity of mother and son that alarmed Chen Lin, who rushed the child away and returned to the principal palace.

Liu was sunk in deep thought when the child returned. There were traces of tears on his face, and, when she asked why he had been crying, he did not dare deceive her.

"We passed by Cold Palace," he said, kneeling before her, "and seeing how grief-stricken Madame Li looked was unbearable to him. That is the reason I beg Empress Mother to persuade the emperor to lift Madame Li's banishment to comfort his son's sorrowful heart."

Liu was alarmed by his words and, putting up a pretense, praised him and lauded his concern.

"What a virtuous and humane excellency you are! Don't you worry. I will speak to him at the first opportunity."

The child then departed, following Chen Lin to Eastern Palace. But how could Liu drop this matter.

"As soon as he entered my quarters, he reminded me vividly of Li," mused the empress. "And now he comes begging to me on her behalf right after seeing her! There is something suspicious in this. Six years ago I told Kou Zhu to strangle that infant and throw it under Gold Water Bridge. But did she do it?" A thought struck her. "I remember that Chen Lin was coming from the imperial gardens with a box in his hands that same day. Did she dare to deliver the heir to Chen Lin? Worthless creature! I'll interrogate Kou Zhu and get to the bottom of this!"

The more Liu thought about it, the more suspicious it seemed. Finally, she summoned Kou Zhu. Liu had her undressed and flogged while she hurled questions at her. But Kou Zhu could not be persuaded to deviate by so much as a word from what she had said six years before.

Liu was furious, and she had Chen Lin brought in and questioned too, but there was no change in his story either. He corroborated everything Kou Zhu had said.

Liu decided to fight fire with fire. "Chen Lin shall torture Kou Zhu. Let one of them pay for what they both did and surely there will be a confession." She gave the order and had the instruments brought.

But Liu's deep treachery was no match for Kou Zhu's resolve. The servant faced death as a return home, and, though her pitiful body was bloodied and beaten nearly senseless, she confessed not a word.

Liu's inexplicable viciousness was interrupted by an imperial summons to Chen Lin. Liu, fearing to delay Chen and thereby leak this affair, ordered him to go. The dying Kou Zhu knew that Liu would continue in Chen's place, and, rather than endure more slow torture, she threw herself into the railing — and was dead.

Liu had the corpse removed and buried secretly behind Yuzhen Palace by another attendant, who was Kou Zhu's good friend. Liu had beaten Kou Zhu and driven her to suicide without reason, but she did not dare report this to the emperor — nor did she dare to investigate her suspicion further.

But her jealousy deepened as the suspicions festered, and Liu became obsessed by hatred of Li. She conferred secretly with Guo Huai in hopes of discovering some ill-will on the part of Li, by which she might be rid of her. Ironically, there was something in the air.

Li had grieved daily since seeing the heir. Fortunately, Qin Feng was there to console her. When he told her in confidence

the story of the child, she felt as though awakened from a dream
and was overjoyed. She began to burn incense every night and
pray for his well-being. This behaviour was secretly observed by
Guo Huai, who reported it to the emperor. He said that Li harboured resentment in her heart and burned incense nightly to put
a curse on him. It would be difficult to forgive her for this,
suggested the spy.

Enraged at this report, the emperor sentenced Li to death by
suicide. He ordered that she be sent a seven-foot long white silk
cord and commanded her to use it at once.

Qin Feng, devastated when he heard the news, rushed to report
it to Madame Li, who fainted away on the spot. In the midst of this
confusion Yu Zhong rushed in, crying, "We mustn't delay! Un-
clothe her and give me her garments. I am happy to die for her!"

Li came to suddenly, and, hearing this, burst into tears. Emo-
tion robbed her of her voice, and Yu Zhong would not allow her
to refuse. He took off his flowered hat, loosened his hair from its
net, and then tied it with a piece of silk. He removed his own
clothes and begged Madame Li for hers. His loyalty made Qin
Feng's heart fill with sadness and, at the same time, admiration,
and he made a resolve to do his best to persuade Li to agree to the
exchange. It was done.

"You two are my great benefactors," she said through her tears,
and then she fell senseless again.

Qin Feng spirited her quickly off to the lower room, where he
made it look as if she were Yu Zhong, sick in bed. No sooner had
he finished, when Meng Caibin, sent to observe the death, arrived
with the fatal decree.

Qin Feng greeted her and had her wait in the side hall.
"Madame Li has ascended to the heavens. You may inspect the
corpse now," he told her. Meng Caibin was very young, and she
feared to look too closely, for she remembered that Li had always
been kind and generous, and she grieved for her. The idea that
someone else might be dying in Li's place never crossed Meng's
mind.

When Qin called her in to see, her face was already covered
with tears and she could not bring herself to approach the body.

"I will go to report to the emperor now."

Because Yu Zhong looked so much like Madame Li, the deception passed, and Yu Zhong was buried with the proper rites.

That was not the end of the matter, of course. Qin Feng must now report that "Yu Zhong" was sick in bed, and he did so. Guo Huai, who had never liked Qin, was happy to hear that Qin Feng's right-hand man was out of the way. He refused to permit "Yu" to be cared for in the palace, compelling him to return home and become a commoner. Qin Feng personally carried "Yu Zhong" out and delivered "him" to a trusted intimate, who took his charge to Qin's home in Chenzhou. This will be recounted later.

From that time on Qin Feng stuck to himself, lonely and bereaved. Often he thought upon his disciple's death — so pitiful and yet admirable — and he worried about Li's finding life difficult in his home.

One night, alone in the palace with his sad thoughts, Qin Feng heard a sudden roaring of flames on all sides. He thought to save himself, but he knew in his heart that the fire must have been set by Guo Huai as a plot to remove the root of the problem and to give vent to his hatred. Qin Feng knew too that, were he to survive the fire, he would not escape punishment for the destruction of the palace.

"I'm better off burning to death," decided the brooding man, who had not the energy left to endure a confrontation with Guo Huai. He therefore made no attempt to save himself and went to his death in the Cold Palace fire.

The fire was indeed the work of Guo Huai. And from that point on, both he and Madame Liu felt secure against repercussions, since the child heir knew nothing and no one dared to enlighten him. The emperor ordered Chen Lin to take charge of Eastern Palace and to manage everything so that no miscellaneous people entered it. Peace and order were restored.

Chapter 9

The Pig-Head Purchase; Magistrate Bao Investigates Public Welfare

Magistrate Bao reached Three Star Village that day. Seeing everything peaceful and quiet, he concluded that the local officials must be very moral. No sooner had the thought crossed his mind than he heard someone cry "Injustice," though he saw not a soul. Bao Xing dismounted and went toward the sound, which emanated from the willows along the road. A person with a document atop her head revealed herself and bowed low. Bao Xing took the document and passed it into Bao's carriage.

When Magistrate Bao had finished reading he spoke to the woman. "In this plea, you say there is no one at home besides you. Who wrote this document?"

"Pen and ink hardly ever leave my hands," she answered. "I learned to read as a child. My father and brothers had degrees, and my husband was also a First Level Graduate."

Marvelling, Bao had Bao Xing give his paper, pen, and inkstone to the woman and asked her to rewrite the plea from memory. Without the slightest hesitation, she picked up the pen, wrote it all down, and handed it to Magistrate Bao, who read it with many a nod of his head.

"Go home and wait there to hear from me," he told her at last. "I will investigate this matter for you."

"Many thanks to Your Excellency, who is as omniscient as Heaven," said the woman, and she kowtowed to Magistrate Bao.

The carriage started off in the direction of the posthouse.

If you want to know what transpired, read on.

Chapter 10

A Pig's Head Leads to Calamity; A Brave Beggar Catches a Thief

The woman from whom Magistrate Bao received the plea in Three Star Village had been surnamed Wen before she married into the Han family. She was widowed and had one son, Ruilong, now sixteen years old. They lived in three rented rooms in Bai Family Village. Madame Han did needlework and taught her son to read. He studied in the east room, while she sewed in the west room, and they lived by themselves without servants of any kind, making the best of this kind of life.

One evening Han Ruilong was studying by lamplight and looked up to see a man in a green robe and red shoes open the curtain to the west room and enter it. Han Ruilong followed him at once. But all he saw was his mother, plying her needle under the lamp.

"My son, have you finished today's lesson?" she asked him.

"I want a quotation, which I can't, for the moment, recall correctly," Ruilong answered. "I have come to look it up."

He rushed over to the bookcase. While pretending to look for a book, he covertly searched the room. Not finding anything, he took a book and left, extremely puzzled. He feared a thief was hiding in his mother's room; yet he dared not make a fuss for fear of alarming her. Consequently he did not sleep a wink all night.

The next evening, he was again studying, when suddenly everything became dim. Again, the curtain to the west room was parted, and again the man wearing red shoes and a light green robe entered.

"Mother!" Han called out, rushing into her room.

Startled, she chastised him. "Why don't you study instead of fussing over nothing?"

Han couldn't think of anything to say except the truth. "I saw someone walk into this room — but now that I am here, I don't see him. The same thing happened last night."

"How terrible if there is some wicked person hiding here!" cried Madame Han. "Son, take the lamp and look around."

Han did so, and when he looked under his mother's bed, he exclaimed, "Why is the earth under here raised so much?"

Madame Han stooped down to look. Indeed, there was a mound of earth under her bed. "Let's move the bed aside," she said, "and have a closer look."

They pushed the bed away and dug into the loose dirt. Soon they came upon a trunk, which surprised them greatly. They got a crowbar, pried it open, and found it brimming with gold and silver. Ruilong was overjoyed and said that it must be a gift from Heaven.

"This looks like a case of 'Wealth seeks out the man,'" he cried.

"Nonsense!" shouted Madame Han. "It isn't ours. It would be wrong for us to keep it."

Han, however, was young and loath to give up so much gold and silver. "Mother," he said. "it is often the case that people come upon buried gold. Now we have neither stolen it nor found it after someone lost it. It belongs to no one. Why is it wrong to keep it? I think Heaven has taken pity upon us, foresaken and impoverished as we are, and sent it to us."

"There may be something in what you say," replied his mother. "Let us buy sacrificial foods tomorrow and make an offering to the god. Then we can decide what to do with it."

Han, beside himself with joy, smoothed over the loose earth and replaced the wooden bed. Then they both retired for the night. But how could Han sleep? He tossed this way and that, indulging in wild fancies of spending the money. It was a long time before he finally began to dream. But his mind was restless and soon he woke again with a start.

It was beginning to get light, and he got up hurriedly and told his mother that he was off to buy the sacrificial foods. He dashed out into the light of a moon shining as bright as day. Seeing how early it was, he slowed down and took his time. Passing Butcher

Zheng's shop, he noticed a light on inside. He knocked on the door, calling out for a pig's head, but suddenly the light went out. No one answered, and, after a long time, he turned toward home.

Just then Butcher Zheng's shop door opened. Han turned at the sound — and the light was on again.

"Who wants to buy a pig's head?" asked Butcher Zheng.

"It is I," Han said. "I want to buy a pig's head on credit."

"Oh, it's you, Master Han. Why didn't you bring along something to carry it in?"

"I rushed out in a hurry and forgot," Han answered. "What shall I do?"

"No matter," said Butcher Zheng. "I'll wrap it in an apron. You can return it to me tomorrow."

On the way home, Han felt tired, so he put the parcel down and rested. Resuming his journey, he encountered a night watchman, who perceived that Han was short of breath and that there were blood stains on his parcel. His suspicions aroused, he asked Han what was in the apron.

"It's a pig's head," Han replied, but his breathlessness made his words indistinct. The watchman stooped down and untied the apron to see for himself what was inside. In the brightness of the moon and the light of the watchman's lantern was glaringly revealed the head of a woman, disheveled and dripping blood.

The watchman, without giving the dumbfounded Han time to explain, took him straight to the district yamen to wait for dawn, when the case could be reported. Because human life was involved, court was convened at once. Han was brought before the local magistrate, who saw at a glance that it was a frail and delicate student he had to examine.

"What's your name?" he demanded. "Why did you commit murder?"

"My name is Han Ruilong," Han said tearfully. "I went to Butcher Zheng's shop to buy a pig's head. I forgot to bring a container, so Butcher Zheng wrapped the head in an apron and gave it to me. Afterwards, the night watchman questioned me, opened the parcel — and there was a human head in it!" Han began to cry uncontrollably.

The magistrate immediately issued a warrant for the arrest of Butcher Zheng. But the butcher not only denied knowing anything about that head; he even denied that he had sold a pig's head that day. Asked about the apron, he said Han had borrowed it from him three days before. "I never thought then that he would wrap a human head in it and try to frame me," said the butcher indignantly.

Pitiful young scholar! He was no match for the wicked butcher — but the local magistate was. Han did not look like a murderer to him, and he was reluctant to apply torture. He had them both put in jail while he looked further into the case. In the meantime, Magistrate Bao was accepting Madame Han's plea. When Bao reached his temporary quarters, the local magistrate was already waiting to present his respects. Bao rested and had some tea, then called in the local magistrate and questioned him about Han Ruilong's case. The magistrate replied that the case, unsolved as yet, was under investigation.

Magistrate Bao decided to hold court at once and ordered the prisoners brought before him for interrogation. Han Ruilong was questioned first. With a tear-stained face and a trembling knee, he knelt before the Magistrate Bao.

"Why did you take a human life?" demanded Bao. "Confess!"

"I bought a pig's head at Butcher Zheng's shop," stammered Han through his tears. "I forgot to bring a basket to carry it in, so the butcher wrapped it up in an apron for me. I never thought that it would turn into such a calamity!"

"What time did you buy the pig's head, and when did you run into the night watchman?" asked the commissioner.

"It wasn't yet dawn," answered Han.

"Enough!" cried Magistrate Bao. "For what purpose were you out buying a pig's head at such an hour?"

No longer able to conceal the facts, Han told Magistrate Bao the whole story, with loud crying and wailing.

Magistrate Bao thought it over, nodding to himself all the while. "This boy's family is very poor, and his desire for wealth overcame him. But from the looks of him, he is surely no murderer." Bao ordered Han taken away and addressed the local

magistrate: "Would the honourable magistrate please send someone to Han Ruilong's home to search for the wooden trunk and
get to the bottom of this case?"

The local magistrate took some men, mounted his horse, and
left. Then Magistrate Bao had the butcher brought before him.
One glance at the wicked eyes and fierce brows convinced Bao
that Zheng was not a good sort. But his answers were the same as
before. Greatly angered, Bao had the man slapped in the face
twenty times and given thirty blows with the heavy bamboo. But
the wicked soundrel was able to endure it all silently, and he
refused to say a word. Bao had him removed.

The local magistrate returned and presented his findings. "I
followed your instructions, and when I opened the trunk in Han
Ruilong's house, I found it filled with paper money for the dead,
and, when I reached more deeply into it, I found the headless
corpse of a man."

"What instrument was the cause of death?" demanded
Magistrate Bao.

Startled by this question, the magistrate had to admit that it had
not occurred to him to look into the matter of the weapon.

"You went there to investigate. Why didn't you do a thorough
job?" shouted Magistrate Bao.

"I am careless, very careless," apologized the local magistrate.

Bao dismissed him, and he retired at once, in a cold sweat.
"What a formidable commissioner!" he thought. "I must be more
careful from now on."

Magistrate Bao had Han brought back again. "Han Ruilong," he
asked, "are the rooms in which you live family property or were
they built by you?"

"Neither," Han said. "They are rented. We haven't been living
in them long."

"Who lived there before you?"

"I don't know."

Magistrate Bao sent Han and Zheng to their cells and
withdrew, very puzzled indeed. A woman's head and a man's
body — how should one handle such a case?

Bao summoned Gongsun Ce, who suggested another

investigation incognito, given Bao's recent success with the method. But the commissioner decided not to overwork that scheme and dismissed Gongsun Ce, promising to think it over.

Gongsun Ce retired and discussed the case with Wang, Ma, Zhang, and Zhao, but they had no suggestions either, and in the end he returned to his quarters.

"Since we arrived in Kaifeng and entered the service of the commissioner," said Zhao Hu to his fellow braves, "we haven't done anything worthwhile. Now we have run into a very difficult case, and we are duty-bound to share the problem with the commissioner. I propose to make a secret investigation."

His fellow officers burst into laughter. "This is a *delicate* affair. Anyone as crude and rustic as you mustn't even think of such a thing. You will only make yourself ridiculous!" they said and again went off into peals of laughter.

Embarrassed, Zhao Hu slunk off to his room. When his servant, who was clever, learned of his master's trouble, he volunteered an idea.

"You should make a secret investigation to *spite* them," he said. "But disguise yourself skilfully. If you succeed, then it will be to your credit. If you don't, no one will be the wiser and there's no loss of face. What do you think?"

"You scoundrel!" Zhao Hu cried with delight. "Go and take care of it for me."

When the servant returned a good while later, he said to his master, "I had to spend a great deal of time on this business. It wasn't easy to dig up all these things, and they cost sixteen and a half ounces of silver."

"Never mind the money! All that matters is that the plan works."

"Everything will be just fine," said the servant. "Let's find a secluded spot where I can put on your disguise."

When they reached a quiet place far away, the servant had his master disrobe. From the bundle he took some soot and smeared it all over Zhao Hu's face, body, and hands. He set a tattered hat on Zhao Hu's head and put an old, tattered shirt on his back. He replaced his master's pants with a ragged pair of trousers barely whole enough to cover his privates. He pasted a medicine patch on each leg and smeared on some red and green colouring to simulate oozing sores. He took off Zhao Hu's shoes and put on some down-at-heel wooden clogs. He completed the outfit with an earthenware begging bowl and a stick for keeping off dogs. Zhao Hu really as much looked like a patchwork quilt as a beggar. No one should have paid thirty-six cash for the stuff, let alone sixteen and one half ounces of silver — but the servant knew only too well how little his master cared about costs, especially when they were for official business.

"At the beginning of the watch, I will be waiting right here for you," the servant told Zhao Hu as he set out on his mission.

Zhao Hu nodded and, taking the bowl in his left hand and the stick in his right, set off for the next town. He walked and walked, until a sudden piercing pain in his toes caused him to stop. He sat down on the front step of a small temple and removed the clogs. A nail had pushed through the sole of one. By hitting the nail against the stone step, he managed to knock it out, but, he was so busily engaged in the task, he never thought of the noise he was making. The monk in the temple thought someone was knocking at the temple door and, naturally, came out to investigate. All he saw was a beggar hitting his shoe on a rock.

When he saw the monk, Zhao Hu blurted out, "Do you know where the headless female corpse and the corpseless male head are?"

"It's a madman!" said the monk at this and, without answering, he closed the temple door again.

Zhao Hu realized his error at once and laughed at himself. "I am on a secret mission," he thought, "so why am I blurting out whatever pops into my mind? I am really dumb! Let me hurry away from here and get on with my business."

But it then occurred to him that, if he were to be a beggar, he ought to call out like one. "But I don't know what beggars cry," he thought. "So what! I'll give it a try anyway. See what happens."

"Take pity on me!" he shouted. "One bowl, half a bowl, even burnt rice will do!"

At first he was quite happy doing this, since he felt it was part of his "secret mission." Soon he noticed, however, that no one was paying any attention to him.

"How will I *ever* find out *anything?*" he thought. He began to feel a little worried. Moreover, the sun was setting and it would soon be nightfall — though, because it was just past the full, the moon ought to rise soon.

Zhao Hu walked on to the next village, and by a happy coincidence he was just in time to see a shadowy figure climb over the back wall of someone's house. This seemed strange and he decided to investigate. "It's only just now dark. How can a thief be about already?" he wondered.

He put down his bowl and stick and removed his clogs. Then, crouching low, he sprang up and caught the top of the wall. After pulling himself up, he noticed a pile of firewood on the other side and eased himself down over it. A man was hiding beside the wood pile. Zhao Hu grabbed him by the throat and warned him, "One word and I'll choke you to death."

"I won't cry out, I won't. Spare my life!" the man begged.

"What's your name?" demanded Zhao Hu. "What have you stolen? Where have you put it?"

"My name is Ye Qian'er, and I have an eighty-year-old mother at home without any means of support. This is the first time I've done something like this, old man."

"You mean you haven't stolen anything?" said Zhao Hu. But he looked around anyway and caught sight of a piece of white silk sticking out of the ground. He pulled on it. It was tied to a pair of "gold lilies!"* Pulling harder, he dragged from the earth a headless female corpse.

"This is fine!" cried Zhao Hu. "You've *killed* someone! Well, I am none other than Zhao Hu, officer of His Excellency Bao, the Prefect of Kaifeng, and I have come under cover to investigate precisely this case!"

----

* "Gold lilies" were the much-prized tiny feet that resulted from foot-binding.

Ye Qian'er was terrified. "Lord Zhao," he beseeched, "It is true that I am a *thief,* but I never *killed* anyone!"

"That's what *you* say! I'll tie you up and then we'll see about it." Zhao Hu tied him with the white silk and even ripped off a piece and stuffed it in his mouth to keep him quiet.

"Stay here quietly until I come back," he ordered and then climbed back up the wall and jumped down outside. Abandoning his bowl, stick, and shoes, he flew straight to Magistrate Bao's headquarters in his bare feet.

He arrived just in time for the first watch, and his servant was waiting. He recognized his master despite his bare feet and pattering approach and rushed up to ask about the investigation.

"I'm delighted!" said Zhao Hu, rushing on toward the commissioner's quarters. But there the doors were closely guarded, because the commissioner was in residence. When the guards saw a beggar trying to enter, they stepped forward to intercept him, shouting, "Impudent wretch! How dare you come here! Where do you think you are going?"

But Zhao Hu swung his arms sideways, nearly knocking them flat, and pushed his way in. Only then did his servant arrive, crying, "That's our Fourth Master. Stop shouting everybody!" The guards were thoroughly mystified by these events.

Zhao Hu, dashing on, careened right into Bao Xing. He seized Bao Xing, giving him quite a scare, and shouted, "You've come at exactly the right time!"

"But who are you?" said Bao Xing.

"It's our Fourth Master," said the servant, rushing up from behind.

Bao Xing could not see clearly in the dark, but he recognized Zhao Hu's voice when it said, "Please tell His Excellency that Zhao Hu begs to see him."

"What a scare you gave me, my dear Zhao Hu," cried Bao Xing, bursting into laughter at Zhao Hu's strange disguise revealed in the lamplight.

"Now stop laughing at me," Zhao Hu said impatiently. "Hurry! I have something urgent to report to the commissioner. Hurry! Hurry!"

Bao Xing realized that it must be something important and took Zhao Hu to Magistrate Bao's study at once and announced him. Magistrate Bao called him in and, he, too, seeing Zhao Hu dressed in that strange garb, thought it was ridiculous. "What is this all about?" he asked.

Zhao Hu then told Bao from beginning to end and in great detail how he had gone on a secret investigation, how he had run into Ye Qian'er, and how he had found the headless female corpse. Magistrate Bao was pleased by Zhao Hu's report, for he had been unable to make any progress in the case.

If you do not know what transpired, then read the next chapter for clarification.

Chapter 11

❦

A Trial and a Sentence

When Magistrate Bao heard how Zhao Hu had caught Ye Qian'er, he dispatched four runners — two to guard the corpse and two to apprehend Ye Qian'er. He commended Zhao Hu enthusiastically and told him to change his clothes.

Zhao Hu, immoderately pleased with himself, withdrew to his room, where his servant had a basin of water and fresh clothes ready. He presented his servant with ten ounces of silver, saying, "Thanks to you, you rascal, I have made an important arrest."

The runners returned shortly with Ye Qian'er all tied up. The commissioner called the court into session and had the prisoner brought before him.

"What is your name?" he demanded. "Why did you commit murder? Speak!"

"My name is Ye Qian'er and I have an old mother at home. It's only because we are so poor and miserable that I became a thief. I never expected to be caught the very first time. I beg Your Excellency to spare me."

"Thievery is crime enough," cried Magistrate Bao sternly. "Why did you also murder?"

"That I'm a thief is the truth. But I didn't *kill* anyone!"

"What a hardened scoundrel you are!" Magistrate Bao shouted, striking the table resoundingly with the gavel. "You won't confess without torture. Drag him out and give him twenty blows with the heavy bamboo."

The flogging left Ye Qian'er battered and bloody. The wretch mumbled to himself, "What rotten luck! This is exactly what happened *last* time. What have I done to deserve it?"

These words were not lost on Magistrate Bao. "What happened last time?" he demanded.

Ye Qian'er, realizing that he had betrayed himself, refused to say another word.

"Slap his mouth! Give him a good beating!" ordered Magistrate Bao.

"I'll talk! I'll talk!" cried Ye Qian'er. "Please don't be angry! It was all because of Mr. Bai, whose name is Bai Xiong, who lives in the Bai Family Village. On his birthday, I went to his house to volunteer my services, hoping to earn a little money. After I finished my work, I expected to get a bite to eat. But the steward Bai An was even stingier and meaner than his master. Not only did he not give me a tip, but he didn't give me any leftovers either. I was so angry that that very night I went to rob his house."

"You just told me this was the *first* time," Magistrate Bao said. "Now it appears that it was the *second*."

"Robbing Mr. Bai was the first time."

"Tell me how you robbed him," Magistrate Bao ordered.

"Since I know my way around his house, I slipped in through the main gate and hid in the east room. It was occupied by Yurui, Bai Xiong's concubine, and contained many trunks full of valuables. From my hiding place, I heard someone tapping softly on the door.

"Yurui opened the door and the steward, Bai An, entered. The two of them laughed merrily and jumped into the canopied bed. After they had gone off to sleep, I opened the wardrobe stealthily and felt around until I came upon a heavy wooden box. I grabbed it, jumped over the wall and returned home. The box was locked, but the key hung on its side. I was beside myself with joy.

"But when I opened it, I was shocked to find inside a human head! And this time, again, I have run into a corpse. That is what I meant. Isn't it a simple case of bad luck?"

"Was the head male or female?" demanded Magistrate Bao.

"Male."

"Did you bury the head or did you report it to the authorities?" Magistrate Bao asked.

"Neither," answered Ye Qian'er.

"Then how did you dispose of it?"

"There is an old fellow in my home village named Qiu Feng, who once caught me stealing his melons ..."

"Stealing melons!" Magistrate Bao exclaimed. "This is the *third* time then!"

"Stealing melons was actually the first time," Ye Qian'er explained. "Old man Qiu was really mad at me. He whipped me good and hard with a wet rope. Since then, I have harboured a grudge against him — so I threw the head into his house."

Magistrate Bao made out two warrants and dispatched four men — two to bring in Bai An, and two to bring in Qiu Feng. He decided to interrogate everybody on the following day. Ye Qian'er was then taken to his cell.

The next day, before Magistrate Bao had finished his toilette, the runner who had been guarding the female corpse returned and reported.

"Last night I followed your instructions," he told the magistrate, "and stood guard over the female corpse. When daylight came, I found that the courtyard where it had been found was, in fact, the backyard of Butcher Zheng's shop. The front door was locked, so I returned immediately to give my report."

Magistrate Bao realized at once what must have happened. "I am informed," he said, and dismissed the runner. He had Butcher Zheng brought in.

"You worthless rogue!" cried Magistrate Bao. "You have committed murder, yet you try to implicate someone else. You say you know nothing about the female head? How is it that there is a headless female corpse in your back courtyard? Confess!"

"Confess! Confess!" shouted the guards from every corner of the courtroom, hoping to overawe him. Butcher Zheng believed the commissioner had sent someone to look for the corpse and was so frightened that he became as mute, as a piece of wood.

"I will confess," he said at last. "It started on that day at the fifth watch. I had just gotten up and was about to slaughter a pig when I heard someone knocking at the door and crying for help."

"I opened the door and let that person in. I heard the sound of pursuers, too, and a voice said, 'She has hidden in someone's house. We must wait until daylight to make a more thorough search.' The pursuers went away at last and things became quiet, so I lit the lamp. My visitor was a young woman. I asked her why she was fleeing in the middle of the night.

"She told me her name was Jinniang and she had been kidnapped and forced into a house of prostitution. 'But I am from a good family,' she said, 'and I would not comply with the Madame's wishes. Later the son of Magistrate Jiang came along. He was very rich and powerful and bought me as his concubine. I pretended to comply, and poured wine and made eyes at him until he was very drunk. Then I ran away.'

"She was very beautiful and bedecked with jewels, and desire welled up in me. But she screamed and would not let me have my way. I grabbed the knife, meaning only to frighten her. The knife barely touched her neck, but her head just dropped off. She was dead, so I took off her outer clothing and buried her corpse in the rear courtyard.

"Later, when I was removing the jewels, someone knocked, wanting to buy a pig's head. I blew out the lamp and kept quiet. But then I thought, why not wrap up her head and have that person get rid of it?

"I must have lost my mind for the moment, because, without thinking further, I wrapped the head up in an apron and lit the lamp again. I opened the door and called the customer back. It was Mr. Han and he hadn't brought his own basket, so I gave him the head and he went away.

"But after he had gone I regretted it. It would certainly lead to complications. If he were to get rid of it, well and good, but, if complications arose, I decided I would simply deny everything. I never imagined that Your All-Seeing Excellency would discover the corpse. How unjust it is! It was only an accident — and I never got a chance to touch her jewels!"

When Magistrate Bao was satisfied that he had made a clean breast of things, he had him sign a confession and ordered him removed. Then the runners brought forward Qiu Feng, and Magistrate Bao asked him why had he buried the head instead of reporting it.

"That night I heard a noise outside," said Qiu Feng, not daring to deceive Magistrate Bao, "and I rushed out to see what it was. When I saw a human head, I was terrified, and I ordered Liu San, my hired man, to take it away and bury it. But Liu San refused unless I would give him one-hundred ounces of silver. I gave him fifty, and then he agreed."

"Where did he bury it?" Magistrate Bao asked.

"Ask Liu San. He will tell you," answered old man Qiu.

"Where is he."

"At my house."

Magistrate Bao ordered the local magistrate to take the old man and find Liu San. They had not been gone long before the other runner returned and reported that Bai An had been brought in. He was taken straight to the courtroom. He was a well-dressed, handsome young man, and admitted at once to being Bai Xiong's steward, Bai An."

"How does your master treat you?" asked Bao.

"Like his own flesh and blood," answered Bai An. "I am infinitely grateful to him."

"You are an incestuous dog!" Magistrate Bao shouted, slamming down his gavel. "Why then do you commit adultery with your master's concubine?"

"But I have always been law-abiding," stammered the frightened steward. "I certainly have not done such a thing!"

Bao then summoned Ye Qian'er, who went straight to Bai and muttered, "Uncle Bai, there is no use denying things. It's best to own up. I've already explained that, when you tapped on Yurui's door and jumped into bed with her, I was in the room watching. When you went to sleep, I opened the closet and stole a wooden box, thinking it was full of valuable loot — but there was only a human head in it. You'd better confess. Even if you don't, it probably won't help you."

Bai An's mouth fell open, and he began to sputter. By the time Ye had finished, his expression had changed completely. Magistrate Bao pressed him about the head.

"I'll confess," he said at last, taking a half step forward. "That is the head of my master's cousin, Li Keming. When my master was still very poor, he borrowed five hundred ounces of silver from Li and never returned them. One day Li Keming came to our house for a visit, and he tried then to collect the debt. My master wined and dined him, and, when Li Keming got tipsy, he confided to my master that along the way he had met a mad Buddhist monk by the name of Tao Rangong.

"The monk had told him to be on guard because there was an inauspicious aura about him. The monk also gave him a magic pillow to be delivered to the 'Star Incarnate.' Li Keming didn't know what that meant, so he asked my master, who didn't know either. But after Li described the wonderful things found in the magic pillow, my master became covetous and decided to kill his cousin to gain possession of the pillow and at the same time get out of paying the old debt.

After the deed was done, he asked me to bury the corpse in the storage room. I thought, 'I've been carrying on all this time with Yurui. What if he discovers our affair? If I cut off the head, preserve it in mercury, and hide it in Yurui's wardrobe, I can use it to blackmail my master if need be.' I never thought that Old Ye would steal the head." He finished speaking and kowtowed.

"Where is the room in which you buried the corpse?"

"After I buried it there, the place became haunted, so I put up a partition wall between it and the rest of the house and rented it out."

When Bao heard this, everything became clear. He had Bai An sign the confession and wrote up a warrant for Bai Xiong's arrest.

By this time, the local magistrate had already returned to the courthouse. "I rounded up Liu San," he reported, "and went to dig up the head supposed to be buried near the well. Liu San pointed out the mound to me — but we found a whole male corpse in there instead. The victim had been struck in the head with an iron instrument. I asked Liu San about it, and he said we had dug up the wrong place. So we dug again and, indeed, we found a male head, preserved in mercury. I didn't dare take it upon myself to proceed further, so I've brought Liu San and several others here to serve as witnesses."

Magistrate Bao was extremely pleased to see how careful and diligent the local magistrate had become. He thanked him for all the trouble he had taken and sent him home to rest. Bao then had Liu San brought in and questioned him about the male corpse buried near the well.

Liu San kowtowed at once, pleading, "Do not be angry, Your Excellency. I'll talk. That corpse is my own cousin, Liu Si. He accidently saw me take the fifty ounces of silver from the master to bury the head, and he threw it up to me. I offered him ten ounces of silver, but he wasn't satisfied. Then I offered him half, but still he wasn't satisfied. He said he wanted forty-five, which meant only five for me.

"That made me furious, but I pretended to agree. I made him help me dig a deep hole, and, when he was bent down shovelling, I hit him with my spade. The sun was in his eyes and he couldn't see me. I buried him in the hole and then dug another hole for the head." He bowed deeply toward the commissioner, who ordered him to sign the confession and sent him away.

By this time, Bai Xiong had been brought in. His confession was the same as Bai An's, and, moreover, he presented Magistrate Bao with the "Pillow of Wandering Immortals." Bao examined it and then had Bao Xing put it away in a safe place. He passed judgment on the case at once:

> Butcher Zheng is to forfeit his life for the woman. Bai Xiong is to forfeit his life for Li Keming, and Liu San for Liu Si. All are to die by decapitation.
> Bai An, for offence against his superior, is sentenced to death by strangulation.
> Ye Qian'er is sentenced to ten years' penal servitude on the frontier.
> Old man Qiu, for secretly burying a head and bribing people to escape punishment, is to serve a prison term.
> Yurui is to be sold into slavery.
> Han Ruilong, for not listening to his mother and coveting wealth and thereby making trouble, should be punished. However, in view of his youth, he is hereby set free and enjoined to

take care of his widowed mother and devote himself to his studies.

Madame Han, who has raised and educated her son, who has chosen to do what is right in the face of strong temptation, and who has taught her son in the correct way, is hereby rewarded with twenty ounces of silver to be paid by the local magistrate. The local magistrate, who deserves to be impeached for his initial negligence, is hereby allowed to retain his position because he has since been industrious and hardworking and has learned to be meticulous during the handling of this case.

Magistrate Bao had handled the case with brilliance and justice, and his fame spread far and wide. He rested one day, and then he set out for Chenzhou.

Now let us return to Zhan Zhao, the Southern Hero from Encountering Hero Village in Wujin District of Changzhou Prefecture. After he parted from Bao in Dirt Dragon Ridge, he wandered around enjoying famous mountains and historical sights, having a marvellous time everywhere. One day he returned home to visit his mother, who was extremely well — mostly because their old servant Zhan Zhong took care of the household and kept everything in perfect order so that his mistress need not worry the least little bit. Zhan Zhong was also straightforward and upright and he frequently scolded Zhan Zhao, who, allowing for his good heartedness and advanced age, never took offence. As far as his mother was concerned, Zhan was attentive to her at all times, carrying out his filial duties.

One day, Mother suddenly felt some discomfort in her chest. Zhan brought the doctor immediately and never left his mother's side. Day and night he stood at her bedside, not expecting that, in the evening of her life, she would never rise again. The medicine proved useless, and she passed away. Zhan Zhao was beside himself, wailing and crying, calling on heaven and earth. All the burial arrangements had to be made by Zhan Zhong and Zhan Zhao's mother was buried with all the appropriate pomp and ceremony. Zhan stayed home in mourning the requisite one-hundred days. But he was, after all, a gallant and a hero — how could he continue to stay cooped up at home? After briefing Zhan Zhong on all family matters and leaving them in his care, he left home, to enjoy the beauties of nature; whenever he met with injustice, he condoled and aided those in trouble.

As it happened one day he came across a group of refugees, crying and holding on to each other as they walked. It was a truly grievous sight. Zhan distributed his money among the refugees and asked them from whence where they were escaping.

"Master, sir," they responded in one voice, "please don't mention it. We are law-abiding folk from Chenzhou. It's all the fault of Marquis of Peace and Joy, Pang Yu! When he was appointed to distribute welfare in Chenzhou, he not only did not help us but, relying on his father's clout at court, conscripted our strongest young men to build himself a garden and stole our women, the pretty ones for wives and the dull ones for servants. For poor people whose life is already unbearable, this makes our days a living hell. That's why we are fleeing — to drag out our frail lives a little bit longer." After this speech, he let out a wail.

"I've nothing to do really," Zhan Zhao thought, his heroism stirred by the plight of these people. "Why don't I go to Chenzhou and have a look around?" Having thus made up his mind, he headed straight there.

Along the way, Zhan Zhao happened upon a gravesite, where an old woman was sobbing tragically.

"A woman of such advanced age," he thought. "What problem has caused her to cry so grievously? There is something peculiar in this."

He wanted to approach her, but he feared that she would be upset because of the taboo on contact between males and females. But there on the ground was a piece of charred paper, so he picked it up to use as an excuse.

"Old Mother," he said, "don't grieve so. Here's a piece of paper that hasn't burned yet."

The old woman stopped her cries, took the paper, and threw it in the pile.

"What is your name?" asked Zhan casually. "For whom are you weeping here?"

"We were such a fine family," she cried, tears streaming down her face. "And now, after all the commotion, I'm the only one left. How can I not cry?"

"Your entire family has met with misfortune?"

"If everyone were dead, I would simply resign myself. But this unclear situation — they're not dead, yet not really alive either — it's unbearable," she explained through her tears.

"Mother, why don't you tell me about your difficulty?" suggested Zhan, made anxious by the confused nature of her words.

"My surname is Yang," she said, after drying her eyes and seeing that Zhan was dressed as a gallant and did not look like a bad type. "I am Tian Zhong's wife," she continued and then told the story of how Tian Qiyuan and his wife had come to harm. All this while her nose ran and her eyes flowed. "My husband, Tian Zhong, went to the capital to press charges and I've had no word from him at all. Our master is suffering in jail and I've no way to send him food."

"No need to cry, Mother," Zhan said, angered by the story she told. "Tian Qiyuan and I are old friends. I've been away from home visiting friends, so I did not know about this. Since you are in economic straits, please take these ten ounces of silver for the time being." He gave her the silver and left immediately for the Imperial Gardens. What happened there is told in the next chapter.

Chapter 12

❦

Gallant Zhan Cleverly Switches Secret Spring Wine; Treacherous Marquis Pang Plans Vanity Hall

What happened when Master Zhan arrived at the Imperial Gardens? There he saw a brand new plaster wall with all kinds of levels. He counted the paces to the gardens and then picked lodgings nearby. At the second watch, he changed into his night clothes, blew out the lamp and listened for some time until he was certain that there was no movement at all. Quietly he opened the door, pulled it shut from behind, and put down the door curtain. He flew up the side of the building and over to the garden (having already measured the distance during the day). He estimated the distance and threw up the all purpose rope that he had removed from his bag of tricks. He was perfect from practice, and the rope landed on top of the wall and caught; he flew up it, using his toes to grip the bricks. On the wall, he crouched and took a stone from his bag. Listening carefully, he threw the stone down. He was "throwing a stone to test the road." No matter what was below — ditch, water, or solid ground — he could tell from the sound. Zhan turned the iron claw around, grabbed the silken line, and let himself down. His back was flush against the wall as his feet hit ground. He looked all around him before he shook the rope down and put it back into his bag of tricks. Stepping stealthily on tiptoe — bird walking — he arrived at a spot light enough for him to see clearly three rooms — an outer and two inner ones.

The eastern room was bright, and human shadows were projected on the window — two people drinking wine, a man and a woman. Zhan Zhao stood quietly under the window and heard the man say: "You can drink all you want of this wine here, wife. But absolutely don't touch the stuff in the other room."

"What's the name of that wine?" his wife asked.

"It's called Secret Spring wine — a kind of love potion. If a woman drinks it, she'll do anything you ask, even immolate herself. The marquis has been desperate for a way to win over Jin Yuxian, the woman he kidnapped. But she would rather die than give in to him, so I suggested he get some potion that would make her do whatever he wanted her to do. The marquis told me to find one immediately. And I told him that the preparation of such a potion would cost him three-hundred ounces of silver!"

"What kind of wine could possibly cost *that* much?" his wife interrupted.

"You don't understand, wife," he responded. "The marquis is furious at not being able to have this woman. How can we ever get rich if I don't take advantage of such an opportunity to get some of his silver? Believe me, it cost no more than ten ounces to make up this potion. Our fortune is made!" With this he laughed loudly.

"We may make a fortune, but won't it be immoral? Besides, she is a chaste and brave woman. Why should you help to abuse her?" his wife said.

"I am pressed by need. I can't help it," he responded — but, as they spoke, a voice was heard outside, calling, "Mr. Zang! Mr. Zang!"

Turning, Zhan saw a light peeping through the branches of the trees, so he slipped into the room and hid behind the curtain.

"Who is it?" asked the husband, getting up to see. "Wife, you'd better go hide yourself in the west room. Don't show your face," he instructed and she disappeared.

When Mr. Zang came outside, Zhan Zhao went in. He picked up the jug of wine there and carried it into the other room, where he found, on a table, a tiny jade bottle full of more wine and an empty red wine bottle as well. At once, he poured the wine from the jug into the red bottle, he replaced the wine in the jug with that from the jade bottle, and finally poured the wine from the red bottle into the jade bottle. Returning the jug to the other room and slipping out, he crept up the eaves and stood watch.

The person who had just arrived was Pang Fu, a man in the

marquis' service. He had come to pick up the potion and settle the account with Mr. Zang. This Mr. Zang's name was Zang Neng and he was a failed, poor scholar. Somewhere along the way, he had read some medical books and remembered some prescriptions, so he set himself up in the marquis' territory to be of use to him. When he came out of the house, he saw Pang Fu and asked, "What have you come for, Manager?"

"The marquis sent me to pick up the potion. He wants you to go personally to collect your silver. But, sir, can you really intend to swallow all three-hundred glistening ounces by yourself? Must I run around killing myself for nothing? No matter how much, a little will do. What do you say, sir?"

"Of course, certainly. Can't have you running around for nothing. When I get the silver, I'll treat you to some drink."

"You really are an enlightened, easy-going gentleman, sir. Fine. We'll have an exchange — if you, sir, will go get the wine."

Zang Neng went for the jade bottle, locked the door, and followed Pang Fu straight to Vanity Hall. How could they know that Zhan Zhao, hearing and seeing them leave, had leaped down the wall and was secretly following them?

Mrs. Zang now came out of the west room and sat down in her original place.

"My husband commits such immoral acts — they are all inhumane," she thought, becoming more and more aggravated. Unconsciously, she raised the jug of wine, poured a cup, and drank slowly by herself. She had no idea that the wine was the potion, and that it would take effect as soon as she drank it and make her even more agitated. She was speculating wildly when someone knocked on the door and walked in. It was Pang Lu, bringing the three-hundred ounces of silver. Mrs. Zang invited him in. He handed over the silver and was turning to leave when Mrs. Zang stopped him. He sat down and they chatted about this and that, until suddenly they heard a cough outside that signalled Zang Neng's return.

"The three — three-hundred ounces," stuttered Pang Lu, going out to greet the husband. "I've already given it to sister-in-law." And then he left.

Zang sized up the situation and rushed into the house to find his wife red in the face and sitting in a stupor on the *kang*.*

"What is this all about?" he demanded angrily, seating himself opposite her.

"You!" she answered, startled out of her stupor. "You plot to harm the wives of others, yet you overprotect your own. Just think about it — do they hate you or not?" This remark shut him up. He poured himself a cup of wine and drank it off in one swallow. Soon he too felt agitated and desirous.

"Bad! Strange!" he said, picking up the jug to smell the wine. "Terrible! Terrible! Quick! Get some cold water."

But he was too anxious to wait. He went to get the water himself, drank some down, and had his wife drink some too.

"Did you just drink this wine?"

"Yes. After you left I had just this cup of wine — " And she swallowed the rest of her answer. "I didn't expect that you would come back just as Pang Lu was bringing the silver into the room."

"Could have been worse. It's okay. Thank the Buddha for watching over us. I was almost cuckolded! But the potion was in the *jade* bottle — how did it get into *this* jug? Extraordinary!"

Suddenly the wife realized that she had drunk the love potion and very nearly lost her reputation.

"It's all your fault!" she said weeping. "You go about doing evil deeds, you plot to kill and, instead, you've harmed only yourself."

"Don't remind me. I'm such a scoundrel. It looks like we won't be able to stay here for long. Now that we have the three-hundred ounces of silver, I'll make up some excuse and tomorrow we'll return to our old family home."

In the meantime, Zhan Zhao followed Pang to Vanity Hall, where he saw Pang Yu, holding the jade bottle, go to Hall of

---

* *Kang* is the flat top of coal-heating stoves on which northern Chinese sleep to keep warm.

Sweet Fragrance with his servant, who lighted the way. Passing a bronze incense burner, Zhan grabbed a handful of ashes. He took the fly swatter out of a flower vase and stuck it in his collar. Following the smell of the incense to Hall of Sweet Fragrance, he hid behind a curtain. Inside he could hear the voices of all the concubines urging Jin Yuxian to give in.

"When we were first kidnapped, we also refused. But we were pressed until we were neither dead nor alive, so we finally gave in. And then at least we got good food and drink."

"You are a pack of shameless hussies!" cursed Jin Yuxian before they could finish. "For me there is only death!" At which she burst into loud sobbing. The concubines were standing speechless when two servant girls appeared leading Pang Yu, who said, all smiles, "You have tried to persuade her, yet she won't give in. So, I have here a cup of wine for her to drink. Then we will let her go."

He walked up to Jin Yuxian and offered her the cup, but, fearing close contact with him, she stuck out her hand and knocked the cup to the floor. Infuriated, Pang ordered the concubines to seize her.

Just then thunder sounded on the steps, and the maid Xinghua appeared, panting for breath. "Pang Fu," she said, "asked me to report to Your Excellency that Governor Jiang Wan has something urgent to tell you and begs to see you immediately. He is right now waiting for you in Vanity Hall."

Pang Yu realized that, for the governor to come in the middle of the night, it must be something very urgent.

"Give her some more guidance!" he ordered the concubines. "I won't forgive her if she's still this stubborn when I get back." He started toward the stairs, but, suddenly, only one step down, he felt dust flying around in back of his head. He lost his footing and went tumbling down, the two maids following suit behind him. The three of them rolled to the bottom of the stairs, each grabbing on to the other, and it was quite a job for them to get untangled and stand up on their feet.

"Scared me to death!" exclaimed Pang as they headed for the door. "What was that creepy thing. It was terrifying!"

The two girls raised the lamp and saw that Pang's head was completely covered with ashes. So were theirs'!

"Bad! Terrible! We've run into a ghost! Hurry!" The girls, scared senseless, followed along, in big and little steps until they reached Vanity Hall.

Pang Yu went to greet Pang Fu and asked him on what errand he had come.

"Governor Jiang Wan has something extremely urgent to discuss with you. He's waiting in Vanity Hall." Pang Yu, after dusting himself off and straightening his clothing, went in to see the governor, who paid his respects and sat down.

"What urgent matter has brought you here in the middle of the night?" asked Pang Yu.

"I received a letter this morning informing me that the emperor has sent Magistrate Bao, Academician of the Imperial Sketch Pavilion, to visit us here and audit the accounts. He should arrive within five days. I was startled by this news and came here to inform you so that you could prepare for it."

"Blackie Bao is a disciple of my father. He would not dare touch me."

"Your Excellency should not say such things," warned Governor Jiang. "I have heard that Magistrate Bao is upright and impartial and does not fear those in power. Moreover, he has three guillotines, which the emperor personally ordered him to construct, and they are awesome." He leaned forward. "Can you really believe that he does not know the things you have done?"

"Even if he knows, what can he do to me?" Pang Yu replied with bravado, though he felt a certain trepidation saying it.

"'The superior man takes precautions against calamity,'" Governor Jiang said anxiously. "This is no small thing — unless Bao were to die and the whole matter be dropped."

"What's the difficulty in that?" said the evil marquis, struck by Jiang's remark. "I have under me now a famous gallant by the name of Xiang Fu. He can fly over eaves and walk up walls. I can send him at once to ambush Bao at one of his earlier stops and assassinate him. Wouldn't that take care of the matter?"

"That would be excellent! But speed is of the essence!"

Pang then had his evil slave, Pang Fu, summon Xiang Fu. Before long Xiang Fu was before them, paying respects to Pang and the governor.

All this time, Zhan Zhao had been outside the window listening and hearing all their plans with perfect clarity. He had never seen Xiang Fu before, so he peeked through the window. He was indeed a good specimen of a man — large and imposing. What a pity that he had taken up with the wrong people.

"Do you dare to assassinate someone?" Zhan heard Pang ask him.

"You are my great benefactor. Never mind assassination, I would happily go through fire and water for you."

"Who would have guessed from his looks," Zhan thought, "that this strapping fellow would be a toadying cur? What a pity he is not living up to his physical inheritance."

"Governor," Pang went on, "Take this fellow with you and give him instructions. You must keep everything top secret."

Jiang agreed and took his leave, Xiang Fu following him. They had not gone more than a few steps before Xiang Fu said "Governor, please wait a moment. I have dropped my hat." The governor stopped and watched Xiang retrace his steps quite a ways before picking up the hat.

"How did the hat fall off so far away?" he asked.

"I think a branch from that tree must have knocked it off," responded Xiang, and they continued on their way. But, after a few more steps, Xiang Fu exclaimed, "How strange! It's fallen off again." But when they turned around there was no one there. The governor was bewildered by it.

They arrived at the front gate, where the governor got into his carriage and Xiang mounted his horse. Together they headed for the yamen.

Do you know why Xiang Fu's hat fell off twice? It was Zhan Zhao, testing Xiang to see how skilled he was in his profession. The first time, Zhan, hiding behind the tree, knocked his hat off as he passed, without Xiang noticing a thing. The second time, Zhan hid behind the Lake Tai stone and knocked the hat off as he passed the stone. Xiang merely turned around to look; he did not search the place. You could see from this that he was careless and his talents unrefined. Relieved, knowing there was nothing to fear from Xiang, Zhan went back to his lodgings to rest.

If you don't know what happened next, read on.

Chapter 13

❦

In Peace Town, Fifth Rat (Bai Yutang) Alone Practices Chivalry; In Miao Family Village, Twin Heroes Split the Silver

Zhan Zhao left the garden and returned secretly to his lodgings. It was already the fifth watch of the night when he quietly entered his room, took off his night clothes, wrapped them up, and put his head down to sleep. The next morning, he took leave of the innkeeper and headed for the governor's yamen to investigate. Tied up to the outer wall was a black horse wearing a bright and shiny saddle from which was hanging a package and also a moneybag. Near it, a young man sat on the ground with a whip in his hand. Zhan realized that Xiang Fu had not yet set out, so he sat down upstairs in the wine shop across the way, drinking and watching for Xiang. Shortly, Xiang Fu could be seen coming out of the yamen. The man with the whip jumped up, took the horse over to Xiang, and gave him the reins. Xiang Fu mounted the horse and, with a flick of the whip, was on his way.

Zhan left the wine shop and followed him stealthily. When they reached Peace Town, there was a wine shop on the west side of the road. Its plaque said "Pan Family Shop." Xiang Fu tied up his horse and went in for lunch. Zhan followed him in and saw him seat himself at a table facing south. Zhan sat down facing north. The waiter wiped Zhan's table clean and asked for his order, which Zhan gave without thinking. The waiter went downstairs to put in the order and Zhan sat there looking about idly. He noticed an old man on the west side, sitting in offended dignity, as though he were a country gentleman who felt that this environment was abominable and the vulgarity insupportable. Soon the waiter brought Zhan his food and drink and arranged it on the table. Zhan had just begun to drink the wine when he heard a noise on the steps and saw a young man enter. Martially attired, he was a handsome and brilliant youth. Zhan unconsciously put down his wine cup to offer silent praise to this young man. He was increasingly impressed as he scrutinized him more closely. Just as the striking fellow was about to sit down, Xiang Fu rushed over to greet him, crying, "Elder Brother Bai, it's been a long time!"

"Brother Xiang," replied the gallant without hesitation. "How fortunate to meet today after so many years."

They gestured to each other to be seated. The gallant sat in the seat of honour after only a token refusal. "Such a marvellous young man," thought Zhan angrily, "and he is acquainted with that one." He listened to what they were saying. "They are as different as day and night."

"Since we parted," said Xiang Fu, "more than three years have passed. I have wanted to go pay my respects to your family many times, but I've been terribly busy. Your honourable elder brother is well, I take it?"

"My brother has passed away," said the gallant, with a grieved look and a sigh.

"How can my great benefactor be gone?" said Xiang, looking shocked. "What a terrible pity!" He went on to make all those unimportant expressions of sympathy.

Who was that handsome man? He was, in fact, that Fifth Gallant from Tumble Void Isle, named Bai Yutang, nicknamed Brocade Coat Rat. Bai Yutang was acquainted with Xiang, who in the past had engaged in showing off his martial arts and selling salves on the street. When he had accidentally killed someone, Bai Yutang's elder brother, Bai Jintang, had helped Xiang out of the lawsuit against him. Bai Jintang, seeing that he was a decent-looking fellow, away from home, took pity on him and gave him the funds to go to the capital to establish himself. Xiang had hoped to get to the city and find a way to advance himself, but, as luck would have it, along the way he bumped into Pang Yu, the marquis of Peace and Joy on route to Chenzhou to distribute welfare. After making inquiries about these people, he first ingratiated himself with Pang Fu, who then recommended him to

Pang Yu. Since Pang Yu was just then seeking someone to help him carry out his evil plans, he retained him. Xiang, himself, felt he had reached the heights of glory. A person such as he is truly a denizen of the low life.

But let us stop rambling and get back to the conversation between Xiang Fu and Bai Yutang. An old man, haggard and dressed in rags, came up the stairs. He rushed up to the other old man, sitting on the west side, and knelt before him. His eyes overflowed with tears as he entreated the seated man, who shook his head in refusal. Zhan found the scene unbearable and was about to look into the matter when Bai Yutang himself went over to inquire, "Why are you begging him like this? What's it about? Why not tell me?"

Seeing that Bai was someone quite out of the ordinary, the old man responded, "You don't know the whole story, sir. Just because I owe him some money, he wants to take my daughter in exchange. That's what I'm begging about. But he won't change his mind. Please, sir, help me settle this."

"How much does he owe you?" asked Bai, looking at the seated man.

Seeing Bai Yutang's angry face, he replied, "Originally he owed me five ounces — but he's accumulated three years of interest, which is thirty ounces, so he owes me thirty-five ounces all together!"

"So he owed you five whole ounces," laughed Bai. "And it's three years since he borrowed the five ounces, and the interest is thirty ounces. Aren't you afraid you might be undercharging him?" Bai turned to instruct his manservant to count out thirty-five ounces.

"Did you have a written contract?" he asked the old man, who, delighted to hear that he was getting his money back, jumped up crying, "Yes!" He took it from his pocket to give to Bai. Bai's man handed the silver to Bai, who gave it to the old man, saying, "Today we are exchanging the silver for the contract in front of all these witnesses. The debt is cancelled!"

"Cancelled! Cancelled!" the old creditor said with delight and, with a good-bye wave, he left at once.

"With such an interest rate, you'd best not borrow from him again," Bai said to the other old man as he returned his contract.

"I wouldn't dare!" the debtor said with a kowtow. Bai Yutang went back to his seat and the old man, thanking him profusely, started to leave.

Zhan stopped him as he passed his table.

"Old sir, don't be in such a rush. Have a cup of my wine to fortify yourself. It won't delay you."

"I don't know you. How could I dare trouble you?"

"That other person spent silver on you," Zhan said, laughing. "Can it be that I can't even treat you to a glass of watery wine? Please don't take offence — sit down."

"I accept your gracious offer," said the old man, sitting down. Zhan ordered a jug of wine for him.

"What's the name of that old man and where does he live?"

"He's from the Miao Family Compound. His name is Miao Xiu. His son, Miao Hengyi, was head clerk in the governor's yamen before he was enfeoffed. He cheats all the villagers, and his interest is very heavy. It's not just because he cheated me that I'm saying these angry words. If you don't believe me, ask around. You'll learn that I'm telling the truth." Zhan committed all this to memory, and the old man left after finishing his drink.

Zhan resumed monitoring Bai Yutang's conversation with Xiang Fu about recent events.

"I am most grateful," he was saying, "to your dear brother for helping me out of that fix and giving me money to go to the capital to establish myself. I unexpectedly met up on the way with Marquis of Peace and Joy, who was impressed and decided to retain me. I am on my way today to Celestial Glory Village on special assignment."

"Which Marquis of Peace and Joy?" asked Bai.

"Can there be two? It's Pang Yu, son of Grand Tutor Pang and Marquis of Peace and Joy," said Xiang, flushing a little in embarrassment. If Bai had not learned of this, nothing would have happened, but, hearing about it, he flew into a rage. His face became livid and he said with a sardonic smile, "You dare throw in your lot with *his!* So be it!" His man paid the bill, he rose, and left at once.

Zhan immediately understood and praised Bai to himself. "That's more like it!" he thought. "Xiang Fu just said that he was going to Celestial Glory Village to wait there for Magistrate Bao. But I've just inquired, so I know that the magistrate won't arrive for a few days. Why don't I take this opportunity to go to the Miao Family Compound and have a look around?" So Zhan paid his bill and left too.

Zhan Zhao is truly a practitioner of good deeds and righteous acts. He feels at ease everywhere. It isn't really that he must eradicate all evils, but once he sees an injustice he cannot leave it alone. It is as though it becomes his own personal affair and that, precisely, is why he is worthy of the name "Hero."

After the first watch that night, Zhan changed into his travelling clothes and penetrated the Miao Family Compound, going straight to the home of Miao Xiu. We need not go into detail again about how he flew over eaves and walked up walls. Zhan saw that there were three parlors inside, all brightly lit, and he heard the sound of voices. With stealthy steps, he took himself over to the window where he listened to what they were saying.

Miao Xiu was talking to his son, Miao Hengyi. "I made a small fortune today at the Pan's," he said, "but it was only thirty-five ounces." Then he told his son how he had met up with a noble person who paid the old man's debt for him. He laughed and so did his son. "Where did you get all *that* silver?" the old man asked his son.

"Dad, you put out the capital, but earned only thirty ounces; I put out nothing and got myself three-hundred!"

"How'd you manage it?" asked his father, laughing with delight.

"Yesterday, after the governor gave Xiang Fu his orders, he kept the marquis behind to discuss a plan. He said that, if Xiang Fu succeeded, fine. But, if he failed, he suggested that the marquis go in disguise by a secret route to the capital to hide out at his father's place. When the results of Bao's investigation are made known, then he can decide what to do. Moreover, he prepared some trunks and is smuggling Jin Yuxian into the capital by way of a boat docked near the Goddess of Mercy Temple. He asked me how much silver would be needed for this expedition and I told him that I would take care of it — he needn't worry — so he went straight to his office and weighed out three-hundred ounces for me to take care of the matter. I thought to myself: 'The marquis' activities are all godless and lawless. Now, as he leaves, he has arranged for the woman he kidnapped to be taken secretly into the capital; futhermore, he has all those trunks with him. I will tell the boatman to get payment from him when they reach the capital. If he doesn't pay up, then the boatman can confiscate his trunks as collateral. Since the marquis would not want the nature of his activities made known or investigated, he will have no choice.' These three-hundred ounces were given me by the governor — how will the marquis know anything about it? So, can't it be said that I got them for nothing?"

Zhan, listening outside the window, thought to himself: "That old saying about evil people feeding on each other is really true!" He turned suddenly to see the shadow of someone flash by, someone who looked very much like that gallant he had seen in the inn that day, the one who had paid the old man's debt.

"So," he laughed to himself, "he pays debts for people during the day and comes to settle the account at night." He saw a light in the distance; fearing discovery, he crouched down to hoist himself up over the eaves. He saw that the gallant had also concealed himself.

"Why don't I creep up that pole and we can do the 'Two Dragons Play with the Pearl' routine?" he amused himself thinking. But just then, the maid, greatly agitated, came running into the parlor: "Master, trouble! The mistress is missing!" At this news, father and son rushed in great fright to the rear of the house. In the meantime, Zhan crept down the pole and entered the parlor. He saw six large packets of silver on the table, and one small one, so he took three packets and left three large ones and the little one for the gallant who had paid the debt. "Let him have a little interest on it!" he thought, turning toward the rear of the house.

That shadow was indeed Bai Yutang. He had seen that there

was someone listening at the window, who then climbed up to the eaves. Bai silently praised his skill, knowing that this man was his equal. Then he had seen the lamp being carried along by Mrs. Miao and her servant girl as they headed for the outhouse. In the space of time the maid took to get some toilet paper for her mistress, Bai had threatened Mrs. Miao with his sword: "One scream and you'll taste the sword." Mrs. Miao had gone completely limp and could not make a sound. He had pulled her out of the outhouse and ripped off a piece of her skirt to stuff her mouth with. Oh, that cruel Bai Yutang! He sliced off both her ears and threw her in the grain bin next to the outhouse, while he hid himself and watched. The maid, returning and unable to find her mistress anywhere, had rushed to the front parlor to report the disappearance to the master and his son, whereupon they had rushed out to look for her. Sneaking into the parlor, Bai saw at once that only three bags of silver were left, plus the small packet. He knew immediately that it was that other fellow who had taken half and left him half. He accepted the gesture, picked up the silver, and left.

Father and son rushed to the rear of the house. They shone the lamp around as they questioned the maid. Approaching the grain bin, they heard a low moaning — and there they found the mistress, her body covered with blood. Seeing the gag, they pulled it out. It was a moment before she revived. She brought forth an "Aiya!" and told them what had happened. Only then did they notice that both her ears were gone. The maid was told to take her to her room and give her some sugarwater to drink. Suddenly the son remembered the silver in the parlor: "Bad! We've fallen into the trap of 'luring the tiger out of mountain.'" He flew back to the front of the house, his father close behind, where they saw that every bit of the silver was gone. Father and son stood dazed for some time, but there was nothing to be done. They were pained and angry.

How did things turn out? Read the next chapter.

Chapter 14

❦

Little Bao Xing Steals a Try at the Pillow of Wandering Immortals; Zhan Xiongfei Aids in Capturing the Marquis of Peace and Joy

Now when the Miao father and son saw that their silver was gone, they had to suffer in silence, since it was stealthily gotten and they feared scandal. Bai Yutang had taken his silver and gone on his way; Zhan had taken his share and headed straight for Celestial Glory Village.

But let me tell you instead about Magistrate Bao, who was unoccupied at the moment, having finished his case in Three Star Village.

Bao Xing was thinking about that "Pillow of Wandering Immortals." "Wouldn't it be great if I stole a little nap on that pillow tonight?" he said to himself. So, after he had seen to all of his master's needs, he spoke to Li Cai: "Brother Li," he said, "may I impose on you? I haven't slept for days, so I'll take off tonight, okay? You must stay alert though. If the master wants tea, get it for him. Tomorrow I'll take your place."

"Don't worry about a thing," responded Li. "I'm here! We are both in his service — why distinguish between your turn and my turn?"

Bao Xing smiled and went to his room. He took out the pillow, looked it over, and suddenly felt very sleepy. No sooner did he put his head down on it than he entered the world of dreams.

He went out of his room and saw a black horse. The saddle was also black. On both sides of the horse were servants. Bao Xing mounted the horse and, at an incredible speed, arrived at a spot that greatly resembled the main hall in the Kaifeng yamen. Puzzled, he dismounted: "How can I still be in the yamen?" he wondered, catching sight of a plaque above that said "Yin Yang Hall." What did it mean? Just then, a judge from the underworld came up to him and demanded, "Who are you? How dare you impersonate the Star Ruler and come here to make trouble?" Someone else called out, "Take him away!" When a strong man in armour appeared, Bao Xing woke up in a fright. His body was covered in perspiration. "The judge said that I was impersonating the Star Ruler," he thought. "I think that only he can sleep on this pillow in the future! No wonder Li Keming said that he had to give it to the Star Ruler."

Bao Xing couldn't sleep for turning these things over in his mind. Angrily, he got up and heard the sound of the fourth watch. Rushing into Bao's room, he spied Li Cai sitting in a chair, his head rocking back and forth in sleep. He noticed also that the snuff of the candle had grown long, so he used the snuffer to trim it. Seeing a note on the table and picking it up to have a look, he exclaimed, "Where did *this* come from?"

Li Cai was startled awake. "I didn't fall asleep," he protested.

"If you weren't asleep, where did this note come from?"

"What note?" asked Bao, before Li Cai could answer. "Show it to me."

Bao Xing went to show it to Bao as Li Cai held open the door curtain.

"What time is it now?" Bao asked, having read the note. Bao Xing shone his lamp on the clock and said that it had just entered the fifth watch.

"Time to get up anyhow!" Bao said.

Bao Xing and Li Cai helped Bao get dressed and washed, after which Bao summoned Mr. Gongsun, who came quickly. Bao showed him the note, on which he saw written "Tomorrow at Celestial Glory Village, beware of assassin. Divide your men, take two routes: one route to East Marsh Forest to arrest the evil Pang Yu; one route to Goddess of Mercy Temple to save a brave, chaste woman. Urgent! Urgent!" There was a line of smaller characters that said, "The brave, chaste woman is Jin Yuxian."

"Where did this note come from?" Gongsun asked.

"We needn't inquire into its origins. We'd best just increase the security tomorrow on our way to Celestial Glory Village. And send extra men to check out both routes."

Gongsun withdrew, promising to discuss the entire plan with the four braves — Wang, Ma, Zhang, and Zhao — and to impress upon everyone the need to be very careful.

Who left the note? Well, Zhan Zhao had gone straight to Celestial Glory Village after leaving the Miao Family Compound. Bao had not yet arrived. "I fear that Bao will rush here and I won't have time to warn him," Zhan had thought. "I'd better go meet him and alert him to the assassination plot so that he can be fully prepared."

What a hero! Taking no account of the extra trouble, he had gone all the way to Three Star Village. It was just the third watch of the night when he had arrived and found Li Cai fast asleep. Deciding not to wake him, Zhan had left the note and headed back to Celestial Glory Village to wait.

Bao arrived in Celestial Glory Village on the following day. His men entered the official residence and searched every corner. Mr. Gongsun instructed his two best men — Geng Chun and Zheng Ping — to stand guard and check out every person coming and going. Wang, Ma, Zhang, and Zhao were sent to surround Bao's quarters and patrol. He, himself, Bao Xing, and Li Cai were to guard Magistrate Bao. If there were any disturbances, everyone was to be informed so that they could act in concert. After completing the instructions, he looked around and noted with satisfaction that the place was lighted as though it were daylight and the guards had mounted a ceaseless patrol outside. Everyone thought there must be an imperial officer on a special mission residing there — how could they know that all these were precautions against an assassin?

Inside the residence, Wang, Ma, Zhang, and Zhao, full of energy, were busily preparing secret weapons to help them capture the assassin. They were going to be ready for anything.

But nothing at all had happened by the third watch. Outside the sentries were patrolling non-stop, illuminating the walls with their lamps. Inside Zhao Hu was going from one place to another, peering into everything, following the moving light outside the wall all the way to an elm tree. Suddenly he looked up and shouted, "There's someone here!" Wang, Ma, and Zhang came flying. The sentries outside stopped marching and rushed over to the elm tree with the lamp. There was, indeed, a black shadow there, which might have been cast only by the tree. But when the man in the tree saw so many shouting people below and the brilliant light of the lamps, he moved. The crowd saw him and rose up in anger.

"He's jumped down!" someone called out. "Take care inside!" The man took advantage of the commotion to grab onto the tree branch, raise himself up, and climb onto the eaves, where he crouched down and scrambled toward the front of the house.

"Thief! Where are you going?" Zhao Hu called out, a moment before he ducked to avoid a piece of flying tile. But, in ducking, he used so much force that he did a somersault. The man on the roof got into position and was about to jump over to the other side, when he screamed "Aiya!" and came rolling down, to fall right in front of Zhao Hu. Zhao turned and held him down while everyone rushed over to see. They grabbed his dagger, tied him up with rope, and dragged him off to Magistrate Bao.

By this time Magistrate Bao and Gongsun had changed into their proper clothes.

"What a noble gallant we have here! I daresay he is a bold hero!" exclaimed Bao, his face suffused with smiles. "Sir," he said to Mr. Gongsun, "loosen his bonds for me."

"This man came to assassinate you!" Mr. Gongsun said, feigning alarm. "How can we let him free?"

"I am dying for worthy men. How can I not desire such a marvellous specimen? Besides, this fellow and I have no enmity. Why should he try to kill me? Surely he has been exploited by some rogue. Hurry! Undo the ties!"

Gongsun ordered Zhang and Zhao to loosen the bonds. Wang pulled out a poison arrow that he spied in the assassin's leg, and Bao ordered Bao Xing to guard him.

"Did you hear that?" Gongsun asked the fellow. "The magistrate is treating you magnanimously — how will you repay his kindness?"

The assassin could not help being moved by Bao's kindness and the fierceness of the men in waiting.

"I had heard," he thought, his conscience activated "that Magistrate Bao is upright and is a good judge of heroes. It was no empty rumour." He prostrated himself on the floor. "I have committed a crime against Your Excellency," he said. "I deserve to die."

"Please rise, good fellow," Bao said. "Sit down so that we can talk better."

"How dare I sit when Your Excellency is here?"

"Never mind that. Just sit down, why not?"

He sat with a bow, and Bao began the conversation, asking "What is your name, young man? Why have you come here?"

"My name is Xiang Fu," he said easily and naturally, seeing that Bao was treating him so well. "It was Pang Yu who commissioned me ... " he began and went on to tell the whole story. "I had no idea that you would be so generous — I am horribly ashamed of myself."

"The emperor has made much of me and spread my name far and wide. For this people hate me and my detractors are many. In the future, if you, good fellow, could testify about this when I confront the marquis, it would show that I haven't forgotten my teacher-disciple relationship with the Grand Tutor."

Xiang Fu agreed and Bao then instructed Mr. Gongsun to tend to Xiang's arrow wound, which he did.

Bao had a secret conversation with Wang Chao. He told him that they would pretend to release Xiang Fu but, in actuality, detain him. Wang showed Bao the arrow that had wounded Xiang and told him that it belonged to Zhan Zhao.

"So," remarked Bao, "it was Hero Zhan helping me secretly. That note I received the other day in Three Star Village must have been written by him." Bao was deeply moved and full of admiration.

By this time, Mr. Gongsun had taken care of everything. He had instructed Ma Han to take Geng Chun and Zheng Ping, the heads of the local militia, to the Goddess of Mercy Temple to rescue Jin Yuxian and had also sent Zhang Long and Zhao Hu to East Marsh Forest to arrest Pang Yu.

Now let us concentrate on Ma Han, who took Geng Chun and Zheng Ping to the Goddess of Mercy Temple. As soon as they got on the mule cart, they flew straight to the temple, where there was a man who asked them why they were late.

"Elder Brother!" said Ma Han, recognizing Zhan Zhao. "Where did that cart go?"

"I have intercepted it and put Jin Yuxian in a safe spot in the temple. You have come just at the right time. Let's change places now."

As he spoke, Geng Chun and Zheng Ping arrived with the mule cart in tow. They opened the mountain gate to the temple, and an elderly woman and a nun walked toward them. The elderly woman was Tian Zhong's wife, Mistress Yang. The two men got down from the cart and lifted Jin Yuxian gently out. Yuxian and Mistress Yang, mistress and servant, held each other and cried. (It was Zhan Zhao who had arranged for Mistress Yang to be waiting there.) They also removed Yuxian's jewels and clothing from the cart.

"Why don't you two wait here until your master's case is settled. I'll have him come here to get you," Zhan said to Mistress Yang. "Please take good care of them," Zhan said to the nun, "Master Tian will reward you lavishly." Then he turned to Ma Han. "Little Brother, return now. Please pay my respects to the magistrate and say to him that Zhan Zhao will report to him another time, and we will surely meet again. Please fill him in on everything that has happened to Jin Yuxian. She is truly a brave and chaste woman and there's no need to question her. Please do this for me." Zhan strode away after giving these instructions, and Ma, who did not dare to detain him, returned with Geng Chun and Zheng Ping by the same road and went at once to report to Bao.

Zhang and Zhao arrived at East Marsh Forest and saw no activity at all.

"Can that fellow have already passed through here?" asked Zhao.

"There's an endless expanse up ahead and no one's tracks to be seen. He can't have come through."

As they spoke, a group of people could be seen approaching in the distance.

"They've come! They're here!" Zhao said. "Brother, let's do this and that and we'll be all right."

Zhang agreed, and, with the messenger, they hid behind a tree. The group of people pressed their horses forward until they reached that very spot. Zhao rushed out in front of the horse and fell flat on the ground. Zhang Long came out from behind the tree and shouted, "Bad! Bad! You've killed him!" He grabbed hold of Pang Yu and Ma Huan and shouted, "You've killed him. Where do you think you're going?"

Pang's servants all crouched forward, demanding, "You've got your nerve! How dare you intercept the marquis?"

"Who cares whether he's a marquis or a duke — you had better bring our man back to life," Zhang Long said.

"What impudence! This is Marquis of Peace and Joy, the son of Grand Tutor Pang. He is dressed in ordinary clothes because he's out on a private visit. You've offended the heavens by blocking his way!" shouted the evil slaves.

Once Zhao, still on the ground, heard that this was, indeed, Marquis of Peace and Joy — no mistake about it — he pulled himself up and slapped the last speaker in the face.

"So, we've offended the heavens, have we! We were, in fact, waiting just for *you* who have offended the heavens!" Zhao Hu shouted back. He dragged Pang Yu off his horse and the runner locked him in fetters. Pang's men sized up the situation, saw that it was not leading anywhere good, whipped their horses into motion, and disappeared without a trace. Zhang and Zhao, knowing it was hopeless, did not even try to go after them. Pang Yu was their only concern, and him they escorted under heavy guard all the way to Bao's residence.

For the details, read on.

Chapter 15

❦

Pang Yu Decapitated, First Use of the Imperial Guillotine; Meeting the Dowager Empress, Late Night at Celestial Piety Temple

Zhang and Zhao brought Pang Yu in custody to Bao's official residence and immediately into the courtroom. Bao saw the chains around his neck. "You people are too stupid," he said. "How can you have put the marquis in fetters? Don't just stand there — remove them!"

The guards rushed forward to remove the chains. Pang Yu automatically began to kneel, but the magistrate stopped him.

"No need for that. Though we must act officially in spite of a personal relationship, I am connected by disciple-teacher ties to the Grand Tutor. You and I are brothers in the same generation — family friends. But we have this case here, unfortunately, so I must question you face to face and you must answer with complete honesty so that we can deal with it. You must not keep anything back out of fear." Bao then called forward ten elders, Tian Zhong, Tian Qiyuan, and the plundered woman. He interrogated Pang about each and every one.

Pang felt that Bao's words implied a willingness to protect him and that his amiable face was an indication that Bao would try to save him. He decided that he had better confess and rely on his father's clout to get Blackie Bao to go easy on him — have him promise to reform and then forget the whole case.

"Your Excellency, Magistrate Bao, no need to go into detail. I did all of those things in a moment of stupidity, and now it's too late for remorse. I beg you to forgive me with a stroke of your pen, and I will be eternally grateful."

"Since you have already confessed to these other crimes,"

returned Bao, "let me ask you about one more thing. Who sent Xiang Fu?"

It was some time before the evil rogue pulled himself together after this shock.

"Xiang Fu was sent by Governor Jiang," he said, finally. "I know nothing about it."

"Bring Xiang Fu in!" Bao ordered.

Xiang Fu walked in dressed as usual, not in prisoner's garb.

"Xiang Fu," Bao said, "you confront the marquis."

"Marquis, you needn't try to deceive him. I have already told everything. You just tell him the truth — he has his plan."

The evil marquis realized that there was nothing for him but to confess. He admitted that he had sent Xiang Fu and, having reached that point, could not avoid signing the confession.

The witnesses — human evidence — were brought in after he signed the confession. Bao asked that everyone come forward to acknowledge each other: there were fathers who recognized daughters; older brothers and younger sisters; husbands saw their wives; and mothers-in-law their daughters-in-law. All kinds of people were among those plundered by the marquis, and the wailing and sobbing among them was hard to bear. Bao had them wait on the two sides of the courtroom to hear the sentencing. He also sent someone to bring in the governor.

"The crimes you have committed," Bao said to the evil marquis, "would normally be dealt with in the capital. But the road is long, and you would no doubt suffer along the way. Moreover, once in the capital, you would be subject to provincial judges and laws, and it would be hard for you to avoid physical torture. If the emperor is angry about this, then he will have to resentence you, and who knows what will develop? It would be best for me to resolve this case right here; it would be most expeditious that way, don't you think?"

"It is all in your hands. I dare not disobey," replied Pang.

"Bring the imperial guillotine," Bao said, and his face lowered blackly, his fierce eyes stared angrily. Those few words mobilized the guards, who shouted the orders along. The courtroom resounded, and four guards carried the guillotine into the room and placed it in its proper position. Wang Chao removed the imperial cloth cover to reveal a brilliantly-flashing, brand-new metal blade, one to strike fear in anyone.

The marquis was scared witless. He was about to say something, but, before he could say a word, Ma Han had thrown him on the floor. The four guards stuffed a wooden bit into his mouth, removed his clothing, wrapped him up in rush mats, and tied him up with a rope. By this time, the evil rogue could not even try to resist. Zhang Long and Zhao Hu carried him over to the guillotine, put his head through the opening, evening out both sides. Ma and Wang made sure that the black side faced in. They lifted the sheath with their right hands and fixed the blade with their left hands, looking expectantly up at Bao. With a wave of his sleeve and a nod of his fierce head, he uttered the two words, "Administer punishment!" Wang positioned himself over the blade to exert great force on both sides and brought it down. *Kecha* was all you heard — and the evil rogue was chopped in two parts. The four guards in white waistbands rushed up and from the front and back in one movement lifted the body and took it away. Zhang and Zhao, using white strips of cloth, cleaned the blade of all traces of blood. In the courtroom, Tian Qiyuan and his servant, as well as Mrs. Tian and the villagers, saw that Pang Yu had been guillotined — and they knew then that Magistrate Bao was truly devoted to the country, committed to saving the people. There were those calling out the Buddha's name, those feeling a great sense of satisfaction, and those more timid ones who had not dared to watch.

Now, who would have guessed that the next trip Magistrate Bao was contemplating would lead to an earthshaking, heaven-rocking affair?

Do you know what affair that was? When Magistrate Bao finished bringing relief to Chenzhou's distressed, he was determined to investigate each and every other locale along the way. He therefore refused to return by the same route, choosing a different way home. One day's ride brought him to east of the Grass County Bridge. He was rocking along slowly in the carriage when he heard a loud crack — *lozi*. Bao Xing stopped the carriage at once and dismounted to have a look. Both axles had splintered. If the chair had not come to rest on firm ground, the axles might have split clean in two.

Bao Xing informed Magistrate Bao, who demanded the horse, grabbed it, and mounted. Before going more than a few steps, however, he reigned in and told Bao Xing to call for the local headman.

The headman soon appeared and knelt before the horse. He was a man of some thirty years of age, carrying a bamboo pole in his hand. He presented himself:

"This humble person is the local headman, Fan Zonghua. I kowtow to Your Gracious Imperial Commissioner."

"'What' is the name of this place." Bao asked.*

"It's not 'what' place. Its name is Grass County Bridge, though it has only a flat crossover and no real bridge at all; nor is there any grass anywhere. You're wondering how it got this name, right? Even I am puzzled by it."

"Be brief! Be brief!" The escort guards called from all around.

"Is there some kinds of official residence here," Bao asked.

"This is a town of many streets, but it is not a market town or port. It is merely a barren and isolated spot, not even a road stop. How could it have an official residence?"

"If there is no official residence," Bao Xing snapped from his horse, "say so and have done. Why go on so?"

"What is that tall building up ahead?" asked Bao, pointing with his whip.

"That is Celestial Piety Daoist Temple. It is called a Daoist temple, but it has the full line of Buddhist accessories — Gentleman Halls, Madame Halls, even an altar to the earth god, in that structure right next to it. There is no income from incense and paper money, and it can support only one old Daoist priest."

"You talk too much! Who asked you for all of these details?"

---

* The following conversation is reminiscent of the Abbott and Costello routine "Who's on first."

"Head for the temple," Bao ordered.

Agreement was heard all around and Bao went straight to the temple.

Bao Xing remounted, shook out the reins, and went on ahead to drive away loiterers. He arrived and gave instructions to the priest: "The Great Imperial Commissioner will be passing through here. He will not need any tea. After you have burned your incense, please remove yourself. Our commissioner likes quiet."

"Yes," said the priest repeatedly. As they were conversing, Magistrate Bao arrived. Bao Xing rushed forward to take hold of the horse, and Bao entered the temple. He ordered Li Cai to set up a seat for him on the veranda of West Hall, and he himself went with Bao Xing to the main hall. The old Daoist prepared the incense and candles, and, his worship completed, withdrew when Bao signalled him with his eyes. Bao then left the main hall, went to the western veranda, and sat in the official seat. He sent everyone away to rest, keeping only Bao Xing at his side. Then he told Bao Xing to fetch the headman secretly.

Fan Zonghua saluted Bao Xing on one knee.

"You appear to be a clever fellow," said Bao Xing, "but you are too talkative. When the magistrate questions you, answer briefly. Why ramble on, adding branches and leaves everywhere?"

"I feared that if my responses weren't clear," Fan answered smiling, "the magistrate would scold me. So I went in the direction of great detail. I never thought I would overdo it. I beg you to be lenient with me."

"Who's scolding you? I am merely alerting you. Being verbose will, on the contrary, make the magistrate scold you. He has summoned you again, so this time answer just what you are asked — don't be wordy!"

Fan agreed and followed Bao Xing to the western veranda, where he knelt on both knees to pay his respects.

"Does anyone live in this area?" asked Bao.

"On South End Pass Avenue there is Elm Forest to the east and Yellow Earth Mound to the west. In the north is a dilapidated hovel. All together there are not quite twenty families here."

The magistrate then wrote on the plaque carried by the

headman, "Notice!" and told him to inform those families that they were to come straight to Celestial Piety Temple if they had any grievances to air.

"Yes," said Fan, and off he went to Elm Forest. Meeting the Zhang's, he asked, "Do you want to sue anyone?" Bumping into the Li's, he asked, "Li the Second, do you have a grievance to air?" Everyone was startled by his questions, and became suspicious.

"As headman," said one, "you want us to sue each other so that you can extort money from us." "We pass our days happily and uneventfully," said another, "and you come along knocking on our doors looking for lawsuits. If it's suing you want, we will sue *you*! What a character. Get out of here! You bring a bitchy smell of bad luck! Some headman. Scram!"

Fan proceeded to Yellow Earth Mound and was shouted out of there too. Undaunted, however, he went on to the dilapidated hovel and called out again: "Today Magistrate Bao is holding court at Celestial Piety Temple. Is there anyone here with a grievance? Please come forward and ... "

"I have a grievance," interrupted a woman, "Take me to him."

"Aiya," exclaimed Fan. "What grievance do you have, my dear madame?"

Fan Zonghua was acquainted with the woman, though he knew nothing of her background. She was somehow related to Manager Qin of the imperial household. Do you remember back when Yuzhong gave his life as a substitute for the imperial mother, Empress Li? Qin Feng rescued Empress Li by disguising her as Yuzhong and having a trusted friend take her to his home in the country leaving orders that she be treated like his own mother. But Empress Li never stopped thinking of her son and cried herself blind. At that time, Fan's father, Fan Sheng, nick-named "Sheng fan" or "Leftovers," was doing odd jobs around the Qin household. Loyal, generous, honest, and a do-gooder, he was often rewarded by Empress Li and felt very much in her debt.

When Qin Feng was later burned to death, his own mother died shortly thereafter of grief — so none of the Qin family knew that the woman brought by Qin was really Empress Li. The proverb says it well: "Out of sight, out of mind."

The imperial mother, therefore, could not go on living with the Qins, yet she had no other place to go. Fan Sheng wanted to keep her in his home, but she would not hear of it. Fortunately, the dilapidated hovel was available. Fan Sheng fixed it up a bit and escorted her there to live. She was most fortunate to have his constant attention. Whenever it rained, he delivered her food and, fearing that others might take advantage of her, he had his son, Fan Zonghua, put up a little shed outside the hovel to keep guard at all times. All this he did out of gratitude for her kindness to him, never once suspecting that she was the persecuted imperial mother.

When Fan Sheng was near death, he told his son, "Take good care of the old woman in the hovel. Long ago she was sent here by Manager Qin of the imperial household and must be someone of quality. You must not neglect her." That Fan Sheng had raised such a filial son was, after all, a result of a life of good works. Since his father's death, Fan had, indeed, carried out his wishes, attending to the "Old Madame" and sometimes even calling her "Mother."

Now she wanted to make a charge, and he asked, "What has happened?"

"My son is unfilial."

"You are truly unlucky. These many years, I never heard you speak of a son — and today, suddenly, you want to bring charges against him."

"This son of mine," she said, "can be judged only by an incorruptible official. People say that Magistrate Bao is good at deciding cases involving the underworld and that he is incorruptible. All these years my case has been delayed because Magistrate Bao never passed through. Now he has come, and so I am seizing this opportunity."

"Since it is thus," Fan said after she had finished, "I will take you to him. When we get there, I will tug your cane as a signal for you to kneel to him. But please don't blame me however it turns out."

Taking up the bamboo cane, he led her to the temple. He went in first to announce her arrival and then escorted her in.

When they reached the foot of the official seat, Fan tugged at the cane, but the old woman paid him no heed. He tugged at it again — at which she surprised him by snatching it away from him entirely. Fan was beside himself with worry when she said to the magistrate, "Ask everyone to withdraw. I have something to say."

Magistrate Bao did as she bid and said to her, "There is no one here now. Please tell me about your grievance."

"Aiya!" she burst out. "Minister Bao, your Empress has suffered abominably!"

Her exclamation startled Bao, and Bao Xing, standing nearby, was chilled by her words and shuddered. Even Bao's normally dark-skinned face paled, and Bao Xing thought, "My Heavens! Good God! What a commotion! We have ferreted out an empress! How will this end?"

If you do not know what happened, read the next chapter for clarification.

Chapter 16

❦

The Loyal Scholar Falsely Takes a Mother;
Filial Madame Bao Prays for Sight-Restoring Dew

Magistrate Bao, hearing the words "Minister Bao" from the mouth of an impoverished old woman calling herself "Empress," wondered how an ordinary person would dare to speak like this. Tears flowed ceaselessly from her eyes as she told her story, which alarmed him and made him suspicious.

"Can you prove the truth of what you say?" he asked, rising.

She took an oil-stained little bundle from her inner garment. Bao Xing went forward to receive it, gathering his shirt up into a receptacle because, out of respect, he dared not use his unworthy hands.

"Release it, please," he said.

She opened her hands and the bundle fell into his shirt. He rushed it over to Magistrate Bao. When the wrapping was opened, a golden ball was revealed on which were engraved the words, "Palace of Yuzhen," which was, indeed, the official name of the empress. Bao rewrapped it, had Bao Xing return it, and rose from his seat. Bao Xing, understanding knelt on both knees to the empress and returned the bundle by placing it on top of his head, so as not to touch anything belonging to an imperial personage. He then led her by her cane to the official chair. When she was properly seated, Magistrate Bao paid her the respect that was her due.

"Rise, Minister Bao," she ordered. "My grievance is entirely in your hands."

"Rest at ease, Your Grace. Your loyal servant will do everything in his power to avenge his ruler. But there are many eyes and ears here, and I fear it would be unfortunate if this were to get out.

Forgive my presumption — but I would for the moment have you thought of as my own mother to avoid speculation. What is the imperial opinion on this?"

"I rely entirely on my son."

Magistrate Bao kowtowed again to express his gratitude. He rose and gave Bao Xing secret instructions.

Bao Xing ran out of the temple just in time to hear the district magistrate scolding the headman. "The imperial magistrate is putting up right here," he was shouting. "Why didn't you inform me of this immediately?"

"The minute he arrived," said Fan defensively, "he asked about this and that and sent me all over with a proclamation — I didn't have a free minute. Do you acutally think that I know the trick of being in two places at the same time."

This answer infuriated the district magistrate.

"Rotten slave!" he yelled, "You make a mess of your job and then dare to argue with me! I ought to have your dog legs beaten."

Luckily it was just at this point that Bao Xing came out.

"Oh, forget it, District Lord Magistrate," said Bao Xing. "It was My Lord Bao's mistake. He should be blamed. But he was so busy that he simply didn't get around to informing you."

"This must look bad in front of Magistrate Bao," the district magistrate said, smiling with embarrassment.

"The imperial magistrate won't scold you, so don't go on like this. He asks that you prepare a sedan chair, and find two capable servant girls, as well as an outfit of quality clothing and hairclasps and bring them all here immediately — at once, at once. Moreover, this official residence must be divided into inner and outer chambers. Please keep an accurate accounting of your expenses and the imperial magistrate will pay you back as soon as he returns to the capital."

"Get up now," he said, turning to Fan. "No need to go on kneeling. The elderly lady has been reunited with her son, Imperial Magistrate Bao. She says you have taken good care of her all along, and she wants to take you with her to the capital. You will be in her service there."

Fan Zonghua heard this news with great joy. He was in seventh heaven over the prospect.

"Will the district magistrate terminate Fan's responsibilities here then?" Bao Xing asked. "The imperial magistrate has ordered that he is to return with us to the capital to take care of 'Old Madame Bao' along the way. And we must somehow get him dressed properly. For that we need your help."

"Fine, fine," said the district magistrate, agreeing to everything.

"First bring the clothing, the accessories, and the maids," urged Bao Xing, "with the greatest of speed." The district magistrate was off in a flash.

Bao Xing re-entered the temple and reported to Magistrate Bao. He also instructed the old Daoist priest to clean up Cloud Hall. When the maids arrived, they escorted "Old Madame Bao" to Cloud Hall to bathe and change. Magistrate Bao rested in West Hall, writing several letters which he sealed securely and gave to Bao Xing to deliver immediately to the capital. He cautioned him to be extremely careful along the way.

Bao Xing left and Fan, after kowtowing to the magistrate, reported that the sedan chair and the horses were ready and that the district magistrate was arranging for official stopping places along the way. "Clothes do make the man," thought Bao, seeing Fan all got up in his new attire. Magistrate Bao instructed him to be meticulous in his ministrations to "Old Madame Bao," although, since she now had two maids, he was not to enter the inner chambers without good reason. Fan, who had a proper understanding of etiquette, agreed and withdrew. The old woman from the hovel had turned out to be the mother of an imperial magistrate, and the situation was now entirely different. How could he suspect that, in fact, she was nothing less than the mother of the emperor!

The next day, Fan brought the sedan chair around to the gate of Cloud Hall and the maids helped the madame mount. Bao steadied the chair pole with his own hand, and together they left the temple. The preparations were meticulous: four runners were to accompany the madame, and Fan, who merited a horse, was to bring up the rear. The district magistrate had also sent four guards to serve as an escort all the way to the capital.

After Magistrate Bao had walked the distance of a shot arrow, he said: "Mother, you enter the house first when we arrive, and your son will follow."

"Son, you needn't be so ceremonious on the road. You should also be carried in a chair."

"Yes, yes," he agreed and withdrew.

The others mounted their horses and started out only after they had seen Magistrate Bao withdraw.

Back in Kaifeng others might be fooled on an important matter like this, but not Mr. Gongsun. He was filled with suspicion, though he could not puzzle it all out. Bao Xing, he thought, deep in Magistrate Bao's confidence, had been sent back to the capital before the others to deliver a letter. This looked like a big affair, one he dared not inquire into too deeply. Neither could he mention it to Bao's four braves, Wang, Ma, Zhang, and Zhao. But he continued wondering about it.

Bao Xing, travelling through the night, arrived in Kaifeng with the confidential letters. Those guarding the magistrate's residence knelt before him and asked after their master. This we need not go into in great detail. When the steward had led the horse away to be fed and brushed, Bao Xing knocked on Madame Bao's door. Seeing that it was Bao Xing, her lady-in-waiting sent one of the maids to inform their mistress at once.

Madame Bao, nee Li, had been in a state of great anxiety, fearing reprisal from Grand Tutor Pang ever since Bao had executed his son Pang Yu. She could not help being alarmed when Bao Xing returned unexpectedly and alone, so she had him brought to her at once. She asked first about her husband, and Bao Xing, rushing through his respects to her, made haste to tell her.

"Master is fine and sent me to you with this confidential letter," he said, offering it to her respectfully. The maid received it and gave it to Mistress Li, who looked first at the two words, "Safe and Sound," on the outer sheet. Inside she saw a small envelope, on which was written "Madame Bao, Confidential." Using her gold hairclasp, she opened the envelope and pulled out the letter which said that Bao was pretending that Empress Li was his

mother and asked that East Room of Buddha Hall be prepared for
the visit of the empress. Mistress Li was to greet the empress in the
manner befitting a daughter-in-law greeting her mother-in-law, so
that everyone would be kept in the dark about her being the
empress — which must not under any circumstances be revealed.
The final sentence was, "Burn after reading." She asked Bao Xing
whether or not he was to return to Chenzhou. He informed her
that he was, in order to escort Magistrate Bao and his "mother"
back to the capital.

"Tell your master that I shall do exactly as instructed in this
letter. Everything will be taken care of — he needn't worry. Also,
it would be inconvenient to write a reply at the moment." She had
the servant give Bao Xing twenty ounces of silver, for which he
expressed his thanks.

"If you have no further instructions," he said, "I will head back
as soon as the horse is fed."

"Go, then," she said, giving him her final instructions. "Take
good care of your master — you don't need me to tell you that.
But tell Li Cai he musn't be lazy. He must return home as soon as
his task is completed."

Bao Xing agreed and withdrew to dine with some good
friends. He wiped his face and thanked them, and they all sat
down to eat. Business came up, and he talked about how they
warded off assassins along the way and how they executed Pang
Yu, at which point he inquired, "Has there been any reaction at
court from Old Pang?"

"Of course!" answered one of his companions. "When he came
to memorialize the emperor, the emperor was furious at first.
Pang dashed his son's confession to the ground, but he knew in
his heart there was nothing to be said, so in the end he asked for
pardon. The emperor was generous and gave it. Magistrate Bao
has probably planted an evil seed there. Better take some precautions against Pang."

Bao Xing nodded in agreement. He told them of how
Magistrate Bao met up with his mother in Chenzhou, just to put
their minds at rest and prevent questions when the empress
arrived. Then he finished his meal and mounted the horse

brought by the steward. Waving goodbye, he took hold of the whip and rode off to catch up with his master.

Mistress Li busied herself with preparations exactly as instructed in the letter. Every day she waited in an attitude of great respect and sincerity for the arrival of Empress Dowager Li. Finally one day, two messengers arrived and went straight to her quarters and knocked on her door.

"Supreme Mistress Bao passed through the city gate and is not far from here," they reported.

Mistress Li put on her festive clothing and went out to wait respectfully in Third Hall with her servants. The big chair was brought in and put down. Runners and chair-bearers withdrew. Mistress Li shut the door to the private quarters before she stepped up to the sedan chair. The curtain had already been lifted by one of the maids, and Mistress Li herself removed the hand rest and dropped down respectfully before the empress, saying, "This unfilial daughter-in-law, surnamed Li, wife of Bao Zheng, welcomes Mother and begs forgiveness."

The empress stretched out her hand, which Mistress Li quickly grasped, and they embraced each other.

"Rise, my dear daughter-in-law."

Mistress Li handed the empress out of the chair and took her to Pure Chambers in Buddha Hall, where she seated her in the principal seat and gave her tea. Then she instructed all the maids to withdraw to another room to rest. As soon as everyone was gone, Mistress Li knelt again before the empress.

"Your humble servant, named Li," she said, "wishes Your Grace a thousand years, a thousand thousand years of long life."

The empress extended her hands to raise her up and said, "My child, you are by no means to do this. We will treat each other as mother-in-law and daughter-in-law. It would be most unfortunate if, in trying to obey the rules of etiquette, our secret were found out. Let us wait until Minister Bao returns before we decide what is to be done. Anyway, both you and I are surnamed Li — so we actually are mother and daughter! You are not my *daughter-in-law*; you will be my *daughter*!"

Mistress Li thanked her and then the empress told her the

ancient story of her betrayal. The old empress was unaware that tears fell from her nearly-blind eyes as she spoke.

"These two eyes have been ruined from crying over my son and missing my husband. Everything is a haze — what can I do?" she cried.

Mistress Li stood near her, crying as well. Suddenly, she remembered something.

"I have a thing that will cure blindness," she thought. "If I can, with extreme sincerity, pray down some heavenly dew to cure the empress's eyes, I will truly have made myself useful and loyal and the object will not have belonged to me in vain." She was about to tell the empress about it — but what if, in the end, it proved ineffectual? Yet if she weren't told, she might be unwilling to wash her eyes with the dew. She thought about it for some time. Finally she forced herself to speak.

"Your humble servant has an Ancient-Modern Basin," she told the empress. "On it there are two openings — one for Yin and one for Yang — which receive sight-restoring dew from the heavens. Shall I pray for some dew this evening?"

"What a virtuous wife!" the empress thought. "She has seen my grief and found this way to comfort me. I mustn't appear ungrateful."

"My child," she answered, "if your sincerity can reach to the heavens and help my eyes, it would be marvellous!"

They chatted casually for a bit longer and after the evening meal was finished she withdrew.

Lighting the lantern, she washed her hands and brought out the Ancient-Modern Basin. She instructed the maid to bring candles to the garden, where she burned incense and worshipped heaven and earth with the greatest reverence. Holding the basin in her hands, she requested some heavenly dew. And, because her loyal heart moved heaven and earth and also because the difficult period of the empress's destiny was ended, there was a moistness in the basin. Then little drops of dew formed, just like condensed vapour. Gradually, they became bigger and bigger. Soon the basin filled up with dew rolling around like drunken pearls, swirling madly left and right until every drop flowed into the

Yinyang openings and became still. Overjoyed, she took up the basin and went straight to Pure Chambers.

But she was tired. Her arms were numb and aching and perspiration drenched her. The empress had not yet gone to bed, so Mistress Li held the basin so she could wash her eyes with the dew. A chill penetrated the empress's bosom, a fragrance surrounded her. Some drops of perspiration appeared on her temples, and she felt a rolling movement in her eyes. She closed them to rest, but then she felt joy in her breast and a lightening of her heart. The eyes, after all, are the flame of the heart.

She opened her eyes. The film was gone from them, the black and white of her eyes were distinct once again, and the moistness of youth had returned to them. The empress was beside herself with joy — and so was Mistress Li.

The empress grabbed Mistress Li and took a good look at her. There were many servants about, so she said only, "Thanks to the power of your sincerity and your filial heart, you have been able to restore my sight." But, as she spoke, she was overcome by a sudden sadness. Mistress Li rushed to comfort her. "Mother," she cried, "your illness was caused in the first place by excessive grief. Now that you are newly-cured, you must be only happy, not sad."

"You are so very right," the empress replied, nodding her head. "I won't grieve any more. My child, go rest. We can talk tomorrow. Now that my eyes are cured, I must close them and nourish my spirit."

Mistress Li withdrew. She had the maids carry out the golden basin and instructed everyone to take good care of her "mother." She sent, in addition, two more servants, and then returned to her bedroom.

The next day Bao Xing reappeared to report, "The master has already put up at Temple of the Statesman. Tomorrow, after an audience with the emperor, he will return."

"I am informed," Mistress Li said, and Bao Xing withdrew.

Read on to find out what happened next.

Chapter 17

❦

General Manager of Kaifeng Visits Bao; Empress Li Recognizes Imperial Concubine Di in Southern Purity Palace

The empress, her sight restored, was greatly indebted to Mistress Li, who daily comforted her in myriad ways and who, in every-thing — whether it was food, drink, anything at all — tried to please her. Mistress Li was coaxing the empress back to health, colour, and spirit, and she was becoming utterly different from the person who had lived in the hovel. But, because Bao Xing had said that the Magistrate Bao, now at Temple of the Statesman, was to see the emperor the next day, Mistress Li was anxious. If the Pang Yu case were mentioned and Bao's replies to the emperor were blunt and honest, the emperor, she feared, would be angry. She was extremely uneasy about this.

Who could have anticipated that on the next day, when Bao, during his audience with the emperor, told him everything, the emperor would praise him highly for having handled the affair justly. He even rewarded him handsomely with a ceremonial robe embroidered with five claws, a string of pearls, a four-happinesses white jade ring, and a pair of beaded coral bags. Bao thanked him, and headed back home after the court was ad-journed. Everyone there bowed in welcome, as he, still wearing his court attire, headed straight to the inner chambers.

His wife came out to him and, after the proper greeting, he said to her, "I would like to have an audience with the empress. May I trouble you, Madame, to ask her permission?"

Mistress Li, knowing that Bao would certainly want to see the empress when he returned, had already had the servants withdraw. She now took him to Pure Chambers in Buddha Hall, she leading the way up front, he walking behind. At the outer room, Bao halted while his wife raised the curtain, entered, and knelt in supplication. "The Imperial Sketch Academician and Magistrate of Kaifeng, Your Grace's loyal servant, Bao Zheng, has returned from his mission," she told the empress, "and he has come to pay his respects to Your Grace."

"Where is my son?" the empress asked.

"In the outer room."

"Bring him quickly."

"Bao Zheng pays respects to Your Grace," said Magistrate Bao, kneeling outside the curtain. I wish Your Grace one thousand years, one million years of long life! My humble home is cramped and crowded — Your Grace is greatly inconvenienced here. I beg forgiveness," at which he threw himself prostrate on the ground.

"Raise your head, my son," said the empress.

Bao raised himself to a kneeling position, and the empress, who had previously only heard his voice, could now see his face: a square face, large ears, a generous mouth, fine beard; a glowing black face with flashing eyes. He had the look of the blessed and the stern. She could see that he would be tall when standing. A sincere and upright, exalted person — and, by the look of that dark face, a demon chaser.

The empress was happy with what she saw. Her son, Emperor Renzong, was blessed because he had such a minister. But, then, suddenly, she recalled her own grievance, and the tears flowed uncontrollably.

"I am so grateful for everything you and your wife have done for me," she cried out. "My affairs are entirely in your hands."

"Do not worry, Imperial Mother. This humble officer will think of a plan. We must get rid of the evil and put the empire in order."

The empress wiped her eyes as she nodded at what he said.

"Raise yourself, My Minister. Go, get some rest."

Bao thanked her, bowed, and withdrew. Mistress Li let the curtain down and comforted the empress for a while. The maids re-entered after they saw Bao leave.

"Daughter-in-law," the empress said to Mistress Li, "Your

husband has just come home — why don't you go too. You must
see to his needs."

The empress, merely expressing her affection for the pair,
unwittingly embarrassed Mistress Li, who, to the empress's
amusement, became red in the face. The maids lifted the curtain
and Mistress Li withdrew, returning to their bedroom.

The household help were receiving the luggage and, when
Mistress Li arrived at her room, Magistrate Bao was having his tea.
He put the cup down, stood up, and said with a smile,* "I have
troubled my wife." His wife also smiled and said he must be tired
from the journey. They exchanged a few commonplaces, and
then he sat down. Mistress Li asked him about his trip.

"I have been extremely worried because of the Pang Yu affair,"
she said. She also asked him secretly how it came about that he
was pretending that the empress was his mother. Bao told her the
general outline, and she did not dare ask for details. Food was
brought, and husband and wife shared a meal. Drinking tea, they
chatted casually, and then Bao went to his study to take care of a
few official matters.

"The Grass County Bridge Runners are returning home," Bao
Xing reported. "Has My Master instructions for them?"

"How much silver do we owe for the clothing and accessories
we required at Celestial Piety Temple? Have them take it back
with them. Have Mr. Gongsun write a note of thanks, too."

Bao, who had after all just gotten off his horse, could not
respond immediately to all the matters demanding his attention.
He returned to his chambers to rest. About this we need not go
into detail.

The next morning, performing his toilette, he heard Bao Xing,
who was standing under the veranda, cough lightly.

"What is it?" Bao asked.

"Manager Ning of Southern Purity Palace has come especially

* The Chinese have a saying that Magistrate Bao's smile is rarer than
clear water in the (eternally muddy) Yellow River.

to send his regards and asks to meet with you in person," Bao Xing reported through the window.

Bao, who never received domestic officials, frowned.

"About what?" he asked. "I am conducting official business and cannot see him. If it is urgent, we will see each other in the antechambers before court tomorrow."

"Just a moment," said Mistress Li. Bao Xing stood waiting, until, after a while, Magistrate Bao said, "My wife is right." He then called Bao Xing back and said "Take him to the study for tea. When I have finished my toilette, I will see him there." Bao Xing turned and left to deliver this message.

Do you know what Mistress Li just now said to the magistrate? It was precisely something on behalf of the empress's case.

"Empress Di," Mistress Li had told her husband, "is in Southern Purity Palace. Why not see Manager Ning and find out why he has come? Perhaps the empress can meet with Empress Di, and then we might have something to talk about." Only because of this advice was Bao willing to go along with the meeting, so he finished his toilette and went straight to the study.

Bao Xing had already gone to convey the message to Manager Ning: "Our master is right now in the middle of his toilette. Please wait a little and he will meet with you. Would Imperial Counsellor please come to the study and have a seat?"

Manager Ning was so happy when he received Bao's message that his eyes lit up, and he said, "May I trouble you to lead the way? I said, didn't I, that as long as we have come, it couldn't be that we would not be shown a little respect. Given our relationship, how could he not grant us a meeting?"

Chatting away, he arrived at the study. Li Cai rushed to raise the curtain for him to enter the room. It was elegantly simple — a few adornments here and there, and that was all. A cry of approval escaped Manager Ning.

Bao Xing brought tea at once and motioned Ning to a chair, where he stood by and kept him company. Manager Ning knew that Bao Xing was Magistrate Bao's confidante and had frequently seen him at court, so he dared not be condescending.

In a flash, Magistrate Bao was heard outside, asking Li Cai if

Manager Ning had been invited in, so Bao Xing went out to greet the magistrate, raising the curtain for him as he entered. Manager Ning had risen from his seat.

"We have come especially to ask after Your Excellency," said Ning. "It was a long, difficult, and tiring journey. We ought to have come yesterday, but, knowing that Your Excellency was exhausted, we came today instead. I fear that Your Excellency may have business to attend to after breakfast. Has Your Excellency rested up then?"

He fell on the floor and saluted Bao. The magistrate returned the greeting.

"I am grateful for your thoughtfulness," said Bao. "I am uneasy that, before I have been able to pay my respects, Empress Di has already troubled herself to show concern for me." Bao indicated that Ning should be seated. He ordered fresh tea.

"What instructions do you bring for me on this gracious visit?" he said to Ning. "I look to you for enlightenment."

"We have come this time not for any official business," Manager Ning said, beaming, "but rather because Empress Di has so often heard her son, Prince of the Six Harmonies, praise with great reverence Your Excellency's loyalty, uprightness, worthiness, and talent. Empress Di is delighted with you. In this recent affair of Pang Yu, by executing first and memorializing the emperor afterwards, Your Excellency has demonstrated the forceful patriotism, sincerity, and fearlessness of a true statesman. The prince told the empress about this when he returned from court, and she was overjoyed. This one, and only this one, is a virtuous minister who can put our country in order and regulate the empire, she said to him. Then she counselled her son by saying that he was young and must always learn from Your Excellency how to become a pure-hearted, upright, and virtuous minister, and not show ingratitude toward the emperor. Our prince admires Your Excellency exceedingly. It is just that he cannot approach you without some official excuse. So we thought that, since Empress Di's illustrious birthday is coming up, Your Excellency might prepare some presents of the edible sort and go to celebrate her birthday. That will allow you to become closer, more intimate. On the one hand, you will be able to repay the good will of the empress and, on the other, our prince will be able to learn something from you. Isn't it an excellent idea? And I have come today with the express purpose of delivering this message."

Bao fell into deep thought. "I never receive powerful nobles from court. Only because of Empress Dowager Li have I done it today. Up to now it has been believed that Empress Di is the birth mother of the emperor. Who could have known that the true one was so unjustly treated? We'd best play it by ear. With luck, we will save a lot of trouble. Moreover, Prince of the Six Harmonies is benevolent. Some contact with him would be no disgrace to me."

"But," he said out loud, "I don't know the exact date of the birthday."

"Tomorrow is the celebration, and the day after the actual birthday. Why, otherwise, should we have rushed here as though chasing after a deer? The day is upon us and I have come expressly to issue this invitation."

"I dare not disobey," replied Bao. "But one thing. It is not fitting that we external officers personally pay our respects to the empress on her birthday. Just now my mother happens to be here. Would it not be even friendlier to send the gifts tomorrow and, on the next day, which is the birthday proper, have my mother go in person? Is this possible?"

"Aiya!" the manager exclaimed. "Your *mother* is here! That's even better. We will report this to the empress when we return."

"Again I am troubling you," Bao protested, thanking him.

"Well said! Well said! Well, now we will return. But first, please send our regards to the Supreme Madame. When we are all in the palace together, we will be able to show our hospitality."

"When my mother is in your palace, I look to you to take care of her needs," Bao added.

"Need you even mention this, Your Excellency? We will do our utmost to serve the Supreme Madame. Our friendship is the important thing here. Please don't see me out, please stay your steps." But the magistrate saw him out as far as the middle gate, until he finally departed, still protesting.

Bao returned to his chambers and told his wife all the details.

He asked her to report them to the empress in private, which she did immediately. Back in his study, Bao instructed Bao Xing to prepare appropriate birthday gifts to be sent the next day to Southern Purity Palace. He also charged him to take good care of Fan Zonghua. He must, under no circumstances, leak the real story to Fan. When the matter was fully advanced, a solution would present itself naturally. Bao Xing understood how important secrecy was, so he hoodwinked even Mr. Gongsun and the four braves, not to mention Fan.

Next day eight different presents were ready for Bao to cast his eye over. There was the usual liquor, candles, walnuts, birthday noodles, etc., which Bao Xing instructed the runners to deliver to Southern Purity Palace. He himself would follow behind on horseback, all the way to Southern Purity Palace Cross Street.

Doing so, however, he encountered in front of the palace a great conglomeration of people, horses, carriages, pole carriers, and carters. The noise was chaotic, and the road impassable. He dismounted and ordered his men to wait until the clamour subsided before they tried to enter the palace. He himself walked to the main gate, where he saw many officials sitting on the heated platforms of stoves on all sides of the five palace gates. Presents were arriving from all over, and everyone was holding name placards and talking in low tones. Bao Xing decided that it would be useless to wait until someone noticed him, so he walked right up the steps and went straight to one of the prince's officers. As he pulled the placard out from his gown, he said: "May I trouble you, Old Sir, to report for me — " "Who are you?" interrupted the fellow, eyeing him suspiciously.

"I am Kaifeng Prefecture's — " But he had barely gotten out these few syllables when that fellow stood right up and said:

"It must be Magistrate Bao's presents."

"Precisely!" said Bao Xing.

"Good Brother," said the officer, grabbing Bao Xing, "You have gone to a lot of trouble! This very morning our Manager Ning sent up a proclamation saying that His Excellency Magistrate Bao's people would be delivering presents today. I am here waiting just for that. Please come in. We'll sit inside." He turned and called out to the prince's runners, "The gifts from His Excellency Magistrate Bao, where are they? Display them, will you! Where are His Excellency's gifts? Bring them over here!"

Bao Xing was led into the study and given tea. The officer sat with him saying, "Our prince gave us instructions this morning to notifiy him as soon as His Excellency's gifts arrived." Then he added, "Would you like to have an audience with the prince?"

"Since I've come, I daresay it would be a good idea. But that means putting you, Venerable Old Sir, to more trouble."

"You can drop the 'Venerable Old Sir!' We are brothers. My name is Wang Xingsan. I am a few years older than you — call me Third Elder Brother. Always ask for 'Bald Wang the Third,' and that will be me! I unloaded my hair at such a young age that everyone calls me that," he chuckled.

When all the presents had been brought in, Wang looked them over. He picked up the name placard, took leave of Bao Xing, and went inside to make his report.

Before long Third Wang came back out and told Bao Xing that the prince had asked him to wait in the hall. Bao Xing followed him to the hall, went up the steps, and walked around the open space, going all the way outside the gate. There he saw a rolled-up screen, and facing front on a Grand Tutor's chair sat a prince. His hair was tied back under a ceremonial golden cap. He wore a ceremonial robe and jade belt. On both sides of him stood in-numerable domestic servants. Bao Xing kowtowed at once, and he heard the prince say from above:

"Return home to take care of your master. Tell him I send my regards. The great care he took, the many presents he prepared I accept and acknowledge. I will see him some other time at court. Thank you again!" To his own men he ordered, "Return the original name placard and give them a thank-you card. Reward Bao Xing with fifty ounces of silver."

The servants handed everything over to Wang the Third, who said confidentially "Thank them for the reward." Bao Xing kow-towed, then rose and followed Wang the Third until they finally exited from the hall. Manager Ning, all smiles, came over to greet him.

"So, you've come, Manager," said Ning. "Yesterday we really tired you out. When you get back and see His Excellency, tell him I have memorialized Empress Di, so he can send along the Supreme Madame tomorrow. Empress Di will not consider it a formal celebration — they will just chat."

Bao Xing nodded, and Ning said, "Forgive me for leaving now."

"Don't let me keep you from your work, Manager Sir."

Wang the Third wanted Bao Xing to sit for a bit in the study, but Bao was unwilling, so Wang gave him the placard and the silver. Bao Xing thanked him as they walked to the gate, where he encouraged Wang to go back. But Wang insisted on staying with Bao Xing until he had mounted his horse.

They went down the steps and saw that the horse had already been brought over. Bao Xing secured his feet in the stirrups and mounted.

"I kowtow to you," he said. Bao grabbed the whip and galloped off, thinking, "We spent twenty ounces of silver for the presents, and the prince has given us fifty in return. He is truly generous to his inferiors."

Shortly he arrived at the Kaifeng yamen. He met with the magistrate and recounted everything in detail. Bao nodded and then went to talk with his wife:

"What was the empress's reaction to what you told her?" he asked her.

"At first, she was in a dilemma — 'What shall I wear?' 'What is the right way to greet people?' So I said, 'Madame, for the time being your Phoenix Body must be inconvenienced by the clothing of the mother of a first-ranking official. Once you get there, Empress Di may not necessarily require you to perform a special ritual greeting. When the time approaches, just play it by ear and you'll finesse your way through it. With luck, the truth will come out. You are there ostensibly to celebrate her birthday, but it is really just an opportunity to get you into the palace. How does Your Grace feel about this?' The empress said, after some thought, that there was nothing to do but what I suggested and that she had best just go to Southern Purity Palace tomorrow."

Magistrate Bao was delighted that the empress dowager had agreed to the plan. He told his wife to send along two clever maids as well, as an escort.

The next day the empress mounted the sedan chair that was brought for her to Third Hall and was carried out. The middle gate was shut by the bearer. By that time Mistress Li had taken care of all of the empress's needs. But, while she had been helping her dress, tears had streamed endlessly down the empress's face. Only after Mistress Li had said a few words of comfort, stressing the importance of the real mission, had the empress come around. Mistress Li had instructed everyone go to Third Hall to wait, and, as soon as they had left, she had paid her respects to the empress again, this time in the proper way. Both Mistress Li and the empress could not stop crying. They wiped each other's tears and were both so choked they could not speak. Mistress Li forced herself to regain control.

"During this visit," she enjoined the empress, "please, I beg Your Grace, do whatever the situation calls for ritually if you want to have the chance to reveal the truth. You must not, because of petty matters of deportment, mishandle the important thing."

"I was grievously wronged at twenty," the empress said, nodding her head. "Now I am greatly indebted to you and your husband. If I can re-enter the palace during this visit and see my son, I will simply tell him the whole story."

"This humble servant is duty-bound to help you," Mistress Li responded, and then she helped the empress out the gate and walked with her slowly to Third Hall. She helped her mount the chair, secured the hand rest, and, as the maids lowered the curtain, heard the empress say, "Daughter-in-law, why don't you go back?" Her voice was full of sadness. Mistress Li assented and withdrew behind the room curtain. The bearers came in, lifted the chair, and slowly went out the middle gate. There was Magistrate Bao, kneeling in wait. He rose, and went forward, taking hold of the chair pole, and followed them out the yamen gate.

"Go back, my son," said the empress, understanding his intention. "There's no need to see me off."

"Yes," Bao said, and stopped in his tracks. He watched from

there as the chair was carried down the steps and saw Fan Zong-hua kowtowing toward the chair in the distance.

"Fan is not only lucky," Bao thought, "but is also very well-behaved." He could see Bao Xing on horseback bringing up the rear escort that surrounded the chair protectively.

Bao returned to the inner chambers where he found his wife with red and swollen eyes. Knowing that its cause was her leave-taking of the empress, he did not ask for details. He quietly discussed with her what might happen when Empress Li met Empress Di. They speculated for a while and then chatted idly about other matters. They would simply have to wait for news.

"Empress Li is compassionate and benevolent," Mistress Li said. "She is generous to others. It's unimaginable that she should have come to such great harm." Bao nodded, sighed, and returned to his study to take care of some official business.

If you don't know what happened during the visit of the empress, please listen to the explanation that follows.

Chapter 18

🐞

Grave Illness, A Mother Recognized; A Secret Mandate, A Righteous Minister Tries Guo Huai

Now let us return to Bao Xing, who went along as escort to the empress. Today was yet different from yesterday. Today most of the sedan chairs there were from the imperial ministry. Wives and concubines, imperial consorts and princesses came in a steady stream to the palace.

Bao Xing understood protocol, so he pressed his horse ahead and dismounted in front of the gate to the prince's residence. He tied his horse to a mulbery tree and headed for the gate. As luck would have it, he spied Bald Wang the Third and extended his hand in greeting.

"Third Lord Wang, Our Supreme Mistress has arrived."

Wang flew inside at these words and shortly there appeared two domestic managers, who announced to all those waiting, "Empress Di proclaims her thanks for your trouble and asks that you all return home at once. She requests to see only Supreme Mistress Bao from Kaifeng yamen."

Everyone nodded assent immediately. Bao Xing had the carriage taken in by his own two bearers and went himself with the palace managers. Then Wang the Third came out to accompany him to the study for tea. He was even friendlier than he had been the day before.

Now the empress's chair was carried to the second gate, from which she saw four eunuchs come toward her, change places with the other carriers, and take her to the third gate. They put her down only after they had passed through the middle door. Manager Ning raised the curtain and said, "My regards to Supreme Mistress Bao." He removed the hand rest, and the empress was

helped down by the maids she had brought with her. She looked
Ning over and returned his greeting: "How do you do, Uncle?"
Manager Ning then led the way to the inner chambers.

Empress Di was waiting outside the gate to welcome her. Di
was startled and bewildered to notice, even at a distance, that her
face was familiar, extremely familiar, but, for the moment, she
could not recall whom she resembled. When the guest reached
her and was about to pay her respects in the way befitting an
inferior to a superior, Empress Di stopped her and said: "Please
don't stand on ceremony." The empress dowager did not respond
with false humilty. They took each other by the hand and sat
down together.

Empress Li now observed that Empress Di had aged consider-
ably. Empress Di, taking a close look at the other woman, realized, suddenly, that she greatly resembled Concubine Li. But, Li
had long ago committed suicide — so she could not imagine who
this woman was. It made her uneasy.

When tea was over, they began to chat. Supreme Mistress Bao's
conversation flowed like water, her bearing was natural and easy,
graceful and refined. Empress Di was thoroughly delighted with
her and felt they were truly destined to be friends. She invited her
to stay in the palace for a few days, so that she could find out more
about her. This invitation was exactly what Empress Li most
wished for, so she agreed. Empress Di then summoned her
domestic managers and instructed them, "Tell the sedan chair
bearers and all the others that they needn't wait. I am keeping
Supreme Mistress Bao here for a few days. Reward all the runners
according to custom."

At this point a meal was served, and Empress Di insisted that
she and Li sit side by side to facilitate their conversation. Empress
Li, again, did not respond with false or excessive humility, and so
gave the impression of being straightforward and dignified.
Empress Di liked this about her particularly. While they were
drinking wine, Empress Di lavishly praised Magistrate Bao for his
loyalty, uprightness, and virtuousness. "This is the good result of
your moral teachings," Di told Empress Li, who modestly dis-
claimed the praise. Then Empress Di asked her her age, to which

she replied "I am forty-two." But when she asked then, "And how old is your honourable son?" the empress was struck dumb. Her face turned red and she could not answer the question. Empress Di did not press her, but glossed over it on the pretext of reheating the wine. But Empress Li would not take any more wine, so, after finishing the meal, they sat and chatted casually. Then they strolled around the palace enjoying the views in company. The more Empress Di looked at her, the more she resembled the departed imperial concubine Li. Di was extremely puzzled.

"How could she be unable to answer just now when I asked her her son's age?" she thought. "She turned red from embarrassment. There isn't a mother in the world who doesn't know the age of her own son. There is something suspicious in this. Is she deceiving me? No matter! Since I have already asked her to stay, we will sleep together tonight to make her think that I desire intimacy. But I will observe her discreetly." While her mind was working like this, she was noticing that the manners, gestures, and bearing of Supreme Mistress Bao were with increasing certainty those of Imperial Concubine Li. Yet she felt even more undecided about what to do.

Evening came, and, after the evening meal, the two women sat chatting as before. Empress Di ordered Quiet Hall cleaned up and pillows and quilts brought. She would while away the long hours of the night in conversation with the supreme mistress, she told them. This was exactly what Empress Li desired. When the time came for them to retire, no servant was allowed to enter the room unless summoned.

So, Empress Di now was able to bring up what had transpired earlier:

"How can it be that you don't know your son's age?" asked Empress Di, who pursued the issue by asking why the supreme mistress had deliberately deceived her. It was crucial that she explain.

"Imperial Sister!" the empress cried out. "Don't you recognize your sister-empress?" She spoke these words twisted by agony.

Empress Di could not help being shocked by what she heard.

"Can it be that Supreme Mistress Bao is actually Empress Li?"

But the empress was, by then, dissolved in tears and could not reply.

"We are completely alone," Empress Di urged her. "Why don't you just tell me everything?"

The empress, controlling the grief in her voice, proceeded to recount the entire tale, from how she was persecuted at the very beginning, how Yu Zhong died in her stead, how she was escorted to Chenzhou, how she met up with Magistrate Bao, who then falsely acknowledged her as his mother, how she came to stay at Bao's residence, how, thanks to Mistress Li's entreaties, heavenly dew was bestowed on her and cured her blindness, and, finally, that the reason she came today to celebrate Empress Di's birthday was precisely for the purpose of disclosing all of this.

Shocked by this story, Empress Di also burst into tears. When she could speak, she asked "Have you some proof of this?" The empress took out a golden ball and handed it to her. Empress Di examined it carefully under the light. Trembling, she handed it back and fell on her knees. "This humble concubine did not know that Your Grace was to arrive here," she said. "I have committed a breach of etiquette. I beg the empress dowager to forgive me."

Empress Li returned the initial greeting and then said, "Imperial Sister, please don't be formal with me. Help me find a way to let the emperor know."

Empress Di thanked her and told her not to worry. "I have a way." She described how Empress Liu and Guo Huai had plotted to replace the newborn heir, Empress Li's son, with a skinned cat and how Kou Zhu had carried the heir out and given him safely to Chen Lin, who straightaway hid him in a hand box and took him to Southern Purity Palace to be raised. When Empress Liu's own son died, he had been made heir-apparent to continue the line.

"One day," said Empress Di, "wandering around, he saw you in Cold Palace and felt instinctively a connection with you. He returned with tears on his face, which made Empress Liu suspicious. She tried to interrogate Kou Zhu, but that loyal woman committed suicide by smashing her head against the steps. Because of this, Empress Liu slandered you to the previous emperor. That's why he requested that you commit suicide."

Empress Li listened to this story like one in a dream. She came to suddenly and, greatly distressed, began to cry. Only after much comforting from Empress Di could she be calmed.

"How can we let the emperor know all this so mother and son may be reunited?" she asked at last.

"I will pretend to be sick and have Manager Ning inform the emperor. He will certainly come himself to see me — and then I will tell him."

The empress thought it was a good plan. Early the next morning, Manager Ning was sent to report, "Empress Di suddenly took sick in the middle of the night. It is extremely serious." Ning did not understand, but he dared not refuse to make this false report. Empress Di herself explained things to Prince of Six Harmonies.

Emperor Renzong at the fifth watch was just about to hold court when the manager of Benevolent Longevity Palace came forward to inform him that Empress Dowager Liu had taken sick and spent a sleepless night. Renzong decided to go first to Benevolent Longevity Palace to pay his respects to the empress dowager, but instructed everyone to keep this quiet for fear of alarming her. With great quiet strides he entered her bedroom. He could hear her groaning. Suddenly she said, "Kou Zhu, how dare you be so unreasonable!" Then he heard an "Aiya!"

The attendants lifted the bed curtain and the emperor approached the imperial bed. Startled, the empress dowager woke from her dream. Seeing the emperor, she said, "I have caused you anxiety. I have merely gotten a chill. It's not serious. Please don't worry." The emperor ordered the imperial physician to treat her at once. He said a few words of comfort to raise her spirits and then left.

He had gotten as far as Branch Palace Hall when the manager of Southern Purity Palace appeared, and, kneeling before him, said, "Empress Di took ill during the night and I have come particularly to inform you." The emperor was startled by this news and headed straight for Southern Purity Palace. The prince came out to greet him, so he asked right off about his mother's illness. The prince mumbled, "Your mother took ill during the night, but now she is somewhat better." The emperor felt a little comforted by this, and this was precisely what the prince had hoped for.

The prince then led the emperor forward to the imperial bedroom, which was still and deserted. Not a sound could be heard. Not a single maid was to be seen. The brocade curtain was hung high on the imperial bed, and Empress Di lay facing the wall.

The emperor sat by the bed and asked how she was. She turned over and spoke suddenly. "Your Majesty, what is the most important, most exalted thing in the world?"

"Nothing is greater than filial piety," he answered.

Empress Di sighed. "Can it be, then, that a son does not know whether his mother is alive or dead? And, even more, has there ever been a son who is the supreme ruler, yet does not know that his mother is drifting abroad?"

The emperor found these two questions incomprehensible and decided his mother was delirious.

"This humble concubine knows the answers to these questions — but I fear Your Highness will not believe them."

When the emperor heard his mother referring to herself as a concubine, he was alarmed.

"Empress Mother, how can you speak so?"

Empress Di took from within the curtain a yellow case and asked, "Does your Majesty recognize this?"

Renzong opened it. Inside was a piece of cloth with the imperial seal stamped on it and the imperial sign written in the hand of the former emperor. Renzong rose in agitation.

Chen Lin, standing nearby, was grieved at the sight of this thing and began to weep, remembering. The emperor was startled to see Chen Lin sobbing, and he asked about the cloth.

Empress Di told him everything — how Empress Liu had plotted with Guo Huai to gain the throne, how they had devised a plan to destroy Empress Li, and how thanks were due in all of this to two loyal and righteous people — Jinhua Palace attendant Kou Zhu and Chen Lin. This was the cloth used to wrap up the heir-apparent and deliver him secretly to Chen Lin. Renzong glanced at Chen Lin, who by this time was dissolved in tears.

"Chen Lin took great risks," continued Empress Di. "You, the heir, were removed to Southern Purity Palace, where you were raised for six years. When Your Majesty was seven, you inherited the throne because of the lack of any other heir. When, accidentally, against all odds you saw your real mother — in Cold Palace — you cried. This made Empress Liu suspicious, so that she cruelly caused the death of Kou Zhu and tried to force Empress Li to commit suicide. Two loyal servants, the little eunuch Yu Zhong, who gladly died in her place, and Qin Feng saved her, and she went safely to Chenzhou.

"When Qin Feng let himself burn to death in the palace fire and there was no one in his family left to care for her, the empress had to leave. She wound up in a broken-down hovel begging for food. Fortunately Magistrate Bao, distributing welfare in Chenzhou, met and acknowledged her as Imperial Mother. To keep the secret, he pretended she was his own mother, and yesterday I was able to see her because she came to celebrate my birthday."

Renzong was in shock, and his tears flowed like a river.

"Where is my mother now?" he cried.

From behind the screen was heard a mournful voice and then appeared a woman dressed in the clothes of an official's family. Renzong was stunned.

Empress Di, fearing the emperor's doubts, at once took out the golden ball and gave it to him. He saw it was the same as Empress Liu's, except that on it was engraved "Yuzhen Palace" and Empress Li's personal name. Renzong forced himself to go forward and kneel. "Your son's lack of filial piety has made My Imperial Mother suffer terribly." Great sobs shook him and he could say no more. Mother and son embraced and wept.

By this time Empress Di had kneeled on the ground and was asking for forgiveness. The prince and Chen Lin were also on the floor trying to comfort each other. After mother and son had spent their grief, the emperor thanked Empress Di and raised her and Chen Lin by his hand. "Were it not for your loyalty," he said, holding Chen Lin's hand, "I wouldn't even be here today." Chen could not utter a word, so tearfully moved was he. Everyone stood up.

"I have been emperor in vain if my mother has suffered like this," said Renzong. "How can I face all the officials? Have I not offended the whole country?" There were resentment and anger in his voice, and Empress Di tried to comfort him.

"Your Excellency should hold court," she said, "and send down a decree which Guo Huai and Chen Lin will take to Kaifeng's Magistrate Bao to be read aloud. Academician Bao will take care of the nest."

This was the plan that Magistrate Bao had asked his wife to convey to Empress Di. The emperor approved immediately, but continued to comfort his mother for some time before he returned to his palace.

There he set about writing a decree to be read aloud in the Kaifeng yamen. Guo Huai thought that it must be a decree enfeoffing Magistrate Bao, and happily went along with Chen Lin to Bao's yamen.

Bao Xing had returned home and shortly reported to Bao. "Empress Di has kept the supreme madame for a few days," he explained. So I have come back with the empty chair. They gave the runners all a twenty-ounce bonus and the bearers twenty strings of cash."

"Tomorrow at the fifth watch," Bao said, nodding his head, "go back to inquire, but be discreet. If anything is up, return immediately to report to me."

Bao Xing was already back at the crack of dawn. He coughed lightly under the balcony of the magistrate's bedroom.

"What have you found out?" asked Bao.

"I learned that Empress Liu had a bad night, so the emperor rushed there to see her. Then he went straight to Southern Purity Palace, where he heard that Empress Di was also taken sick. Probably he has not yet returned to his palace yet."

"Good," Bao said, and Bao Xing withdrew.

"This must be," Bao said to his wife, "because Empress Di's plan has disclosed the truth." Husband and wife were secretly delighted.

They had just finished breakfast when the arrival of an imperial decree was announced. Bao changed at once into his formal attire and went to the courtroom. Up front was Guo Huai, with Chen Lin behind him holding the decree. Guo Huai felt that, as General Manager, he should be the one to read the decree aloud, so he opened the imperial seal and, after the three salutations to Magistrate Bao were completed, read aloud "The emperor, entrusted by Heaven with the care of the empire, decrees: Now we have before us the eunuch Guo Huai." It was his own name. He could not go on.

Chen Lin took over. "Now we have before us the eunuch Guo Huai," he read, "who plotted against the throne and whose treachery is fathomless. The emperor lacked an heir and Liu and Guo plotted secretly against Empress Li when she was with child. Disobeying Empress Liu's orders, Kou Zhu secretly carried the heir to safety — her bravery was infinite. A bright and shining, newly-formed pearl was to die a violent death by order of Empress Liu. Chen Lin delivered the heir to Southern Purity Palace, demonstrating unwavering loyalty. Later, the heir's instinctive reaction upon seeing his real mother created suspicion. False curses and slanderous words killed our young and dignified Yu Zhong, who died in place of the empress. Guo Huai forced our revered Imperial Mother from her rightful place and caused her twenty years of deep suffering. Only because of the incorruptible Magistrate Bao's ardent loyalty have we this 'Day of Returning the Pearl.' This case must be tried with gravity and great care."

"Long live the emperor!" cried Bao, standing up to receive the decree. "Take him away," he ordered, whereupon Zhao Hu rushed to lay hands, mistakenly, on the virtuous Chen Lin. "You brazen thing." Bao shouted at Guo "You still don't withdraw!" Zhao Hu was stupified and it was, in the end, the four braves who took off Guo Huai's clothing, cap, and shoes and dragged him off to the open court where he was made to kneel. The imperial decree was presented and Bao arranged two seats, the official one for himself on the left and, next to it, one for Chen Lin. On that very day Magistrate Bao held court and said to Guo Huai, "You'd better make a complete confession of everything that transpired years ago."

If you want to know what happened, please read on.

Chapter 19

❦

A Cleverly-Extracted Confession, An Imperial Decree, and A Royal Restoration

Magistrate Bao brought Guo Huai down and called for order. He sat in the official seat and seated Chen Lin near him.

"Guo Huai," he demanded, "confess your plot to switch the heir and betray Empress Li."

"How can Your Excellency say such things?" responded Guo Huai. "Concubine Li bore a monster and the emperor was furious, so she was exiled to Cold Palace. Why is there talk of some switch?"

"If there were no switch," Chen Lin continued, "why did you order Attendant Kou to take the heir, strangle him with your waist band, and throw him under Gold Water Bridge?"

"Manager Chen, why do you bear witness against me? We are both imperial attendants. Don't you know Empress Liu's temper? You won't be able to bear the punishment when she sends down her edict against you."

"Guo Huai," said Bao, with an icy smile, "Are you using Empress Liu to threaten me? I would have let it go, but, since you bring her into this, then you will suffer for it."

Bao ordered Guo Huai taken away and given twenty blows with the heavy bamboo.

The court guards as one man pushed him to the floor. The strokes split his skin and rent his flesh, while he grit his teeth and grimaced, screaming unceasingly.

"You still refuse to confess, Guo Huai?" asked Bao.

Guo Huai hardened his heart, determined not to confess.

"It was Concubine *Li* who produced a monster. She brought this upon herself. It has nothing to do with *me*."

"Why was Attendant Kou killed?"

"Because Kou Zhu crossed Empress Liu, she had her killed."

"Bah" said Chen Lin. "When you interrogated Attendant Kou, it was I who held the stick to beat her! Empress Liu questioned her about where she had put the heir! How can you say it was a matter of crossing her?"

Guo Huai stared at Chen. "If you held the stick, it was by your hand that she died. You beat her until she could bear it no more. She crashed her head into the steps and died. Why do you accuse *me?*"

"Villain! You are lying! Guards!" Bao called "Squeeze his fingers."

The guards seized Guo Huai's hands and put on the press. They pulled both ropes and Guo screamed like a pig being slaughtered.

"You still won't confess?" asked Bao.

Guo gritted his teeth. "There is nothing to confess," he said, sweating like a bamboo steamer and going white in the face. Bao ordered the press released and the imperial torture instruments applied. Again and again Guo screamed until he became delerious and they had to stop the torture. Chen Lin was asked to write up that day's interrogation.

Magistrate Bao withdrew to his study and had Mr. Gongsun brought to him. He arrived knowing the details of this affair and, after greeting the magistrate, sat down.

"Guo Huai won't confess," Bao told him. "When I used the presses, he sweated horribly and paled alarmingly. I feared serious harm. This is a crime against the imperial family, but he couldn't bear up under the heavy torture. Help me think of a way to make him confess by torturing only his skin and flesh and not harming his muscles and bones."

"I will draw a diagram," said Gongsun, withdrawing.

After he had thought it all out, he made a quick sketch, gave it a name, and went back to Bao's study. The drawing was of something that looked like a large iron, but the surface was not flat. Nails with round heads had been soldered on. It was to be heated red-hot and applied to the fleshier parts of the body. Only the skin and flesh would be harmed, not the bone and muscle.

"Does this instrument have a name?" Bao asked.

"Its name is 'Apricot Blossom Rain'," because of the red dots that appear."

"Such a vile instrument with such an elegant name," said Bao smiling. "You, sir, are truly a man of talent."

Gongsun called the iron worker to construct this instrument immediately. By the next day it was done. By the third day, Bao re-adjourned court.

Guo Huai had been in terrible pain in jail, groaning and refusing to eat or drink. Within two days he had become extremely haggard. "I've been here three days now," he wondered. "Why hasn't Empress Liu's decree arrived?" Then he remembered. "The empress has been ill and she probably hasn't heard about this yet. I will grit my teeth and not confess under any circumstances. Without an oral confession, Blackie Bao can't settle this case. But why was the emperor suddenly reminded of this matter? *That* I can't figure out."

Just then the jailor came along and ordered him to court. Guo Huai's heart beat wildly as he followed the guard into the courtroom. Something was burning in a bed of red hot coals — what was it? He knelt down and listened to Bao.

"Guo Huai, why did you plot to harm Empress Li? And substitute a skinned cat for the newborn emperor? Confess — or your flesh will suffer."

"That never happened!" Guo cried. "If what you said had happened, it would have leaked out sooner or later. I beg Your Excellency to investigate it closely."

Bao's hair stood on end in outrage. He smacked the gavel and denounced Guo. "You villain! Even the emperor knows of your treachery, yet you go on telling lies. You are truly despicable. Guards, remove his clothing."

Four guards bared his back, and two held him down. A third used a cloth to press down his head and hair, and the fourth took the "Apricot Blossom Rain" from the hot coals and stood behind the villain.

Guo hardened his heart and said not a word. Bao ordered the torture to begin. The "Apricot Blossom Rain" scortched the skin and flesh. The stink was not pleasant. Guo screamed and went into convulsions, panting for breath. Bao stopped the torture and began the interrogation. Guo had fallen paralysed on the ground, and the guards had to support him. Bao had him taken away. Mr. Gongsun instructed the guards to take him to Prison Spirit Temple.

There the jailor, all smiles, offered him a bowl of something, whispering, "Venerable Lord, you have been greatly disturbed. This humble person has nothing to offer but this pain-killing pill and a jug of yellow wine I have prepared for you. Please take them, Venerable Counsellor. They will settle your spirits." Guo, hearing the warmth in his words, took the bowl without thinking.

"I am indebted to you. If I ever have a come back, I won't forget you."

"Old Lord, if you should ever leave Kaifeng, all you need do then is lift your hand, and I will follow." This flattery delighted Guo, who took the medicine and wine and felt better immediately.

"Is there any more of this wine?" he asked.

"Yes, yes," the jailor answered. "There's plenty." He ordered it brought immediately and respectfully poured it for the villain.

Guo Huai liked this meticulous and thoughtful fellow.

"Have you heard any court news these few days?" he asked as he drank.

"Just that Empress Liu was ill because Attendant Kou was haunting her. But she is completely recovered. The emperor visits her every day. Probably in a day or two her decree will arrive, and then you will be fine. Even Our Excellency Magistrate Bao dare not disobey a decree from the empress."

Guo Huai was so overjoyed by these words that he downed several cups of wine in quick succession. On an empty stomach, the wine made his heart beat wildly and his face turn red; his eyes glassed over and, when he got up, he weaved back and forth. The jailor took the wine and withdrew, leaving the villain by himself, reserved and self-contained in spite of his drunkenness. This matter weighed heavily on his mind. He could not shake it off. "Just now," he thought, "that jailor said the empress was ill because Attendant Kou's ghost had taken possession and was haunting her. She is better now, and her decree will arrive before the day is out." And then he thought, "Attendant Kou's death was unjust. No wonder she is making trouble."

His imagination began to run away with itself. He felt a gust of cold wind. The dust was blown about and landed on the window-sill. Suddenly a human form appeared, far away and near at the same time, making a humming sound.

Guo Huai, frightened, started to call for someone when the apparition came right up to him and said, "Guo Huai, don't be afraid. I am Kou Zhu, come to ask you one question. Yesterday the empress said this affair was planned mainly by you, so I released her to return to the palace. Moreover, I have discovered that you and the empress are down for long lives and, since I cannot remain here in limbo forever, I came today to clarify what happened so I can be released from my suffering."

Horror seized Guo Huai. The apparition before him had dishevelled hair and tracks of blood all over its face. Its voice was thin and frail, and he knew it was Attendant Kou's ghost, confirming what the jailor had just told him.

"Attendant Kou," he said involuntarily, "you died unjustly. I arranged with midwife Yu to substitute a skinned cat for the newborn heir in order to betray Empress Li. You didn't know the situation, so you died crying injustice. Since I am scheduled to have a long life, if I can get out of prison, I will have the loftiest Buddhist monks and Daoist priests help get you released from your suffering."

The ghost cried out "Counsellor Guo, you have good intentions, and I am endlessly grateful. In a little while we can go to the Hall of the King of the Underworld, and, if you explain what happened back then, I will be released. No need for monks and priests to release me. But, if you are not sincere in your confessions, you will create evil effects."

The wailing sound of ghosts was suddenly heard, and a small ghost appeared. It was grasping a Soul Warrant Placard that said, "The King of the Underworld and the emperor have convened court and now summon the living soul of Guo Huai for interrogation." The villain was bewildered, so he followed and did what he was told without question. Twisting and turning, they arrived finally at a hall, pitch black and gloomy.

"Kneel down," said the little ghost, and the villain knelt at once.

"Guo Huai," was then heard, "the things that you and Empress Liu did are written in the record. You ought, by rights, to be transmigrated, but your earthly life is not yet done and you must return to the world of the living. But consider the aggrieved ghost of Kou Zhu. We cannot yet accept this wandering female in the next world, so you must tell us everything that happened so she can be released from her suffering."

Guo Huai kowtowed toward the dais and told the entire story of how Empress Liu plotted to become empress and how they substituted a skinned cat for the real heir to betray Empress Li.

Suddenly the lights went on. Seated on the dais was none other than Magistrate Bao. Both sides were lined with guards, and it was like a hall in the underworld. One scribe had already given Magistrate Bao a copy of the confession, while a scribe from Prison Spirit Temple handed up a transcript of everything said by Guo Huai and the female ghost. Magistrate Bao looked over them both, then ordered Guo to sign them. The villain realized there was nothing for it — he had fallen into their trap — so he signed.

Do you know who the female ghost was? Gongsun Ce had summoned the singing girl, Wang Sanqiao, from Balustrade Hall. Gongsun coached her to impersonate a female ghost and elicit the truth from Guo. She was rewarded with fifty ounces and sent home.

Bao had Guo jailed with a strict guard. At the fifth watch the next morning, court was convened and the emperor memorialized. The confession was given to him to inspect and he put it in his sleeve. Court adjourned and he headed for Benevolent Longevity Palace. There Empress Liu was in delirium, her hands and feet twitching wildly, as though she were fighting off something. She awoke suddenly and, seeing the emperor, said, "Guo Huai is an old servant. I look to you, my son, to be lenient with him."

Renzong responded by throwing Guo Huai's confession in front of Empress Liu. The empress fainted away upon first glance. Her breath choked in her throat. Terror seized her and, terrified, she gave up the ghost. Renzong then ordered her carried to the side hall and buried as befits a concubine with whose body no great care need be taken. He also decreed that the palace be cleaned immediately.

The next day at court, after the three salutations were given by all the officials, the emperor summoned Magistrate Bao. "Empress Liu died of fright. I request that Minister Bao proclaim this far and wide for me and bring order back to the empire."

Then did the masses of people, the internal and external ministers learn that the imperial mother was surnamed Li, not Liu. The emperor had the court astronomer pick an auspicious day on which he abstained from meat and cleansed himself, so that he could go to each and every temple to offer sacrifices. After that he called for the imperial chariot and, taking with him all the military and civil officials of the court, went personally to Southern Purity Palace to invite the empress dowager to come home. Concubine Di (formerly Empress Di) rode along in the imperial chariot. We need not describe all the pomp and ceremony that went along with the return of Empress Li.

After Emperor Renzong brought the empress dowager in, he sent away the chariot and waited on her himself. At this time concubine Wang and all the others stood in line to receive the empress. She entered the main hall, and, after receiving congratulations from her place on the throne, she got up to change her clothing. She summoned Mistress Li, wife of Magistrate Bao, Academician of the Imperial Sketch. The empress dowager greeted Concubine Di with the ritual appropriate between sisters, and gave her even more gifts. The emperor also rewarded her, but we need not go into detail about this.

The emperor decreed that Guo Huai was to die by dismemberment. Midwife Yu was already dead, so her corpse was now, according to regulation, disgraced. He also decreed that a memorial hall, called Hall of the Loyal and Brave, be set up on the land near Long Life Mountain and Blessed Sea to commemorate Kou Zhu on the left and, on the right, to commemorate Yu Zhong, and these two halls were to be called Hall of the Righteous Twins. The writing finished, he personally burned incense in worship.

One day Prime Minister Wang Qi handed in a statement saying that, since he was old and feeble, he wished to retire. The emperor sympathized with the elderly statesman, bestowed upon him food and money, and granted his request for pension. Then he appointed Magistrate Bao Prime Minister. Bao memorialized the emperor about the merits and achievements of Mr. Gongsun and the four braves. The emperor responded by appointing Gongsun to be Registrar and promoting the four braves to sixth-rank lieutenants to continue working in Kaifeng. Empress Dowager Li decreed that Chen Lin would be promoted to General Manager and Fan Zonghua was to be Secretary. The Broken Hovel was to become a shrine with one-thousand ounces of silver and one-thousand acres of land for incense burning. Fan Zonghua was permanently to be the head of the shrine and in both spring and autumn take care of all sacrificial matters.

Chapter 23

❧

A Liberal Gallant, A Disastrous Event;
A Tiger Fight and a Chance Meeting

News of the special imperial examination reached Huguang
Province and came disturbingly to the ears of the scholar Fan
Zhongyu, who lived in Peaceful Goodness Village of Jiangxia
District in Wuchang Prefecture. His was a family of three — him-
self, his wife, Mistress Bai Yulian, and their seven-year-old son,
Jinge. Despite his reputation as a man of learning, Fan was very
poor, and his family was just managing to get along.

He returned one day from his literary study group beset by sighing and depression. Mistress Bai feared her husband was angry at
someone and asked, "My Lord, what has made you so unhappy?"

"Today at the study group, my classmates and I did no lessons,"
he replied. "Instead each and every one of them were packing
bags and preparing to leave. 'Where are you off to in such a
terrible hurry?' I asked them.

"'You mean you still don't know, Brother Fan?' said one. 'the
emperor has announced an unscheduled exam (in a special
memorial). We heard it might happen long ago. If we are planning to go to the capital to take this exam, you must even more so.
Why you will certainly come out first if you do!'

"It was these words that depressed me and sent me home, dear
wife. We are so poor. How can I go anywhere?" he sighed.

"So that's it," said Mistress Bai. "Well, there's no use worrying
over it. It has been many years since I parted from my mother, and
I had long cherished the hope of accompanying you when you
went to the capital to take the exams. You could have taken the
exams and I could conveniently have visited my mother. But,
because of our difficulties, I long ago put any such hope aside."

Mistress Bai comforted her husband with such words as she could, and Fan, thinking it over, realized that it was indeed a hopeless situation. Worry would serve no purpose, and he too had best forget the idea.

Early the next day, in the middle of his toilette, Fan heard someone knocking. He hurried to the door and was delighted to find his very close friend, Liu Hongyi. Fan clasped his hand and took him inside.

Liu Hongyi was an elderly person, loyal and upright, and Mistress Bai had never felt obliged to withdraw when he came to visit. She came forward to greet Uncle Liu, as did Jinge, and old Mr. Liu was very pleased to see them. They offered him a seat and Mistress Bai went to brew some tea.

"Today," Liu told Fan, "I have a particular matter to discuss with you. Have you heard that the emperor has added an extra imperial exam?"

"I found out just yesterday when I went to my study group," Fan answered.

"Then what are your plans?"

"I can deceive others," sighed Fan, "but not you. Elder Brother, look at how poor we are. What would you have me do?"

"Little Brother, don't feel sad," Liu said, hearing the dismay in Fan's voice. "But how much would it cost to go to the capital?"

"Just talking of it makes me uncomfortable," said Fan.

Fan went on to tell Liu about Mistress Bai's dashed hopes of visiting her mother, and Liu nodded and said, "There is nothing greater than filial piety, and that is as it should be. But how much would you need then?"

"Yesterday I calculated all the particulars, and, for three people, the journey would cost seventy or eighty ounces of silver. But I cannot possibly raise that amount. I must give up the idea!"

Liu hummed for some time, and then he said, "That being the case, let me make some arrangements. Wouldn't it be wonderful if I could work things out?"

Fan thanked him profusely, and, when Liu rose to leave, Fan refused to part with him, insisting that he stay for lunch.

"Eating is of no consequence now," Liu said. "I worry only

about delaying the important thing. Let me depart early — it's crucial that I begin making arrangements."

Fan saw he could keep him no longer, so he escorted him to the main gate.

"Till tomorrow then," said Liu. "You must wait here at home for my news." They bid each other farewell, and Liu took his leave.

Fan escorted his friend home, and he was both delighted and sad. Things seemed to be taking a lucky turn, but it was at the cost of involving a good friend in his own difficulties.

Back home, Fan and his wife again began to build castles in the air. On the following day, Fan was on pins and needles waiting and hoping, and no position he took was comfortable for more than a second. Noon was forever in coming, but come it did at last and brought someone to the door. Fan opened it at once, and there was Old Mr. Liu, his face covered with sweat. Wheezing and gasping for breath, he led in a black donkey.

"Good old black donkey!" cried the old man. "I haven't ridden him for quite some time, so he's acting up. He knocked me out all the way. I'm drenched with sweat." He entered the room and dropped onto a seat.

"Everything's taken care of," he said. "You really are lucky!"

He took the money bags off the donkey and put them on the table. He removed two envelopes and laid them there too.

"There are one-hundred ounces of silver here. Little Brother, you can go — all of you."

"So much!" exclaimed Fan joyfully. "But I don't know where you borrowed it. May I ask for an explanation and instructions?"

"Don't worry," said Old Mr. Liu. "I borrowed this from a very good friend and there is no interest — even if there were, I would take care of it. Yes, this is a bit more than you need — but take it. Remember the old saying: 'Frugal at home, Liberal on the road.' Another thing — if I may say an inauspicious thing — if you fail, stay in the capital. Don't come back, because next year is the regular exam, and that way you can save yourself trouble. It's always better to have a little extra."

Fan knew what he said was reasonable. He knew too that Liu

was both generous and straightforward, so he did not express thanks, but merely felt deep gratitude.

"Get up, Brother," Liu cried. "We must take care of the necessities for the trip."

"With the silver, it's easy," replied Fan.

"Let's plan the details. I won't go home today — we'll go shopping instead. Tomorrow is an auspicious day for your departure."

Off they went, dragging the black donkey, through the main gate and into town. Mistress Bai stayed at home to pack for the trip. By evening, Old Mr. Liu and Fan had returned, and the three of them packed everything, not resting until the third watch. They asked Old Mr. Liu to keep an eye on all the bulky stuff after they left and then tried to get some sleep.

But Old Mr. Liu was getting on in years and could not sleep. Neither could Fan, for anticipating the trip. The two chatted leisurely through the night. Old Mr. Liu gave Fan much good advice and Fan took note of it all.

At the crack of dawn, the cart came, and they loaded it at once. Mistress Bai bade Old Mr. Liu a tearful farewell, and then mother and son got onto the cart.

"There is one more thing," Old Mr. Liu told them, pointing at the donkey. "This donkey I have raised these many years. Please take him and ride him into the capital."

"You are so kind. How can I refuse?"

Fan went out through the gate with the donkey. He and Old Mr. Liu clasped hands, and neither could bring himself to let go of the other. Fan could not speak for his tears, and it was finally Liu who hardened himself and urged Fan to mount.

"Forgive me for not seeing you off," he said, and then he turned and went back through the gate. Fan went sadly on his way, while Old Mr. Liu went back to seal the doors and windows and inspect the house one last time.

They travelled during the day and rested at night on the way to the capital. They ate when hungry, drank when thirsty, and arrived at the capital without incident.

Fan settled his family into lodgings, and then he suggested

going at once to Compleat Mountain to look for his wife's mother. Mistress Bai, however, dissuaded him.

"My Lord, there is no rush. We came primarily for the examination. It would be better to go after it is over. We haven't seen my family for so many years that we will not be able to avoid a great many formalities, and that would be distracting for you. Gather your mental energies now, and later we will all go together. My family and I have been separated for so long already, what difference will another little while make?"

Fan felt the wisdom of his wife's words and determined to throw himself into his books.

The time for the exam drew near, and Magistrate Bao was sent by the emperor to administer it, which he did in an absolutely upright and impartial fashion.

Fan finished all three sessions feeling very satisfied with his performance and then turned his thoughts to his wife.

"My wife came along to visit her mother, but she sacrificed her visit for me, and we have delayed until today. She has been separated from her mother for so long and now, so near home, still has not seen her. I would be heartless if I were not now considerate of her."

He thereupon prepared the black donkey and went in search of a cart, which he promised to return after taking his family to Compleat Mountain the following day. As soon as they arrived at the mountain, they sent the cart back and went on in search of Mistress Bai's home, supposing they could find it with ease. But no passerby they asked had so much as heard of the Bai family.

Fan began to worry, and he regretted having sent the cart back. His original plan had been to put his wife and son on the donkey and walk beside them the remaining few miles. It had never occurred to him that he would be unable to find the place.

He had his wife and son rest on a black rock and put the donkey out to graze while he hastened ahead toward Eastern Mountain Pass, asking everyone he met for directions to the Bai house. But not a single person could help him. Fan was frustrated and anxious about his wife, and, to add to his problems, his legs were killing him. The only thing to do was head back to the place where he had left his family.

But when he got there, neither wife nor son was to be seen. Shocked and surprised, Fan searched desperately for some trace of them, his anxious eyes as large as brass bells. By this time, he was screaming. His voice sounded all over the mountain and echoed in the valley, but there was no answer.

Finally his voice gave out. Hoarse, dry-mouthed, and exhausted, Fan sank down on the rock and heaved great sobs.

Terror seized him — and then he saw an old forester in the distance. Fan rushed up to the man, crying, "Have you seen a woman with a child?"

"I did indeed see a woman, but there was no child," replied the forester.

"Where was the woman?" Fan asked at once.

"To tell the truth, it was a terrible thing. Five miles from this mountain, in a place called Lone Tiger Village, there is a violent marquis named Ge Dengyun. He is cruel and plunders the womenfolk of the people. Just now I saw him returning from hunting with a crying woman across his horse." Without so much as an answer, Fan turned and ran with flying feet down the mountain toward Lone Tiger Village.

Do you know what happened to Jinge? Ge Dengyun had brought a hoard of retainers to the mountain to hunt wild beasts, and they were surprised by a fierce tiger who sprang from a thicket of bushes.

The tiger, seeing so many people all carrying weapons, beat a hasty retreat down the mountain. But as it passed the black rock where Jinge and Mistress Bai were sitting, it opened its jaws and snatched up the child. Mistress Bai fainted dead away. All of this had just happened as Ge Dengyun rushed down the mountain. He took one look at the prostrate woman and ordered her put on a horse and taken home with them.

The tiger, meanwhile, travelled west across two small peaks. He passed under a tree in which a woodsman was cutting dry fire wood. When the man saw the child in the beast's jaws, he acted swiftly. "Tight situations breed wisdom," as the saying goes. He aimed the axe at the rushing tiger's head and threw it. The tiger received it right between the shoulders and the beast collapsed under the heavy blow, opening its mouth as it fell. Jinge dropped to the ground.

The woodsman, seeing that the tiger was wounded, climbed quickly down the tree. He grabbed his carrying pole and with all his considerable strength laid it across the tiger's haunches. With a great roar, the animal decamped over the mountain peak.

The woodsman hurried to pick up the little boy and held him in his shirt. Jinge was still breathing and his wounds were not serious, but the woodsman had to call to him for quite some time before he recovered consciousness.

The woodsman breathed a great sigh of relief. Afraid of running into other wild beasts, which would be no joking matter, he held the little boy firmly, found his axe and stuck it in his waistband, picked up the pole, and walked down the mountain. Heading southwest, he reached Eight Jewel Village in a short time and made his way to his home. At the gate, he called out, "Mother, open the door. Your son has come home."

An older woman with graying hair opened the door and cried out in surprise, "Where did you get this little boy?"

"Come inside, Mother, and I'll tell you all the details."

The mother took the pole and locked the door, while the woodsman placed the child gently on the bed and removed his axe.

"If you have any hot water, please bring some," he said to his mother, and she brought a cup at once. The woodsman raised the child and made him drink a little of the hot water. Only then did Jinge take a deep breath and speak. "Aiya! I was scared to death," he said.

The old woman looked him over carefully. Although he was covered with dirt he was a fine-looking child and she was disturbingly drawn to him. The woodsman described his rescue of the boy, and the old woman, shocked to hear of the child's narrow escape, stroked his head and said, "You were saved from the mouth of a tiger and will have a marvellous long life. Rank and wealth for all your days. Don't be afraid. Take your time and tell us where you are from."

"My surname is Fan, my name is Jinge, and I am seven years old," he said.

"And do you have a father and mother?"

"My father's name is Zhongyu and my mother's surname is Bai," he answered.

"Where is your home?" asked the old lady, amazed by what she was hearing.

"I am not from the capital. I am from Peaceful Goodness Village, Jiangxia District, in Huguang, Wuchang Prefecture."

"Is your mother's childhood name Yulian?" the woman asked breathlessly.

"That's right!" cried Jinge.

"Aiya!" shouted the woman, embracing the child. "My precious! My heart aches for you!" And then she began to cry.

Jinge was shocked and confused.

"There is no need to be startled," explained the woodsman. "My name is Bai Xiong. The Yulian just mentioned is my sister, and this woman is our mother."

"If that's so — then you are my grandmother," said Jinge, putting his little hands around the woman's neck, "and he is my uncle." Then he too began to cry.

If you want to find out what happened, read on.

Chapter 24

❦

The First Candidate's Madness; A Bearded Drinker's Death

While Jinge and his grandmother cried for a long time, Bai Xiong held back his own tears and comforted them.

"Your parents, having come to the capital," asked old Mrs. Bai, "why didn't they come here right away?"

"It was because we were looking for you that I was carried off by the tiger," Jinge answered, explaining how they had come to the capital both for the examination and to visit grandmother.

"My mother and father decided we would come to you after the examination, and that's why we came to Compleat Mountain today. We never expected that no one would know who you were, and, when no one did, Mother and I waited on the black rock while Father went looking for you. Then the fierce tiger came and I fell unconscious before I was rescued by Uncle. But what state must my parents have cried themselves into by now? They will be sick with grief!" Jinge began again to cry.

"But Eight Jewel Village — our village — is many miles from Compleat Mountain, and you were looking for us on the western mountain pass, so how could anyone have heard of it? Don't cry, Nephew. It's already late today, but tomorrow morning I will go to look for your parents."

Bai Xiong prepared some food and then he and his mother attended to Jinge's wounds. They cleaned off the dirt, washed him, and combed his hair. Bai Xiong applied medication with his knife, and they comforted him in myriad ways lest he grieve over his father and mother.

At dawn the next day, Bai Xiong stuck the axe in his waistband, picked up the pole, and headed straight for Compleat Mountain.

At the black rock, he looked all over but saw no trace of anyone. Then suddenly a man rushed at him, hair disheveled and face bloodied. In one hand he held a piece of cloth, and in the other a pair of vermillion shoes. He came forward in great confusion, and Bai Xiong tried to speak to him.

The man, however, raised the shoe as if to hit Bai Xiong and cried out, "You cur! Beat up the old man! Kill the old man!"

Bai Xiong dodged the blows and remarked to himself that the man bore a close resemblance to his own brother-in-law, Fan Zhongyu. He called out that name, but the man seemed not to know the name and responded crazily.

"I will get my nephew and bring him back to identify this man," decided Bai Xiong. "You crazy man," he said to the fellow, "you wait here a bit. I'll be right back," and he turned and headed straight for Eight Jewel Mountain.

Do you know who this crazy fellow was? It was indeed Fan Zhongyu. The previous day after hearing the forester's words, he had rushed into Lone Tiger Village and shouted at the gate of the violent marquis, insisting that his wife be returned. That hateful villain did not return his wife, but instead had Fan brought in and cleverly calmed him down with promises.

Thus the marquis kept Fan there, and in the evening accused him of murdering a family member and ordered him beaten until he died. The villain had a crate made and put Fan inside. At the fifth watch, the crate was to be thrown into the wilds.

The marquis' henchmen, however, ran into a group of messengers along the way, which caused them to drop the crate and flee. These messengers had been sent to announce that Fan Zhongyu had come in first in the exams. When they had found no one at his home and the house all sealed up, they had made inquiries and learned that Fan and his family had gone to Compleat Mountain, so they had continued their mission into the night.

Encountering, in the middle of nowhere, men with a crate who dropped it and ran, the messengers deduced a midnight theft. They suspected they might well have come into an unexpected fortune, and they untied the rope and opened the crate with some excitement.

Out leaped Fan, who had been prematurely judged to be dead. He straightened his body, grabbed the vermillion shoes, and began to attack everyone in sight. Frightened by his sudden appearance, his bloody face and wild hair, the messengers decamped. Fan bolted on, riven with anxiety, and step by step made his way toward Compleat Mountain, where he bumped into Bai Xiong.

Meanwhile, Bai Xiong had reached home, told his mother everything, hoisted Jinge onto his back, and set off again for Compleat Mountain. But, when he got there, the crazy man was long gone, and the only solution was to turn around and go back home. Once there, he questioned Jinge as to where he had lived in town, and, since he was not a man to shirk difficulties, he then set off at once on the forty-mile trek to the city.

Distance did not deter Bai Xiong, and, without stopping once, he made his way to the place his sister and her family had stayed. He found it, of course, sealed up, and though he had come, as the saying goes, "on the wings of hope," he was forced to return "with a heavy heart."

But no sooner had he turned again toward home than he heard a cry being raised in the streets. Everybody was shouting, "Where is the new number one candidate Fan Zhongyu?"

Hearing this raised Bai Xiong's spirits immensely.

"If he came out first, it's an official matter — and there will be an official investigation to find him. He'll certainly be found. I'll take this good news home and also question my nephew for more details."

But when Jinge heard that his parents were missing, he cried so bitterly that it took his grandmother a very long time to coax him to stop. Then the child answered all of Bai Xiong's questions, describing in detail how his mother and he had ridden in the cart, how his father had ridden the black donkey down the mountain, how the donkey had been put out to graze, how he and his mother had waited on the black rock, how his father had gone to Eastern Mountain Pass to make inquiries, and how he had been carried off by the tiger. Bai Xiong committed it all to memory and made plans to take up the search again the next day.

Bai Xiong's decision was indeed heroic. He had just spent a hard day covering one-hundred and forty or fifty miles — but dwelling on his hardships will delay our story, and, as the unofficial histories say, "One mouth is hard put to tell the tale of two separate stories." There were many reasons for his difficult day. Would you not like to know about them?

Do you know what they were? Well, on the west side of Drum Tower Street in the city sits Prosperity Timber Factory, which is run by two brothers from Shanxi — the elder one named Qu Shen, the younger one Qu Liang. Qu Shen was not very refined-looking, and he sported a very disorderly beard, so that everyone called him "Qu, the Beard." He loved his drink and was daily besotted — a habit that earned him yet another sobriquet, "The Dregs." Yet his drinking never interfered with his business and, with the help of Qu Liang, he made it solidly prosperous.

One day, Qu Shen consulted with Qu Liang.

"I've heard that the new shipment has arrived. I'm going to go have a look. If it looks okay, let's buy some. It'll be a bargain, don't you think?"

Qu Liang was willing, so Qu Shen put four-hundred ounces of silver into his moneybag and hired a mottled donkey the colour of soy sauce. It was an eccentric donkey that delighted in following crowds. If there were no other donkeys on the road, it was hard to get him to move, but show him another donkey and he would set off at once in pursuit. Qu Shen put the moneybag on the saddle, mounted, and started for South Compleat Mountain.

He arrived at the lumberyard, whose proprietor he knew well, but, no matter how much lumber he looked at, the dimensions were all wrong. He made, in the end, no purchase, but the etiquette of business prevented any hard feelings about it, and the proprietor proffered food and drink as usual.

It took but one look at the drink to set Qu Shen off, and it was left a cup and right a cup as they talked and laughed. In the end he got so drunk he forgot about going home until, looking up at the declining sun, he suddenly declared, "I must get to the city. It's very late, very late."

He continued to mutter about how late it was while standing

up, bowing a salute, and grabbing hold of his soy-coloured, mottled donkey. He mounted and turned the donkey in the direction of Compleat Mountain.

But the donkey would not budge. Qu Shen got more and more upset. He whipped the animal on the left and on the right, scolding him all the while.

"Stinking shitegg from the swamps!" he cursed. "You nourish a solider one-thousand days so as to use him on only one — and there's nothing under the sun worse than not even getting your one!"

He was still shouting when the donkey suddenly perked up its ears, cried out "Ma," and began prancing madly in all directions. Qu Shen knew his donkey and surmised that it must have heard another donkey's cry. So he held tight to the reins and let it go where it wished. Anything was better than the stupor from which it had just awakened.

Finally there appeared before them another donkey, running back and forth. As soon as Qu's donkey saw this donkey, it began kicking wildly. Qu Shen was unable to stay in the saddle and slid off the donkey's rear end. He picked himself up and gave the donkey a good whipping. Then he grabbed its bit, turned it around, and tied it to an elm tree.

He saw that the other donkey was a black one, complete with saddle and flaps. The black donkey — the very one Fan had ridden, put out to graze, and forgotten about in his troubles — had not eaten all night and had wandered aimlessly, following its reins until it wound up outside Eastern Mountain Pass eating grass.

"Whose donkey is this?" cried Qu Shen after staring at it for some time. He called out several times, but there was no answer.

"What a fine donkey it is," he said to himself, looking at the mouth, the four teeth, the sleek and plump body, and the bright and shiny saddle.

"No one's around," he thought. "I'll exchange the mother." So he put his moneybag on the black donkey, grabbed the reins, and mounted. The animal galloped off as though it had wings, and Qu Shen was delighted with his bargain.

But soon a violent wind blew up and the dust irritated his eyes

so that he could barely open them. It was growing dark, too —
already time to light a lamp — and Qu Shen grew fearful.

"I'll never get into town under these conditions. But I still have
four-hundred ounces of silver. If I meet a ruffian up ahead at
Compleat, it would be a real mess. I'd better rent a room from
someone and stay the night."

No sooner had this thought occurred to him than he noticed up
ahead a slight slope, on the south side of which he saw a light. He
got off the donkey, led it to the slope, and stopped in front of a
gate. He heard a woman's voice.

"Jiahan, Jiahan," she was saying, "get dressed and eat. Do
people starve their wives?"

Then a man's voice said, "*You're* hungry? Who said *I've* eaten
anything?"

"You don't *eat* anything!" the woman cried. "You just *drink*
your 'yellow soup'!"

"Nobody told you not to drink!"

"If I could drink, I would long ago have started. You finally get
some money and you forget all about the food and the firewood.
All you do is drink it up."

"That's hard to say. It's just that I have a lucky mouth," the man
said.

"Since you like ready-made dishes so much, I'll make a point of
arranging for you to have junk food tomorrow. You can enjoy
yourself a bit."

"Don't talk nonsense," he said. "I may be poor, but I'm a good
fellow."

"And just where in town is there a good fellow like you?"

Qu Shen was reluctant to knock, but there was not another
light in the darkness, so he tapped on the door with his whip and
called out softly.

"Excuse me. I am looking for lodgings."

Suddenly, all sound from inside stopped.

Qu Shen called again, and finally the woman asked, "Who're
you looking for?"

"I'm a traveller. Pardon me, but I am looking for a place to stay
because it's gotten dark. Tomorrow I will thank you lavishly."

"Wait a minute," said the woman.

After another long silence, a man came out carrying a lantern and asked, "What are you up to?"

"I was just passing through," Qu Shen said, "and because it got dark, it's hard to walk and I was a little disturbed, so I'd like to find a place to stay. I'll thank you lavishly tomorrow."

"So that's it," said the man. "No big thing. Come in and sit down."

"I also have a donkey," said Qu Shen.

"Bring it along," said the man. He tied the donkey to a tree on the east side and, carrying the lamp, led Qu to the inside room.

Qu Shen picked up his moneybag and followed him. When he entered, he saw that there were two inner rooms and one outer, a three-room hut. Qu Shen placed the moneybag on the brick-bed and again greeted the man.

The man returned the greeting and said, "It's just a poor grass hut — don't laugh at us, boss."

"Well said," Qu Shen responded.

"Your honourable surname?" he asked. "And where is it that you made your fortune?"

"My name is Qu, Qu Shen. I have a timber factory on Drum Tower Street in town. And your honourable name?"

"Li, Li Bao."

"Oh — Big Brother Li. Forgive me, forgive me."

"Well said, well said, Big Brother Qu. Pleased to meet you. Pleased to meet you."

Do you know who Li Bao was?

Li Bao was the one sent by Magistrate Bao's father-in-law to accompany the magistrate to the capital to take the examination. Later, when Magistrate Bao was fired, Li had decided Bao would never return to office, and he had run off with all their luggage and silver. Every day he frequented places of ill-repute and in short order had spent everything.

He wound up in this place and set up in Old Li's store. He seemed at first, to old Mr. and Mrs. Li, to be an industrious and careful sort, and, since they had no sons, they had him marry their daughter, so he could take care of them in their old age.

But he could not change his character, and he continued to philander, gamble, eat, and drink. He literally infuriated the old couple to death. He took over the store and became even more unscrupulous, giving in to dissolute ways.

Mistress Li was no better than her husband — gluttonous and imprudent — and, before two years were out, they had to close the store. Later they had to sell all the furniture and equipment in the store, and finally they broke down the store front and sold the pieces. All that was left was the grass hut. At present they were seriously impoverished. And now luck brought them the unfortunate Qu Shen as a lodger for the night.

While Li Bao was drawing him out, he noticed that there was no oil in the lamp. He rose, lifted a torn curtain, and went to the east room to get some. As he passed his wife, she whispered, "What was it that he just put on the brick bed that made that jingling sound."

"It's his moneybag," Li Bao answered.

"Then we'll be rich! And don't we deserve it," said the woman happily.

"How so?" asked Li Bao.

"You silly rabbit! He has only one moneybag and it's very heavy. He must have hard cash in there. Offer him a drink — if he drinks, we are eighty per-cent made. We've got plenty of drink. Do your best to get him drunk and I'll take care of the rest."

Li Bao understood her and took out the oil jar and added some oil to the lamp, so that it lighted the whole room. Then he talked up a storm — Big Brother this, Big Brother that — until finally he inquired, "Big Brother Qu, do you drink?"

The question made Qu Shen salivate, such a craving for drink did he have. "Where can one get liquor in the middle of the night?"

"We have it right here," Li Bao said, "To be honest about it, I love drinking more than anything else."

"Right!" cried Qu Shen. "I feel the same way. We are bosom buddies!"

While he spoke, he warmed the wine. The two sat facing each other. Qu Shen did indeed love to drink — but Li Bao had an ulterior motive. He pressed wine on him once, twice, three times, until Qu Shen was blind drunk and sat rocking back and forth, unable even to speak. He pulled the moneybag close to him, and, as soon as he put his head on the pillow, he fell into a deep sleep, snoring sweetly.

Mistress Li now made her appearance.

"He's drunk all right — what's your plan?" asked Li Bao.

"Go find a rope."

"What for?" asked Li Bao.

"Stupid! To strangle him with and be done with it."

"'Human fate is governed by the heavens,'" protested Li Bao, shaking his head. "It's nothing to fool around with."

"You want to make a fortune," she said angrily, "yet you haven't the stomach for it. Spineless bastard! Do you really want me to starve to death with you?"

She nagged him until he no longer cared about the laws of his country. He brought the rope. His wife had already moved the broken brick bed away, but, when she saw Li Bao shaking and trembling, she knew he could not do the job. The evil woman grabbed the rope from him. She gave one end to Li Bao, got on the brick bed, wrapped the rope once around Qu Shen's neck, and then told her husband to pull hard.

Qu Shen's hands and feet struggled as he tried to get free, and Li Bao had to use all his strength, in spite of his fear. Before long Qu Shen stopped struggling — at which point Li Bao became paralysed. The evil woman opened the moneybag and drew out packet after packet — eight in all — and she was ecstatic.

If you want to know what happened, read on.

Chapter 25

❦

Mistress Bai Resurrected, Bad Yin, Worse Yang; Qu Shen, Possessed, Dies Inebriated and Revives in a Dream

Let us return now to Li and his wife. By the light of the lamp, Mistress Li lifted the lid of the brick bed and hid inside the packets of silver from Qu Shen's moneybag. Then the two murderers left the room and turned their attention to the corpse.

"It's late and no one is about," said the wife. "Let's carry him to the northern slope and throw him behind the temple. Who will know?"

Li Bao could see no other way, so he had his wife get back up on the brick bed to lift the body onto his back. Only when he stood up did he realize how heavy Qu Shen was, and it was not long before they both collapsed on the floor. Li Bao struggled to his feet again, however, and exerted all his strength. The wife quietly opened the door, looked around, and said, "Go while there's no one here. Take him away quickly."

Li Bao secured the body on his back and struck out for the northern slope. He had not walked far when a black shadow made his hair stand on end and his eyes see stars. He threw the corpse to the ground, and ran straight to the southern slope, stopping for nothing.

"I'm here! Where are you running?" his wife demanded.

"Scared me silly!" he said, gasping for breath. "Just now, not far from the northern slope, I saw someone. I threw the corpse to the ground and ran back. I didn't think I would run past the house."

"That was your fear creating hidden devils. You have forgotten that small willow tree on the northern slope. You took it for a person."

Realizing his mistake, Li had his wife close the door at once.

"But the deed is not done yet," his wife said.

"What else is there to do?"

"If we keep that donkey, it will be seed for disaster."

"Yes," Li Bao said, "What do you think we should do?"

"Can't you handle even this tiny matter? Let's just chase it away!"

"What a shame, don't you think?" Li Bao said.

"You have come into an enormous fortune and you're still thinking of a donkey?"

Abashed, Li Bao rushed out into the courtyard, untied the donkey, and led it outside. Once in front of the gate, however, the donkey refused to budge. Li Bao's cruel wife then picked up the gate-bar and smacked the donkey hard on its haunches. In pain, the donkey pulled to the end of its tether. The wife struck it a second time, Li Bao let go, and the animal fled down the hill.

The evil woman motioned her husband back inside and finally locked the door. Li Bao's heart was pounding wildly, but his wife was bold and self-satisfied.

"Tomorrow we will act perfectly normal — just 'draw water from the well.' If someone discovers the corpse, you go along to have a look lest people get suspicious. When things calm down, we'll start using the money. What do you say — have we done a clean job of it or not? Secret enough?" Her cockiness emboldened Li Bao.

Just then, the cock crowed three times and day dawned. People were already walking on the road, and it was not long before one of them spotted the corpse. More people gathered, and a busybody went to inform the local headman, who came as soon as he heard that there was a corpse in his jurisdiction.

"It's a case of strangulation," said Kutou, the headman, who examined the rope around the corpse's neck and found it loose and untied. "Fellow villagers, watch it for me. Don't let any wild animals get to it. I'm going for my helper. He can take care of it while I report to the district." And he left, heading west.

He had walked only a few steps when the villagers all began to cry, "Come back! Come back! He's alive! He's come back to life!"

"Don't horse around," Kutou said, turning his head. "This is a terrible thing. Why are you carrying on like this?"

"He really has revived! We're not joking!"

Kutou turned back, and, indeed, the curled up hands and feet of the corpse were opening up and the man was reviving. They helped him sit up, with his legs crossed, and after a long while he cried "Aiya" in a very faint voice.

Kutou knelt before the man.

"Friend," he said. "Wake up. Wake up and tell me whatever is on your mind."

Qu Shen's eyelids fluttered and he looked up at Kutou, then at all the others.

"Ya!" he cried suddenly in a delicate, feminine voice, "Who are you all? Why are you talking to me, a humble woman? You don't even keep a distance!" He covered his face modestly with his sleeve. Everyone stared at him and burst into laughter.

"A fine 'humble woman,'" they laughed. "A fine 'humble woman' you are!"

But Kutou held them off.

"Don't laugh," he admonished. "He has just revived and his spirit is not in order yet. Please be quiet. Let me question him thoroughly."

The laughter stopped, and Kutou said, "Friend, who tried to kill you? Who strangled you? Tell me about it."

"This humble woman hung herself of her own free will," said Qu Shen, hanging his head shyly and delicately. "I was not strangled."

"But you were!" shouted the villagers. "You didn't hang yourself — there is still a rope around your neck and you are lying here!"

"Quiet, everyone," said Kutou. "Let me question him. Friend, why did you hang yourself?"

"My husband and son and I were on our way to visit my mother, and a cruel marquis kidnapped me and hid me upstairs in the rear building of his house. He wanted me to sleep with him. I pretended to agree, got rid of the maid, and hung myself."

"You all heard this, right?" said Kutou, turning to the villagers.

He stuck up his thumb. "Someone else is involved in this. It is really strange. To look at his appearance and listen to his speech, the inside doesn't quite match the outside!"

He was still pondering the puzzle when he heard something behind him and received a blow on the back of his head. He grabbed the hand of his assailant and whirled around, crying, "Aiya, who are you?"

He found himself face to face with a crazy man, holding a shoe and hitting people with it.

"I get up at the crack of dawn," muttered Kutou, "and find one mixed-up person lying on the ground and another who hits me with a shoe. What a mess!"

"The man with the shoe is my husband!" cried Qu Shen. "Please hold him."

"Good friend," laughed the villagers, "no one with a face like *yours* could get a *husband*!"

The laughter was interrupted by the shouts of two people who suddenly appeared on the road struggling over a dappled donkey.

"Headman, headman," they called. "We want to fight this out in court!"

"Damn it!" said Kutou. "What luck! One case isn't even done before another comes along."

"Let go of each other," he commanded. "Now, you two take your time and say whatever you have to say."

Do you know who those two fellows were — Qu Liang and Bai Xiong, fighting over a donkey. The day before, after Bai Xiong had returned home, he set out again for Compleat Mountain early the next morning. He came out Eastern Mountain Pass looking all over for his brother-in-law. When he caught sight of a soy-coloured donkey tied to an elm tree, he took it to be his brother-in-law's donkey. (Jinge had not said the donkey was black, nor had Bai Xiong thought to ask the colour of the coat.) Figuring that with the donkey it would be easier to find his relatives, he untied it and took it with him. But, very shortly, he bumped into Qu Liang.

Now Qu Liang had become quite uneasy when his brother,

who was carrying four-hundred ounces of silver, had not come home. He made up his mind to rush straight to the boat factory to make inquiries as soon as the city gates were opened in the morning. When on the way he ran into Bai Xiong leading a dappled donkey that was exactly the donkey that his brother had ridden, he accosted him.

"Where are you taking our donkey?" he shouted. "Where is my brother? And our silver?"

"This is my relative's donkey," Bai Xiong answered, looking the stranger over. "And I might ask *you* where my brother-in-law and sister are!"

One thing led to another, and they finally went in search of the headman to press charges. They soon bumped right into him, as we have seen.

"Let go of each other," ordered Kutou a second time. "I said take your time and tell me what's on your minds."

But just then Qu Liang spotted his brother sitting on the ground and called out to him. He dropped Bai Xiong's hand and ran to his brother's side.

"OK, OK, isn't this my brother here?"

"Brother, what are you doing here?" he cried. "And how come this rope is around your neck?"

"Keep your distance!" said Qu Shen. "Who are you to dare to be so rude to me?"

When Qu Liang heard a woman's voice coming from his brother's mouth — and not even using their Shanxi dialect — he was covered with confusion.

"What's wrong with you?" he demanded. "We Shanxi people are 'hearty fellows.' How can you face people in your present condition?"

Ignoring Qu Liang, Qu Shen called out to Bai Xiong, "Aren't you my brother Bai Xiong? Aiya, Brother! Look at what trouble your sister is in!"

It was Bai Xiong's turn to be thunderstruck.

"Step aside!" shouted someone. "Quick! That crazy man is back!"

Bai Xiong realized at once that it was the very same man he had encountered two days before.

"Brother," said Qu Shen in his high feminine voice, "that's your brother-in-law Fan Zhongyu. Stop him!"

Bai Xiong, fed up with the confusion, handed the reins of the donkey to the headman and grabbed firm hold of the crazy man. Everybody helped, and finally they subdued him.

"I can't make heads or tails of this case," cried Kutou. "You two needn't fight over the donkey. I'm going to take you all to the district yamen. You can tell your stories there."

He saw an old man coming toward him and called out to him to hurry.

"How can you dawdle at a time like this, my dear sir?"

"I came as soon as I heard!" replied the man.

"Quickly, find two carts. That one was almost killed and can't walk, this one is crazy, and those two there are also involved. Hurry!"

The old man turned, left immediately, and returned before long with two carts. He told Qu Shen to get up, but Qu Shen insisted on being lifted in by Bai Xiong — who, however, refused. But everyone urged Bai Xiong on and, having no choice, he raised Qu Shen up. Those large feet of Qu Shen's coyly and coquettishly moved forward in two-inch steps, as though they were precious three-inch Golden Lilies. Everyone burst into laughter.

Qu Liang, watching all this, was mortified and sighed audibly. When Qu Shen finally got on the cart, Qu Liang elected to ride in the same one as his brother — but Qu Shen hooted him off and Bai Xiong got on instead. Qu Liang was told to ride with the crazy man, who hit him on the head with the shoe and drove him off the cart.

He started, in desperation, to mount the dappled donkey, but the headman would not allow it.

"We haven't determined yet whether or not this donkey is yours — and if it isn't yours it's best that I ride it."

There was no other solution but for Qu Liang to run alongside the cart, and so in this way they all headed straight for Lucky Charm District.

Along the way, they encountered a black donkey, and the

dappled donkey took off after it. The headman hung on gamely, but it was clear he would not keep his seat long. Qu Liang rushed forward, grabbed the bit of the donkey, and explained, "You don't know about this donkey's eccentricity. As soon as he sees another donkey, he chases after it."

Suddenly, from behind the black donkey appeared a short, dark man, his shirt open in front. He and a companion were closely following the donkey. Do you know who this man was? None other than Fourth Brother Zhao Hu. Because of the disappearance of the man who had come in first in the civil service examination, Magistrate Bao had gone to memorialize the emperor and then had initiated an investigation in Kaifeng. Having adjourned court and set out in his carriage, he was startled by the sounds of people up ahead. He turned with his foot on the carriage step and tapped his baton.

"What's that clamour up ahead?" he demanded, and Bao Xing and the others dismounted and rushed ahead to find out. They discovered a riderless black donkey, complete with saddle and flaps. It headed straight for Bao's carriage, and they could not drive it away.

"Can it be that this donkey has some sort of grievance?" Magistrate Bao asked himself. He ordered his men not to restrain the donkey, but to wait and see what it did.

Released, the donkey ran straight to Bao's carriage. Bending its front legs, it nodded three times in Bao's direction.

"Strange," muttered everyone else — but Magistrate Bao understood and spoke again to the donkey.

"Black donkey, if you have a grievance, let your head face south and your tail north. I will appoint someone to go along with you."

Without hesitation, the donkey stood up, turned around, and indeed, faced its head south and its tail north. Once again, the magistrate understood.

"Come!" he said.

But Zhao Hu had long before risen onto his toes and was leaning forward and listening closely, knowing that the magistrate would call for help. The minute he heard "Come!" he rushed over to Bao's carriage. "Follow this donkey," ordered Bao. "Observe the situation. If you notice anything strange, report to me."

And so Zhao Hu had set off after the donkey, who led the way. When they reached the city limits, Zhao Hu was puffing and panting, and he dropped onto a rock to rest a bit. His perspiring servant came panting up shortly afterward.

"If Fourth Master wants to accomplish this mission," said the servant, "he must plan it out a little. How can two feet keep up with four? And where is the black donkey?"

"He was ahead, and I behind. I don't know where he's gone off to," answered Zhao Hu.

"What kind of mission is this? How can you accomplish your mission without the donkey?"

As they talked, the black donkey appeared again, running back toward them.

"Ya, ya, ya!" said Zhao Hu, addressing the animal. "If you really have a grievance, you'd better walk a little more slowly, so that Old Zhao, here, can keep up with you. Or how would it be if I ride you a bit, then walk a bit?"

The black donkey contracted his ears, put his legs together, and stood still — so Fourth Master mounted, and they travelled thus a few miles. In a surprisingly short time, they reached the slope on Compleat Mountain. The donkey ran straight to the northern side of the slope.

Fourth Master was at that point walking, and had become hot, so he had opened up his shirt and taken his time. But he had followed the donkey closely and thus in due course had arrived at the northern side. The donkey stood stock-still at the back wall of a temple. The servant arrived shortly thereafter, looked around without seeing anything unusual, and joined his master in standing in some puzzlement beside the motionless donkey.

"Help!" came a sudden shout from inside the temple. Fourth Master had his servant bend down so he could stand on his shoulder and get onto the wall for a look. What he saw was a poorly-made coffin with its lid askew. Nearby, a beautiful woman was beating up an old Daoist priest. Fourth Master leaped down, heedless of the height, and rushed over to protest.

"You!" he shouted. "Men and women aren't allowed to touch. Why are you beating up this man?"

"I was murdered by someone," said the woman in a Shanxi accent. "They wanted my four-hundred ounces of silver. I don't know how I wound up in this coffin, but this old Daoist came and opened it up. How can I not beat him?"

"If that's the case," said Zhao Hu, "let go of him. I'll question him."

The woman stood aside, and the Daoist crawled up to Zhao Hu.

"This is the family temple of the violent marquis. Yesterday they brought in a coffin, saying that in it was Manager Ge Shou's mother, who had died of illness. They ordered me to bury it at once, but there is just now a taboo on earth, so I placed it temporarily here in the rear courtyard. This morning I heard noises inside — so of course I pried off the lid. I never expected this woman to get out and beat me up, and I don't know why."

Zhao Hu then turned to look at the woman. Although her appearance was clearly that of a woman's, there was something strangely masculine about her. And she had a Shanxi accent and spoke of a plot to kill for wealth. Zhao Hu did not understand this very well, and it made him somehow impatient.

"Old Zhao, here, has no time for your silly affairs," he said. "I'm here on a mission for Magistrate Bao. You'd best follow me to Kaifeng and tell your story there."

He untied the Daoist's waistband and used it like a rope to harness him so he could just be pulled along. He had the woman follow behind. They reached the main gate of the temple, removed the bar, and opened it. The servant had already brought the donkey around.

If you do not know what transpired after they left the mountain, read the next chapter for clarification.

Chapter 26

❦

Look and Listen, Distinguish Good and Bad;
Exchange of Faces, A Confusion of Gender

Fourth Master Zhao Hu came through the temple gate, handed the priest over to his servant, and took hold of the donkey. Suddenly the woman was heard to speak.

"That man over there — on the southern slope. He looks like the one who injured me!" She came forward a few steps and reiterated her accusation. "Indeed it is!" She ran straight at the man, grabbed him, and began to shout. "Good old Li Bao! You strangled me to death. Where are my four-hundred ounces of silver? Return them to me at once and that will be the end of it!"

"What rudeness!" cried Li Bao. "Woman, I never saw you before in my life, and I don't know anything about your four-hundred ounces!"

"You rotten bastard," screamed the woman. "You killed me for my money and now you pretend innocence."

Zhao Hu rushed to prevent them from going further. He had his servant tie Li Bao up with the other end of the rope that bound the Daoist, and marched them all off toward Kaifeng.

Meanwhile, out of respect for Fan, First Place Exam Winner, the Lucky Charm District Court did not dare interrogate those involved in this case, but sent them all to Kaifeng. Magistrate Bao immediately convened court and had Fan Zhongyu brought in first.

The guards escorted him in, as he protested loudly.

"Curs! Beat me up! Kill me!" he shouted, still waving his shoe, with which he attempted to beat up anyone who got close to him.

But the civil servants were fast, and they snatched the vermillion slipper away. Fan Zhongyu then began to shout nonsense.

Registrar Gongsun recognized these as signs of temporary insanity, and told Magistrate Bao that he must treat Fan with medication. The magistrate nodded in agreement and had a messenger escort Fan to Gongsun's chambers.

Bai Xiong was called up next. He knelt before the court.

"Who are you," asked Bao, "and what do you do for a living?"

"I am Bai Xiong. I live in Eight Jewel Village in the northwest section of Compleat Mountain, and I am a hunter. The other day I saved a little boy from the mouth of a tiger and, when I inquired about his home and name, I found that he was my very own nephew. He told me that his father had ridden here on a donkey, and so I went in search of the father all the way to Eastern Mountain Pass. There I saw a dappled donkey tied to a small elm tree and took it to be the one on which my brother-in-law had ridden here. But a man from Shanxi that I met on the way said the donkey was *his* and then demanded I produce his brother and a great deal of silver. Finally we decided to take our quarrel to the local headman, but, when we got there, we saw a group of people surrounding someone — who turned out to be the Shanxi man's brother — but changed. When the man went forward to greet his brother, he answered in the voice of a woman and refused to acknowledge the man as his brother, saying that *I* was his brother. I beg Your Honour to decide this matter."

"What is your brother-in-law's name," Bao asked.

"Fan Zhongyu. He is from Jiangxia District in Huguang, Wuchang Prefecture."

Bao recognized at once the name and town of the new first graduate. He nodded his head and had Bai Xiong withdraw.

Qu Liang was next. He knelt and said, "My name is Qu Liang. My older brother's name is Qu Shen, and we own Prosperity Timber Factory on Drum Tower Street. My brother took four-hundred ounces of silver and went to the southern section of Compleat Mountain to buy a load of timber. When he did not return all night, I got worried, so I waited until the city gates opened and rushed outside Eastern Mountain Pass. There I saw a man leading my brother's donkey. When I demanded the donkey, he not only wouldn't give it to me, but he demanded his brother-in-law from me. That's why we went looking for the local head-man together and there I saw my brother sitting on the ground. I don't know how this change came over him, but he didn't recognize me as his brother. On the contrary, he called that one named Bai his brother. I beg you, Lord Magistrate, to settle this case."

"Are you sure that this dappled donkey is yours?" asked Bao.

"How could I not recognize it? This donkey has a peculiarity. As soon as it sees another donkey, it chases it."

Magistrate Bao also asked him to withdraw for the time being and gave another order.

"Bring in Qu Shen. Bring in Qu Shen," the court guards echoed on both sides.

But Qu, the Beard, did not budge. The messenger had to go up to him and speak.

"The magistrate is calling you to the courtroom," he said, whereupon Qu Shen, bashful and shy, coy and coquettish, walked in delicate tiny steps into the courtroom. Before he knelt, he wiped the floor with his hand as elegantly as you can imagine. The yamen runners on both sides did not dare to laugh — but they wanted to.

"Who tried to kill you," asked Bao. "Tell us."

"This humble woman's name is Bai Yulian. My husband is Fan Zhongyu and he went to the capital to take the civil service examination. I came along with him so that I could visit my mother. After the exam, we took our son, Jinge, and went to Compleat Mountain looking for my mother's home. My husband went into the mountain to inquire, while my son and I waited on a black rock. But suddenly a ferocious tiger came along and carried my son off. I fell unconscious from the shock. Then a group of people came by, and their leader said "Take her!" They put me on a horse and took me to this leader's home they locked me in a room and that's when I hung myself. Then, confused and unclear, I felt a cool breeze go suddenly through my body — and when I opened my eyes there were many people around me. Then I saw that I had changed into this shape."

Bao was puzzled. He called Qu Liang up again and asked if he recognized the man.

"He's my older brother," Qu Liang answered. But Qu Shen denied knowing Qu Liang.

Bao had Qu Liang withdraw and recalled Bai Xiong.

"Do you know this person?"

"I do not," Bai Xiong replied.

"I am your blood sister!" Qu Shen said at once. "How can you not know me? How can that be?"

But Bai Xiong stood there in total bewilderment. Bao began to suspect that it was a case of two souls — male and female — attaching themselves to the wrong bodies. How, he wondered, was he to deal with something like this? He had them all taken away.

In a few minutes, Zhao Hu, bringing with him all those involved in the case, appeared to make his report about the black donkey. Bao called up the Daoist priest, who bowed and stated his case.

"I am in charge of the family temple of the violent marquis," he said. "My name is Ye Kuxiu, Painstaking Cultivation. Yesterday the marquis had a cheap coffin brought to the temple from his house. He said it was Ge Shou's mother, who had died of illness, and he ordered me to bury it immediately. But there is a taboo right now on earth, so I had it placed in the rear courtyard ..."

"Nonsense, you cur!" cried Magistrate Bao. "What special day is it that you dare irreverently speak of an earth taboo? Slap his face, guards!"

"No need to get angry, Old Lord," sputtered the Daoist. "I'll tell the truth, I'll tell the truth. When I heard it was the manager's mother, I figured that there must be jewels and clothing in the coffin. My greed overcame me for just a moment — and that's why I spoke wantonly of an earth taboo. But as soon as I removed the cover, the woman came back to life. She grabbed hold of me and beat me in earnest. She spoke a mouthful of Shanxi dialect and she was very strong. I was scared and called for help, and at that point someone jumped over the wall and tied me up."

Bao had him sign a confession and on the instant wrote up a subpoena to bring Ge Shou in for questioning. The Daoist was then taken away.

"Bring in the woman," cried the guards, left and right. "Bring in the woman. Bring in the woman."

The woman, however, did not budge, and the guard was forced to go up to her. "Madame," he said, "the magistrate has called you up."

"I'm a good fellow," said the woman indignantly. "*Who* is a woman? Cut out the joking!"

"You're a woman now. No one is joking with you. Go into the courtroom, please."

Annoyed, the woman entered the courtroom with enormous, wide strides and, with a loud klunk, knelt on the floor.

"Madame, what is your grievance? Tell us," Bao said.

"I am *not* a woman," said she. "My name is Qu Shen. It's all because I took four-hundred ounces of silver with me to buy some lumber on Compleat Mountain. I didn't expect the deal to fall through. It was late when I ran across a black donkey without an owner — one with four teeth too! — so I tied my dappled donkey to a small elm tree and rode the black one, thinking I had found a real bargain. But a big wind came up, and, since it was even later by then, I found a room to spend the night on the southern slope in the home of Li Bao. He got me drunk and then strangled me to death. I was trying to catch my breath when suddenly I saw light. It was a Daoist priest who had opened the coffin lid. I don't know how I wound up in the coffin. But my four-hundred ounces of silver were missing — so I beat up the priest. As we left the temple gate, I saw someone drawing water, and it turned out to be Li Bao, who had tried to kill me. I grabbed him and brought him along. We people from Shanxi have come a long way — it wasn't easy. I want my four-hundred ounces of silver. But look at what's happened to me — how can this be?

Then Bao had Bai Xiong brought up again.

"Do you know this woman?" he asked Bai Xiong.

"Sister Yulian!" cried Bai involuntarily. He was about to go up to her and acknowledge her when the woman said.

"Who's your sister? I'm a good fellow."

Bai took great fright on hearing this, and Bao had him with-draw. He called for Qu Liang and asked her, "Do you know him?"

The words had hardly left his mouth when the woman cried, "Aiya, my brother! Somebody tried to kill me, your big brother. You must think of our silver!"

"What's this all about?" asked Qu Liang. "How long have I had *this* kind of brother?"

Bao motioned them all away, since he had already realized that there was a problem of male and female souls attached to the wrong bodies.

When Bao had Li Bao brought in, he saw that he was the very same evil servant who had run away from him during his time of trouble. He did not question him about past matters, however, but asked only why he had killed for the silver.

Li Bao, faced with the majesty and awesomeness of Bao, and seeing that Bao Xing and Li Cai were both officials of the seventh degree, was ashamed and wanted only to die. Holding back nothing, he made a complete confession. Bao had him sign it, sent someone to get the stolen money, and had Mrs. Li brought in.

But another messenger preceded her.

"Ge Shou has been brought in," he reported, and Bao ordered him brought to court immediately.

"Who was in the coffin that was carried to the family temple of your master?" he demanded of Ge Shou.

Ge Shou was terrified. He paled and said, "It was my mother."

"You have been manager of the marquis' household for many years; you must be a trusted person. If it was your mother, why was she being buried in such a cheap coffin? Even if you did not have the means, you ought to have requested some money from your master. But you are hard-hearted and careless. You are unfilial!"

Bao turned to the guards. "Drag him down and give him forty blows with the heavy bamboo." They did so, beating him until he rolled wildly on the floor.

"How old are you this year?" Bao asked.

"I am thirty-six this year," he responded.

"How old is your mother?"

Ge Shou's mouth fell open, but nothing came out of it. Only after a long while did he manage to say, "I — I don't remember."

"Nonsense!" shouted Bao. "How can there be a son who doesn't remember how old his mother is? Your mother has no place in your heart — you are unfilial! Take him down, and give him another forty blows."

"My Lord Magistrate, no need to get angry," said Ge Shou hastily. "I'll tell the truth."

"Speak!" Bao said.

"Hurry! Talk fast!" They pressed him from both sides.

Under all this pressure, the evil slave felt compelled to tell the truth.

"My Lord Magistrate, I don't really know whose corpse that is in the coffin. Two days ago, on a hunting trip, the marquis encountered a woman sobbing loudly on Compleat Mountain. She was quite attractive. His intimate, whose name is Diao San, made a display of diligence before the marquis, and then they kidnapped the woman and locked her up with two maids to console her. But then someone named Fan came looking for his wife. Diao San plotted again with the marquis to invite Fan to the study to keep an eye on him, while pretending to look for his wife."

"Where is Diao San now?" asked Bao.

"He died that very night," was the reply.

"I think you had some grievance against him — and that you killed him! Take him down and beat him."

"I did not kill him! He died on his own!" protested Ge Shou.

"How?" demanded Bao.

"I'll force myself to tell you. It was because Diao San had plotted with the marquis to keep Fan in the study. At the third watch, Diao San, with a sharp sword in his hand, went to the study to kill Fan, but, when he hadn't returned by the fifth watch, the marquis sent someone to check on him. He had tripped over the threshold and fallen on his own sword, which pierced his throat, and he was dead. Then our marquis sent a servant to the study to claim that Fan had, for no reason at all, killed a family member. He had Fan beaten to death. The body was put in an old suitcase, and under cover of darkness the case was abandoned somewhere on the mountain.

"And the woman? How did *she* die?"

"She gave in to the marquis — or seemed to — after being urged and persuaded by the maids. But she was only pretending. Within the wink of an eye she had hung herself. Our marquis was pretty upset that three people had died and he hadn't even gotten his way with her. But he got a coffin, said that it was my mother, and had it carried to the family temple to be buried. This is everything that happened — I don't dare lie about it."

Bao had him sign a confession, and then he took everyone into custody. Mistress Bai — a woman's body inhabited by a man's soul — and Qu Shen — a man's body inhabited by a woman's soul — were placed in separate rooms in the women's prison. Profanity and horseplay were forbidden. Bao then sent Wang Chao and Ma Han, along with some yamen runners, to arrest Ge Dengyun, who was to be tried the next day. After these orders, court was adjourned and everyone filed out.

The headman, Kutou, had been most put upon that day. From the crack of dawn until now, an entire day, he had not only gone hungry, but he had been stuck looking after the two donkeys, and no one paid him any heed. He was in sore need of an audience to listen to his troubles, so he stopped a man leaving the court.

"Has Lord Magistrate Bao adjourned court?" he asked.

"He has," answered the man.

Kutou was just about to mention the donkey when the man walked on. He asked many people in succession, but everyone ignored him. Sighing and groaning, he scratched his ears and his cheeks in frustration.

He forced himself to wait for Fourth Master's servant, and, when he came out, Kutou beseeched his help. The servant took pity on him and told him to take the donkey to the stables. But leave it to that dappled donkey to be mulish. Its eccentricity acted up and it refused to move. Fourth Master's servant had to help Kutou drag it all the way to the stables. There everything was explained to the man in charge, and the donkey was fed and secured. The servant told the headman to go home and come back bright and early the next day to hear the proceedings. With heartfelt thanks, the headman took his leave.

Magistrate Bao had his dinner and sat in his study contemplating this affair. It was clearly a case of bad Yin and worse Yang, but he could not think of a way to solve it.

"The Yin errs, the Yang is off. But what can I do about it?" he muttered over and over, sitting there with knitted brows and distress in his eyes.

Bao Xing saw his master thus and knelt before him.

"As I see it," he offered, "to solve this case you must go to the Yin Yang Hall."

"Where is this Yin Yang Hall?" asked the master.

"It's in the underworld," replied the servant.

"The underworld!" shouted Bao. "You cur! Why are you talking nonsense?"

If you want to know what happened, read on.

Chapter 27

A Magic Pillow Brings Dreams, Exchange of Souls in an Ancient Mirror; Zhongyu Wins First Place

"Idiot!" said Magistrate Bao to Bao Xing. "'The underworld indeed!'"

"Now, would I dare to speak nonsense to you?" protested Bao Xing. "I've been there."

"When did you go there?"

Bao Xing reminded Magistrate Bao of the story of the murder of Li Keming, who had been killed by the head of the Bai household because he wanted Li Keming's "Pillow of Wandering Immortals." Afterwards, he related, the pillow was submitted in court, and, while the magistrate was resting his horse in Three Star Village, he, Bao Xing, secretly tried out the pillow. It sent him to the Yin Yang Hall, where they said that he was an imposter of Star Lord, and he was chased away by the spirits.

The words "Star Lord" struck a bell in Bao's head, reminding him of the "Case of the Black Basin" and the "Case of the Cold Palace Ghost." He had been called "Star Lord" when he had solved both of those cases. Bao Xing's remarks began to seem a little less like nonsense.

"Where is this pillow now?" asked Bao.

Explaining that he had put it away safely, Bao Xing went at once to get it. He returned quickly and Magistrate Bao noticed that the pillow was very carefully wrapped.

"Open it so I can have a look."

Bao Xing opened it and presented it to the magistrate with both hands. It was made of what looked like a piece of rotten wood. On it were carved — not very clearly — tiny characters. Bao examined it carefully and made no comment about using it or not, but only nodded. Bao Xing understood his master at once, and offered him the pillow. He went into the inner room, hooked up the bed curtain, and placed the pillow squarely in the centre of the bed. Then he made the magistrate a cup of tea.

Bao sat for a while and then got up. Bao Xing brought the lamp at once and led him into the bedroom. The magistrate saw that the curtain was raised and the pillow was placed right in the middle of the bed — just as he would have it — so he got onto the bed and lay down with his clothes on. After letting down the curtain and removing the lamp, Bao Xing waited quietly outside.

Although Magistrate Bao was trying to rest, he found he had too much on his mind to sleep. Absently, he turned over to face the wall. When his head touched the pillow, the curious thought came to him that he was in a wide-open hall. Near him two yamen runners appeared leading a black horse with a black saddle and black flaps.

"Star Lord," said the runners, "please mount."

So Bao got on and shook the reins. The horse took off as if it had wings, and all Bao could hear was the whistle of the rushing wind. The places he passed were all blurred and confused, but, despite the dark, he could see quite clearly. He saw before him a city moat, and behind it gates closed tightly. The horse ran straight up to the closed gate, and Bao's stomach dropped as he realized they were going to crash into it — but they did not. They simply passed through it like lightning. Shortly after leaving the gate behind, they arrived at a huge yamen. They entered the courtroom, whereupon the horse stopped and two red and black-robed judges came out to welcome Bao.

"Star Lord," said one, "please convene court."

Bao dismounted and walked into the courtroom. A large plaque on the dais read "Yin Yang Hall." The chair and table and all the implements on the table were black. Magistrate Bao, not taking the time to look these over carefully, sat down in the official seat.

"The Star Lord must be here for that case in which the Yin is off and the Yang is in error," observed the red-robed judge, who handed Bao a register. But there was nothing at all written on it.

Bao was about to ask what it meant, when the black-robed judge took it from him, turned a few pages, and put it down on the table. Bao looked again, and this time he saw eight lines of crudely-drawn speech, very reverently couched.

"Where *chou* should have been, *mao* was used; and where *yin* should have appeared, *chen* was employed," he read. "Mistakes were made in the upper division, and so two souls were improperly exchanged. To clarify this issue, rely on the Ancient Mirror from the well. Just as you are about to look in the mirror, prick you finger and drip the blood on it. Mix the blood together with your fingers and you will see the reflection."

Nothing more was written, and Bao was about to ask a question when the two judges took the register from him and departed. The black horse also disappeared.

Bao felt very nervous. He called out, waking up at the same time. Bao Xing rushed in with the lamp, and Bao asked what the time was.

"The third watch was just struck."

"Bring me a cup of tea."

But Li Cai entered just at that point and announced, "Mr. Gongsun would like to see you," so Bao Xing raised the curtains and Bao got off the bed and went outside.

"Fan's illness," explained Gongsun, "has been cured."

"What prescription did you use?" asked Bao in delighted tones.

"I used five woods soup."

"What is five woods soup?"

"I boiled pieces of mulberry, elm, peach, locust, and willow into a soup and then put it into a washbasin. I covered it tightly and hung it so that it steamed his face and body until he broke out in a full sweat. When the body fluid and blood separate, you know, one becomes clear again. Right now he is just a little weak.

"You, sir, have marvellous hands and wonderful prescriptions," cried Bao. "Since I have already troubled you, would you continue his care?"

Gongsun agreed and withdrew.

Bao Xing arrived with the tea, and Magistrate Bao requested the Ancient Mirror. He also had Li Cai inform the officer of external affairs to wait in the second hall. Bao Xing brought in the mirror and was told to hang it up in the second hall. Magistrate Bao followed him and ordered Qu Shen and Mistress Bai brought at once.

Bao placed the man on the left, the woman on the right and told each to prick a middle finger, smear some blood on the mirror, and then look at the reflection. Qu Shen obediently bit the middle finger of his right hand — which did not hurt him in the least because he did not recognize it as his own hand — and spotted the mirror with his blood.

Mistress Bai realized she too must comply, bit a small opening in the middle finger of her left hand, and added her blood to the mirror. The bloodstains on the mirror swirled wildly. The over-hanging clouds were torn away, and light began to flash all around, so brightly that it was difficult to keep one's eyes open. A chill swept over everyone.

Then Bao ordered the man and the woman to look into the mirror. When they did, they saw that one had hung herself and one had been strangled. Both felt the breath choked out of them and their hearts pierced by a thousand arrows — and then, sud-denly, they fainted and dropped to the floor. The flashes of light from the mirror gradually receded. Everyone there was stunned — this was one function, then, of this Ancient Mirror.

Magistrate Bao handed over the Ancient Mirror, the Pillow of Wandering Immortals, and the Old and New Basin to Bao Xing for safekeeping. When he then glanced at the prostrate figures, Qu Shen began to move his hands and feet, and then his eyes popped open.

"Good Old Li Bao! You stole my four-hundred ounces of silver. Give them back!"

After this outburst, Qu Shen paused and looked himself over thoughtfully. Suddenly he scratched his beard and said happily, "Wo! It is! It is! This is really *me*!" Then, kowtowing toward the magistrate, he said, "I beg Lord Magistrate Bao to settle this. It was four-hundred ounces — that's no joke!"

By this time, Mistress Bai had also come to and was feeling shy and anxious. Bao ordered Qu Shen removed to the outer office and had Mistress Bai taken to the tea room, where there was a woman who would look after her. Then he himself withdrew from the courtroom and took his rest.

He rose early the next morning and called Bao Xing at once. "Ask Mr. Gongsun," he ordered, "whether or not Fan can move around." Before long Gongsun himself entered the study, bringing Fan with him. Fan greeted the magistrate in the ritual way and thanked him for saving his life.

Bao stopped him, saying, "You mustn't do this. You mustn't do this."

Fan looked haggard, Bao decided, but not crazy, as he had before. The magistrate was greatly pleased and took time to be seated. Gongsun allowed Fan to sit and Bao explained the situation to him, adding that his wife was fine and that he should do his best to get well.

"When you have some time," said Magistrate Bao, "write down the examination questions, so that I can show your answers to the emperor. That will insure that you don't lose your position as first graduate."

This was delightful news to Fan, and he expressed his deepest thanks to Magistrate Bao. Magistrate Bao commended him to the care of Gongsun, and the two of them bid goodbye to Bao and left.

Wang Chao and Ma Han came to announce that Ge Dengyun had been brought in. Bao convened court at once and interrogated him. Ge Dengyun, relying on his power and his position as a marquis, as well as on people's fear of him, was confident that, even were he to make a complete confession, Bao could do nothing to him. So he confessed arrogantly to everything and denied nothing. Bao had him sign the confession.

Then Lord Magistrate Bao, who feared no one, lowered his head and said, "Bring in the imperial guillotine."

Wang, Ma, Zhang, and Zhao had understood the situation all along and were ready at once with the guillotine. They removed the imperial wrapping and revealed the tiger-head blade. This blade had never before been used, and no one had foreseen that it would be used to settle accounts with Ge Dengyun.

The villain's face went ashen, but, before he had time even to repent his actions, he died under the guillotine. The dog-head blade was used for the execution of Li Bao, and Ge Shou was sentenced to await beheading in prison. Li Bao's wife, Mistress Li, was sentenced to await strangling in prison. Ye, the Daoist priest, because he had tried to rob a corpse, was sent to Yan'an in Shanxi to become a soldier. Qu Shen and Qu Liang took their silver home right then and there. Because Qu Shen, greedy for a small gain, had exchanged his dappled donkey for the black one, his dappled donkey was confiscated to be used for the court. The black donkey, because it had achieved merit by presenting the grievance, was to be kept by the court and nourished with respect.

Fan and Mistress Bai kowtowed their thanks to Bao there in court and then went to Eight Jewel Village with Bai Xiong to rest and wait for instructions. Fan's reunion with his son and Mistress Bai's reunion with her mother were as full of grief and joy as all such meetings are, and there is no need to go into detail here.

The next day, Bao, having solved this case, memorialized the emperor. He reported the execution of the violent marquis, Ge Dengyun, perpetrator of much evil, and announced that the new first graduate, Fan Zhongyu, was still convalescing because of a misfortune encountered on the way to visit relatives. Bao requested a waiver of ten days for Fan and then arranged a feast in the Imperial Garden to honour the new first graduate.

Emperor Renzong was delighted with this document and commended Magistrate Bao heartily for having eliminated evil, re-stored order, and done everything in the proper way.

Chapter 32

❧

A Servant Is Saved, A Scholar Travels; A Poor Scholar Is Discovered, A Guest Rhapsodizes

Master Zhan's thoughts sped like an arrow toward home. Already he had reached Wujin District, and it was only the second watch of the day. He could make it home if he travelled throughout the night. But, as he reached an elm forest, he heard someone call out, "Help! I'm being beaten! He has a pole!" Zhan followed the sound and found an old man with a bundle on his back, gasping for breath. From the forest came another cry: "Someone swiped my bundle!"

Sizing things up, Zhan said to the old man, "You hide! Let me stop him." The old man hid himself behind a tree and Zhan crouched down. The oncomer, intent on catching up, did not see Zhan stick out his leg. There was a loud *kerplunk* and the runner got a mouthful of dirt.

Zhan rushed forward, grabbed him, undid the pouch at his waist, and tied him up. Then Zhan stuck the stranger's cane into his belt and propped him up on it.

"What's your name?" he called out to the old man. "Where's your home? Take your time and tell me everything!"

The old man, who by this time had caught his breath, bowed his thanks. "My surname is Yan," he replied. "My full name is Yan Fu, and I live in Elm Forest Village. My master plans to visit relatives in the capital, and so he sent me to his good friend Jin Bizheng to borrow clothes and money. Mr. Jin is good-hearted and had me stay for a meal. Then he gave me thirty ounces of silver for my master's travel. My age and poor eyesight delayed me in returning, and, when finally I reached Elm Forest, I heard someone call out to me about a toll for passing.

"I was scared to death, and I ran until I got very short of breath. Fortunately, you came to my rescue — or my long life would have ended at this man's hands."

"I must pass through Elm Forest Village on my way, so why don't I escort you home?" offered Zhan. Yan Fu again bowed in gratitude.

Then Zhan turned on the stranger. "You plunder people in the dark and then scream about somebody stealing your bundle! You're lucky *I* caught you, because *I* won't harm you. I'll just leave you here to rest a bit, until someone comes along and rescues you." He told the old man to pick up his bundle, and the two of them left the forest and headed straight for Elm Forest Village.

Eventually they reached the gate of the Yan home. "This is it," said the old man. "Please come in and have some tea." He pushed the door open, and from inside could be heard the voice of his young master, saying, "It must be Yan Fu, just come home!"

"I won't stay for tea," said Zhan, hearing this. "I have to get on my way." And, taking enormous strikes, he departed, heading straight for Village of the Heroes.

Yan Fu, hoisting his bundle, called out, "I'm back!" Then he went inside and closed the door.

Yan Fu's young master was also surnamed Yan. His other name was Chasan and he was twenty-two. He passed his days with his widowed mother, Mistress Zheng, and the old servant. His father, Old Master Yan, had been an upright man who was once chosen as District Governor. Poor as a churchmouse, however, he had died after a protracted illness, leaving the family in some difficulty financially.

Yan Chasan had always had an ambition to master book-learning and had already memorized a bellyful of the classics. He daydreamed often about going to the capital and taking the government examinations — but his family was too poor. Another exam year was coming up, however, and his mother had a plan.

"Your aunt's family is wealthy," she reminded her son. "Why don't you visit her? You can study hard — and you can also complete your betrothal. Why not kill two birds with one stone?"

"That's a good idea," admitted Yan Chasan, "but we have heard nothing from Aunt's family for years. When Father was alive, he often wrote and sent his regards, but, when he died and we sent a messenger to them with the news, they never even sent condolences. Uncle has taken a new wife, and we haven't heard anything from them since.

"If I were to go to the capital, you would have no one here to look after you. And we don't have enough money for the travel expenses. Anyway, I haven't yet made a name for myself. Things being what they are, it would be useless for me to go. It's hopeless."

While they were talking, Yan's good friend, Jin Bizheng, knocked at the door. He was greeted happily, and when he heard about Yan's mother's idea, he swept aside all objections by offering to finance the whole enterprise. Chasan was thrilled and his mother was infinitely grateful to Jin Bizheng, who at once took Yan Fu off with him to purchase the necessary items for a trip to the capital. Mother and son went on making plans, and Mistress Zheng wrote a letter of entreaty in her own hand so that Yan's aunt would have no reason for not taking him in.

When Yan Fu had not returned by the second watch, Chasan had urged his mother to go to sleep, while he himself read by lamplight. By the fourth watch, Chasan had become quite anxious, but shortly thereafter Yan Fu had appeared and presented his master with the clothing and silver. Chasan was delighted, but the old man was exhausted from travelling and from his great fright and could no longer stay awake. Chasan sent him off to bed, and he took his leave, saying that they could chat tomorrow.

The next day Chasan showed the clothes and silver to his mother, and they began to plan the trip.

"Will the young master go to the capital alone?" asked Yan Fu.

"I will go by myself," Chasan said. "You must stay here and look after my mother."

"You can't go by yourself!" cried the old man.

"Why not?"

Yan Fu described his encounter with the robber, and, when

Mistress Zheng heard about it, she agreed. "I would have no peace of mind. You two must go together."

"But with no one at home to take care of you, I would be the one with no peace of mind," insisted Chasan.

Just then, someone rapped on the door. Yan Fu opened it and found a young boy, who said: "You, old sir, did you get home all right last night? It was really late." Yan Fu screwed up his eyes. "What are you looking at, old sir? I'm from Master Jin's. I poured the wine for you yesterday."

"Oh. Oh, yes, yes! I seem to have forgotten. What brings you here?"

"My master sent me to see Master Yan."

So the old servant took him inside, where he greeted Yan and paid his respects to the mistress.

"What is your name?" Chasan asked him. "And why have you come?"

"My name is Yumo. My master knew that you have no servants here and was afraid that the long trip to the capital would be inconvenient for you, so he sent me to accompany you. He says that this venerable caretaker is getting on and his eyesight is poor. He should stay at home to manage the household and look after the mistress. This way, everyone can be easy. He also sent ten ounces of silver for the road. It's always better to have a little extra."

Yumo spoke clearly and intelligently, and his news was delightful. "How old are you?" asked the mistress.

"Fourteen."

"Can such an infant even walk?"

"Mistress, from the age of eight, I have been on the road with my father doing business. Walking does not confound me, nor even the customs of various places. The raising of brows and lowering of eyes are things that I can handle. I know all the roads, especially the way to the capital. Otherwise, why would my master send me to you?"

The mistress was delighted, and so Chasan bid his mother farewell. She could not help crying, but she gave Chasan the letter she had written, saying, "When you get to Lucky Charm District in the capital, ask about Twin Star Lane and you will find your aunt's house."

"There is a Twin Star Lane, in the southern part of Lucky Charm District. It is also called Twin Star Bridge. I know it," said Yumo.

"That's excellent. You must take very good care of him," said the mistress.

"I know it."

Chasan gave Yan Fu some final instructions, handing him secretly ten ounces of silver for the support of his mother. Yumo had already picked up their pack, and master and servant set out at once.

Chasan had never left home before, and, after ten or twenty miles, his feet hurt. "I guess we've walked fifty or sixty miles already," he said to Yumo.

"The young master has never left home before. It's hardly any time since we started out — how could we have walked fifty or sixty miles? If we had, we'd be flying. We haven't even walked *thirty* miles," said Yumo.

"Then it is really a long and difficult road," Chasan said, with alarm.

"Master, calm down. There is a method to walking. If you get more and more anxious because you haven't arrived yet, then walking becomes extremely difficult. Calm yourself, be neither tense nor slow. Imagine you are on a pleasure trip in the mountains. There are no scenic spots along this road, but let us consider each village and temple as an elegant scene and a marvellous view. A rock or a piece of wood can be the detail of a beautiful site. Walking like this, your heart is wide open, your eyes are bright, and you forget your weariness. This way you can cover many miles."

Chasan paid attention to what Yumo said and began to enjoy the trip. They covered ten or twenty miles very quickly. Then Chasan said to Yumo, "I'm not tired now, but my stomach feels empty."

"Isn't that an inn over there?" said Yumo, pointing ahead. "Let's stop there for something to eat."

When they arrived at the town, Chasan wanted to go into the

first restaurant he saw, but Yumo stopped him. "The food isn't ready-made here — it will take a while. Master, please follow me." Yumo was a shrewd young fellow, and roadwise, and he took Yan into a small grocery, which was both cheaper and quicker.

After master and servant had eaten, they travelled on, covering a good ten miles and stopping from time to time to rest under a tree or just by the roadside. Toward evening, they reached a bustling town called Double Righteousness Town.

"Master," Yumo said, "Let's stay here overnight. It is getting too late to go on." Chasan readily agreed, and then Yumo cautioned him, "Master, I will arrange the lodging. Please don't you say anything." Yan nodded his head.

As soon as they arrived at the inn gate, the innkeeper called out, "Clean rooms! It's late. If you continue on your way, it will get too late to find a place at all."

"Do you have single rooms? Or a side room will do."

"Please come in and have a look."

"If you *have* such rooms, then we have something to look at. If you *don't*, then we will head for that inn over there," Yumo said.

"Why not just come in and have a look? If there's nothing to your liking, you can leave — how about it?"

"Let's take a look then," Chasan said.

"Master, you don't understand," Yumo answered. "Once we go in, he won't let us out. I know how things are done at inns."

As he was speaking, another servant of the inn came out. "Please go in," he said, "there's no need to be suspicious. We won't deceive you."

Chasan had already started walking in, and Yumo could only follow. "Sir, please have a look at these three excellent upper rooms — new paint and paper, clean and bright," said the servant.

"Is that so," Yumo said. "As soon as we're inside, it's the three best rooms in the house. We have very little luggage. If you gave us your three best rooms, wouldn't that be swindling us? It's a single room or side room, or nothing."

With that, Yumo turned as if to go, but the waiter grabbed him, saying, "What a fuss, my young master! Those three best rooms have two with windows and one inner one — but we'll charge you for one room only, all right?"

"Let's leave it at that," Chasan said.

"*First* we must be thrifty and *then* magnanimous," said Yumo. "Now that we've cleared that up, I will indeed pay for that one room."

When master and servant were shown to the best suite, they went into the inner room and put down their luggage. The waiter dusted the table in the outer room with his hand and said, "Why don't you eat in this room. Isn't it more spacious?"

"Don't try to seduce us," Yumo said. "Even if we ate in the outer room, we would still sleep in the inner one. What's more, we don't drink and we ate early. We merely want a place to stay."

Seeing there was little business to be had here, the waiter said, "Shall I brew a pot of good jasmine tea for you?"

"We still have a full supply of the water we got on the road," said Yumo. "We won't take any tea."

"Let me light a candle for you."

"Your inn has no oil lamps?"

"It has, but I was afraid that the smell of a lamp would get on your clothes and you gentlemen would dislike it."

"Just bring it along. We don't mind."

Finally the waiter turned to leave.

"He is really shrewd!" Yumo said. "We spend money on the *candle*, and he saves on the *oil* — I dare say he's very clear about what's *his* and what's *ours*."

The waiter gave Yumo a look over his shoulder and was gone a long time before he brought the lamp.

"What will you two gentlemen have to eat?" asked the waiter.

"We want a little, nothing more. Just bring us a snack."

The waiter calculated that there was no business in a snack and left without a word. As they waited, they got hungrier, and finally they called out to him.

"It's not ready yet," came the reply. After another wait, they called to him again. "In a minute," he called back. "They're making it right now. In a minute. In a minute."

Then someone began to shout outside. "How *dare* you be so contemptuous here!" they heard. "How can a little plate of vegetables cost so much? I'm trying not to humiliate you, but not only won't you let me stay here, you insult me as well, you monster! I'm going to set this dog's house of yours on fire."

"This person is venting a little anger for us," Yumo said. "Serves them right!"

Then they heard the innkeeper. "We're full," he said. "We don't have any rooms. Do you expect us to build one on the spot for you?"

"So dog farts don't smell!" shouted back the man. "Bullshit! Build one on the spot! Build one on the spot — and I would have to wait! You really are out to insult educated people."

At this point, Chasan stepped out the door.

"Master!" Yumo cried. "Don't get involved!" Yumo was about to stop his master, when the man in the courtyard turned to Chasan.

"Elder Brother," he said, "you be the judge of this. That he won't let me stay here and tries to get rid of my kind is not incomprehensible. But now he wants to build me new rooms on the spot — it's outrageous!"

"Would it please you to stay in *this* room?" Chasan inquired.

"'Duckweed meets in unexpected places.' But I can't impose on you."

Yumo thought, "This is bad. My master is going to be swindled." He rushed out to find his master and the man already walking up the steps arm in arm. They came to the rooms and sat down in the lighted one.

To find out what happened next, read on.

Chapter 33

❧

A True Gentleman's Meeting with Bai Yutang;
The Handsome Hero Tests Yan Three Times

Chasan and the man entered and sat down. In the lamplight,
Yumo could see that the man was wearing a tattered scholar's
turban and a torn blue shirt. On his feet were a pair of down-at-
the-heels, frayed black boots. His face was covered with dirt, and
he looked more like a good-for-nothing than a scholar. Yumo was
scheming to get rid of him when the innkeeper entered and
apologized to the fellow.

"No need," said the stranger. "'Great people do not remember
the transgressions of petty men.' I forgive you."

"What is Elder Brother's honourable name?" Chasan inquired
after the innkeeper had taken his leave.

"I am Jin, Jin Maoshu."

"Jin, is it? Gold?" said Yumo to himself. "It is my former
honourable and righteous master whose name is 'Gold.' One in
as poor a state as *this* fellow isn't even worthy of the surname
Yin (silver). There's an old saying. 'A Jin without gold will be
broken by poverty.' Master Yan is about to be taken in by this
character."

"I haven't asked your name," the man said to Chasan, who
gave it in turn.

"Ah, Brother Yan. But I have been negligent — have you
eaten?"

"Not yet. Have you, Brother Jin?"

"No. Why not share a meal? Let's call the waiter."

The waiter was summoned and appeared with a pot of jasmine
tea, which he put on the table.

"What do you have here in the way of food?" Jin asked.

"Our first-class meal is eight ounces of silver, the middle-class meal is six, and the lower-class — "

"Who eats lower-class food?" interrupted Jin. "Let it be first class food! What are the delicacies on the first class menu?"

"Two large bowls, two pewter, six big bowls, four medium-sized bowls, and also eight small plates — chicken, duck, fish, meat, wings, sea slugs, and more, seasoned to your taste."

"Live carp?" Jin asked.

"We have huge ones — one ounce two cash per fish."

"Since we fancy it, we don't care about the price. But let me tell you, carp that doesn't exceed one catty is called 'kidnapper,' not carp. Only those that are more than one catty are carp. Not only do we want a live one, but the tail must be red as rouge — only then is it fresh. Bring it in for me to look at. Now, what kind of liquor do you have?"

"Merely the ordinary variety," answered the waiter.

"We don't want that kind. We want the aged Chaste Maiden Shaoxing," insisted Jin.

"We do have ten-year-old Chaste Maiden Shaoxing, but we sell it only by the jug. At four ounces of silver each."

"You *are* petty-minded. Forget the ounces, just bring us a jug. Open it here, and I'll taste it. Mind you, I want it golden red, rich, and fragrant. Only the pure, amber-coloured kind. And when you pour it into the bowl, it should stick to it."

"You can taste it, and, if it's not good, there's no charge — all right?"

"Well, sure," said Jin.

The waiter disappeared and returned in a trice with two candles. He was clearly in his element, very happy and extremely diligent. Next he brought in a kidney-shaped basin of wood, in which a huge carp thrashed about wildly.

"My Lord, look. How about *this* carp?" he said.

"This fish is, indeed, carp. I should have anticipated the basin. On the one hand, it makes the fish look big, and, on the other, it is so shallow the fish must bang around and show it is alive. That's the trick of selling things. Don't take it away. Open its belly right here. We'll have no substitutions."

Thus challenged, the waiter dispatched the carp right in front of them. Jin continued his instructions.

"Dress it right away — and, let's see, what spices and sauces? Black mushrooms and white mushrooms, and also some laver. And I want 'tip on tip'." The waiter looked puzzled at this last. "How can you not know?" asked Jin. "'Tip on tip' is the very tip of the tip of young bamboo shoots. They must always be tenderly boiled and then cut into strips. And they must be crisp and crunchy when eaten."

The waiter took down all these orders, and before long he brought up a cask of wine, together with the awl, siphon, and porcelain basin. Right in front of them, he pierced the cask, siphoning from the top and bottom, and the fragrant wine poured forth.

Chasan tasted it and pronounced it good. The waiter poured out a bowl and put it into the kettle to warm. He arranged the cold dishes and then brought on the others one by one. Jin did not even touch his chopsticks; he merely tasted the pickled vegetables and drank the wine slowly, waiting for the carp. The two of them drank and chatted, and, the more they talked, the more they saw eye to eye. Chasan was delighted.

Before long the fish arrived in a large platter. Jin raised his chopsticks and motioned to Yan: "Fish must be eaten hot. Once it gets cold, it gets all fishy." He gave Yan a piece and then separated the fish down the middle with his chopsticks. He asked for vinegar and ginger and, alternating between the fish and wine, he called out with delight: "Marvellous! Marvellous!" After one side was consumed, he stuck his chopsticks in the gills and flipped the fish over. He and Yan finished off the second side in the same fashion as before, and then Jin asked for a medium-sized bowl. He crumbled six pieces of steamed bread into it, ladled some fish soup over it, and noisily ate it all, topping it off with three spoons of soup.

"I am full," he said. "Brother Yan, take your time — don't stop, don't stop."

But Yan was also full. They left the feast and Jin gave instructions for Yumo's meal. "Steam what needs to be steamed — we can't let him eat cold leftovers. And there is still some wine. If he wants to drink, give him as much of it as he wants."

The waiter nodded and Jin and Chasan went into the inner room to chat. There were many leftovers, but Yumo touched nothing. He knew they would not be able to take any with them when they left, and, though it broke his heart, he could not eat a bite. All he had was two cups of wine by himself. Then he went to the back room, where Jin, on the brink of sleep, sat rocking back and forth with his toothless mouth opened wide.

"Brother Yan," muttered Jin, "you are tired. Why not rest? I, too, will retire."

Jin lay on the bed, and soon there was a *klunk* as one of his boots fell to the floor, and then another, followed by thunderous snoring. Yan signalled to Yumo to remove the lamp, and he himself also slept.

Yumo sat in the lighted room, annoyed and unable for a long while to get to sleep. He was awakened by footsteps and was startled to discover that it was already dawn and his master was coming out from the inner room.

"Go get the wash water," said Yan in a low voice. Yumo brought it and Yan washed his face.

When they heard coughing from inside, Yumo rushed in and found Jin stretching his lazy bones and yawning. His dirty feet were sticking out — he probably had no socks — and he was reciting something. "Who awakes first from the great dream? I alone know my fate. I sleep my fill in Grass Hall, while the sun rises languidly through the window," he murmured. Then he dragged himself up, mumbling, "You take a short nap and the sun is up!"

"The inn people have brought your wash water," Yumo said.

"I never wash my face. Water is bad for the skin. Have the waiter write up the bill and bring it to me."

"Interesting," thought Yumo. "He's going to pay the bill after all."

The bill came to thirteen ounces, four cash, and eight cents.

"Not much. Not much." said Jin. "Add two ounces for the waiter, the cook, and the houseboy."

The waiter thanked him.

"Brother Yan," Jin said, "I won't stand on ceremony with you. I will take my leave first. See you in the capital." And, with a *tala, tala*, he left the inn.

"Yumo, Yumo!" Yan called. It was a long time before Yumo responded.

"We'll leave after you have paid the bill," said Yan.

Yumo hesitated. "Hm!" he grumbled, stalking over to the counter with the silver. He wrangled and hassled over the bill, giving in the end fourteen ounces for everything. Then he and his master left the inn.

When they reached the outskirts of the village, Yumo asked, "Master, what sort of a person do you take Mr. Jin to be?"

"A good man of learning," Chasan replied.

"Master, you have never left home before!" exploded Yumo. "You don't know the dangers of the road. There are swindlers and snatchers. There are even those who ambush and kill people! Bizarre things can happen. If you take Mr. Jin to be a good person today, you will certainly fall into his trap tomorrow. As I see it, he is nothing more than a freeloader."

"Stop this nonsense!" snapped Chasan. "A young person like you making such terrible accusations! In Mr. Jin's reserve is the air of a hero. His destiny is not ordinary. Even if he were a swindler, then we have merely wasted a few ounces of silver. Why is that so important? Stop minding my business for me."

"Bookworm!" Yumo thought and laughed to himself. "I am interested in his welfare and he gets into a huff. I'll have to work this out later myself."

They had not walked long before they arrived at a place to eat. Yumo, still angry, ordered a fried roll, and they left right after eating it. Toward evening, they arrived at Prosperity Village and took lodgings. As before, they were given three rooms at the top for the price of only one, but at this establishment the waiter was far more agreeable.

They had just sat down, hardly even warmed up the seat, when the waiter came in smiling from ear to ear and asked, "Is the master's surname Yan?"

"How did you know?" Yumo asked.

"There's a Master Jin outside looking for you."

"Invite him in at once, at once!" Chasan said.

"That's the limit," Yumo said to himself as he went out to greet the fellow. "He's found himself a sugar daddy. He gets all the ideas, we spend all the money. It's not too late, though. Tonight I'll take care of him."

"Master Jin has arrived," he said. "Wonderful! Wonderful! My master is here waiting for you."

"Extraordinary coincidence! To bump into you like this again," said Jin.

Chasan waved him to a seat and they chatted for a while, even more cordially than before. Finally Yumo interruped to say, "Our master has not yet eaten. Master Jin surely has not yet eaten either? Why not eat together? Let's call the waiter to discuss it and have him start preparing."

"Absolutely right! Absolutely right!" said Jin. Summoned, the waiter appeared with tea and placed it on the table.

"What do you have in the way of food?" asked Yumo.

"We have different classes. First-class is eight ounces of silver, middle class is six, lower-class — "

"*Who* eats lower-class food?" cried Yumo. "We'll have first class. And I won't ask about the delicacies — no doubt there's chicken, duck, fish, pork, wings, sea slugs, and so on. But do you have live carp?"

"Yes," the waiter said. "But it's expensive."

"Do you think we care about the price? If carp is under one catty, it is called 'kidnapper.' It must be more than one catty before it is carp. And only when the tail is rouge-red is it fresh. Bring it and let me see it. Then there's the wine. We don't want the ordinary stuff. We want the ten-year-old Chaste Maiden Shaoxing — which, I suppose, will be at least four ounces per jug."

"Yes. How much would you like?" inquired the waiter.

"Niggard! What do you mean, 'How much?' Bring a jug and we will taste it — but let me make it *perfectly* clear that it must be golden red and richly fragrant. It must stick to the bowl like amber. If you bring the wrong kind, I won't take it."

The waiter nodded, and before long a lamp was brought up. The waiter presented the fish and Yumo inspected it.

"The fish, indeed, is carp," he declared. "And of course you would put it in only half a bowl of water, so that it looks big and must thrash about and show itself very lively. That is the trick of selling. Open its belly here. No substitutions, please. And dress it freshly. Season it with dried black mushrooms, fresh ones, and laver. And you have 'tip on tip'? I'm sure you don't understand. 'Tip on tip' is the tip of the tip of young bamboo shoots. They must be tender and cut into crisp, crunchy strips that go *kezhi, kezhi* when you eat them."

The waiter nodded and brought the wine. Yumo ladled out a cup, gave it to Jin, and said, "Master, have a taste. I guarantee it will be drinkable."

"Quite good. Quite good," Jin said. Yumo did not give Chasan a taste, but poured it into the kettle to warm first and then gave them each a cup. The waiter arrived with the cold dishes and arranged them on the table.

"Put the citron on this side," Yumo directed, "This master loves it."

"You should rest a bit after they bring us the food," Jin said, glancing at Yumo, "Come back later." Yumo withdrew until after the hot dishes, when the waiter came out with the fish. Yumo followed him into the room and ordered, "Bring ginger and vinegar."

Yumo raised the wine pot, and, standing near Jin, poured him a full cup.

"Master Jin, pick up your chopsticks. The fish should be eaten hot. Otherwise it tastes fishy." Jin glanced at him again.

"First give my master a piece," Yumo said.

"But of course," Jin murmured, serving Chasan with fish. He was about to take another piece with the chopsticks when Yumo stopped him.

"Master Jin, you haven't separated the fish down the middle with the chopsticks."

"I must have forgotten," Jin said, and he separated the fish along its spine. Then he dipped a piece into the vinegar and

ginger mixture and ate it. Washing it down with a cup of wine, he
finished it in one swallow.

"I will pour the wine," Yumo said to Jin. "You need only
concern yourself with eating the fish."

"Marvellous! Marvellous! That saves me a lot of work." He
continued to drink a cup of wine with each helping of fish.

"Wonderful! Wonderful!" said Yumo.

"Extremely wonderful! Extremely wonderful!" said Jin.

"Now stick the chopsticks inside the gills."

"But of course," said Jin, flipping the fish over. "I will give a
piece to your master and then separate it lest you waste your
words reminding me."

When the fish was nearly gone, Yumo asked the waiter for a
medium-sized bowl. "Master Jin," suggested Yumo when the
bowl had been brought, "Let us break up the steamed bread and
soak it in the fish juice."

"Yes, yes," said Jin. While he was eating it, Yumo held onto the
plate, lifted up one end, and said: "Master Jin, ladle out three
spoons from this side and drink them — then you will be full. No
need to keep our master company."

"When our masters have finished," Yumo told the waiter, "you
decide what must be reheated or steamed — I refuse to eat cold
food. I'll get the wine myself."

The waiter agreed and was removing the food when he heard
Mr. Jin say abruptly: "Brother Yan, this little manager of yours
could save me a lot of talking. How wonderful if he were to come
with me."

Chasan laughed — but that day Yumo finally did accept the
situation. He sat crosslegged outside and had the waiter serve
him. Afterwards, he sat down in the lighted room and waited for
the snoring, which came as expected. He removed the lamp and
then, without the least bit of rancor, went to sleep himself.

At dawn on the next day, Chasan again woke first. Yumo
brought him his wash water as before, and as before Jin began
to cough in the inner room. Yumo rushed in before Jin, who
was stretching and yawning, could speak and cried, "Who
awakes first from the great dream? I alone know my fate. I sleep

my fill in Grass Hall while the sun rises languidly through the window."

Jin opened his eyes wide. "You are really clever," he said. "You remembered it all. Very good."

"No need to get wash water — it's bad for the skin," said Yumo. "Let's have the bill. We'll take care of it."

The bill came to fourteen ounces, six cash, and five cents.

"Master Jin, that's not much. Let's also give the waiter and the others two ounces."

"Just so! Just so!"

"Master Jin, don't stand on ceremony. Please feel free to go on your way. We shall see you in the capital."

"Quite right, quite right. I will leave first."

He then extended his hand to Chasan and, with a *tala, tala*, left the inn.

"What a thick skin!" said Yumo to himself. "Like a catty of meat in a dumpling wrapper! *I* wanted to annoy *him* — but I think *he* has annoyed *me* instead." He laughed and then heard his master calling.

If you want to know what transpired, read on.

❦

Chapter 34

Geneologies Are Revealed, The Hero Is Recognized; Mrs. Yan's Letter Gets Read, The Impoverished Scholar Is Despised

Seeing that Jin had left, Chasan instructed Yumo to settle the bill.

"We don't have enough silver," replied Yumo. "We're short four ounces. Let me run down our expenses. We left home with twenty-eight ounces of silver. Two days, two breakfasts, and miscellaneous expenses used up, all together, one ounce and three cash. Night before last, the meal cost fourteen ounces, and sixteen ounces, six cash, and five cents went on last night's meal. We have spent thirty-one ounces, nine cash, and five cents. Are we not short almost four ounces?"

"Well, let's pawn some clothing to get more silver. After we have paid the bill with it, we will use the rest for travel expenses," said Yan.

"We've been away for two days and already we are pawning things," said Yumo. "After we pawn this clothing, what do we have for tomorrow?" But Chasan brushed his objections aside.

It was some time before Yumo returned.

"I pawned the clothes for a total of eight ounces of silver. After paying the bill, we will have four-odd ounces left."

"Let's go then," said Chasan.

On his way through the inn gate, Yumo began to mutter to himself. "At least we're rid of that *heavy* bundle," he said. "We're light and lively now. What are we waiting for?"

"No need to go on so," Yan said. "We have merely spent a few extra ounces. It's not important. Tonight we'll do whatever you suggest, okay?"

"That Mr. Jin is strange," Yumo said. "You could say he is a sponger — but why does he order all that food and not even lift his chopsticks? If he's a wino, his capacity is lousy. He ordered a whole jug of wine and drank only a little! It was all left over, and the inn made money on us. If it's the fish he loves, why doesn't he order only fish? One might think he had some score to settle with us — but we only just met him and we haven't quarrelled. Is it that he wants to eat and drink at our expense and then say nasty things about us? Even less likely. I just can't fathom him."

"As I see it," Chasan replied, "he is an unconventional man of learning, a bit Bohemian, but nothing more."

Master and servant chatted along the way, and, as before, took breakfast, rested, and then travelled straight on until they reached a place to lodge. An idea struck Yumo.

"Master," he said, "Let's stay at a small inn tonight and have a simple meal. Each of us will spend a mere two cash and there will be no more waste of money."

"As you like, as you like," agreed Chasan, and they chose lodgings at a small inn.

No sooner had they sat down than the waiter came in and announced, "There's a Master Jin outside looking for Master Yan."

"Fine," Yumo said. "Invite him in. We'll spend two more cash. He can't hatch any great schemes in this small inn."

Jin was shown in and cried, "My Brother Yan — this is truly a case of 'The accumulated good fortune of three lives.' Wherever I go, I bump into you."

"Truly, our destinies are intertwined," responded Chasan.

"Then, let us make a pact and become sworn brothers."

"He is pulling a fast one," said Yumo to himself. Aloud, he said, "This little inn isn't suitable for the ritual ceremony of swearing brotherhood. You'd best postpone it."

"No matter," said Jin. "Supreme Harmony Inn, next door, is a big place. They have everything. Not only the proper ritual items, but also food and drink. Let's go over there."

The frustration was almost more than Yumo could bear. "They will certainly be set on making money on us," he thought, stamping his foot. "Someday *he'll* get *his*! Someday he *has* to get *his*!"

Jin called over the waiter from Supreme Harmony Inn and instructed him to prepare a pig's head and the three sacrificial meats for the ceremony. He ordered the most expensive dishes and told the waiter in great detail how he must dress the fish and how he must bring a jug of aged Chaste Maiden Shaoxing. All was exactly the same as the previous two times. Yumo stood to the side, listening. He looked on as Yan and Jin laughed without the slightest care in the world — very much like brothers with different surnames.

"Our master is truly a bookworm," Yumo thought to himself. "Let's just wait and see what he does tomorrow when he gets hungry."

Before long, the three ritual meats were prepared and Jin and Chasan burned incense in order of age. Who would have guessed that Yan was two years older than Jin?

"And now the little brother will eat the big brother," Yumo thought. There was nothing for it but to stand on the side and wait on them. After swearing brotherhood, they burned paper money and it was Yan who sat in the seat of honour.

"You will be called 'Noble Elder Brother,'" said Jin, taking the other seat, "and I will be called 'Honourable Little Brother.'" They seemed more intimate now, and Yumo, listening to it all, was annoyed.

The food and drink arrived shortly and — the reader will not be surprised to hear — all progressed as before. Yumo wasted no words, but simply waited for them to finish before he went outside and sat crosslegged, saying, "It's all the same whether I eat or don't eat. So let me live for the moment and have a good time." Then he called for the waiter. "Bring over the wine," he cried, "I have an idea. We've got lots of wine and food here. Call the waiter from next door, and we servants can feast together. Consider it a small token of my respect for you. How about it?"

The delighted waiter was at a loss for words, and went immediately to get the waiter from next door. The two of them served Yumo and ate at the same time. Suddenly, Yumo was quite happy. When he had finished, he went in as before to wait for the masters to finish. Then he removed the lamp and went to sleep himself.

When Yan came out in the morning to wash his face, Yumo

whispered, "Master, you shouldn't have sworn brotherhood with Mr. Jin. You don't know where he is from. You have no idea who he is. What if he is just a sponger? Won't your reputation be ruined?"

"You rotten slave!" exploded Chasan. "How dare you butt in? Stop this nonsense! You are not to say such things! He's not the kind of person you say he is. Mr. Jin's behaviour is different from the usual. He speaks of matters of chivalry. We have sworn brotherhood, and we are bound to help each other despite all difficulties."

"It's not a matter of my butting in," rejoined Yumo. "How are we going to pay for all this food and drink?"

Just then, Jin lifted the curtain and joined them. Yumo hurried forward, crying, "Master Jin, how is it that this morning you have stretched your lazy bones and gotten up before reciting your poem?"

"If *I* recite it, what will *you* recite?" Jin said with a laugh. "I was saving it for you. I never thought you too would forget it."

When he finished, he called for the bill. "This is bad," thought Yumo. "He's about to fly off."

The bill came to eighteen ounces and three cash, including the ritual items.

"Not much," said Jin, when Yumo showed it to him, "Not much. We'll give the waiter two ounces. We didn't use anything from this inn, so we give only one ounce here." Then he turned to Yan.

Yumo pricked his ears up immediately. "Now he's going to say, 'We won't stand on ceremony.' And where am *I* going to go to get twenty ounces of silver?"

But this time Jin did not say those words. "Noble Elder Brother," he said to Chasan, "are you going to the capital to see your relatives looking like this? Won't they look down on you?"

Chasan sighed. "I am simply obeying my mother's orders," he said. "I myself did not want to make this journey. My aunt and uncle have not written to us for years, and when I get there I will have to do a lot of explaining."

"You must make a few arrangements," suggested Jin.

"He's really concerned," thought Yumo, "now that they've sworn brotherhood."

Just then a man entered the inn. He was a big man in a large goose-winged hat. He wore a short black jacket tied at the waist with a leather belt, a pair of pull-on black boots, and he carried a whip. Yumo was about to ask if he were looking for someone when the man dropped to the floor and kowtowed to Jin, saying, "My master feared that you lacked funds for the road, sir. He sent me to offer you these four-hundred ounces of silver." Now Chasan understood.

"How can I possibly need so much silver when I travel?" said Jin. "But I accept the good wishes of your old master as far as two-hundred ounces. Take the rest back, and thank him for me."

The man put down his whip and from his girdle-pouch drew forth envelope after envelope — four in all — and arranged them on the table. Jin opened one envelope, took out two silver ingots, and gave them to the messenger, saying, "You have been greatly troubled, coming all this way. Please accept some tea money."

The man dropped to the floor and kowtowed again before picking up the envelope. He was reaching for his whip when Jin stopped him and asked, "Wait a moment, please. Did you ride an animal here?"

"Yes," answered the messenger.

"Good. I know that 'one guest should not trouble two hosts' — but I have another little job for you."

Then Jin turned to Chasan. "Noble Elder Brother," he asked, "Where did you put the ticket from the pawn shop in Prosperity Village?"

"How could he know that I pawned my clothes?" wondered Chasan, but he asked Yumo for the ticket.

Yumo had for some time been in a stupor-like trance, trying to absorb all this. "How can it be that anyone would send the likes of Master Jin so much silver?" he wondered. "Indeed, my master has good judgment. Today I have learned a lesson."

When he realized that Chasan was asking for the pawn ticket, he took out a pouch from his waistband and passed the entire thing, including the leftover four ounces of silver, to Jin. Jin took another two ingots of silver and said to the man, "Take this ticket to Prosperity Village and retrieve what he pawned. You may keep what's left over after paying the capital and interest. Leave your own pouch here until you return. I'll be waiting for you at the Supreme Harmony Inn next door." The man agreed, took the whip, and departed.

Jin took out two more ounces of silver and called to Yumo, "You have been put to a lot of trouble these two days. Take this silver. I am not a sponger — right?"

Yumo dared not say a word, but only kowtowed his thanks.

"Noble Elder Brother," Jin said to Chasan. "Let's go over to that inn."

"I rely on you, Honourable Little Brother."

Jin asked Yumo to wrap up the rest of the silver on the table. Yumo did so and then stopped to pick up the heavy pouch as well.

"Don't be silly," laughed Jin. "You have been smart in every-thing else. How is it that now you have become stupid? We'll have the waiter carry it over to the inn next door for us."

Yumo laughed in turn and called the waiter to take the pouch, and master and servant left the small inn together. The Supreme Harmony Inn was large and spacious. Yumo strode swiftly to the best rooms and immediately laid out the silver he had wrapped up and put beside it on the table the heavy pouch the waiter had brought. Chasan and Jin took chairs on either side of the door while the waiter diligently prepared tea.

Jin announced that he intended to buy a horse for Chasan, as well as some proper clothing, shoes, and a hat. Nor did Chasan refuse. By evening, the messenger had returned, given Chasan the pawned items, had picked up his pouch, and gone on his way.

The drinking and eating this time were unlike the last few times. They ordered only what they wanted to eat and there was just enough left for Yumo.

By the middle of the following day, eighty or ninety of the two-hundred ounces had been spent on a horse, the pawned items, new clothing, tips, and other bills. The remaining silver Jin gave to Chasan, who was loath to accept it.

"Noble Elder Brother, please take it," urged Jin. "I have acquaintances all along the road who will meet my expenses. I have no need for silver. I will, as before, depart first and we will meet in the capital."

So saying, he waved goodbye and, with a *tala, tala,* left the inn. Chasan was sad to part with him and saw him out with eyes full of longing.

Yumo's energy picked up astonishingly. He packed their knapsack, hiding all but four ounces of the silver in a secret place. He had the waiter fasten the luggage to Chasan's new horse and, when everything was ready, invited his master to mount. Mounted, Chasan looked quite affluent and very comfortable. Yumo wrapped up the rain gear to carry in a tiny bundle on his shoulders and mounted the mule Chasan had rented for him. He crossed his legs and rode all day that way.

Toward the end of the day, they arrived at Lucky Charm District and headed straight for Twin Star Bridge. There they inquired about the Liu family, whom everyone knew, and got directions. When master and servant arrived at the gate what they saw was indeed the home of a wealthy man.

Chasan's uncle, Liu Hong, was a landlord by profession. He was a stubborn and stingy man who cared nothing for people and everything for wealth. He used his abacus in all matters. He and Old Mr. Yan had been brothers-in-law, but they were as different as fire and ice. Nonetheless, because Old Mr. Yan was a respected District Governor likely to make a mark, Liu had betrothed his daughter, Liu Jinchan, to Yan Chasan in infancy.

Liu had not foreseen that, when Old Mr. Yan died and the family sent word, he would feel some regret about the betrothal. It was a reaction that embarrassed his wife, Mistress Yan. Three years later, however, Mistress Yan suddenly took sick and gave up the ghost — whereupon Liu made up his mind to break with the Yans entirely and stopped all correspondence with them. He took a second wife, named Mistress Feng, who had a good face but an evil heart. She doted on the young daughter, but it was an affection with ulterior motive.

Liu Hong was in the habit of sighing and groaning whenever

Chasan's name came up, by way of laying the groundwork for reneging on the betrothal. Mistress Feng understood and secretly harboured her own devilish scheme. She had a nephew, Feng Junheng, of the same age as Jinchan, and she wanted him to be the son-in-law who would care for her in her old age. Thus, if Liu Hong were to pass away, this bit of the Liu estate would not escape from the Feng family. Mistress Feng herself especially doted on Jinchan and saw to it that Feng Junheng also made a great show of being diligent and attentive in front of Liu Hong. The master liked this, but it did not compensate in his mind for Feng Junheng's decidedly unrefined appearance, so he did not suggest a betrothal.

When Liu Hong's daughter came of age, he inquired as to Chasan's whereabouts. Though he could get no information, he had heard that the family was in financial straits, and he feared for his daughter's comfort if she went to them. He *must* devise a way to withdraw from the commitment. While he was in his study pondering this very question, one of his servants announced the arrival of Master Yan from Wujin District.

Alarmed, Liu Hong was momentarily at a loss, but he recovered himself quickly and told the servant to say he was not at home. The servant turned to leave, but Liu called him back and asked, "In what condition has he come?"

"He's wearing new clothes and riding a gallant steed. He has with him a young companion, quite orderly."

"Yan must have gotten rich," Liu thought, "and he has come for the express purpose of confirming our relationship. Lucky that I was careful and didn't mess up this important business." He re-instructed the servant to invite the guest in at once, and he himself went out to welcome him.

He found Chasan clad brilliantly in handsome garments and bearing himself with grace and refinement. His servant was a lively young lad, leading a sleek white horse, and Liu could not help admiring his nephew. Chasan greeted him as a nephew ought to greet an uncle, with great politeness, but Liu modestly refused two and then three times and then accepted the ritual greeting only halfway.

They sat down and exchanged commonplaces, while the servant poured tea. Chasan related his family's misfortunes and his mother's instructions to come here to prepare for the examinations. He mentioned the letter personally penned by his mother (which Yumo produced in a flash), and presented it to Liu Hong with a salute.

By this time, Liu Hong had on his black face and was no longer happy. But he had to read the letter — after which he felt even more annoyed. Chasan's request to pay his respects to his aunt was received churlishly. "My humble wife has not been feeling well these last few days," said Liu, "You can see her another time." He ordered his servant to escort Yan to Secluded Studio in the garden, where he was to stay. Sizing up the situation, Chasan submitted to being led there.

If you want to know Liu Hong's plan, then read about it in the next chapter.

❦

Chapter 35

Old Liu Reneges, Evil Hearts Plot;
Feng Rhymes Couplets, A Dog Fails to Fart

Liu Hong, with a worried look on his face, put the letter in his sleeve and went to the inner rooms.

"What has made the master so annoyed?" asked Mistress Feng.

Liu Hong told her about Chasan's visit. At first, she was very alarmed, but she pretended to be delighted, and congratulated her husband. "This is a wonderful thing," she said. "Something you ought to do."

Liu turned on her in fury. "A *wonderful* thing! You always understood before! Why do you get muddled today? Look at the letter. She would have him study here until the exams next year. How much do you think that will cost us? And if he passes, we will have still more social obligations to fulfill. If he doesn't pass, she would have me arrange his marriage here and after a month send the two of them to Wujin District. You figure it out. I would lose both the person and the money. How can you say that I should do it?"

Mistress Feng was a clever woman, and she set about sounding out Liu's desires. "According to the master, then," she asked, "how should this affair be handled?"

"I don't have any plan. I merely would like to renege on the betrothal and find another, richer son-in-law, lest our daughter suffer and I get involved later on."

Mistress Feng heard Liu Hong's words "renege on the betrothal," and she quickly adapted her own evil plan to the circumstances. "Let us, then," she suggested, "neglect Yan for a few days in Secluded Study. I guarantee that within ten days he himself will renege on the betrothal and leave of his own free will."

"If you can do that," Liu Hong said happily, "it will relieve me of a great burden."

The two plotters were unaware that their daughter's old wet-nurse, Mistress Tian, had passed by the window as they spoke and had stopped to listen. She didn't miss a word and afterward rushed to Jinchan's chamber and told her everything.

"My Young Lady," she warned, "should not be restricted by vulgar proprieties and so perpetuate the attitudes of the women's quarters. You must save Master Yan and Old Mother Yan. This is a matter of no small importance. You must not help your mother and father subvert your betrothal because of petty concerns of etiquette. My Young Lady must come up with a plan right away."

"But my own mother is dead, and I have no one to turn to," said the young woman.

"I have a plan," said Mistress Tian. "They calculated that he would not be able to bear it after ten days. Do not refer to Master Yan as husband just now, but talk like brother and sister. Write a note and have your maid, Xiuhong, arrange for you to meet him at night in the study and explain everything to him. Give him some of your pin money, so that he can find another place to stay. Have him wait until he takes the exam and establishes himself to complete the betrothal. Then there would probably be no way for the master not to give his permission."

At first the young lady absolutely refused. But Mistress Tian and Xiuhong entreated her so eloquently that, in the end, she assented.

All people have their own secret plans, and the one hatched by the wet-nurse and the maid was designed to help Chasan and to protect the young lady. Secret plans ought to be devised from the goodness of the heart, as this one was, but there is another kind of secret planner. His plans agitate him to the point of madness, and he is as restless as an ant in the tropics.

Such a planner was Junheng. From the minute his aunt suggested he be betrothed to Jinchan, he started haunting their home, intruding at inopportune times. He always pretended to be humble and refined whenever he bumped into the master, but he had an unbearably toadying laugh that drove Liu Hong wild. If the master were not around, he would gossip wildly and slander others to his aunt, begging her, even on his knees, to settle his betrothal as soon as possible.

As luck would have it, Liu Jinchan one day went to pay her respects to Mistress Feng, and, while mother and daughter were chatting, this fellow rushed in. The young lady did not have time to hide herself, so Mistress Feng said, "You two are cousins, the same flesh and blood — you can see each other. Greet each other properly."

There was nothing for it but to hold up her sleeve in the ritual greeting and wish him good luck. He bowed in return, staying bent for quite a long time. But his sneaky eyes looked straight through her. Xiuhong, standing nearby, could not bear to look on and urged the young lady back to her maidenly chambers.

Feng was awestruck for a long time, wearing an expression that was not quite human, and, from that day on, he plotted and entreated with increased fervour. He burned to get his hands on Jinchan. He went everyday to the Lius' to visit. When he saw the white horse tied up in the courtyard, he asked about it.

"It is the one ridden here by Master Yan from Wujin District," answered the servant.

The news fell on Feng like a bolt of lightning, and it was a long while before he came out of his stupor and asked himself how on earth he was going to handle this. He went to the study to see Liu Hong, who was clearly very troubled by something. "It must be this affair," Feng realized. "Yan must be terribly poor. I'll meet him and see how the land lies. If he really is not up to snuff, then I'll make a fool of him and set myself to rights at the same time."

He explained to Liu Hong that he wanted to meet Chasan, and Liu Hong, unable to refuse, took him to Secluded Study. Feng, the would-be foolmaker, found a handsome and noble-looking Yan dressed in brilliant new clothes. Feng felt keenly the contrast with his own appearance, and Chasan's elegant and sophisticated conversation so unnerved him that he was unable to string together a complete sentence. Feng wished desperately for a place to hide.

Liu Hong, looking at the two of them, was also struck by the contrast between the beautiful and the ugly, and he thought to himself, "Yan has the looks and talent to be a good match for my daughter. What a pity that his family is so poor." But he looked at Feng Junheng's shoulders and saw how he wrinkled his brows and rolled his eyes and decided that Junheng could not possibly do either. Liu Hong felt embarrassed and he left, muttering, "You two continue your chat. I'll go take care of my work."

Feng Junheng scratched his head and looked perplexed. He sat for another little while and then returned to his room, where he looked at himself in the mirror and said, "Feng Junheng! Oh, Feng Junheng! Just look at you. If my parents wanted a fine son, why didn't they spend a little time on him, teaching him, training him, so that when he meets people he is not afraid to open his mouth?" He bemoaned his fate for a while and then reminded himself, "Yan is a human being and I'm also a human being. Why should I fear him? That's degrading. Tomorrow I will gather my courage and test him a bit." With these thoughts running through his mind, he fell asleep in the study.

The next day after breakfast, he hesitated again. But he soon hardened his will and went to Secluded Study. He met Yan and they sat down.

"May I ask how old you are?" Feng Junheng inquired.

"Double ten plus two," replied Chasan.

Feng Junheng did not understand what Yan had said, so Yan traced it on the table for him.

"Oh" cried Feng, "I dare say it is the simplified way of writing twenty. In that case I also am double ten."

"So Elder Brother Feng's honourable teeth are twenty?"

"Oh, teeth. Well, no, I have twenty-eight, including molars. My years, however, number twenty."

"Honourable teeth," Yan said, laughing, "means age."

Knowing that he had answered incorrectly, Feng pleaded, "Older Brother Yan, I am a crude person. Don't play literary games with me."

"Elder Brother Feng," Yan inquired, "what lessons do you do at home?"

Now Feng Junheng understood the word "lessons," so he said, "I have a tutor at home, a man of learning, who has taught me some kind of poetry — five words to a line, four lines to a verse, and there's some kind of rhyme or non-rhyme. How can I possibly write such poetry on my own, I thought. But once I got the hang of it, it came very smoothly — but I could only write half a stanza. No matter how hard I tried, I couldn't finish it. My teacher gave me the words 'flock of geese' to start with, but could I compose anything? What a job that one was!"

"Do you still remember it?" asked Chasan.

"I remember it extremely well. It was no easy thing to compose it — how could I forget it? 'In the distance a flock of geese/Dive into the river on seeing people.'"

"And what follows?"

"I told you, all I could compose was half a verse."

"Shall I finish that one for you?" offered Chasan.

"I dare say that would be fine," said Feng.

"White feathers divide the green water/Red-palmed feet move on blue-green waves."

"That sounds really good," said Feng. "There was yet another one. Our study courtyard had a loquat tree, so my teacher picked that as a topic for me. What I came up with was, 'There's a loquat tree/Two sloping wood slabs.'"

Feng Junheng stopped talking about regulated poetry. "I most love to match rhyming couplets," he said.

"Why?"

"Because, when you compose poetry, you must consider even and oblique tones and rhyme, but when you match couplets, you think them up out of nowhere. If there is a first line, then you just match up the words — that's all there is to it. Elder Brother Yan, why don't you come up with a couplet for me to match?"

"Today is the Double Ninth Festival," reflected Chasan, "and the wind is sounding and the trees are roaring." So he wrote, "Ninth day, double ninth/Wind blows leaves."

Feng looked at this line for a long time. "Eighth month, mid-autumn/Moon lights up the terrace," he said at last. "What do you think of that? How about another?"

"He lacks an understanding of proper behaviour," thought

Chasan, whose next line was, "In reforming and cultivating one's person/Who can compare with Ziyou and Zixia?"

Feng Junheng responded with, "In making friends and meeting acquaintances/I dare compare with Liu the Sixth and Liu the Seventh."

Yan then resorted to barbed praise. "Three ancient records, five former rituals/You are a chest of one hundred treasures," he wrote for Feng Junheng.

Feng pondered this and then matched with, "One turn, two dazzles/A kaleidoscope."

Chasan, pressed for another, lost his patience, and said, "I would teach you, but there's no door to enter by," a line clearly implying that Feng was unworthy of learning from him.

Feng Junheng foolishly took this line seriously, however, and cried triumphantly, "I have matched it! 'I dare not follow/I have a window.'"

Chasan took out a fan brushed with elegant calligraphy and began to fan himself. Feng asked to see the fan, and Chasan handed it over.

Feng praised it lavishly, saying, "Beautiful characters! Beautiful characters! Like 'fighting dragons and sparring tigers'." But when he turned it over and saw only blank paper on the other side, he said regretfully, "Why don't you paint a few people on this side? Take a look at my fan. One side has a painting, but the other has no characters. May I beg Elder Brother Yan to write a few characters for me?"

"These characters were written by a very good friend who gave me the fan," Yan said. "The inscription here is proof. I would not dare to deceive you. My calligraphy would defile your 'honourable waving' of the fan."

"We said we would not play literary games, so what's this 'honourable waving' rigmarole?" objected Feng. "My fan was also given by a friend, so I beg Elder Brother Yan's compliance. Once you write something, it will be perfect. Just look at how excellent the spirit is."

Chasan took the fan and inspected the painting, which depicted a woman rowing a boat with an oar.

"Look at that man holding a pair of binoculars on the other side of the shore," said Feng. "He is bent over with laughter and really looks alive. Please write some words on the other side. I will take care of your fan while you inscribe mine."

Yan could see no way to avoid taking Feng's fan, which he put in his pen holder.

Feng then took leave of him and returned to the study, thinking, "Yan didn't even have to think about finishing those half verses — he just opened his mouth and out they came. He is much more learned than I am. And he is handsome. If he stays, he will steal my cousin!"

He conveniently forgot that the two were originally betrothed, and thought only of how to keep them apart. The greedy, evil fellow wracked his brains for the best way to hurt Chasan. All night, he tossed and turned with his plots, but he could not come up with a plan that suited him. The next day after breakfast, he headed once more for the study.

If you want to know what happened, read on.

Chapter 36

❦

Gold Is Given, A Maid Loses Her Life;
The Corpse Is Robbed, A Servant Is Ungrateful

Now when Feng Junheng reached the garden, he saw a woman coming toward him. Looking more closely, he observed that it was Xiuhong. Suspicions welled up within his heart, and he accosted her.

"Why have you come here to the garden?" he demanded.

"The young mistress sent me here to pick flowers," she answered.

"Where are the flowers you picked?" he asked.

"The flowers haven't bloomed yet, so I am returning empty-handed. Why are you interrogating me? This is the Lius' flower garden. It's not yours. We don't need you minding our people's business! It's uncalled for!" She swept her sleeves back and left without turning her head, leaving a furious Feng Junheng, unable to answer her back, staring angrily at her retreating figure.

This encounter increased Feng's suspicions even more, and he rushed to the study. Yumo had just gone out to brew some tea, and, Feng noticed, Chasan had a note in his hand, which he seemed just about to open and read.

Chasan suddenly raised his head and, seeing Feng, offered him a seat, at the same time slipping the note into a book. They chatted for a while, and then Feng asked if he might borrow some easy-to-read poetry books from him.

Chasan went over to the bookcase to look. While his attention was diverted, Feng noticed that a corner of the note Yan had just slipped in the book was sticking out, so he extracted it carefully and put it in his sleeve. When Chasan came back, he grabbed the profferred book, stuck out his hand in goodbye, and returned to the main study.

Feng entered the study, put the book down, and then took the note from his sleeve — the very note that the wet-nurse had urged be written to Chasan, appointing him to meet the young mistress in the inner courtyard at the second watch that evening so that she could secretly give him some money. After one startled glance at it, he said to himself, "This is really something! I almost messed up a very important matter. If they had been able to meet tonight, the young mistress would certainly have given herself to Yan and my conjugal destiny would have flown away. That would not have been good!" Feng's thoughts soon shifted, however, "No matter, no matter. The note has fallen into *my* hands, and Yan probably fears that I am now wise to him. He won't dare to go."

Then a plan occurred to Feng, and the more he thought about this plan, the more marvellous it seemed. "Why," he asked himself, "don't I impersonate Yan? If I go there at the second watch and get my hands on her, then it will be *my* marital fate. The affair is bound to leak out, and, if she won't give in, I'll use this note as evidence. Even if my uncle were to find out, he would be forced to 'open his door to welcome the robber.' He couldn't do anything to me!" Feng could hardly wait for the second watch to come.

Now, Liu Jinchan did have Xiuhong give the note to Chasan and she also secretly prepared some money and clothing for him. But, when the time of the assignation came, she instructed Xiuhong to carry the parcel to Chasan. Mistress Tian begged her to go herself, but the young mistress was firm.

"I have already transgressed the code of proper behaviour in this matter," she said. "If I were to go myself to meet him, then I would be violating the code even more seriously. I refuse to go."

There had been no moving her, so Xiuhong had set off with the parcel. As she approached the corner, she saw someone hunched over and coming toward her. Looking carefully, she saw that it was not Chasan, so she demanded, "Who are you?"

"I am Yan," she heard that person say, and then he came toward her as if to lay hands on her. Xiuhong knew trouble when she saw it and called out, "Thief!"

Feng Junheng stuck out his hand as though to cover her mouth. It was a clumsy movement, but forceful, and the young maid, who was small and weak, fell backwards under it. The evil devil had no time to take his hands away, but fell down on top of her, his hands hard against her throat. By the time he got up, the maid had breathed her last, dropping the parcel and the silver on the ground. When Feng realized that she was dead, he picked up the packages and the money, threw Chasan's fan and the note down near the body, and hurried back to his study.

The young mistress and the wet-nurse were waiting anxiously upstairs, and, when Xiuhong did not return, they began to worry. The wet-nurse decided to go to the meeting place herself. In the meantime, the watchman had discovered the dead maid and reported it at the house. The news terrified the wet-nurse and she ran back to the maiden's chamber to tell the young mistress.

With lamps and fires, the servants were all heading to the scene of the crime. Liu Hong shone the lamp on the body and, sure enough, it was Xiuhong. He saw that near the body was lying a fan, and a distance away was a note. He picked both things up at once and, when he opened the fan, saw that it was Chasan's. He was very annoyed at this. But when he looked at the note, he grew furious. He said not a word, but ran straight to his daughter's chambers. Mistress Feng, not knowing why he was like this, followed behind.

"Look at what you've done!" Liu Hong shouted at his daughter, throwing down the note before her. By this time, the young mistress knew that Xiuhong was dead, and, seeing her father in such a state, she felt ten-thousand arrows pierce her heart. It was difficult to explain — all she could do was sob bitterly.

Mistress Feng sized up the situation, picked up the note, and read it. "Oh, so *this* is what it's all about," she said. "Master, you are really scatterbrained. How do you know it's not Xiuhong who made all this trouble? Her handwriting, in the first place, has always been just like our daughter's. Our daughter has never yet set foot out of her maiden's chamber, and Xiuhong died outside the gate — how is it that you can't distinguish black from white and have instead blamed our daughter? It is just that I wonder why

Yan, having already gotten the money and things, had to choke her to death? I really don't know what this all means."

Liu Hong, awakened to his error, began to blame Chasan for everything that had happened. He sat down at once and wrote a document accusing Yan of having killed the maid without cause. He did not, however, mention the matter of the silver for fear that it would harm his own reputation. Then he sent Yan to Lucky Charm District.

Poor Yan! Because he had not the slightest inkling of what was going on, he was driven to wild surmises about what was happening to him. Fortunately, Yumo, who was a clever lad, discreetly investigated the matter and explained it to him. When Chasan understood it, he made a vow to himself that no one should interfere with his intention.

After comforting her step-daughter, Mistress Feng ordered the wet-nurse to take good care of her and then returned to her own quarters and began to scheme. She decided to insist on Chasan's death and vowed to do her best to incite Liu to do the evil.

It happened to be just what Liu himself wanted, and he waited anxiously for the district magistrate to come for the investigation. Xiuhong was duly found to have been choked to death, and no other injury was discovered. Liu Hong set his teeth and insisted Chasan had done the murder and that he must pay for it with his life.

The district magistrate returned to his yamen, convened court immediately, and had Chasan brought up. Looking him over carefully, he saw that he was a frail student sort, nothing like a murderer. Wanting to be gentle, he asked, "Yan Chasan, why did you kill Xiuhong? Confess!"

"I did it," replied Chasan, "because Xiuhong did not listen to me and disobeyed my orders. Yesterday, when she disobeyed me again, I lost control and in my anger pressed her toward the rear gate. I just touched her throat. It never occurred to me that she would fall over and die. I look to you, sir, for a decision, and I will have no complaints." When he finished, he kowtowed.

The magistrate took note of how Chasan confessed willingly and without excuse. There was nothing remarkable in what he had said — yet the magistrate could not help feeling that something was wrong.

"He doesn't have the look of a murderer," he thought. "Is he subject to fits? Are there details he can't reveal and would die to keep secret? This case must be investigated very carefully before it is settled." He ordered Chasan taken back to his cell and withdrew to the rear chamber, where he had another matter to contemplate.

Why had Yan confessed to a murder he did not commit? He had, he felt, greatly wronged the young mistress. His carelessness in losing her note, sent to him out of the goodness of her heart, had brought about the death of Xiuhong, for one thing. For another, if all this were to come out in court, the young lady's reputation would be ruined. If she had to make a public appearance, it would violate the code of the maidenly chamber. These thoughts filled Chasan's mind, and he was aware of little else. Certainly he was not conscious of how terribly Yumo was suffering on his account.

When his master was taken away, Yumo scrounged up some silver and headed for the district office to make surreptitious inquiries. It terrified him to hear that his master had confessed to everything, and tears streamed down his face. Later, when he went to see Chasan in jail, he took a small gift to present to the warden, with the result that he was given permission to stay inside and take care of his master. Yumo then gave his silver to the jail guard, saying that Chasan must be looked after in every way. The sight of the white and shiny silver enchanted the guard, who agreed to everything.

Finally, Yumo was taken in to Chasan, and he scolded him through his tears, crying, "My master should not have confessed to murder!"

Chasan smiled slightly, completely indifferent, and Yumo did not understand.

At Liu Hong's place, everyone had heard that Chasan had confessed. The old scoundrel was delighted and as happy as if he had just recovered from a terrible illness. But it was tragic for Jinchan, who, when she heard, knew that Chasan would die.

"It is *I* who have harmed him," she said. "Since he has no future, why should I live on alone? My death will pay for his." She got rid of the wet-nurse by asking her to brew a pot of tea — and then she hanged herself from the beam of her chamber.

Returning to a closed door, the wet-nurse knew that something was wrong. She called out, but there was no answer. Through a crack in the door, she saw the young mistress suspended and terror seized her again. She ran crying and staggering to inform the master and mistress.

Liu Hong called for servants and ran upstairs and threw open the door of the maidenly chamber. He rushed in and clasped the young girl in his arms. While the servant was loosening the sash, Mistress Feng arrived. Husband and wife thought that they might yet save her, but her breath was already infinitesimal. Both of them burst into bitter tears, and Mistress Feng began to shout recriminations at her husband.

"It's all your fault, you old turtle!" she cried. "Old murderer! You can't tell red from black, black from white. You have taken your daughter's life for eternity. You've barely sent *that* one to the district court when *this* one hangs herself. What a stink this will make when it all gets out!"

Liu Hong choked back the tears that rose at her words, and shouted back, "Thanks for reminding me! How are we supposed to handle this kind of thing? Crying over it is a small matter. We have to come up with a plan."

"There is only one plan," retorted Mistress Feng. "The only thing to do is to say that our daughter developed a violent illness and is indisposed. Then we must get someone to bring us a coffin secretly. We will say it is for the purpose of warding off evil spirits. We will encoffin her discreetly and put her in the garden hallway while we think of the best way and place to bury her. After three or four days, we will say that she died of the illness. That way, no one will know and no tongues will wag."

Liu Hong could not come up with a better plan, so he ordered the servant to procure a coffin. "If anyone asks," he explained, "just say that our young lady is seriously ill and we are doing this to chase away evil."

The servant nodded and in short order came back with a coffin, which was stealthily placed in the back building.

In the meantime, Mistress Feng and the wet-nurse had dressed the young mistress and had placed her in the coffin with her favourite jewels, hair ornaments, and clothing. The only thing they did not do was play the funeral music. Then they had the servant carry the coffin to the garden pavilion and position it properly. Not daring to sob out loud, the master and mistress could only cry quietly. The gate to the garden was locked lest anyone see the coffin, and the household servants were given four ounces of silver apiece to still their tongues.

Among the servants there was one whose surname was Niu — the Cow — and whose given name was Lüzi, which means donkey. His father, Niu Number Three, was an older servant in the Liu family, and, when he had become blind, Liu Hong, recognizing that he had worked hard for them for many years, had built three rooms outside the garden gate to house the old man, his son, and his daughter-in-law in a place from which they could conveniently take care of the garden. When Donkey Niu came home on that day with four ounces of silver, his wife, Mistress Ma, demanded to know where it had come from.

Donkey Niu described how the young mistress had hanged herself, how the master and mistress had put the coffin in the garden and not played the funeral music, and how the silver had been distributed as payment for keeping all this secret. He went on to tell how many burial items there were in the coffin — phoenix-headed clasps, pearl flowers, kingfisher bracelets, and other wonderful things.

Mistress Ma drooled with envy at this news. "What a pity about those valuables!" she cried. "If you had any guts, when it got dark, with only this one section of wall between it and us, you would sneak in there — "

"Daughter-in-law!" broke in Niu Number Three. "What are you saying? Our master has suffered a tragedy, and we ought all pity him. How can you want to rob the corpse before it is even cold? Little Donkey, Little Donkey — you must not do this thing!" The old man was filled with anger.

During the old man's speech, Donkey Niu had been signalling to his wife. Now he turned angrily to his father and said, "I know all that! We were only talking. I wouldn't do it."

Donkey Niu gestured to his wife to prepare dinner, and he himself went to get some wine. When all was prepared, Donkey Niu began to drink without inviting his father to join them. Mistress Ma served him and ate at the same time. They did not speak to each other, but merely made hand gestures. When they had finished, the two of them put away the utensils. Donkey Niu then found an axe in the courtyard and put it on his belt. When the second watch was struck, he headed straight for the back gate of the garden, where he selected a strategically high spot, took hold of the wall, and leapt over it.

To find out what transpired, read on.

❦

Chapter 37

The Corpse Revives, Retribution Strikes;
A Boy Serves His Master, A Hero Squanders Gold

Now, Donkey Niu arrived at the garden just as the watch was being struck. Holding on to the wall, he climbed up, and leaped over. *Kerplunk!* Donkey Niu dropped into the garden with a thud, giving himself quite a scare. The moonlight shone through the forest, and the shadows of the flowers in the garden swayed to and fro like secret villains. Donkey Niu knew the way and headed straight for the coffin. He had a sudden memory of how it had looked earlier with the young mistress in the coffin, and shivers went up and down his spine. His hair stood on end and he began to quiver.

"This is bad," he thought. "I mustn't blow it." He sat down on the treadle of the hall railing to calm himself. He fingered the axe and thought, "I have come here to make my fortune. All I have to do is go up there, open the lid, and the wealth will be mine. Why am I afraid? My mind is working overtime. Even if a ghost appeared, it would merely be the ghost of a delicate female from the inner chambers — what could she do to me?"

At this thought bravery welled up in his breast and, picking up the axe, he approached the coffin. But his conscience smote him as he stood beside it, and he dropped down on both knees and prayed silently: "I, Donkey Niu … , am truly miserable, a poor fellow. I am just borrowing the young lady's jewels and clothing. When I am in better circumstances, I will burn mountains of paper ingots for her."

He laid down the axe and grabbed the coffin lid from the front with both hands. With a violent pull, the lid came loose. He walked to the other side and lifted the lid again with both hands, so that it moved up and to the right, lying crosswise on top of the coffin. As he was about to reach in, someone cried, "Aiya!" He bolted down the steps of the pavilion in terror, hunched over, shaking and chattering, and gasping for breath. He looked back and saw the young mistress struggling to rise from her coffin. "I have received much guidance from Uncle," she said, and then she fell silent and lay back down.

"Has she come back to life?" Donkey Niu asked himself. "Even if she has, she is in a state of great weakness — if I choke her a little, she will be dead as before. And I will have my fortune."

He stood up and, putting up his hands to strangle her, advanced again toward the coffin. But before he reached the pavilion, something flew through the air and bit sharply into his hand. Not daring to cry out, Donkey Niu clenched his teeth against the pain, swinging his arms about and rolling on the floor.

From behind a convoluted Taihu stone emerged a man dressed in dark, night attire. He headed straight for Donkey Niu, who sensed disaster and prepared to run, but the stranger seized his arm and stopped him. Donkey Niu flung himself to the ground and cried out, "Lord, sir, let me go!"

The man held Donkey Niu to the ground and, flashing his sword, demanded, "Who is in the coffin?"

"The young lady of our household," stammered Donkey Niu. "She hanged herself."

"Why did the young mistress of your family hang herself?" asked the stranger, who seemed startled by the news.

"Yan confessed in court, so she hanged herself. I don't know why. I beg you, sir — let me go!"

"Your intention to rob the corpse may be forgiven. But then you planned to kill her. For that you must be killed — you cannot be spared." As he spoke, the sword was falling, and, by the time he finished, Donkey Niu had entered the soup pot.

Bai Yutang — for that was the stranger's name, though he sometimes called himself Jin Maoshu — saw that he had killed Donkey Niu and that the young mistress had revived. He wanted to go to help her, but he had reasons for not arousing suspicion in the future wife of his sworn brother.

Jin Maoshu had been very busy since parting from Chasan. He went first to Lucky Charm District and made thorough inquiries about Liu Hong. He learned that Liu Hong was very stingy and would certainly despise poverty and lust after wealth. Later, he learned that Chasan had arrived and everything was in good order, and he was delighted. But then he was informed that Chasan had been arrested, so he rushed over to the Liu house to get to the bottom of things. He knew that Chasan had suffered an injustice, but his first knowledge of the young mistress's suicide came from his interrogation of Donkey Niu.

A plan flashed into his mind, and he called out loudly, "Your young mistress has come back to life! Come quickly to rescue her!" Then he kicked the door out, leaped to the upper floor, and set off for Liu Hong's room.

The two men of the early night watch were just making their rounds when they heard Jin's cries. They also heard clearly the *kecha* sound of something being kicked in. Startled, the two ran toward the sound and shone a lantern on the spot. The corner garden gate, frame and all, was askew. Gathering their courage, they entered the garden. Looking first into the pavilion, they saw that the lid was crosswise on the coffin. Coming closer, they saw the young lady, eyes closed, sitting up in the coffin, mumbling. The guards whispered excitedly to each other and quickly agreed that they should take the news immediately to the master and mistress.

One of them turned to go and in so doing caught sight of a dark object beyond the coffin. He shone the lamp on it and discovered a body. He looked more closely and recognized it.

"Isn't this Donkey Niu?" he asked the other guard, "Why is he lying here? Was he left here yesterday after the coffin was laid out? And what's this soggy thing? My foot is soaked. Aiya! There's a hole in his neck! He's been killed! Hurry, hurry to the master!"

Liu Hong ordered the corner gate opened and rushed to the garden when he heard the news. Mistress Feng, who had summoned the servants and maids, was hard on his heels. At the first sound of alarm, the wet-nurse, Mistress Tian, had dashed to the garden before anyone else, propped up the young mistress, and begun to call for help. But the young mistress continued to mumble, "Thank you, Uncle, for your guidance. How can I ever repay you?"

When Liu Hong and Mistress Feng saw their daughter alive again, they were beside themselves with joy. Everyone tried to help. Mistress Tian carried the young lady on her back, and the other servants surrounded her all the way to the maiden's chamber, where she was laid down very gently. They prepared a little ginger soup for her and gradually she came to. Everyone but the wet-nurse, the mistress, and the younger maids was sent away, and the young mistress was kept quiet until she regained her senses.

Liu Hong chided the night watchmen, who were still waiting outside, "Why don't you two go about your business instead of standing here?" he demanded.

"We are waiting to talk to you, sir. There is another matter."

"You won't get a tip," warned Liu Hong.

"We aren't asking for a tip. There's a dead body in our garden."

"How can there be a dead body there?" asked Liu Hong, frightened.

"Come with us and you'll see. It's not a stranger either. It's someone we know."

When they reached the pavilion, one guard raised the lamp high above the blood-drenched ground. Liu Hong looked and trembled for a long time before he spoke. "Isn't he Donkey Niu? How was he killed?" Liu asked. Then, catching sight of the axe, he began to understand. "He came to open the coffin and rob the corpse. That's why the lid was opened."

"But who killed him?" asked one of the watchmen. "It's hard to believe that he slit his own throat when he saw that the young mistress had come back to life."

With a sigh of distress, Liu Hong set someone to watch the body and sent a report of the death to the authorities.

When the local constable arrived, he spoke severely to Liu Hong. "Just the other day a maid was choked to death here, and that case still has not been solved. Now a servant has been killed. All these happy events have taken place in your honourable home. I must trouble you, sir, to come with me."

Liu Hong knew that the constable was taking advantage of the situation and went back into the house for some silver. As he entered the room, he saw with a shock that the cabinet was open and its lock on the floor. He searched the cabinet — the loose silver had not been touched, but he was short ten of the full packets of silver. He was devastated. When he came out of the stupor of despair, he sent the maid for the mistress and weighed out two ounces of silver for the constable, who soon became very agreeable and offered to make the report himself, without troubling Liu Hong, who for his part hurried back to the room and burst into tears.

"What's wrong?" asked Mistress Feng, appearing in the doorway. "Our daughter has come back to life — you ought to be happy. Or is it that you are grieving for Donkey Niu?"

"That grave-robbing thief!"

"Then what are you crying about?"

Liu Hong told her about the missing packets of silver.

"My heart aches for the silver. I want to report this to the authorities. That's why I called you — to discuss it."

"Impossible!" cried Mistress Feng. "There are already two unsolved murders connected with our family. If you report the theft of the silver now, they will see nothing else. And you will alert them to the fact that we have amassed a great deal of money, and then they will start asking awkward questions, and we will have to spend *another* ten packets and it won't necessarily solve the case. We just have to bear the pain and consider it lost money."

When Liu Hong heard his wife's words, he felt that she was right, so he let the matter drop. But every once in a while, his heart contracted in pain.

Meanwhile, Mistress Ma was getting angrier and angrier at Donkey Niu's failure to return with the stolen jewels. When she had incited her husband to rob the corpse, she had envisioned easy success. She never expected to wait the whole night without seeing her husband return. By dawn, she was complaining bitterly: "That abominable son of a turtle! I show him the way to get rich, and he doesn't come home with the money. He has probably

spent it on some woman. And, any minute, his father will ask
about him again and start grumbling on senselessly."

Just then came a knock at the door, and a voice outside cried,
"Third Brother Niu, Third Brother Niu!"

"Who is coming to call so early?" demanded Mistress Ma.

She opened the door and found it was the man with the honey
wagon, Li Number Two, who enquired solicitously whether she
was upset.

"Hah!" she answered rudely. "I get up at this hour and you
expect me not to look miserable. What do you want?"

"You do look grieved. How could you not, when your Donkey
Niu has been murdered?"

Niu Number Three heard these words from his inner room and
cried out, "Old Li, come into the room! What is this all about?"

Li Number Two then went into the room and said, "Older
Brother, Donkey Niu was killed in the flower garden, but we don't
know why. Your master has notified the authorities, and they'll be
here soon."

Niu Number Three whirled on Mistress Ma. "Yesterday I tried
to stop you, but you wouldn't listen, and now he's gotten himself
murdered. Isn't this going to implicate our master? Old Li, take me
there. I must try to prevent the autopsy. Isn't that the right thing to
do? I will not keep my daughter-in-law here. Send her home."

He took hold of his walking stick and concluded sadly, "The
donkey's mourning is in the east, the horse's in the west." Then,
asking Old Li to lead him, the old man headed for the master's
residence. When they arrived, Niu Number Three told the master
about his attempts to stop his son and daughter-in-law. The news
pleased Liu Hong, and he took Niu Number Three under his wing.
He told him what to say, what not to say, how to take care of the
corpse, and how to arrange everything properly.

The official arrived after the young lady's coffin had been
moved to an empty room. Niu Number Three told him what had
happened and asked to be allowed to take care of the corpse. The
official inquired about the details and then assented.

Now let us return to Chasan in jail. Thanks to Yumo's care, he
was not suffering at all. His case had still not been brought up and

he did not know whether it was settled or unsettled. He felt uneasy, and he was startled when the jailor called Yumo out and said to him, "Little fellow, you must leave. I can't go on providing for you."

Yumo felt that the jailor was not saying what was on his mind, so he pleaded with him. "Uncle Jia," he begged, "please take pity on my master, who is suffering an injustice. I *beg* you to be generous."

"We long ago took pity on him," the jailor said. "But you count it up — the expenses are not light. That tiny piece of silver was used up in no time. 'Money in a yamen is like boats in the water,' they say. You must think of a plan. It's hard to believe that your master doesn't have any friends."

"We've come from far away to visit relatives," Yumo said tearfully. "How could we have friends here? We must beg Uncle to take pity on my master. There's no other way."

"That's useless talk," said the jailor. "But here's an idea. Your master has a relative. Isn't he a wealthy man? Why don't you go after his money?"

"He is my master's *enemy*!" cried Yumo, the tears streaming down his cheeks. "How could we get help from *him*?"

"Go talk it over with your master and think of some way to get to this relative. Get some of his money, and we'll be able to take good care of your master."

"Your plan," said Yumo, shaking his head, "is a difficult one. My master won't be able to carry it out."

"In that case, you'd better leave today. I can't allow you to stay here."

Yumo was hard pressed, and he sobbed bitterly. How he wished he could kneel on the ground and beg him!

At that moment, a man standing by the prison gate called out, "Chief Jia, Chief Jia! Come quickly!"

"I'm busy."

"Hurry! I've something to tell you," the man insisted.

"What is it?" asked Jailor Jia, crossing to the gate. "Are you afraid I would keep all the money for myself? Of course not! I would share it with everyone!"

"Who is that you are arguing with?" asked the man.

"It's Yan Chasan's young companion."

"Aiya! Why did you stir him up? Their guardian Bai has arrived, and just now he scattered some change at the yamen gate — about one-hundred ounces. He'll be coming in soon. Make preparations! Take good care of the two of them."

Jailor Jia turned and went back to where Yumo was still crying.

"Old Yu," he cried, rushing up to him. "Why haven't you stopped blubbering? Talk a bit, laugh a bit, wail and blubber a bit. What's wrong with that? Why are you suddenly so serious? Tell me, does your master have a friend by the name of Bai?"

"He does not have any friend named Bai," Yumo answered.

"Traitor! You're still giving me trouble! Right now there is a man named Bai outside who has come to see your master."

As he spoke, the guard on duty approached them, escorting a person wearing a martial turban, a moon-white cloak, and a peach-coloured shirt. On his feet were the boots of an official, and he had the air of a hero. Yumo took a look and thought that he looked very much like Master Jin, but he dared not acknowledge him.

"Yumo!" he heard the hero say. "You are here too. Good boy! This has been really difficult for you."

At these words, Yumo broke down completely and rushed forward to greet the man. His voice was different, but it had to be Master Jin.

How was he to know that Master Jin was Bai Yutang? Fifth Master Bai raised Yumo from his knees, asking kindly, "Where's your master?"

If you want to know how Yumo answered him, read on.

❦

Chapter 38

**A Grievance Is Vented, The Carriage Is Topped;
Danger Is Braved, A Note Is Affixed by a Sword**

Bai Yutang raised Yumo and asked: "Where is your master?"

Jailor Jia hastened to answer for him. "Master Yan is in this room here — we have been taking care of him."

"Fine. Serve him well, and I will reward you."

Jailor Jia said "yes" a good many times.

Yumo went to tell Master Yan, and Fifth Master Bai followed. Chasan was not wearing chains, but he looked haggard and drawn, with dishevelled hair and a smudged face. Bai rushed up to him.

"Noble Elder Brother," he cried, extending his hands, "How did you meet with this injustice?" There was grief in his voice.

"Ai, your stupid brother is ashamed to see you. On what matter has Honourable Little Brother come to this place?"

Seeing that Chasan was neither tearful nor troubled, merely embarrassed, Bai nodded his head and thought admiringly, "Yan is a true hero."

"You and I are boon companions and sworn brothers," he said. "Ours is not a superficial friendship. Do not insist on deceiving me. Tell me how this happened."

Chasan had to comply. "It was all my fault," he said. "When Xiuhong delivered the note, I was not able to read it because someone came to my room just then. So I put the note in a book. Who would have thought that the note would get lost, and, by evening, all this would have occurred? After Liu Hong had me sent here, Yumo made discreet inquiries, and so I learned about the trouble the young lady had gone to on my behalf. I hated myself for losing the note and bringing about this tragedy. Without my confession, her maidenly chastity would have been compromised by interrogation and her reputation ruined. The only solution was for me to die."

Bai Yutang felt the justice of Yan's words. He thought them over carefully. Finally, he spoke, and said:

"My Noble Elder Brother appreciates kindness and repays kindness by sacrificing himself for another. That is the act of a great man. But what about your poor old mother, waiting anxiously at home?"

This one remark released all the agony in Chasan's heart, and he burst into tears.

"When I die," Chasan said after a long while, "I look to you to take care of my mother. Only then, when I am in the Yellow Springs, will I be able to close my eyes."

Chasan was wracked with sobs, and the sight moved Yumo to tears as well.

"What's wrong with you two?" cried Bai Yutang. "Noble Elder Brother, you must be more open-minded. Think all things over carefully. You can be concerned for others — but you must also be concerned for yourself. I have heard that Kaifeng's Magistrate Bao solves cases as though he had supernatural powers. Why don't you go there to press charges?"

"The local magistrate did not obtain my confession through torture," replied Chasan. "I confessed of my own free will. What need is there to go to argue the case?"

"You may feel this way — but perhaps Magistrate Bao will not accept your confession."

"History says, 'You cannot take the will out of a common man.' How much truer is that of me?"

Bai Yutang realized that Chasan had not the slightest intention of changing his mind, so he devised another strategy. He told Yumo to call in the jailor and the warden.

Yumo found them whispering and chattering and waving their hands and feet excitedly. Catching sight of Yumo, they called to him to join them, asking gaily what orders he had for them.

"Master Bai would like to see you both."

The warden and the jailor made haste to obey this summons, trotting along like dogs with their tails wagging. Fifth Master Bai had his companion take out four packets of silver and said to the two men, "I'll give each of you one of these, and the remaining two are for looking after Master Yan. From now on, you are to take care of all of his needs. Do not let me hear that you have neglected him in any way."

The two men bowed and thanked Bai Yutang effusively.

"Everything here has been arranged satisfactorily," said Bai, turning to Chasan. "I would like to borrow Yumo for a few days. Will you allow it?"

"He has nothing to do here. I won't need him. Take him away, Honourable Little Brother."

Yumo, who had long before divined Bai Yutang's intentions, cheerfully took his leave of Chasan and followed Bai out of the prison.

When they were out of earshot, Yumo asked, "Am I to go to Kaifeng to present this case without my master's knowing?"

This question made Bai shout with delight. "How strange," he cried, "that a person so young should be so smart. That is rare. Yes, Yumo, that is my intention. Do you dare to go?"

"If I would not do it, I would not have asked. Ever since the day my master confessed, I have wanted to go to Kaifeng. There was no one else to take care of him, or I would have gone already. I heard you try to bring my master to his senses, and, when he refused to see his mistake and you asked to borrow me, I knew it was for this task."

"So you guessed my intention," said Bai, laughing heartily. "Let me tell you, though, Yumo, your master has fallen into a devilish fix, and it won't be easy to extract him quickly. I will make some discreet arrangements, and tomorrow, when you get to Kaifeng, explain very simply how your master confessed to the murder without reason. Magistrate Bao will have his own way of deciding this case. We ought to be able to get your master out of this mess." When he finished speaking, Bai had his companion give Yumo ten ounces of silver.

"Give me these another time," said Yumo. "I haven't used the two ingots you gave me last time. Anyway, it's not good to carry too much silver when you go to present a case."

"That's true," said Bai, nodding. "Start for Kaifeng today. You can lodge in the vicinity and present the case tomorrow."

Yumo agreed and departed for Kaifeng.

At this same point in time, a strange thing was happening in Kaifeng. Bao Xing and Li Cai were preparing to serve Magistrate Bao, who held court every day at the fifth watch. All the requisite caps, clothes, and teas were ready. While the two were waiting quietly to be called, they heard the magistrate cough. Bao Xing seized the lamp, raised the curtain, and went in to him. As he reached out to put the lamp on the table, he felt suddenly fearful, and a cry of "aiya" escaped him.

"What is it?" Magistrate Bao asked from under the canopy.

"Where has this sword come from?" cried Bao Xing.

The magistrate sat up, threw a wrap over his shoulders, and raised the curtain. There was indeed a bright and shining sword lying across the table. A note was stuck under it. Magistrate Bao ordered Bao Xing to hand him the note.

Four large characters were written on the note — "Yan Chasan's Grievance." Magistrate Bao pondered this for a minute, but did not understand it. He made a mental note to consider the matter further after adjournment. Then he washed and dressed and held court.

At the end of the day, he climbed into his carriage and set out for home. As he arrived at the yamen gate, a child ran out from the throng of people and fell on its knees near the carriage, crying "Injustice!"

Wang Chao was walking close by and turned aside to seize the child. When Magistrate Bao's carriage reached the residence, he alighted and ordered the child brought to him.

"Bring the child," called the man on duty, just as Wang Chao was inquiring as to Yumo's name.

"Don't be afraid when you see the magistrate," Wang Chao said to Yumo, "and don't talk nonsense."

"Thank you, sir, for your advice," replied Yumo.

Wang Chao entered the gate and led Yumo up to the court-room. The boy knelt and kowtowed toward the magistrate.

"What is your name and what matter have you come about?"

"I am Yumo, from Wujin District. My master came to Lucky Charm District to visit his relatives — "

"What is the name of your master?" interrupted Magistrate Bao.

"He's surnamed Yan and his name is Chasan."

These three words rang a bell in the magistrate's mind, and he said to himself, "So there is, indeed, a Yan Chasan."

"Whom was he visiting?" asked Bao.

"Master Liu of Twin Star Village, Master Liu Hong, who is the uncle of my master. We could not know that three years ago his wife would die and he would take a second wife, Mistress Feng. Liu Hong has a daughter — Liu Jinchan — who was betrothed quite young to my master.

"Following his mother's orders, my master came here to see these relatives. He could study here and prepare for the civil service examination next year and, at the same time, fulfill his marriage vows.

"But Liu Hong put me and my master far away in the flower garden area — no doubt he harboured evil intentions. We had been there only four days when, early in the morning, a yamen runner from the local district came and arrested my master, charging him with having choked to death — for no reason — the young mistress's maid, Xiuhong.

"Lord Magistrate, my master and I are never apart. And he never left the study, so how could he have choked the maid to death outside the corner gate? But when they held court, he confessed to *everything*! He said he killed the maid and that he was happy to give his life in exchange. I have no idea why he said that — and so I have come before your Lordship to beg you to decide this case for my master." He kowtowed again after this speech.

Magistrate Bao sighed deeply. He was silent for a time, and then he said, "Since your master is a relative of Liu Hong's, you ought to be able to come and go as you please."

"Liu Hong," said Yumo, "is a very stubborn man. He wouldn't even let my master *see* his second wife. We stayed in the study in the garden for four or five days, and they sent no one to serve us.

I was the one who got all our food and tea and water. They did not treat us at all the way you treat relatives. There wasn't even a *whiff* of meat in any of the dishes."

"Aside from Xiuhong," asked Magistrate Bao, "how many maids are there at the Liu's?"

"I have heard that there was only Xiuhong plus a wet-nurse, Mistress Tian, who is a very good person indeed."

"How so?" asked Bao.

"When I went inside for tea, she said to me, 'The garden is a deserted place — you and your master must be careful while you are living there lest some untoward matter occur. Frankly, I think it would be best if you left here after a couple of days.' And now this calamity is come upon us."

"The wet-nurse knew something," thought Bao. "I'll do a little research and see what transpires."

He had Yumo wait in the hall, and then he gave orders to his messengers. "Bring Liu Hong and his family's wet-nurse here separately. Do not allow them to confer with each other," he told one, and he instructed another to go to Lucky Charm District, get Yan Chasan, and bring him in for questioning.

Liu Hong was brought in after Magistrate Bao had withdrawn from the courtroom, eaten, and prepared for bed. Bao gave orders for the convening of court, and, when Liu Hong was brought up, he asked, "What relation to you is Yan Chasan?"

"He is my nephew, the son of my wife's brother."

"Why did he come here?"

"He is studying in my home in preparation for the exams next year."

"I have heard that he was betrothed to your daughter in infancy. Is this true?"

"How can he know my family affairs?" Liu Hong thought anxiously. "No wonder everyone says he must have supernatural powers." Aloud he said, "They were betrothed when they were very young. Yan Chasan's visit had two purposes — to prepare for the exams and to get married."

"And did you let him stay at your home?"

"I did."

"Did your maid Xiuhong wait on your daughter?"

"She was with my daughter from the time they were young. She was extremely smart — she could write and do arithmetic. It is a pity that she died."

"How did she die?" Bao asked.

"She was choked to death by Yan Chasan."

"When and where did she die?"

"As far as I know it was already past the second watch. She died outside the corner gate."

The magistrate slammed the wooden slab and cried, "*Nonsense*, you old cur! That is what your servants told you. You did not *personally* see who choked her to death. How do you know Yan Chasan killed her? You are blaming him because you loathe poverty and lust after riches. Are you daring to lie to me?"

Liu Hong kowtowed at once. "Please don't be angry, Your Excellency. Let me explain. At first I didn't know who it was who killed the maid. But there was a fan on the ground next to the body, and it had Yan's name on it. That's how I knew he had murdered her." Then he kowtowed again.

"Then Yan must indeed have done this unworthy thing," thought Bao.

A messenger entered and announced that the wet-nurse had been brought in. The magistrate had Liu Hong taken down and Mistress Tian brought up. Mistress Tian had never before laid eyes upon such eminence, and she was shaking from head to toe.

"So, you are young Liu Jinchan's wet-nurse?"

"I — I am," she answered.

"How did the maid Xiuhong die? Confess everything."

Mistress Tian realized that she must tell the truth, so she explained how she had overheard the master and mistress plotting to harm Yan, how she had discussed saving Yan with the young mistress, how Xiuhong had secretly given Yan the money, and the rest.

"Why would Master Yan, having gotten the money, choke Xiuhong to death? But he left behind a fan, and that note. My master was furious when he saw that, and he took Yan straight away to the local magistrate. And who would have thought my young mistress would hang herself?"

"Liu Jinchan is dead?" cried Bao with a start.

"After she died, she came back to life."

"What?"

"It was all because my master and mistress mentioned that it was Yan's first day in jail — the very next day my young mistress hanged herself. She was a young lady who had never married, and, if this news were to get out, the Lius' reputation would be ruined. They gave it out that the young lady was dying and that they wanted to buy a coffin to scare away the evil spirits.

"Meanwhile they encoffined her and put the coffin in the pavilion in the flower garden. But in the middle of the night someone cried out, 'Your young lady has come back to life!' The coffin lid was open, and there she was, sitting up inside."

"Why was the lid open?" asked Bao.

"I heard that the family servant Donkey Niu went to rob the corpse, but *she* had come back to life, and, I don't know how, *his* throat was slit."

"That abominable Yan!" thought Bao. "He is completely transparent. As soon as he got the money, he killed Xiuhong. What a pity that Jinchan's chaste bravery should be so unappreciated. But what is all this about the sword with a note affixed? And why has Yumo come to redress his grievance?" Bao looked up from his thoughts and said, "Bring Yumo in."

When he was brought up, the magistrate chastised him angrily. "You cur!" he cried. "So young and you dare to hoodwink me so boldly! How shall I punish you?"

"Every word I said was true!" protested Yumo, kowtowing deeply to the magistrate's anger. "I would not dare to hoodwink Your Excellency."

"You should be slapped in the face, you dog! You told me that your master had never left his study. How did his fan get to be outside the corner gate? Speak!"

If you want to know what Yumo said in response, read on.

❦

Chapter 39

Junheng Loses His Head, The Scholar Offends

"Now that you mention the fan," began Yumo, "there is a fact you should know. Feng Junheng, the nephew of Liu Hong's present wife, wanted one day to compose couplets with my master. Later he begged my master to write some words on his fan. My master refused, but Feng wouldn't take no for an answer and seized my master's fan, saying he would not return it until my master had finished writing on *his* fan.

"Your Excellency, I would not dare to deceive you. You can send someone to get the fan — Feng Junheng's, the one on which is painted a woman rowing a boat. It is still there in my master's penholder.

Bao laughed loudly, sensing that he had gotten to the bottom of this business of the fan. He was much happier with the way things were going now, and ordered that a warrant for the arrest of Feng Junheng be prepared. Then he had Mistress Tian sent away and left Yumo kneeling in the gallery. He read Yan's confession and spotted the inconsistency at once. He chuckled to himself, "*One* is willing to die for the *other*. The *other* repays *him* by hanging herself. It certainly is a case of 'righteous husband' and 'chaste wife'."

Yan Chasan, who had by this time been transferred to Kaifeng, was summoned next, and was in fetters when he was brought in. He saw Yumo and wondered what he was doing there. The guards removed his fetters, and he knelt.

"Yan Chasan, raise your head," said Magistrate Bao.

Yan did so, and Bao saw that, despite his dishevelled hair and smudged face, he was handsome and looked goodhearted. "Why did you kill Xiuhong?" Bao asked.

Yan repeated precisely the confession he had made in the district magistrate's courtroom.

"Xiuhong was really despicable," agreed the magistrate, nodding his head. "You are Liu Hong's relative, a guest in his home, and she was disrespectful and refused to come when you called her. No wonder you were furious with her. Now let me ask you, when did you leave the study, and what path did you take to the corner gate? What time did you choke her to death, and where exactly did she die? Speak!"

Yan, who could not answer any of these questions, stood before the magistrate in silent awe. "When, indeed," he thought. "I was afraid that Jinchan would have to make an appearance and lose her good name, so I confessed to murder. But I cannot answer these questions about when I left the study and what path I took to the corner gate — what can I say?"

Yan's deep thought was interrupted by Yumo, who cried out, "Master, if even now you don't explain, you truly cannot be thinking of your old mother at home worrying about you."

At these words, shame and anxiety rose from deep within Chasan; tears formed in his eyes and spilled down his face. He kowtowed toward Magistrate Bao. "The real criminal should die for this crime," he confessed. "I beg Magistrate Bao to pardon me with a wave of the pen."

"I have one more thing to ask you about," Magistrate Bao said. "Why did you not respond to the note? Why didn't you go to meet Jinchan?"

"Aiya!" cried Chasan. "Oh, Your Excellency — everything, *everything* went wrong because of *that* note. I was just about to read it when Feng Junheng came to borrow a book, so I slipped it unread into a book on the desk. After Feng Junheng left, I searched all over but couldn't find it. It had disappeared, and I had never read it. How could I know about the assignation at the inner corner gate?"

Magistrate Bao sensed the truth of what he was hearing. Then it was announced that Feng Junheng had been brought in. The magistrate had Yan and his servant taken away and Feng brought in. One look at Feng's rabbit ears and oriole gills, his snake-like brows and rat-like eyes told Bao that he was no good. Bao slammed the gavel resoundingly and demanded of Feng Junheng, "Tell me at once how you impersonated someone for gain and murdered out of lust! Confess!"

The guards surrounded Feng menacingly and shouted, "Speak! Speak! Speak!"

"I have nothing to confess," Feng Junheng said.

Bao called for "instruments of persuasion," and the guards fetched three planks of wood. Feng Junheng broke down in terror and began to babble the whole truth — how he exchanged fans, how he stole the note, how he took the fan and the note and impersonated Yan at the second watch that night, how because Xiuhong wanted to scream he grabbed her throat and killed her, how he planted the fan and the note, picked up the parcel of silver, and returned to his room.

When he was done, the magistrate had him sign a confession and called at once for the instruments of punishment. Wang, Ma, Zhang, and Zhao brought in the dog-head guillotine, and, according to the regulations, Feng Junheng was beheaded then and there. It was so terrifying that Liu Hong, Mistress Tian, Chasan, and Yumo dared not lift their heads to look.

After the floor was swept clean of the corpse and head and the instrument was put away, Magistrate Bao called for Liu Hong. Liu Hong's knees turned to jelly and he was a long time crawling up to the magistrate's dais.

"You cursed old cur!" said Bao. "Jinchan hanged herself, Xiuhong was murdered, Donkey Niu was killed, Yan was arrested, and Feng Junheng was executed — all because *you*, you dog, lusted after money. You have offended the living, the dead, and your daughter, who died and was resurrected. If today you are snuffed out by the guillotine, I think that it ought not be an inconvenience for you."

Liu Hong fell to the floor and banged his head on it. "It would not be unjust," he cried. "I beg Your Excellency to be merciful and forgive this little old man. I will rectify my errors. I shall reform."

"Since you realize you must rectify your errors," replied the magistrate, "listen to my instructions. Today I hand Yan Chasan over to you. He is to continue his studies in your home. All of his expenses will be paid by you. Next year after he takes the exams, whether he passes or not, you will arrange to complete the marriage ceremony. If you neglect Yan in any way, I will have you arrested and you will be executed under the guillotine. Can you do these things?"

"This little old person is willing. This little old person is willing!"

Bao then had Yumo and Yan Chasan brought up. The judgment was explained to them, and Bao instructed Yan Chasan in the proper attitude toward studies. "You must understand what is important. Do not pay attention to small things at the expense of the greater issues. That is not determination, but weakness. Henceforward, you must study very hard. Send me your work regularly, and I will look it over. Whatever success you enjoy, you will acknowledge your debt to Yumo's devotion to you. Day to day, you must take good care of him."

"Respectfully, I shall obey your orders," Yan said, kowtowing. Then master, servant, and uncle all kowtowed. Liu Hong took Yan's hand, Yan took Yumo's hand, and they were happy and sad at the same time. They left the courtroom and returned home with Mistress Tian.

The case was concluded. Magistrate Bao withdrew.

Chapter 81

ఛ

Steal the Imperial Crown, Give It to Ding Zhaohui; Obstruct the Ministerial Carriage, Inform on Ma Chaoxian

Now let us return to Zhi Hua, Black Demon Fox, who had arrived at the Imperial City and, using his all-purpose cord, leaped over the imperial wall. Having gotten inside the protective wall, he gave a full display of his martial arts by walking up walls and flying over eaves. Now these were not ordinary walls and eaves — the walls were high and the building very large. There were story on story of glazed-tile halls, extremely slippery to climb. Moreover, there were guards on duty everywhere. Should they hear the slightest movement, it would be no party. Good Old Black Demon Fox! He moved with light but firm steps. He leaped over roof ridges and snuck into buildings. He left a secret mark wherever he passed to help him on his way back. With a *sou, sou, sou,* he had arrived on the mound behind the square storage house. He counted the tiles and then picked them up and placed them one by one in the proper order. He dug out the earth and put it on the side in a pile. When he reached the beams, he forcefully removed the boards. As before, he arranged them in order, and the beam was clearly exposed. He removed his circular saw from his bag of tricks and sawed it in two, holding the saw at an angle. He put the saw away and used the hook at the end of his all-purpose cord to secure himself. Holding onto the cord, he pulled himself up by a few handfuls until he reached the ceiling. He grabbed onto a beam and followed it along till he felt firm ground under his feet and then slid along on tiptoe, so as not to leave footprints.

Just as he was about to spring into action he saw a light come from the farther wall, heard someone jump down and call out "Here it is, I've found it."

"Bad," Zhi Hua thought and rushed straight ahead to the pit wall where he flattened himself and hid. He listened carefully and heard: "We've got three of them."

"What are they looking for?" Zhi Hua said to himself.

"We've got all six now," someone said suddenly. Zhi Hua climbed back up the wall, jumped over it, and left. It was, in fact, the men on duty next door who were throwing dice and, in their excitement, had thrown some over the wall. Afterwards they agreed to look for them, so they took the lantern and jumped the wall to find the dice. When they said, "We've got three of them" and then "we've got all six now," they were talking about the dice.

After Zhi Hua saw them go back over the wall, he used his torch and shone it on a vermillion-coloured box with many openings which were firmly sealed with strips of red and locked with a metal lock. On each opening was a number with the words "The Best: Number One." It was, in fact, the Nine Dragon Crown that was housed inside. He stuck out his hand and pulled out a small leather jug in which some warm wine remained. He used the wine to moisten the seal and carefully removed it. He felt the lock and discovered the opening had the shape of a horizontal 工, so he took a leather key from his bag and gently tried to open it. He carefully opened the flap and saw inside a crown box wrapped tightly in yellow imperial cloth on top of which was an ivory plaque on which was written "Best Number One Nine Point Imperial Crown," and, in addition, "Official So and So Enters Bowing." He wasted no time inspecting it; he cautiously lifted it out of the case and placed it on his head. He tied it under his chin in a secure knot. He relocked the box and used his sleeve to wipe it clean of fingerprints. He took out a waxed envelope full of paste from his bag of tricks and resealed the seal. He pressed with his fingers all around and shone the torch to check it over; he found it without a suspicious trace of anything. He smoothed out the ground with his feet to remove all footprints and, with the help of his all-purpose cord, climbed back up on the wall. When he reached the ceiling, he used only his hands, securing the cord below with his feet. He stretched up and, leveraging himself on the ceiling, he flipped over and landed securely on the mound. He gathered up the all-purpose cord. He replaced the beam, rubbed off the grease until it was gone; he replaced the boards, repiled and smoothed out the earth, and replaced the tiles. He took out a small wiskbroom and dusted the earth with it so that no trace was left of his visit. After he finished cleaning up, he left the storehouse, and returned the way he had come, all along the way finding his secret markings. By this time it was already the fifth watch.

His only care had been to steal the crown; he forgot completely about Pei Fu, who, by this time, was worried to death, thinking all kinds of crazy thoughts, watching the time go by — from the third watch to the fourth; from the fourth to the fifth, waiting and looking for Zhi Hua until his eyes crossed. When, finally, he thought he saw someone's shadow in the distance, the sudden sound of the night watchman's gongs crashed into his ears and scared him near to death. At that moment, the shadow crouched down out of sight and did not move.

"Who's there?" the night watchman asked.

"That's my son. He's gone to relieve himself," Pei Fu rushed to intercept the watchman. "You go rest, sir."

"Patrolling is an important job. I've no time to rest." He immediately beat the gongs for the fifth watch and left, heading north. Pei Fu rushed ahead and Zhi Hua came forward. "What a coincidence that the watchman should show up again. We almost blew the whole thing." He quickly untied the strings around his chin and removed the crown. Pei Fu opened the bottom layer of the straw basket and Zhi Hua put it in carefully and re-covered it. He took up his night clothes, rolled them into a bundle, and hid them away, using the blanket to wrap them tightly.

Sister Ying was still fast asleep, so Pei Fu whispered his query: "How did you steal the crown?"

After Zhi Hua told him the whole story, Pei Fu was scared speechless.

"Since the deed is done, old sir, why don't you pretend to be ill?" Zhi Hua suggested. When Boss Wang arrived at dawn, Zhi himself pretended to be grief-stricken as he said, 'My father was suddenly taken ill last night. He was sick all night and is now unconscious. I must return home at once."

Boss Wang had to let him go. Sister Ying, unaware of the real situation, believed that her grandfather was truly sick and began a pitiful sobbing.

As they journeyed, Zhi Hua pushed the cart and Ying walked along beside, crying all the way. They heard sighs from people who thought they were escaping from the wilderness. When they reached a spot outside the city gates where no one was around, Zhi Hua called Pei Fu out from hiding and put Ying into the cart. He took hold of the ropes and rushed along to make time. They left Henan, arrived at the Yangtze and took a boat. They had gentle winds all the way down the river.

Arriving at the mouth of the river, they were just about to change boats when they saw three men coming out of a large boat on the other shore. It was the twin heroes, Ding Zhaolan and Ding Zhaohui, and Ai Hu. All were delighted to run into each other, and at once the small boat was hooked onto the large one. Zhi Hua and the others boarded the large boat, changed clothes in the cabin, and sat down to chat.

"What about that matter?" asked the twins.

Zhi told them everything and they were enchanted. The harmonious winds brought their boat home in one day. There they anchored and were received by the village head. Pushing the cart along, they went into the village as a group. At the reception hall, Zhi took down the basket and put it safely away, after which there was the welcome feast.

"I have already prepared a grain basket," Zhaohui responded to Zhi's question about how to deliver the crown. "One side is the crown and the other side is incense, candles, money, and grain. It's simple and handy. We will say that we are going to Tianzhu to burn incense on our mother's orders. What do you think, Brothers?"

"Fine. But where will we stay?"

"An Old Zhou, named Zhou Zeng, runs a tea house in Tianzhu, and I am very close to him. He has a good location. Upstairs it is secluded and quiet — an excellent place for us to rest." These words put Zhi Hua's mind at ease, but only after dinner and in the quiet night when no strangers were present did Zhi remove the nine dragon pearl crown from the case for them to see. They looked it over in awe — pure shining gold with layers of dragons and pearls glistening all around. On the top were nine golden dragons — Oh dear, front and back, each had reclining dragon; left and right, were two dragons in motion; on top, were four dragons with raised tails on which was supported a coiled dragon. Countless pearls surrounded the crown, but from nine enormously large ones an incredible brilliance shot out in all directions. Add to that the flashing of the pure gold, and it was truly difficult to look upon. Everyone was overwhelmed by this object of rare beauty. Zhi rewrapped it carefully, put it back in the case, and closed the lid securely.

At the fifth watch, the younger Ding left Jasmine Village and headed for Middle Tianzhu, from which he returned in a mere few days. He was welcomed by all in the reception hall and asked for the details of his trip.

"I stayed at Old Mr. Zhou's Inn after arriving in Middle Tianzhu. I burned my incense and, in the evening, pretending exhaustion, I retired upstairs very early. Old Zhou feared disturbing me, so he did not come upstairs again. Thus I was able to use this time to steal into Buddha Hall in Ma Qiang's home. Indeed, there were three statues of the Buddha there, and I placed the precious, bejewelled crown behind the partition on the left of the middle Buddha. I replaced the yellow silk curtain so that no one would notice that anything had been touched. By the time I had done all this and returned to my upstairs room at Old Zhou's, it was already the fifth watch. Pretending recovery from my illness, I instructed my servant to pack up and get ready to leave. Old Mr. Zhou was loathe to see me go, however, insisting on making me hot broth and wine to drink and pressing me to accept four-hundred ounces of silver. I refused both and hurried home." These words delighted all present — with the exception, Zhi Hua was quick to observe, of Ai Hu, who sat in silence.

"Well then," Ai Hu finally said, pleasantly, "since Uncle Ding has taken care of the crown, I guess I should be on my way."

These words made the Ding brothers feel Ai Hu's difficulty deeply, and so they said nothing.

But Zhi Hua spoke. "Oh, Ai Hu, my son, we have done this thing to help loyal people and righteous men. Your uncles and I have taken grave risks to accomplish this task. If you were ever to hint at this matter when you get to the capital, not only would all our efforts have been in vain, it would be hard to protect the lives of those loyal and right-minded folk involved."

"Your words are extreme, Brother Zhi," the Ding brothers added hastily, "Dear Nephew, you must, however, act with great care."

"Master and Uncles," responded Ai Hu, "please don't worry. Even if they chop off my head, I will not give up my mission. There is no further reason for the matter not to conclude successfully."

"Well, I hope you mean that," Zhi said. "Here is a letter for you to take there to help you find your Fifth Uncle Bai, who will take care of you."

Ai Hu put the letter in his inner pocket, picked up his bundle and bid farewell to Master Zhi and his two Uncles Ding. Seeing so young a boy taking on such a momentous task, the three men felt both anxiety and love on his account and, before they knew it, they had seen him off all the way to the outskirts of the village.

"Master, Uncles," said Ai Hu, "there's no need for you to accompany me so far. Allow me to take leave of you here."

"Please remember," Zhi Hua instructed again, "that the Golden Crown is behind the left partition of the middle Buddha!"

Ai Hu nodded, hoisted his bundle, and strode away without looking back. Anyone looking on would realize that, in this situation, even an older person could not compare with Ai Hu, a fifteen-year old. Ai Hu was young, but brave and, moreover, clever. "Being resourceful does not lie in age; being unresourceful, one-hundred years may be lived in vain," as the saying goes.

Ai Hu stopped only when hungry or thirsty and made it to Kaifeng in one day. But, passing through the city gate, he did not go first in search of Bai Yutang, but rather flew straight to the Kaifeng Provincial Office to see what it was like. He did not expect to see someone driving idlers away shouting, "The Grand Tutor has arrived!"

"What luck!" thought Ai Hu. "Why don't I just go up and greet him?"

He took advantage of the chaos to push himself forward out of the crowd when he saw the Grand Tutor's carriage approaching.

"Grievance, Lord Magistrate, I've a grievance!" he shouted, kneeling in front of the carriage.

Magistrate Bao, seeing a mere child shouting "Grievance" and holding up the progress of his carriage, told his men to bring the child into the yamen. Four officers came forward, grabbed Ai Hu, and said, "You are mischievous, kid. Do you think Kaifeng is your playground?"

"Please don't say such a thing. I have not come for fun. I really want to press charges."

"Don't frighten him," said Zhang Long, coming forward. "What's your name?" he asked Ai Hu. "How old are you?"

After Ai Hu had answered the questions, Zhang asked, "Who are you charging?" and "What are the charges?"

"Uncle," Ai Hu answered, "you need not inquire further. Only take me to see the magistrate. I have something to report to him personally."

"This kid is interesting," thought Zhang Long. Suddenly he heard someone shout from inside the yamen to bring the child in, so he said: "Let's hurry, then. The magistrate has convened court."

Ai Hu followed Zhang Long to the front gate, where Zhang announced their arrival. In the courtroom, Ai Hu bowed low, stealing a look as he did to check everything out. He saw Magistrate Bao, formal and dignified, seated majestically, flanked on both sides by his court officers. It was awe-inspiring, just like the court of the King of the underworld.

"Young fellow, what is your name?" Bao asked. "Against whom are you pressing charges? State your case!"

"My name is Ai Hu," he responded. "I am fifteen this year, and I am a servant in the home of Mr. Ma, Ma Qiang."

"What brings you here?" Bao asked as soon as he heard the name Ma Qiang.

"I have come specifically to 'inform' about a certain matter. I don't really know what 'inform' means, but I was a witness, and I have heard people say that 'to witness and withhold evidence of a crime increases one's own guilt!' So I came here to bring this to Your Honour's attention and fulfil my own responsibility."

"Tell me everything — carefully," Bao instructed Ai Hu.

"It all started three years ago, when the Old Gentleman returned to his ancestral home because of illness."

"Who is the 'Old Gentleman'?" interrupted Bao.

"Ma Chaoxian, of the Four Finger Treasury," said Ai Hu, holding up four fingers. "He is the uncle of my master, Ma Qiang."

"Hmmm," thought Bao. "He must mean Manager Ma Chaoxian of the Four Branch Treasury. The child mistook four branches to mean four fingers." Aloud he said, "And what happened after he returned home because of illness?"

"The Old Gentleman was carried home by carriage and brought all the way into the Great Hall. He got down from the carriage and ordered all his servants to withdraw. Considering me a mere child, he and my master did not hesitate to speak in my presence. The Old Gentleman removed a package wrapped in imperial cloth from the carriage and whispered to my master, 'This is the nine dragon crown of the emperor. I brought it along with me. You hide it securely in the Buddha Hall. Later on, when Prince of Xiangyang comes to power, this will be our offering to him, and our contribution. You must not under any circumstances leak this affair.' My master received it and gave it into my care. I followed my master to Buddha Hall, all the way carrying this heavy package. My master put it behind the left partition of the Middle Buddha."

Ai Hu's words startled Magistrate Bao and his court.

"What happened then?" asked Bao.

"Nothing much. Time passed, I got older. I had often heard people say that withholding evidence is a serious crime, but I didn't really understand what it meant. Later on someone found out about this matter and questioned me, so I told them what I knew. 'If nothing comes of it, then you can forget about it,' I was told. 'But if something does happen, then you are "withholding evidence."' Then, recently, my master came to the capital, and someone advised me, 'You'd better protect yourself! If your master leaks something about that three-year-old matter on his visit, you are guilty of withholding evidence.' I was really frightened by this — I am no longer the ignorant, innocent lad of three years ago. Now I have some experience, and the more I thought about it the more I realized it was no joke. So I rushed here. I'm really not 'informing,' just explaining. Then it will no longer have anything to do with me."

Magistrate Bao listened to the end, thought it over, and then suddenly shouted, "A curse on you, you cur!" He smacked the clapper on the table and demanded, "Who sent you here to slander your master and the imperial manager to me? Why? Confess everything!"

"Speak now. Confess now!" echoed the court officers lined up on Bao's left and on his right.

If you want to know how Ai Hu dealt with this, read on.

❦

Chapter 82

Imperial Fortune Tried, Little Hero Interrogated; Obeying Imperial Orders, Officers Meet with the Five Ministers

"Astonishing!" thought Ai Hu, hearing Bao ask who was behind this charge. "No wonder everyone says that Magistrate Bao has supernatural detecting powers. It is true!"

Ai Hu pretended fear and said, "I've nothing to say — this is too difficult for me. If I don't inform, my crime will be serious! If I do inform, you say that someone put me up to it. Let's just forget the whole thing. Let's just wait for my master to bring it up, and then I will tell my story, okay?" Having said his piece, he stood up and started out of the courtroom.

"Go back! Go back! Kneel! Kneel!" cried the two rows of officers when they saw that he understood nothing about court regulations.

Ai Hu returned and knelt, only to hear the magistrate say sardonically, "I can see that, in spite of your age, you are quite shrewd. Do you know the rule here?"

"I don't know about any rule," Ai Hu said, alarmed by Bao's words.

"I have a regulation. Whoever infringes on it must have his four limbs chopped off. You have come here today to inform on your master, and you have thereby violated my regulation. You must have your limbs hacked off. Come. Bring on the imperial instruments of punishment!"

Both lines of officers called out in response, and Wang, Ma, Zhang, and Zhao carried the dog-head guillotine into the courtroom and placed it on the floor. They removed the imperial wrapping and the cold shining blade of the guillotine was revealed and placed directly in front of Ai Hu.

"Ai Hu, Oh! Ai Hu!" our Little Hero said to himself at the sight of the blade. "You have come to save the loyal subjects and righteous men. Never mind my four *limbs*— even were they to chop me in *half*— as long as I get the deed done, I must not under any circumstances leak the affair."

"So you still refuse to tell the truth," he heard Bao say to him.

Ai Hu pretended great fright and responded, "I am really terrified. It was just because I feared the heavy crime of 'withholding evidence' that I came to make charges! Oh, Lord Magistrate!"

Bao ordered the removal of his shoes and socks. Zhang Long and Zhao Hu came forward and, amid shouts from both sides, threw Ai Hu to the ground and stripped off his shoes and socks. They thrust his two feet inside the guillotine opening. Wang and Ma secured the blade, adjusted the position, and turned to face Magistrate Bao. It would take only a hand signal from Bao to lower the blade and, with a quick *kecha*, Ai Hu's feet would be chopped off. Zhang and Zhao held Ai Hu down, each on one side, while Ma Han pulled up his head by the hair so that he faced Magistrate Bao.

"Ai Hu, who put you up to this?" Bao asked once more. "You still refuse to confess?"

"I was afraid!" Ai Hu answered tearfully. "No one put me up to it. If you don't believe me, send someone to get the crown; if it's not where I said it was, I will happily confess to my crime."

Finally Bao nodded. "Release him." Ma Han let got of his hair and Zhang and Zhao removed his feet from beneath the blade. Wang and Ma carried the instrument over to the side of the room, and everyone in the courtroom, including the four braves (Wang, Ma, Zhang, and Zhao) relaxed, greatly relieved at Ai Hu's good luck.

Bao continued the interrogation "Ai Hu, is that imperial* crown still in the Buddha Hall at your master's residence?"

---

* The word for imperial is a homonym for jade. Ai Hu is confused

"It is still there. But, Lord Magistrate, it is not a 'jade' crown. My master's master said it was a pearl crown with nine dragons."

Bao ordered Ai Hu taken away. The jailor, Old Hao, collected the prisoner and led him to his solitary jail cell. "Young Master," he said to Ai Hu, "have a seat right here. Let me go get you some tea." He returned shortly with a covered bowl of newly-brewed tea.

"Do they expect some tip under these circumstances?" wondered Ai Hu. "And how come they are calling me, an offender, 'Young Master?' And such excellent tea! What does all this mean?" Then he saw Old Hao whisper something to a boy, and immediately the table was laid with food and wine and sweets. Old Hao himself diligently poured the wine. Ai Hu did not know what to make of the whole thing.

Then Ai Hu heard someone in the outer room laugh, and Old Hao rushed out to greet him. "I have already taken care of the young master and provided him with food and drink."

"Fine," Ai Hu heard the laughing man answer. "I've troubled you. I will give you the ounces of silver tomorrow." Old Hao gave him thanks, and Ai Hu then heard the laughing man say, "You stand guard out here while I go chat with the young master. Don't come in until I call you." Old Hao agreed to everything, turning to stand guard at the entrance. Indeed, to everyone who came, he held up his spread hand to stop them, put on an impressive pout, and waved them off.

Do you know who this fellow was? None other than Fifth Brother Bai. Hearing that a young boy had come to press charges, he had rushed to the courtroom to have a look — and he recognized Ai Hu.

"What has he come for," wondered Bai. Ai Hu's explanation alarmed him. After mulling it over, he decided that Ai Hu's visit must be on behalf of Governor Ni and Brother Ouyang, and he became even more worried. "How could they entrust such a weighty matter to such a young boy?" When he heard Bao calling for the imperial torture machine, he wrang his hands in agony. "It's over," he thought. "He's done for!" He dared not go forward, but stood there with his eyes fixed on Ai Hu. Then, when Ai Hu held his ground and insisted on his story without wavering, Bai Yutang praised him silently: "What a great kid! It is truly a case of 'Strong generals have strong soldiers.' If he gets out of the guillotine this time, he will truly have become a man." When he heard Bao grant Ai Hu's petition, he was overjoyed. He slipped out of the courtroom and found Old Hao, the jailor, whom he instructed: "That child pressing charges in court is my nephew. He'll be down in a bit and you must take good care of him." Old Hao dared not be lax in this, and so he called Ai Hu "Young Master" and waited on him. He knew that Bai Yutang would return to check up on him. He wanted both to do a good job of it and also get something out of it. Indeed, Bai did return and give him ten ounces of silver and ask him to stand guard outside while he, himself, went in.

Ai Hu rushed forward as soon as he recognized Bai Yutang.

"Dear Nephew," Bai whispered to him. "You are very, *very* brave — you dare to come to Kaifeng and create such a stir. You're quite something! But whose idea was this? Why didn't you come to find me first?"

Ai Hu told Bai the entire story. "Just before I came here," he concluded. "my master gave me a letter for you and told me to come to see you. But, I feared that someone would trace my steps and the affair would be leaked — and then I just happened to run into the magistrate as soon as I arrived, so I simply aired the grievance right there."

He took out the letter and gave it to Bai, who read it at once. And was it not precisely a request that Bai help Ai Hu and make sure that he did not get into trouble?

"Clearly," he calculated to himself, "Ai Hu wanted to show off his bravery, so he didn't come to give me this letter first. His arrogance is going to be hard to control in the future."

Aloud he said to Ai Hu, "Well, the critical point has passed. Now you can relax. I heard what you said just now in the courtroom. Tomorrow the magistrate will no doubt memorialize the emperor, so we'll see what he has to say before we make our plans. Have you eaten?"

"The food's not important," responded Ai Hu. "It's just that the wine is …" He did not go on.

"You mean there's nothing to drink?"

"No, there was, but just the *tiniest* little bit. After a mere five or six cups it was all gone."

"Five or six cups is not a small amount," thought Bai. "I dare say this young fellow loves his drink." "Old Hao," he called. "Bring us another bottle of wine."

"In a bit, when the wine comes" Bai advised Ai Hu "drink moderately. You mustn't make the mistake of becoming a lush! You don't know what decree will come tomorrow. You'd best pay attention and protect yourself."

"Fifth Uncle is absolutely right. I'll just drink this last bottle, and that'll be it." Bai laughed. Old Hao brought the bottle, and Bai warned him again, and then left.

Magistrate Bao did present the emperor with a memorial about this matter on the very next day. Renzong read it, thought it over carefully, and suddenly remembered something.

"Minister of the Board of War, Jin Hui, memorialized me about this twice. He said that my royal uncle was plotting rebellion. It made me very angry, so I demoted him. How can it be that in today's memorial Magistrate Bao is also saying this? There is something suspicious here." With these thoughts, he summoned Manager Chen Lin and secretly ordered him to go to investigate the Four Branch Treasury.

Old Chen Lin accepted the task and went to Ma Chaoxian's residence with some of his underlings. There Chen made known that there was an imperial decree, but Ma had no idea what it was about. Seeing that Chen himself had been sent, Ma dared not disobey, so he went along with Chen to the Treasury, where he undid the seal and opened the gates. Starting with the characters of the emperor, they opened the seal and the lock and, finally, the flap. They looked in and what do you think? It was empty.

"Where is the nine dragon pearl crown?" demanded Chen Lin. Ma, seeing that the crown was missing, turned ashen and could in no way respond to Chen's inquiry. His mouth hung open, his eyes were wide, and finally he stuttered, "I don't — I don't — I don't know."

"I was sent here," Chen said, noticing Ma's terror, "precisely to look for this crown. The crown is missing, and I must return to memorialize the emperor about it and get further instructions. Children, guard Manager Ma well."

Chen reported at once to the emperor, who was furious and demanded that Ma be brought for questioning by Chen.

"Ma's nephew, Ma Qiang, is also being questioned in the Hall of Great Principle. Since the uncle has embezzled, the nephew surely knows about it. I must return to the Hall to cross-examine them."

The emperor approved the plan and sent the original memorial along with Ma Chaoxian to the Hall. After the emperor sent off the decree, he feared that difficulties might arise with the interrogation, so he sent also Du Wenhui, Minister of the Board of Punishments; Fan Zhongyu, Head of the Investigative Board; Yan Chasan, Head of the Privy Council; and Wen Yanbo of the Hall of Great Principle — all to help with the interrogation.

The decree came down, and all these heads of government proceeded to the Hall of Great Principle. But when Yan Chasan, Privy Council, was about to mount his carriage, he saw that Yu Hou had a note in his hand as he reported: "This was sent by Fifth Master Bai. Please have a look." Yan took it and read that Bai was requesting that he take care of Ai Hu. "Certainly! I am informed. Please send the messenger back." Yu Hou conveyed Yan's response to the messenger, who then returned to Bai.

"This matter of helping in the cross-examination — it's not going to be easy to be impartial." thought Yan. "I'll just have to play it by ear."

Yan got into his carriage and headed for the Hall of Great Principle, where he found all the ministers gathered together. They read the document and learned that Ma Chaoxian was being charged with embezzlement and that the prince of Xiangyang was plotting rebellion. They were alarmed, and tried to figure out what to do.

"The Palace Manager, Chen Lin, will arrive shortly," said Fan Zhongyu. "We clearly must first find out the truth from that child. We'll examine him, all right?" All were in agreement and they asked Minister Wen to bring them up to date on the case of Ma Qiang.

"Ma Qiang has already confessed to violent and tyrannical acts," said the minister. "But on this one issue he refuses to change his story — he insists that Governor Ni is a thief and robbed his home. Northern Hero, Ouyang Chun, has already been brought in. He is a hero and righteous man, and he saved Governor Ni's life. He knows nothing about the theft and refuses to confess to it. The interrogator questioned him several times and feels that he is an upright man who speaks chivalrously — not the type to rob and steal. The interrogator has already sent someone to look into the matter discreetly. As of now Ai Hu is here and, being of Ma's household, he ought to know something about the theft. We can question him about it." All agreed.

"The Palace Manager has arrived," came the announcement, and all rushed out to welcome him. Chen dismounted and took a few steps forward to address the group. "You all came early. Please forgive my tardiness. The emperor was so angry about this affair that he could not eat. I stayed behind to coax him, and, after he finally agreed to eat, I rushed as fast as I could, but I have still arrived late."

They proceeded to the courtroom and took the seats arranged for them in order of rank.

"You have not begun the questioning?" asked Chen.

"We were waiting for you, sir. But we have made a tentative plan," they said and they told Chen the results of their discussion.

"An excellent plan, sirs!" Chen praised. "Let's do exactly as you suggest." He had Ai Hu brought into the courtroom first.

Ai Hu, who had already been through the terror of Kaifeng and Magistrate Bao, felt quite unafraid of the five ministers about to interrogate him here. He came in, knelt on both knees, and, muttering all the while, looked left and right to see what was going on.

"Goodness!" exclaimed Chen. "I only knew there was someone called Ai Hu. He's actually a mere child — though a sturdy one and quite clever looking. How old are you?'

"I'm fifteen." answered Ai Hu.

"What kind of grievance can a young fellow like you have that you have come to press charges? Speak up so that we all can hear."

Ai Hu told them everything that had happened to him in Kaifeng on the previous day. "Magistrate Bao was going to chop off my four limbs," he added. "I truly did it out of fear for the crime of withholding evidence — I had no intention of harming my master. That's why the magistrate was lenient with me and granted my petition." Ai Hu then knocked his head on the ground.

"You've all heard his story now," Chen said to the group. "Please ask him whatever you have to ask. Although I'm here at the emperor's request, I really don't understand anything about the case — I'm just doing my duty."

"Ai Hu," Minister Du asked, "how many years were you in Ma Qiang's household?"

"I've been there since I was young."

"Did you personally witness Old Master Ma give your master the nine dragon crown three years ago?"

"I saw it with my own eyes. The Old Master first gave it to my master and my master gave it to me to carry up to the Buddha Hall where my master placed it behind the left partition of the middle Buddha."

"It happened three years ago — why did you wait until today to inform about it? Speak!"

"Yes, indeed!" added Chen. "I remember clearly three years ago when Manager Ma asked leave to return home to take care of his ancestral tombs. He took three-months leave. I even have the documents here we can check out. Why do you only now come to tell us about it? Explain!"

"I was only twelve then. I knew nothing of worldly affairs. Now I am fifteen and understand a bit more. Furthermore, now that my master has already been indicted for other things, I fear he will disclose this business too. How could I bear the crime of withholding evidence?"

"Let's drop that," Fan said. "Let me ask you, what exactly did Old Master Ma say to your master when he gave him the crown?"

"I only heard my Old Master say: 'Keep this crown safely. When the prince of Xiangyang raises the matter, we will offer him this crown and will be rewarded with high positions.' I have no idea what 'matter' he was going to 'raise.'"

"You naturally would be able to identify your Old Master?"

This question struck Ai Hu dumb — his mouth fell open and he stared in astonishment.

If you want to know what happened, read on.

❧

Chapter 83

He Sticks to His Story, He Is Shrewd and Clever;
The Proof Is Irrefutable, With No Just Cause,
A True Grievance Prevails

"I'm done for," thought Ai Hu when he heard Fan's question about recognizing his Old Master. "Though I did see him at that time back then, I didn't really pay attention — not to mention that three years have passed! Even if I can't recognize him, how did that minister come upon that one question to stump me? There must be a reason."

"I know my Old Master," he told them.

"Bring Ma Chaoxian in," Fan ordered. Left and right shouted agreement and went out to get him.

Yan, observing carefully, noticed that Ai Hu had answered "I know him" only after a deep sigh. He knew, therefore, that Ai Hu was troubled by the question. Would he make a mistake in the identification? That would be terrible! "Brilliant ideas are born of crises," so he pointed with his hand under the cover of his sleeve and said: "Ai Hu, when Ma Chaoxian comes in a short while, you must confront him. Don't try to protect him." But, as he spoke, he winked at Ai Hu and, though he was unwilling to shake his head as a signal, he caused his gauze hat to move ever so slightly. Ai Hu, already suspicious because of Fan's question, saw Yan's strange behaviour and understood what was happening.

He heard the sound of fetters and stole a look outside. There he saw an elderly eunuch being brought in who, though he was in chains, came into the courtroom with a slight smile on his face. Only when he reached the front of the courtroom did he put on a serious expression and let out a sigh. Moreover, he did not kneel when he faced all the officers; he stood straight as a rod and uttered not a word. This made it even clearer to Ai Hu.

"Ai Hu," Fan asked, "tell your old master to his face what you told us."

"He is not my old master," Ai Hu said, pretending to look him over. "I know my Old Master."

"Good kid," said Chen with a smile. "Sharp eyes!" Chen turned to Fan. "From the looks of it, this young fellow does indeed know Manager Ma. Men, take him away and bring in the real Ma Chaoxian." The officers escorted the imposter away.

Before long they brought up that lying, rebellious, treacherous, immoral Ma Chaoxian, his beady eyes filled with tears. His fetters were removed, and he knelt before the court. Old Manager Chen could not help feeling sorry for him, so he said: "Ma Chaoxian, there is someone charging you with stealing the emperor's nine dragon crown and taking it home with you when you went back on sick leave three years ago. You must confess everything."

"The crown you speak of," said Ma scared to death, "disappeared from the treasury. I know nothing about it."

"Ai Hu," interjected Minister Wen, "you confront him."

Ai Hu repeated his deposition. Then he said, "Old Master, there's no point in denying things now that we have reached this pass."

"You villain!" cried Ma. "You are truly hateful. When did I say I know you!"

"Master, how can you not recognize me? At that time I was twelve, and I waited on you for such a long time. You even praised me often for being so intelligent; you said I would amount to something in the future. Can you really have forgotten all that? Is it really true that 'Men of rank are forgetful.'"

"Even if I know you, when did I give the imperial crown to Ma Qiang?"

Minister Wen interrupted again. "Manager Ma, it's no use denying it. You'd best just tell us everything lest your flesh suffer for it. Your case is one personally decreed by the emperor, and we will have to use heavy torture if you don't confess."

"But I truly know nothing about this! If you must apply torture — whether the whip or the press — please go ahead with it."

"I don't think he will confess with his hands tied. Men, bring out the instruments of heavy torture."

They were about to go to get the instruments, when Ai Hu cried out, "I retract the charges. Let's forget the whole thing."

"Why do you wish to retract the charges?" asked Chen.

"I did it in the first place out of fear, fear of being accused of withholding evidence. That's why I informed — but I never wanted my Old Master, whose age is so advanced, to suffer like this. You're going to use the heavy punishment on him — wouldn't that be the same as if I myself killed him? I simply can't bear it. I'd rather retract the charges."

"Silly boy," Chen said, nodding his head all the while, "this case came by imperial decree — how can *you* decide what to do?"

"No need to apply the torture at this moment," Minister Du said, "take Ma away now. Ai Hu, you go too. Don't allow them to speak to each other." They were removed from the courtroom.

"I wanted to scare him just now," said Yan, "when I asked for the torture instruments. I knew that such an elderly person couldn't bear up under such punishment."

"I was a little suspicious when Ma said he didn't know Ai Hu just now," added Minister Du. "How can we be sure that Ai Hu wasn't put up to this by someone else?"

"He's shrewd," thought Yan, but, since Bai had asked him to look after Ai Hu, he could not watch and do nothing.

"You are quite right to be concerned about that," Yan said to Du. "But Ai Hu is a child — how could anyone have sent him to tackle such an important and grave matter? Moreover Magistrate Bao has already figured that out. That's why he was ready with the guillotine to chop off his four limbs. If somebody else had put him up to it, why should he not confess? Why sacrifice his life?"

"That is probably true, but I have something else on my mind. Why not bring Ma Qiang in, and we can question him?" Everyone present agreed, and Ma Qiang was summoned. He was forbidden to talk to Ma Chaoxian along the way.

Minister Du began the interrogation.

"Ma Qiang, there's someone here submitting a grievance on your behalf — do you know him?"

"But I don't know about whom you are speaking."

"Bring the petitioner in to be identified!"

"So it's that kid, Ai Hu," Ma thought when he saw who it was who came in and knelt. "So he looks out for his master after all — great!"

"That's one of the servants in my household," he then reported. "His name is Ai Hu."

"How old is he?" Du asked Ma.

"He's fifteen."

"Is he from a family of servants that has served your household?" Du continued the interrogation.

"He's been with us since he was little."

That evil Ma cared only to get this information out — not a person in the room did not nod in acknowledgment, and all doubts about Ai Hu's story were completely dispelled.

"Since he's your servant, listen to the grievance he has put forward for you. Ai Hu, tell us quickly about your deposition."

"Don't blame me, Master," Ai Hu said after repeating his story. "I really could not bear the responsibility of withholding evidence."

"I curse you, you cur! What you've said is total nonsense! When did the Old Master give me some kind of crown?"

"This is a courtroom," Chen shouted at him. "It's not a place for you to curse your servants. You have no sense at all! You should have your faced slapped."

"May I tell you, sir," Ma said, crawling forward half a step, "my uncle gave me no crown three years ago when he returned home. This is all a scandalous lie created by Ai Hu."

"You say," Yan rejoindered, "that your uncle gave you no such crown. Ai Hu, here, says that you put it in the Buddha Hall of your home. If we find it there, will you still deny it?"

"If you find such a crown in my house, I will happily confess — I would not dare go on denying it."

"In that case," Yan continued, "let's sign this agreement."

Ma Qiang was certain that there was no such thing in his house, so he was delighted to sign. The ministers looked over the document, had Ma Qiang removed and Ma Chaoxian brought back.

"Well then," they told Ma Chaoxian after reading the signed agreement to him, "Your nephew has already explained everything to us — do you still refuse to tell us the truth?"

"There was no such affair" insisted Ma. "If you actually find the crown in my nephew's home, I will happily confess." They prepared a document for him to sign and then took him away to a separate prison cell.

"What do you know about the robbery in your master's house?" Wen asked Ai Hu.

"I was in the Hall of Gathering Worthies looking after some friends of my master."

"What 'Hall of Gathering Worthies'?"

"The big room in my master's house is called 'Hall of Gathering Worthies.' Lots of people live there. Every day they duel with their guns and clubs. All of them are very talented. On that day my master swindled a literati of the first degree and his old servant, and, because it turned out to be a governor, he and his man were locked up in the empty room there. But, they escaped — no one knew when — and my master rushed out after them when he found out. He brought back only the governor and locked him in the dungeon."

"What dungeon," asked Wen.

"It's actually a cellar. Everything important happens in that cellar. May I tell you, sir, that I don't know how many people have been killed in that dungeon?"

"He dares to have a dungeon!" Chen laughed coldly. "That is really outrageous! The literati was certainly murdered by your master then."

"He was actually intending to murder him when that literati was rescued by someone. That scared my master. Those toughs tried to convince him that it was nothing, that, if something were to come of it, they would all flee together to the protection of the prince of Xiangyang. But that very night, just after the second watch, some tall man came and tied up my master and mistress right in their own bedroom! The fellows in the Hall of Gathering Worthies rushed to rescue them, but all of the fellows together were no match for the tall one. They all ran back to the Hall and hid there. I was scared and hid myself, so I don't know what happened."

"But you do know what time your master was brought here to the yamen, don't you?"

"I heard Yao Cheng say that it was after the fifth watch."

"In that case," said Wen, addressing the group, "Ouyang Chun had nothing to do with the robbery."

"Why do you say that" they asked.

"Because Ma, on the list of stolen items, originally reported that the robbery took place at dawn. If the tall fellow was bringing Ma to us in custody after the fifth watch, how could he also rob the place at dawn?"

"You are absolutely right!" they responded.

"Minister, let's not look into this matter now. It's important to deal first with the Ma Chaoxian affair."

"But this matter is intimately connected to the imperial crown affair. We must clear it up, deal with both of them at the same time. Then tomorrow we can go find those involved and arrest them." With this explanation, he called for Yao Cheng.

Yao Cheng knew that this was a major case as soon as he heard mention of the nine dragon crown. He thus fled far, far away, and the runners returned after quite some time to report that he had fled out of fear of punishment and they had no idea where he was.

"Since the plaintiff himself has fled, something irregular is going on. More and more it looks as though the nine dragon crown affair truly happened, and we must report to the emperor again," responded Wen. The ministers wrote up a report, which Chen took to memorialize to the emperor.

On the next day the imperial degree to arrest all the insurgents of the "Hall of Gathering Worthies" and to search for the crown reached Hangzhou. The insurgents were taken at once back to the capital for questioning. After a few days, the acting governor restored the crown and had it sent to the capital. Mistress Guo, Ma's wife, was also brought in.

Do you know how she was brought in? As soon as the warrant reached Hangzhou, the local patrols got their men ready to help arrest the insurgents and kill them if necessary, but when they arrived at the Hall there was no trace of anyone, so they had to question Mistress Guo.

"They all fled," she told them.

The officer in charge then searched the Hall, where he found many letters that spoke of plots and rebellions with the prince of Xiangyang. They had Mistress Guo accompany them to the Buddha Hall, where they did indeed find the box with the crown hidden behind the left partition of the middle Buddha niche. The acting governor opened the box, confirmed that the crown was in it, and sealed it back up. He readied the golden kiosk to hold the crown. Mistress Guo was taken into custody as a material witness to an important crime.

The ministers gathered in Temple of Great Principle to verify the crown and make a deposition to that effect. Mistress Guo was brought into the courtroom and questioned, "Why was the imperial crown in your home?"

"I truly do not know," she answered.

"Where was the crown found?" Fan asked.

"It was found hidden in one of the niches in the Buddha Hall."

"Did you personally witness the discovery?" Du asked.

"I did personally witness it," she responded.

Du had her sign the deposition and summoned Ma Qiang. The minute Ma entered the courtroom and saw his wife there he knew that things had taken a bad turn. "How does she come to be here?" he wondered, terrified.

"Ma Qiang," Fan began the interrogation after Ma came forward and knelt down. "Your wife has already produced the nine dragon crown — do you still deny everything? Tell your story face-to-face with her at once!"

"Where did you find this crown?" he asked her, trembling with fear.

"In the middle niche of the Buddha Hall."

"So it really was found there?"

"Why are you asking me? If you hadn't put it there yourself, how could they have found it there?"

"You perverse rebel, you!" shouted Wen, interrupting their argument. "Even your wife has confirmed this. How dare you continue to lie!"

"I'll take my punishment," said Ma finally, knocking his head on the floor. "I will happily sign a confession."

He signed the confession, and Yan had husband and wife removed to one side while Ma Chaoxian was brought in and shown
the signed confessions as well as the crown. Ma Chaoxian was
scared senseless, and, after confronting Mistress Guo again, he
said at last, "Okay. Okay. I have nothing to say in my defence.
I'll sign a confession and be done with it." He signed the confession, which was checked over by the court officers, and he and
his nephew were then taken to separate cells. It was thus that
Black Fox Demon's clever strategy succeeded in capturing a
traitorous villain.

Chapter 86

Greedy for Good Wine,
Uncle and Nephew Meet

Now when the emperor saw Ouyang Xiu's copy, he was suddenly reminded, by the surname Ouyang, of Northern Hero, Ouyang Chun, so he summoned Minister Bao and asked about him. Bao told him everything about Ouyang — how upright and brave he was, how moral a person he was, how he carried out good deeds and set store by righteous behaviour. The emperor was awed by this report. When Bao returned to his yamen, he called Lieutenant Zhan into his presence to tell him of this happening, and Zhan, in turn, returned to his residence and reported on it to all the heroes.

"I'd best go get Northern Hero," Jiang Ping volunteered. "No one else can take this on. Within the Kaifeng residence, none of the four braves can leave and Gongsun Ce and Fifth Little Brother have both gone to Xiangyang. Big Brother Zhan must remain here in Kaifeng to take care of everything. If he needs help, there is always Elder Brother Lu. Moreover, right now I am free of all commitments, so, rather than remain idle, I'd like to do this job. I can enjoy myself and visit Brother Ouyang at the same time — isn't that 'killing two birds with one stone'?" After discussing this among themselves, their decision was reported to Minister Bao, who was delighted by the news. He sent for the Kaifeng letter of introduction and gave it to Jiang, who wrapped it up and fixed it to his body. Jiang took his leave, heading for Jasmine Village in Songjiang Prefecture.

During his three days' journey, he did nothing but eat when hungry and drink when thirsty. Near dusk one day he arrived at the Happiness Inn in Laifeng and took a single side room in the eastern wing. He ate dinner after a short rest and brewed a pot of tea that was particularly fragrant. He drank many cups and found, in the middle of the night, that he had to relieve himself. Just as he reached the courtyard he spied a man pushing open a door with his finger and shouldering his way in without a sound, after which he shut the door tightly.

"There's something funny about this," Jiang mused, "I'd better have a look." Forgetting his plan to relieve himself, he leaped, flying, over the wall, and jumped down into what turned out to be the landlord's quarters.

"Little Brother begs Older Brother to help," Jiang heard someone saying. "I have already identified that person staying in the east side room. He is my master's enemy — how can I let him go?"

"True," someone responded, but, "how can I help avenge your master?"

"He is already in a drunken stupor. How about strangling him right now and throwing him in the wilds? Wouldn't that save a lot of trouble?"

"It won't be too late if we wait until he's sound asleep," the other responded.

Jiang heard enough to send him straight over the wall to the east side room. He quietly lifted the cloth curtain and peaked inside. The candle was still burning, and a person was sleeping on the bed, facing the wall. Jiang, who could see that he was not a large man, sidled into the room, snuffed out the candle, and took a closer look. What a shock! It was Ai Hu, Little Hero, lying there stinking drunk!

"Such a young one!" he shouted in Ai Hu's ear. "His lust for liquor is disastrous. If I hadn't shown up here at this inn today, his young life would have been lost. But who is that person who wanted to kill him? Never mind, I'll just wait for him right here." He blew out the candle, *pu*, and held his breath while he sat and waited. But the need to relieve himself was now urgent, and he could bear it no longer. He opened the leaves of the door and urinated just outside. He had been holding it a long time, and the quantity was enormous. The entire ground was soaked.

He had barely finished when he heard noises outside, so he hid himself behind the gate. As the first person stepped forward and then paused, the man following closely behind crashed into him. At this moment Jiang closed the door on them and leapt out from behind it, squashing the two of them under him. He cried out, "Don't beat me. I am Jiang Ping. The two under me are the thieves!"

By this time Ai Hu had awakened, and, when he heard it was Jiang Ping, he got up in a rush. Jiang stood up and told Ai Hu to hold those two down.

The inn boy, having by now heard the shout of "Thief!" had rushed over with his lantern. Jiang had him shine the light on the would-be murderers, who turned out to be the landlord and his friend. Jiang tied them up with his rope and noticed that the clothes of the fellow on the ground were completely soaked with his urine.

"Why did you listen to that traitor and agree to kill my nephew? Why? Speak!" Jiang questioned the landlord.

"Don't be angry, sir. My name is Cao Biao, and this is my friend Tao Zong. He came to me greatly disturbed because his master had been killed. He then noticed that this young guest here was drinking up a storm in my shop, so he became very suspicious. Why would this patron drink so much, he wondered. And he was so young to boot! He stole a look at him and recognized him as the enemy of his master. So he insisted that I come along with him to help."

"So you just agreed, even though '*helping*' meant 'helping to *kill*' someone?"

"Not at all," countered Cao Biao, "he merely asked me to help catch him."

"So you think you can fool me about this?" Jiang said, "The two of you had it all arranged to strangle him and throw him in the wilds. You even said, 'It won't be too late if we wait until he's sound asleep.' Doesn't that make you a full accomplice?"

This shut Cao Biao up completely, although he was mystified at how Jiang knew this.

"You are definitely bad characters," said Jiang. "I am positive that you've killed more than a few folk." As he spoke, he called to Ai Hu, "Drag that one over; I'll question him too."

"Aiya," Ai Hu said, as he got a good look at the man he dragged up from the ground. "So it's you!"

"Fourth Uncle," explained Ai Hu. "He is not Tao Zong. He is Yao Cheng, the very one who escaped charges in Ma Qiang's case against him."

"Since you are Yao Cheng," Jiang pressed, "why did you say you were Tao Zong?"

"My original name was Tao Zong, but I changed it to Yao Cheng when I threw my lot in with Mr. Ma. Afterwards, when all hell broke loose at my master's, I fled to avoid being implicated in his affairs. That's when I took up my real name again — Tao Zong."

"It is clear," said Jiang, "that you are unstable. Can't even make up your mind about your own name. I've no need to question you further."

"Get the local headman," Jiang told the inn boy. "Let me tell you, this fellow is an escaped criminal. Your landlord, on the other hand, has done nothing serious. Just tell the headman that I was sent here from Kaifeng to arrest this person. Tell him to hurry — I shall be waiting here anxiously."

The inn boy did not dare drag his feet. Before long two people entered, came forward, and knelt down on one knee. "We did not know the magistrate's messenger was here," said one. "We've been remiss. Please forgive us."

"Which one of you is the headman?" asked Jiang.

"I, Wang Da, am the headman. He is the guard, and his name is Li the Second."

"Under whose jurisdiction do you fall here?"

"We are all under the jurisdiction of Tang District."

"What's the name of the official in charge?" Jiang pressed.

"His name is Ho Zhixian," answered Wang Da. "May I ask your honourable name, sir?"

"My surname is Jiang. I am here on the orders of Grand Tutor Bao to find escaped criminals," he fabricated. "What a coincidence that I caught two right here in this inn. I've already tied them all up. I'll need to bother you to keep an eye on them, and tomorrow morning we'll go together to the district court and hand them over to your superior."

"Please, Mr. Jiang," said the two in unison, "don't worry about this. Go get some rest, and we will take care of everything. We don't dare to blunder again. Escaped convicts or anything else, we don't dare."

"Fine," said Jiang. He grabbed hold of Ai Hu's hand and returned to the west side room.

If you want to know what happened later, please read on.

Chapter 87

Three Heroes Visit Sha Long on Behalf of a Friend, Four Gallants Neglect Ai Hu to Save a Life

Now, the two local men had agreed to keep watch over the criminal and be very careful. Jiang had risen, taken Ai Hu's hand and gone back, step by step, to his own room.

"Nephew," Jiang asked after they had seated themselves, "how is it that you are here? Where is your mentor?"

"It's a long story," Ai Hu replied. "This is what happened. I went with my godfather to Governor Ni's home in Hangzhou, where we stayed quite a while. My godfather tried to leave many times, but Governor Ni would not let him. It was only after the marriage was consummated that we could leave Hangzhou. Then we went to Jasmine Village to thank the Ding brothers for all their trouble, and we also stayed there for a while. We didn't know that Uncle Ding had sent someone to Xiangyang to make inquiries and that that person had returned after a few days.

"'The prince of Xiangyang,' he reported 'already knows that the court is beginning to be aware of him. He fears that troops will be sent and is worrying how to prepare for them. On the one hand, he has men guarding the overland route; on the other he has men guarding the waterway — these are two strategic junctions. Any movement at court will be reported immediately.' When my mentor and godfather heard this, they were greatly worried. Why? Because they have an extremely good friend by the name of Sha Long, nicknamed Steel Face Budda Warrior, who lives in Sleeping Tiger Ditch. This spot is not far from Black Wolf Mountain, so they were afraid that Uncle Sha might be attacked by the imposter prince or duped into joining their gang. They decided that my mentor, my godfather, and Second Uncle would go to Sleeping

Tiger Ditch, and I would be put in the care of First Uncle. So, I thought to myself: 'They shut me up here in the house and keep me from enlarging my experience by participating in all the excitement — I can't bear it.' I stewed over it for a few days, but Uncle Ding refused to leave me alone for a second, so I had no chance at all to get away. Finally I was able to steal five ounces from Uncle Ding, for road expenses, and I headed for Sleeping Tiger Ditch to see the excitement. I never thought that I would run into my enemy here at this inn."

"What a little devil," thought Jiang, shaking his head. "To him piling up dead bodies is fun. He is really bold, really big-hearted — so why did Brothers Ouyang and Zhi Hua hand him over to Brother Ding? Why didn't they take him with them if he was able to go? There must be some reason for it. Since I've run into him here today, I can't let him go on by himself."

"Uncle Jiang," Ai Hu interrupted his thoughts to ask, "did you come here today to catch the criminal or on some other business?"

"How could it be to catch a criminal? I am here under orders from the prime minister, who sent me to find your godfather. Minister Bao feared that we wouldn't be able to report to the emperor if we didn't know your godfather's whereabouts. That's why I am here. I never expected to catch Yao Cheng."

"Uncle Jiang, where do you plan to go from here?"

"I had intended to go to Jasmine Village. Since I now know that your godfather has gone off to Sleeping Tiger Village, I think I'll head there tomorrow right after taking Yao Cheng in custody to the district court."

"Dear Uncle," Ai Hu cried out joyously, "please, please, you simply *must* take me with you. And, then, if we see my godfather, you can say that you brought me along from the beginning. That way my two elders will not scold me."

"You really know how to sweep it all under the rug," Jiang laughed. "Do you honestly believe that Uncle Ding won't tell them the truth later on?"

"But by then, after so much time has passed, who will remember any of this? Even if he tells them, seeing that things have come to this pass, my master and godfather will have nothing to blame me for."

"Ai Hu, it seems to me," Jiang thought, "is young and likes his drink; in addition, he slipped away from home. I'd better just take him along with me. This will allow me to do what is right and find Brother Ouyang at the same time. But I really must do something about his drinking."

"If I take you, you must agree to one condition," he said to Ai Hu.

"Fourth Uncle!" Ai Hu said happily. "Just tell me what it is, dear sir, for there's nothing I won't agree to."

"It's about your drinking — you will be allowed only three horns of liquor with each meal. You can't have a drop more. Do you agree?"

"Three horns it shall be," said Ai Hu, although only after some thought. "A little is better than none. But I suppose three horns will satisfy my craving," after which the uncle and nephew chatted half the night away.

They soon returned to the east wing room to have a look and heard Cao Biao vigorously venting his resentment against Yao Cheng, who could only hang his head and sigh.

At the crack of dawn, Jiang and Ai Hu washed up and packed their bags. Ai Hu, on his own initiative, picked up the bags and had the headman and the guard escort the two criminals in custody to Tang District. When they arrived at the yamen, Jiang pulled out his official letter of introduction and, before long, was called into the study for an audience.

Jiang told the district magistrate everything, from beginning to end, but, since he himself had to continue his search for Northern Hero, he requested that someone from the district office be sent to escort the criminals to the capital. The magistrate at once had the document made ready and even put in a word about Jiang's trip to Sleeping Tiger Ditch. Jiang took leave of the magistrate and, after rewrapping his official letter of introduction in its protective covering and sticking it in his waistband, he finally left with Ai Hu.

Now the two criminals and their escort reached Kaifeng and offered up the document. Magistrate Bao convened court and used his instruments of torture to extract a complete confession from Yao Cheng. He was actually a water waterway thief, and he had once harmed Ni Ren and his wife. He was further interrogated about the matter of Ma Qiang's collusion with the prince of Xiangyang. Yao confessed that Ma Gang, Ma Qiang's older brother, had previously been spying for the prince. Once the confession was obtained, Yao Cheng was beheaded and Cao Biao sentenced to military exile. We will not go into the details of the conclusion of this case.

Jiang and Ai Hu, having left Tang District, proceeded toward Huguang. Ai Hu, indeed, had only three horns of wine with each meal. One day they arrived in Glossymouth Harbour and hired a boat with Fu the Third and his two boathands. Jiang, feeling expansive and engaged, enjoyed the scenery during the boat ride. As for Ai Hu, his eyes blurred over and he looked like a child rocking in a cradle rather than an adult sitting on a boat. At first, his head swayed back and forth as he tried to remain seated while he dozed, but later he simply put his head down and slept. Only when it came time to drink did his energy return one-hundred fold as he talked and laughed. But the minute he finished those three horns of wine, he began yawning and couldn't even eat properly. Jiang worried about this situation, fearing that Ai Hu might become sick. But, on the boat, he had to let the boy have his way, so he merely kept his eye on him.

Then one day at about 3 p.m., Jiang heard Fu the Third say, as they were going along, "Get hold of the boat quick. Let's find a place to get out of the wind. There's a storm up."

The boatmen did not dare delay; they poled fast and secured the boat on a goose-head rock. This particular place happened to be Jewel Cove, an extremely secluded spot. They let down the anchor and had a meal. Then it was time to light the lantern. There was no movement at all. The wind was down and the waves were still.

"There's no storm here," Jiang thought. "Why did the boatmen say there was one? Aha, yes! He must be harbouring evil intentions — what else could it be? I'd better pay attention."

He could hear the thunderous sounds of snoring coming from Ai Hu's after-dinner nap.

"How can he not mess up with such a craving for wine and sleep?" Jiang mused.

In the middle of these thoughts, there was a huge rumbling and the boat began to rock. A terrific rush of sound rose up. A great wind was rising. Waves and billows roared and swelled, and only then did Jiang come to believe the words of Fu the Third predicting the storm. Fortunately, after a short period of wild gusting, the wind let up and the sky cleared. The moon shone brightly and illuminated the clear ripples of the blue waters. The evening colours became increasingly crisp and clear, so that Jiang was reluctant to go to sleep immediately. He sat alone at the prow of the boat enjoying the beauty of the night. At about the second watch, Jiang, preparing to retire, heard someone weakly call out, "Help! Help!" He looked northeast in the direction of the sound and saw the faint twinkling of a light.

"Could this be some secret plot?" he thought. "I'd better go save that person." In the rush, he didn't bother about his clothes. He merely put his shoes at the prow of the boat and jumped into the water. Treading along, he moved ahead and suddenly heard someone gasping for breath. He pushed toward him, but the current pulled from a northeasterly direction. Jiang hurried forward, passed the drowning man in order to grab hold of him and then lifted him above water. But the man's two hands flailed about wildly in an attempt to grab onto Jiang, which Jiang did not let him do. That, in fact, is the nifty trick of saving a drowning person.

But, of all those who fall into the water, whether it is accidentally or with the intention of suicide by drowning, there is no one who does not seek to be saved when that actual moment of dying is upon him. Such a person's hands will flail about, ready to grab onto anything at all. Should they actually grab hold of someone else it is certain death for both, for, always, he who tries to save a drowning person will be brought down by the one drowning — if he does not understand this principle. This is because the rescuer does not know the trick of saving a drowning person. The drowning person's hands will also be full of the mud seized while struggling for his or her life at the bottom of the water.

Jiang raised him out of the water, let him grope about for a while, grabbed onto his hair with one hand and his waist band with the other, and swam along in this fashion to the shore. Fortunately the time that had elapsed had been short. After choking a bit on the water he had swallowed, he came to and coughed it all up, at which point Jiang was able to ask him his name. The fellow turned out to be Lei Zhen, an elderly man over fifty.

"Is the Lei Ying employed as the prince of Xiangyang's palace guard related to you?" Jiang queried.

"He's my son," the old man answered. "How do you know about him?"

"I've heard his name mentioned often, but I've never met him. May I ask where you live, sir and where you were heading?"

"I live right in the rear of the prince's residence, about two and a half miles from here, in Eight Jewel Village.

"I was on my way to visit my daughter in Ling District. She is very poor, so I was taking her some clothes and hair ornaments. I hired a boat run by two brothers — Mi the Third and Mi the Seventh — but they had evil intentions when they saw my things, so they said a windstorm was coming up and we had to hide out here. First they killed my servant and, when I called out for help, they came after me. In my terror, I pushed open the porthole and jumped into the water. Then I lost consciousness. Thanks to you, I am saved."

"Most likely their boat hasn't left yet. You, sir, wait here a bit and I'll go see about your luggage."

"That would be nice," the old man said happily. "But I don't want to trouble you any further."

"It's nothing at all," Jiang said. "You just wait here — I'll be right back."

He dove into the water and in a flash swam over to the lighted boat.

"Let's open the bag and have a look," he heard one of the two rogues say. "I guarantee it will be interesting."

Jiang grabbed onto the edge of the boat and leapt over. "Thief!" he cried, getting his footing on the boat, "You care only about your fun, not at all about what happens to other people." When

Mi the Seventh heard a man speak from nowhere, he grabbed his dagger and knife. Before he could get his bearings, Jiang had already lashed out with his foot and, though he wasn't wearing shoes, he got him in precisely the right spot, his cheek — so how could he bear it? He tottered, and, as he fell over, the sword dropped from his hands. Jiang was right there to snatch it away, and, taking advantage of the rogue's prostrate position, Jiang settled the account then and there.

Mi the Third saw right away that things were bad for him, so he jumped out of the window broken by the old man in his escape. Jiang, not about to let him get away, jumped in the water and grabbed hold of his legs, pulled them up out of the water so they looked just like a pestle, and dragged him onto the boat. He found a rope, tied him up and held his head down to let him throw up the water. Jiang then swam back to the shore and carried Lei Zhen onto the boat.

"When this crook comes to, I'm going to scare him a bit with the sword, but don't be afraid. He's all tied up. You'll have to wait until dawn to get another boat."

Jiang then dove back into the water and swam over to his own boat, but, when he reached the spot, there was no trace of it at all. Most likely Fu the Third took off as soon as he saw good winds. There was nothing for it but to return to Lei Zhen's boat. As he approached, he heard Lei Zhen saying in a trembling voice: "One move and you get the knife." Jiang knew that the old fellow was terrified, so he called out from a distance: "Old Mr. Lei, I'm back."

"Why, sir, did you go and then come right back?" asked Lei, enormously relieved to see Jiang back on the boat.

"My boat has disappeared. I think it must have left. So, why don't I escort you home?"

"I have put you to so much trouble," Lei answered. "How can I ever repay you?"

"Old sir, how about lending me some clothing so I can change out of these wet ones?"

"Yes, yes, yes! But all I have is the loose kind of gown."

Jiang used a silk cord around his waist to help shorten the garment. At dawn the next day, he used the punt pole to push off and then kicked Mi the Third into the water, giving the old man a fright.

"The heavens decide our fate! This is terrible," said the old man.

"This guy makes his living from the water — who knows how many customers he has robbed and murdered. Now he's met up with me, and it is only right to get rid of him. What's there to be heartsick about?" But Lei Zhen went on sighing.

However, let us not tell about how Jiang Ping escorted Lei home, but rather how Ai Hu, who slept through the night, finally woke suddenly and, not seeing Jiang Ping, rushed out of the cabin looking for the boatman.

"Where has my uncle gone?"

"You two were together in the cabin — why ask *me?*"

Ai Hu was beside himself. He ran around looking and saw a pair of shoes laid out at the front end of the boat.

"Aiya!" the cry escaped him. "Fourth Uncle has fallen into the water. Or, perhaps, you two have killed him."

"You, young fellow, don't know what you are saying. Last night we moored here because of the storm. We stayed on the rear of the boat the entire night, while you and your uncle stayed in the front cabin. I suspect that your uncle went on deck to relieve himself during the night, lost his footing, and fell into the water. Yes, perhaps that's what happened. How can we have harmed him?"

"You say we plotted murder," added the seaman. "Why would we kill only him and not you too?"

"Or maybe you, young fellow, coveting his heavy luggage, killed him — and now you turn around and blame us," suggested another boathand.

"How can you say such a thing!" Ai Hu protested, his eyes bulging. "Nonsense! He's my uncle — why would I want to kill him?"

"Not necessarily. The packages and luggage are now in your hands — so who are you blaming?"

Ai Hu pushed back his sleeves, made his hands into fists, and was ready to beat them up, but Fu the Third stopped him.

"Don't be this way!" he cried. "As I see it, that gentleman was neither killed nor did he loose footing and fall in the water. He went in of his own accord. Everyone, just consider for a moment — if he were killed or fell overboard, how do you explain his two shoes placed nice and neat right here?"

The boatman's analysis woke the others up to their error, and the two hands had nothing to say. Ai Hu, no longer angry, returned to his cabin. He inspected the luggage and saw that nothing had been touched. Even the imperial document was exactly where Jiang had put it. When he inspected the inner garment holding the gold, he found that there was the same amount — just under one-hundred ounces — as before. He rewrapped it, completely puzzled.

"Where has uncle gone to? Could he have gone fishing in the middle of the night?"

"Young man," he heard Fu the Third call out "we have reached our anchoring spot."

Ai Hu tied up his undergarment, picked up the luggage, jumped ashore, and strode ahead. The cost of the boatride had been paid in advance: it was a matter of "the boatman doesn't fight for the cost of the passage."

If you want to know what happened next, read on.

Chapter 88

❦

Robbing Fish and Stealing Wine, Little Brother Visits Elder Brother; Discussing Writing and Debating Poetry, the Old Gentleman Picks a Son-in-Law

After Ai Hu had left the boat, he went on his way wondering, "Uncle Jiang saved me at Happiness Inn. Then he kindly agreed to take me along with him to Sleeping Tiger Ditch. I never thought he would fall into the water and leave me trembling with fear." With this thought, bitter tears came streaming down his face. Then, suddenly, he remembered that Uncle Jiang was an expert as far as water was concerned. Indeed, his nickname was "Overturning-River Rat," so how could he drown? This thought made him joyous. But, as he walked along, his mind turned again in a negative direction: "Bad! Bad! That saying has it right 'Horsemen are the ones who fall off; the ones who drown are swimmers.' I know he's talented and brave; he can overturn a boat in an open ditch. What a shame that a hero of our time should lose his life here in this place." He burst into tears again. Then he remembered that pair of shoes once more. Had his uncle really gone off to catch some fish? If that were so, he would be able to see him again. At this thought, he burst into hysterical laughter. Anyone watching this alternating hysterical crying and laughing would have assumed that the young fellow was insane and kept their distance. Who would dare to provoke such a man?

By this time a myriad worries were gnawing at his heart. Ai Hu forgot his hunger and passed up all resting places. Only when he noticed that it was already dark did he realize he was hungry and, look as he might, there was no place to eat. But he saw a sudden flash of light and, running toward it, discovered a shanty, inside which were two men sitting facing each other and playing guess fingers. He rushed in just as one of the men called "Eight horses!"

Ai Hu stuck out his hand in response, calling "Three dollars!" The two men, who turned out to be fishermen, scolded Ai Hu for rushing in recklessly and crashing their game: "You, young fellow, are very rude. We are having our fun here drinking — how dare you come in and disturb us?"

"Please let me explain," said Ai Hu. "I am a traveller who missed the rest stop. I am so hungry that I had to impose on you and make your acquaintance." Having explained, he was about to pour himself some wine when one of the fishermen stopped him.

"If you want to eat, you must wait for our leftovers. We will give you the scraps."

"I am not a beggar who needs your charity," said Ai Hu. "I have silver to buy your wine — are you willing to sell me some?"

"This is not a wine shop. If you want to buy, go up the road a bit. I don't sell here." With that, the two men took off their turbans and resumed their finger game.

But as soon as one of them called "Match!" Ai Hu stuck his hand out as though to take the wine.

"You rascal you. You are really tiresome!" the other fisherman said furiously. "We've said we won't sell, so why are you being so devious?"

"If you won't sell, then I'll have to steal it."

The fisherman laughed sardonically. "Tell us something else," he said. "Since you are informing us you are going to steal it, then you should know that we won't let you." He stood up and went outside, pulling up his sleeves to be ready for a fight: "Rascal! Let me see how you steal!"

"Don't be in such a rush," Ai Hu said, laughing as he put down his bundle. "Let me explain: if I lose, then I'll listen to you. If I win, then, needless to say, not only do I get enough to drink, but you must also provide me with a meal." The fisherman showed no agreement. He merely raised his fisted hand at Ai Hu, who grabbed hold of it, instead of ducking, and, with a firm twist to the side, brought the fisherman to the ground before he knew what was happening. When the other fisherman saw what had happened, he called out furiously, "You rogue, how dare you start up with us!" and he kicked him from behind. Ai Hu turned and, raising the heel of his foot, knocked the second fisherman's feet out from under him so that he fell down backwards. The two men crawled upright and stood together, but the Little Hero, with a hand to the left and one to the right, knocked them down again. Three times he did this before the fishermen acknowledged that they were no match for him and skulked away in embarrassment.

Ai Hu entered the shanty, picked up the bowl of wine and drained it. About to pour himself another, he noticed a fresh whole carp that had barely been touched — he was delighted. He drank another bowl of wine and, not bothering with chopsticks, grabbed a piece of fish with his hands and stuffed it in his mouth. He poured himself more wine. So it was, a bowl of wine, a piece of fish, and before long the dishes and bowls were cluttered about. The wine ran out just as he was beginning to feel very satisfied, so he picked up the fish platter and swallowed everything down in one gulp, including the soup from the fish. He wasn't completely sated, but he felt relieved. He found a fish net and he wiped his hand on it. As he rose to leave, something bumped his head lightly. He turned and saw a large gourd of wine — delightful — and took it down. Under the lamplight he saw it was a pewter container. It had a screw top — but he couldn't open it no matter which way he turned. He became so agitated that he forced it open by breaking off the neck and then downing its contents straight out of the bottle in four or five gulps. His hand relaxed and the jar fell crashing onto the plate, which broke into smithereens. Ai Hu was not fazed by any of this. He simply picked up his bundle and left the shanty, striding forward with confident steps and giving not a thought to north, south, east, or west. It was a case of "Cold wine leads to blunders."

Not only had Ai Hu drunk on an empty stomach, but he had drunk too fast, and outdoors he was blown upon by the wind. The wine uncontrollably bubbled up in his throat and he staggered on for only a couple of miles before he had to give up. Spotting a broken-down pavilion on the side of the road, Ai Hu threw his bundle down to use as a pillow and, heedless of the dirt, stretched out and immediately began to snore. Indeed, "In his deep sleep, he knew not the day had dawned" describes the situation.

While still asleep he suddenly felt a rush of movement above him and some slight pain. He took a surreptitious look around and saw that the day had already dawned brightly and that he was surrounded by five or six people, each holding a club. He understood immediately. "These are the troops summoned by those two fishermen," he thought. "Actually, it was I who was wrong in the first place. Why not let them beat me up a little to let off some steam and that will be the end of it?"

These men were, indeed, fishermen who had been notified by the two that Ai Hu had scared off. They had all rushed to the shanty with clubs to find him, but, having arrived, saw that, not only was the fish and wine completely gone, the wine gourd was broken and the platter smashed. They were furious and set out to search for him. They were concerned only with the main roads, never suspecting that Little Hero would have wandered around in a drunken stupor and wound up on a small path somewhere. After searching without success for some time, they decided he had outsmarted them. Giving up, they headed for their homes. But some soldiers went by way of the small path, which led them to the broken-down pavilion, where they heard the sound of thunderous snores. By then it was early dawn, yet they could not see clearly — it seemed to be a young person. While someone stood guard over him, they recalled those close by and gathered together five or six, including the fishermen from the shanty.

"It's him!" they said, and everyone got ready to let him have it. But there was one older man among them who cautioned.

"Don't beat him recklessly. You might hit him in a fatal spot and that wouldn't be right. Find a fleshy spot to hit. After all, you only want to warn him not to do this again."

There followed a huge clamour; some of it was the beating of Ai Hu and some was club hitting club. But when Ai Hu didn't budge at all, they became suspicious and feared they had killed him. How could they know that he was deliberately silent, giving them their chance to let off steam. When he realized they had actually stopped, he opened his eyes.

"Why did you stop?" he asked and leaped up, grabbed his

bundle, dusted himself off, and saluted them: "Please! Excuse me!" But they continued to surround him, unwilling to let him go.

"Why are you holding me here," he asked.

"You stole our fish and wine — how can you think it's over just like this?"

"Didn't you beat me up? That should have vented your anger. Now what more do you want?"

"You broke our wine jar and smashed our platter — you must repay us; otherwise don't even think about leaving."

"So I broke your jar and platter. No matter, I'll give you the silver to buy another set."

"I want only my original ones — what good is the silver to me?"

"That's difficult, then," Ai Hu responded. "People have life and death; things have destruction. Since it's smashed, how can it become whole again? If you won't take the silver, then hit me some more to get revenge for your things and thereby settle this matter."

He put his bundle aside, lay himself down on the ground, and began to clown around. The fishermen didn't know whether to laugh or be angry, nor did they think that hitting him would be the right thing.

"This young fellow is really infuriating," the elder said. "Now he's playing tricks on us!"

"Well, then, let me kill him," one of the men said.

"Don't talk like that!" the elder said. "You can't possibly think that we would just stand here and watch you take his life?"

As the elder spoke these words, a young man came along and said to them: "Please excuse me, gentlemen, but what crime has this person committed that you all want to beat him up? Please forgive him on behalf of this humble person." When he saluted the others, the fishermen saluted him back, realizing that he was a very refined young man: "How can we forgive him for stealing our food and drink and breaking our utensils — he is really abominable! But, since you are speaking on his behalf, we'll just have to call it a piece of bad luck." With that, they all dispersed.

The young gentleman took another look at Ai Hu, who, still lying on the ground, was covering his face with his sleeve. He went forward and removed Ai Hu's sleeve only to discover that he was completely red-faced and, without any explanation, burst into uncontrollable laughter.

"Stop laughing! What exactly is going on here? If you have something to say, get up and say it."

"I am truly mortified," Ai Hu said as he rose and dusted himself off. "I have really blundered." He went on to tell the entire story, not glossing over any of the details, and burst out laughing again at the end.

"According to how he tells it, one can see that he is a straightforward and heroic young man," the young man thought admiringly, as he observed the noble features and uncommon bearing of this fellow.

"May I ask Noble Elder Brother's name?" he inquired.

"Little Brother's name is Ai Hu? How about Noble Elder Brother?"

"This little brother's name is Shi Jun."

"Ah, so it is Master Shi," Ai Hu responded. "Please don't laugh at my intolerable situation."

"I wouldn't dare, not at all. 'All men in the empire are brothers.' There is no reason to laugh." But Ai Hu mistook the words "all are brothers" for "all swear brotherhood," so he replied:

"How can such a crude person as I swear brotherhood with such a noble and refined person as you? But, since you are willing, I will take you as my sworn older brother."

Shi Yun was delighted by this remark, knowing that Ai Hu had misunderstood his words. He could see that Ai Hu was a worthy person and honest, so he asked his age. Ai Hu, at sixteen, was a year younger than Shi Jun, so he prostrated himself and kowtowed. Shi joined him, and then they helped each other up.

Ai Hu picked up his bundle. Shi Jun, taking him by the hand, led him out of the pavilion straight toward the forest. There a young boy waited, holding two horses and looking expectantly into the distance. Shi went up to him and called out: "Jinjian, come here and greet your young master."

Jinjian had seen the whole thing — how his master first saw the other fellow, and how, puzzlingly, they had kowtowed to each other. If his master put it this way, he'd best pay his respects at once.

"I kowtow to you, young master."

Ai Hu had never been kowtowed to before, nor had anyone ever called him "Master." He was delighted by Jinjian's show of respect and did not know how to react.

"Get up, get up!" he said, pulling two ingots of silver out of his breast pocket to give to him.

"Go buy yourself some candy," he said to Jinjian, but Jinjian would not accept it until Shi advised him to, after which he kowtowed again to express his thanks.

"But why is he doing that again?" Ai Hu wondered. "Oh, yes! It must be that I didn't give him enough. He's asking for more."

Ai Hu reached again into his pocket. (You see, Ai Hu himself had been a boy retainer, but he had never been taught in the master's etiquette, so he did not understand. Don't think for a moment that the story is contradictory!)

"The silver you gave him is sufficient," Shi said. "Why give him so much? May I inquire, where are you going, Honourable Little Brother?" asked Shi, distracting Ai Hu from the question of the silver.

"I'm going to Sleeping Tiger Ditch to find my master and my godfather. May I inquire where Elder Brother is going?"

"I am going to my Uncle Jin's, in Xiangyang District, to ask his help editing my essay and also to study. How terrible if we cannot go along together chatting happily," Shi replied.

"We both have tasks — we'd best each go our own way — but we'll certainly meet again! Please mount your horse, Elder Brother. Allow me to escort you part way."

"Please don't go a long distance. I am riding on horseback and you are walking — how could you keep up? We'd best just take leave of each other right here."

Thereupon they saluted each other again. Jinjian brought the horse over, but refused to mount because Ai Hu was on foot. He led the horse by the reins and walked. But Ai Hu insisted that he mount and catch up with his master. He stood watching them until they disappeared into the distance before he picked up his bundle and strode in broad steps to the main road.

Now, then, Shi Jun's father's name was Shi Qiao, his style

Bichang and he had done one term as district magistrate before contracting an eye disease that blinded him. He had had to take sick leave and retire to his home in the country. Shi Qiao had two lifelong sworn brothers — the first Secretary of the Military, Jin Hui, who met with censure after being involved in the Xiangyang affair; the second was Shao Bangjie, newly appointed governor of Changsha. The three men, although only sworn brothers, were more like flesh and blood. Old Mr. Shi knew that Old Mr. Jin had a precious daughter whom he had seen many times throughout her youth and, although there had been talk of a betrothal between his son and his friend's daughter, betrothal gifts had not been exchanged. Now grown up, Shi Jun had been sent by his father to Mr. Jin's, ostensibly to study, but secretly to complete his betrothal.

Shi arrived that day at Nine Immortals' Bridge at the foot of Nine Clouds Mountain in Xiangyang. He found his way to Old Mr. Jin's residence and sent in a letter announcing his arrival. Mr. Jin had him brought to the study at once. He observed that Shi Jun was of noble bearing and very learned, that he was humble and gentle, quite an admirable young man. Jin was delighted with him and pleased by the letter his father had written.

"Your honourable father's eyesight must be improving," remarked Jin. "Otherwise, how could he have written this letter?"

"My father can see only some light — he sees nothing else. This letter was written by me at my father's dictation — please, Uncle, be magnanimous and don't laugh at me."

"Your calligraphy is marvellous, nephew. How dare I instruct you in writing? I am long unused to study and my hand is like a horsewhip holding a pen. How can I correct your work? What we can do is let you study hard, and, when you are free, we can converse and chat — learn from each other. We will both benefit."

At this time one of the family servants announced dinner. Jin instructed him to lay the table right there in the study so he could continue his conversation with Shi as they ate. While they drank, Jin questioned Shi on many points of scholarship and Shi answered each and every one naturally and with ease. Jin was ecstatic over this young man and, after the meal, arranged for him to be set up in the study. Self-satisfied and well-pleased, Jin then returned to his own quarters at the rear of the house.

If you want to know what he said to his wife about all of this, then read on.

Chapter 89

Simple-minded Jinjian Hides the White Jade Hairclasp; Foolish Jiahui Loses the Purple Gold Earrings

Now, when Mr. Jin reported to his wife, Mistress He, about Shi's sterling character and excellent learning, she was delighted. In fact, Mistress He was the younger sister of the worthy Mr. He Zhixian from Tang District, and she had borne two children, a daughter of sixteen named Mudan and a son of seven named Jin Zhang. Old Mr. Jin had another wife whose name was Qiaoniang.

"Why did Honourable Nephew come here?"

"Old Shi has gone blind," responded Jin, "so he wrote me a letter asking that his son be allowed to complete his studies here under my tutelage. That is the stated reason, but I can read between the lines of the letter a marriage proposal."

"How do you feel about that?" asked He.

"Actually, my brother Shi mentioned this once years ago, but our daughter was still too young, and I never completed the betrothal. Who would have thought that nephew Shi has already grown into a young man of excellent character and deep learning, worthy of being betrothed to our daughter?"

"Since that is so, why don't you agree at once to the marriage?"

"It's best not to rush into this. He will be staying here for a while, and I'd like to observe his behaviour more closely. If he is truly as good as he seems, it won't be too late to raise the issue of betrothal."

Husband and wife, totally engrossed in their conversation, had no way of knowing that Jiahui, the young servant girl of their daughter, was on her way to Mistress He's bedroom and over-heard everything. Now this girl had been with their daughter since she was small, and, because she was bright, capable, and beautiful, she had been tutored along with her mistress. As a result, she became quite literate and was given the word "enriched" for her name, to which was then added the word "elegant," to convey the idea that she was both superior and beautiful. Since Jiahui was this outstanding, you can imagine how superb were the beauty and learning of the young lady Mudan. So, overhearing how handsome and learned the intended Shi Jun was, she rushed back to the young lady's room and said with a happy smile, "My mistress has great happiness in store."

"What are you talking about?" Mudan queried.

"I have just come from your mother's room, where she was talking with your father. Old Mr. Shi has sent his son here to pursue his studies. Your father said that not only is he very learned, but he is also extremely handsome. Your parents are both delighted and intend to betroth you to him. Is this not a great happiness for you?"

"You silly thing, you!" Mudan said, putting aside her book. "You get naughtier by the day. What is the big fuss? Why do you have to come running to tell me? You are becoming more and more useless — and you continue to stand there! Go away!"

Jiahui's feeling of happiness vanished under her mistress' scolding, and, shame-faced and embarrassed, she returned to her room to mull this over.

"I am a servant to my mistress, but we are like flesh and blood! Why was she not pleased by what I told her? Why did she scold me instead? Perhaps I understand. Often those with talent have not good looks and those with good looks are not talented. Few have both. My mistress probably didn't believe me, and, when I think about it, I did handle it clumsily. I should have investigated a little on her behalf and confirmed the facts. That way I would not appear to be ungrateful for everything she has done for me."

Having reached this conclusion, she could not remain inactive and went stealthily to the study to have a peek.

"No wonder my old master bragged so about him," she thought after looking him over. "He really is quite good-looking. As I see it, he is decidedly both talented and handsome. If my mistress doesn't realize this and takes it into her mind to be stubborn, it will hinder the betrothal. Ai, I'd better manage it for her. How can that be anything but the right thing!"

She returned at once to her own room and took out a hibiscus handkerchief.

"This was given to me by my mistress, so I'll use it as a go-between."

Taking up her pen, she wrote across the handkerchief two lines

> *"Fair, fair," cry the ospreys,*
> *On the island in the river.*
> *Lovely is the noble lady,*
> *Fit bride for our lord.*

then folded it up and put it away.

At noon the next day she found herself free, so she hid the handkerchief in her sleeve and went to the study. As luck would have it, Shi Jun had gotten tired and thrown aside his books. He sat with his head on his desk enjoying a long mid-day dream. Jinjian was nowhere to be seen, so Jiahui quietly approached the desk, threw the handkerchief on it, and turned to leave. But in leaving, she grazed the desk, startling Shi awake for a moment. However, he merely covered his eyes again, turned around, and went back to sleep. In a few minutes Jinjian came in and saw his master asleep with his head on the desk and a handkerchief peeping out from under his wrist. He drew it out slowly and opened it to have a look. An unusual fragrance greeted his nose, and he saw that two lines from the *Book of Poetry* were written on it.

"What is the meaning of this," he thought, puzzled. "Where did this hanky come from? Never mind. I'll just hide it and, if my master asks for it, I'll question him about it." But, when Shi woke up, he neither looked for it nor asked Jinjian about it.

---

* Translation from Arthur Waley, *The Book of Songs* (New York: Grove Press, 1954), p. 81.

"This mustn't be his then," thought Jinjian. "But, if it's not his, where did it come from? I'd better keep my eyes open and find out."

The next morning Jinjian made sure to keep watch, going in and out many times. Indeed, he saw Jiahui come out, head for the study, watch Shi Jun look for a book, and retreat without making herself known. Then, before she could return to the rear quarters, he came forward and stopped her.

"OK," said Jinjan. "Why did you go to the study? You'd better explain fast or I'll scream!"

"Who are you?" asked Jiahui, seeing that it was a young fellow.

"I am Jinjian, who has served my master since youth, who never leaves his side, who says yes to whatever he says, and who follows his every order. Who, then, are you?"

"So, it's Brother Jin," she said with a smile. "Since you ask, I am Jiahui, who has served my mistress since youth, who never leaves her side, who says yes to whatever she says, and who follows her every order."

"So, Sister Jia," Jinjian responded.

"What's this Jia and Jin business — it sounds really strange. Why don't I just call you Brother and you can call me Sister? Let's get rid of the 'Jia' and 'Jin,' OK? Brother, did your master see that handkerchief yesterday?"

"So, that hanky was hers," thought Jinjian. "One can see that 'Great persons have a magnanimous hearts.' Why don't I tease her a bit?"

"Don't be in such a hurry, Sister," he said. "'Matters are best handled with grace! Elder Sister will get a brother-in-law sooner or later. Why rush so?"

"Don't talk nonsense, Brother," Jiahui said, red-faced. "I do this because my mistress has been so kind and generous to me and because Old Master and Mistress have said they want to bring about the betrothal. That's why I brought the handkerchief — to alert your master to propose marriage without delay. The two lines from the *Book of Poetry* mean 'Gather the gems and wait for a good offer.' Did you not understand them?"

"So that's what it is all about! I misunderstood. You don't know, Sister, that my master came here on orders from his father precisely to propose marriage. But, fearing that Old Master would not be willing, he wrote, instead, an earnest letter requesting that my master be allowed to stay here and study. He really just wanted your master to see for himself the character and education of his son. If you want also to repay the kindnesses of your mistress, let's use some real keepsakes — that handkerchief is useless. After all, I am in charge of my master's affairs."

"Don't worry, Brother — I am also in charge of my mistress's affairs. We two will take care of this to show our gratitude," she said, and, after planning to meet again, they returned separately to their own quarters.

Everything has its own underlying principle, which can be neither forced nor plotted. If something was not meant to be, though you try to force or plot for it, you will always do something wrong, and it won't come about. But if it was meant to be, then you merely have to seek it and it will happen. Without the least bit of aggressiveness, it will come about. It is even less possible to force the issue in marriages. Remember the sayings — "Fated lovers will meet though one-thousand miles separate them" and "You cannot break up a true marriage with a club."

But Jinjian and Jiahui were players who would not let things take their natural course, and, because of this, things would inevitably get so complex, to the point of chaos, that lives were almost lost. Certainly their intentions were not evil, nor did they mean to harm anyone. Theirs was an innocent cleverness that did not know how to weigh issues. One was motivated by affection, one by a desire to show off. By the time that everything came to light, these two dared not spill the truth. The remorse they felt for what they had done was intense.

Jiahui explained the situation to Jinjian, who was extremely attentive and thought ceaselessly about their plan. As luck would have it, one day Miss Mudan asked Jiahui to neaten her dressing case, in which Jiahui spied a cunning pair of jade hairclasps. She hid one in her sleeve and secretly passed it on to Jinjian. Jinjian returned to the study and opened up the case of books, but there was no keepsake there for him to take. He spied a purple goldfish pendant hanging on a fan, so he took it off at once and put the jade hairclasp in its place. He opened up the hanky that Jiahui had put there the previous time. As he was about to wrap the purple goldfish in it, he was overcome by a desire to show off his own literary talent, so he grabbed a pen and added: "Modest and retiring is the young lady, a good match for the superior man." He wrapped up the pendant and walked smugly back to Jiahui! "I told you that everything was in my hands. What do you think now?" He opened the hanky for Jiahui to inspect. But she had already waited so long that she was very anxious to leave, and, seeing a return gift in the hanky, she accepted it in a rush.

"Brother, I'll listen to your news another time," she said and, stuffing the present in her pocket, she rushed off.

Soon after, she bumped into the twelve-year-old daughter of Qiaoniang, the master's secondary wife. This young girl, Xinghua, was extremely bright.

"Where are you going?" she asked Jiahui.

"I went to the garden to pick some flowers," she answered.

"Where are they? Give me a few," said Xinghua.

"The flowers were not yet in bloom, so I have returned empty-handed."

"You don't have even one? I don't *believe* you! Let me *look*," she said, grabbing hold of Jiahui.

"You naughty girl," Jiahui said, trying to hide her things. "How *dare* you do this! I already told you I have no flowers — and, even if I did, I wouldn't give them to *you*. Do you think that walking there yourself to get some would give you big feet? Go pick your own!" Jiahui straightened out her clothing and stormed off, head high.

Xinghua, red-faced with embarrassment, called after her, "What's the big deal? I'll go tomorrow to pick some. You think only yours are desirable?" Looking down at the ground, she spotted a parcel. She scooped it up — it was the very same purple goldfish wrapped in the hibiscus hanky that Jinjian had given Jiahui. Xinghua hid it immediately in her sleeve and returned in a fury to her mother's room.

"Where have you come from? Why are you pouting? Who has angered you — tell me."

"That abominable Jiahui. She went picking flowers, so I asked her for a couple, and she refused. She even pushed me. Think of it, Mother, isn't it infuriating? But it happened that she dropped a parcel which I will never give back to her."

"What have you found there," Qiaoniang asked. "Let me have a look." Xinghua gave it to her for a look. Who could have predicted that this one look would give rise to many scandalous complications.

Do you know why? Since being dismissed from his post, Jin Hui had become indifferent to official life. Every day he entertained himself with poetry and spirits, and, as long as he heard there was a place to go to indulge himself, he would go, sometimes for the day, sometimes for half a month. Busy entertaining himself, he would forget to go home. Fortunately, Mistress He was at home, and she was capable and meticulous about taking care of household affairs. But Qiaoniang, though, was flighty, and she waited day and night for the master to return. No one would have guessed that, although Mr. Jin was quite dashing, he actually spent no time in the company of women. Yet Qiaoniang was like an ant on hot earth — she could not bear to be still. Consequently she was not discriminating in her tastes and secretly became friendly with the secretary. A saying has it: "When lewdness gets bold, it is hard to keep secret."

One day when she was in the garden pavilion with him just about to begin their lovemaking, the young lady — Mudan and Jiahui, who had gone there to burn incense, disrupted the happy event. The cowardly secretary, fearing that this affair would become out, packed up and fled the very next day.

Having lost her lover, she did not consider that she was the one who had erred. Rather she hated Mudan and Jiahui to the marrow of her bones. She thought constantly of harming them, but she had not yet found a way to do it. Now she had the handkerchief and the pendant, which exactly suited her plans, so she set about beguiling Xinghua.

"Since this parcel is something you found, why not give it to me? I won't take it for nothing — I'll make you a shirt, OK?"

"Forget it!" Xinghua said. "Last time you had me running back and forth with your presents and notes to that man and you promised to make me a shirt then too. But have you done it yet? How dare you mention the shirt to me again! You are all talk."

"Let's not bring up the past," Qiaoniang said. "This time I will definitely make you a shirt. What's more, to make I'll line it for you up for last time, OK?"

"If you really mean it, then it's fine. Allow me to thank Mother here and now."

"No need for thanks. But you mustn't mention this matter to anyone. I am waiting for the master to return. You must not be around when I tell him — I am going to be keeping an eye on you!"

Xinghua was delighted with the arrangement and agreed to everything.

On a certain day, Mr. Jin came home from his drinking party very late. Mistress He was asleep and, knowing how hard she worked to keep the household going, he could not bear to wake her. He went instead to Qiaoniang's room. Qiaoniang greeted him and offered him a seat. She poured him tea and knelt before him: "Your humble wife has something to tell you."

"What is it?"

"I found out something that has grave implications. Even though I tell you about it, you must not leak it, but rather get to the bottom of it," and with these words she took out the handkerchief and gave it to him with two hands.

Mr. Jin saw a purple goldfish pendant wrapped in the hand-kerchief and also saw clearly the four lines of poetry written on it. He noticed that the handwriting of the first two lines was delicate and graceful, different from that of the last two, which was vigorous and free-style. Jin felt uneasy at heart when he saw this.

"Where did you pick this thing up?" he asked.

"I don't dare tell you," Qiaoniang answered.

"Just tell me and I'll take care of it."

"Sir, you mustn't under any circumstances get angry," she im-plored. "It was when I was returning from my morning visit to Mistress He that I found this over by Mudan's quarters."

His face turned ashen. "That rogue!" he hissed, overcome by rage. "How dare she do such a thing! This is terrible!"

He rewrapped the pendant in the handkerchief and stuffed it in his sleeve, at which point Qiaoniang added a last remark.

"Sir, this matter has implications for our family; you must not noise it abroad. You must investigate it thoroughly. It seems impossible to me that Mudan has done this thing. Perhaps it was Jiahui who was responsible."

Mr. Jin said nothing, merely nodded his head, and went to the study to retire.

Read on to learn how Mr. Jin handled this affair.

Chapter 90

❧

The Marriage Forbidden, Where Can Mudan Turn; Jiahui Impersonates Mudan and Pays Respects to Mr. Shao

Now when Mr. Jin heard Qiaoniang's words, he knew that, although she openly shamed Mudan, the insinuation was to implicate Jiahui. If Jiahui was seen to have committed immoral acts, then how could Mudan be uncorrupted? It was truly a case of "The corruptability of a superior man depends upon his morals." Upon seeing the gold hairclasp, Mr. Jin discarded all thought of Jiahui, went straight to interrogate his daughter, and did not stop until he almost caused her death — so poisonous was Qiaoniang's plan! She had spoken those words implicating Jiahui, knowing full well that, in order to harm the mistress, she must first dispose of the servant girl. But, as it turned out, Mr. Jin was a rash and stubborn man, and her words did not have their desired effect on him. Mudan, a pure and filial child, did not dare argue with her father, and the result was disastrous.

Jin returned to his study, but he did not close his eyes all night. The next morning he stealthily went to the other study to spy on Shi Jun, but Shi had gone out to a study group. Jin took this opportunity to search his room and found, in his suitcase, a jade hairclasp. After careful scrutiny, he decided that it was one of the very pair he had given his daughter. His rage was uncontrollable as he rushed straight to Mistress He's quarters.

"Where is the pair of jade hairclasps that I gave Mudan?" he asked her.

"Since you gave them to her, she must have put them away."

"Get them for me. I want to have a look," he ordered, so Mistress He sent her maid after them.

"When I went to get them from the young lady," she reported

shortly, "she could only find one in her dressing case, though she searched and searched. She asked Jiahui, but she was ill and confused and could not say where the other one had gone to. The young lady says that, as soon as she finds it, she will bring it here."

Mr. Jin grunted, sent the maid away and said to his wife: "You raised *some* daughter! How can this be?"

"Our daughter has lost a hairclasp — let her take time to look for it. Why must you get angry?"

"If she's going to look for it," he said with a sardonic laugh, "she'd better go look in the study!"

"Why do you say such a thing," Mistress He said with great alarm.

"This is all the work of the daughter you raised," he answered, and took out the pendant and handkerchief to show her. "Here's the proof. What have you got to say now?"

"Where did you get this clasp?" she asked him.

He told her he had found it in Shi's case of books.

"I'll give my daughter three days to do away with herself. I don't want to see her again," he said and stormed off, heading for Shi's study.

Mistress He, distraught and pained by his words, rushed to her daughter's room, where she broke into tears at the sight of her daughter.

"Mother," Mudan asked, bewildered, "why are you crying?"

Her mother, sobbing all the while, related the entire affair to her. Mudan's face crumpled, and she also began sobbing.

"How did this happen?" she asked through her tears, her beautiful voice weak and trembling, "I know nothing at all about it. Let's have Mistress Liang, my wet-nurse, go ask Jiahui if she knows anything."

Who could have predicted that from the moment Jiahui lost the handkerchief and pendant, she would fall sick from worry and, on that very day, ask for leave to return to her room to recover.

When Mistress Liang arrived, Jiahui was delirious and incoherent — how could she possibly answer any questions? Mistress Liang had no choice but to return and say that Jiahui, when asked, knew nothing at all about the matter.

"What will come of this?" Mistress He asked, bursting into tears again.

Mudan forced herself to stop crying. "Father has ordered me to kill myself," she said, "and I dare not disobey. But I grieve that I will not live long enough to repay Mother for all her efforts in raising me, and that, though I die, I will not be able to rest in peace."

"My child," cried Mistress He, rushing to embrace Mudan. "If *you* die, *I* might as well die *with* you."

"Mother, don't feel sorry for me. Remember that my little brother is only seven-years old. If you were to die, who would care for him? And wouldn't that terminate the Jin clan?" she said and, clinging to her mother, she sobbed as if she would never stop.

"I have something to say," said Wet-nurse Liang comforting, for she had come up with a plan. "Our young lady is delicate and reserved and has never left her maidenly chamber. I guarantee that she never did this thing. It must be Jiahui's doing, but we can't confirm this because she is too sick now. If we were to wait until she is well, I fear it would not do, since the Old Master is so quick-tempered and impatient. Yet if our young lady is forced to end her life now, then it will be too late for regret when this affair is actually cleared up."

"So what would you have us do?" asked Mistress He.

"The best plan is to have my husband secretly rent a boat, and he and I will take the young lady and Jiahui to my old uncle's place in Tang District for a while. Once Jiahui recovers, we will ask my old aunt to investigate thoroughly to get to the truth of the matter. This plan will allow us to avoid both the greater anger of Mister Jin and the loss of our young lady's life. The only problem is that you, Mistress, must bear some responsibility here to find the right time to entreat the Old Master to understand."

"I will tell him all by and by. But I am worried about how you will fare on the road."

"This matter has come to such a pass that there's nothing else to be done."

"Your plan is marvellous," Mudan said, "but I have never left

Mother before nor have I ever shown myself in the world. I really am not used to such things. Also, such behaviour would be disobedience of my father's command — I just don't feel right about it. It's cleaner and simpler to die."

"Child, this is your wet-nurse's temporary solution to the problem. If you really were to die, would it not make it look that all the more like the truth?"

"I can't bear to leave you, Mother. What's to be done?"

"You are just feeling some anxiety over the imminent separation. You will surely be reunited when the matter is cleared up after a bit. What's wrong about that? If our young lady is afraid to show herself, I have yet another plan for that: we'll have Jiahui dress up as you and on the way say that she is sick and we are taking her to Uncle's to recover. Our young mistress will dress up as a servant girl and who will be the wiser?"

"That is a good idea. Hurry and take care of everything. I will go soothe the old master."

By this time, Mudan was numb, and, although she had a thousand things to say, she could not manage anything but "I will go. Mother, please take care of yourself," after which she burst into tears. Mistress He, in spite of her pain, hardened her heart and left.

Mistress Liang summoned her hero husband, whose name was Wu Neng, actually meaning "clueless." Since she called him her "hero" and his name meant "clueless," he was clearly a "clueless hero." If he had any kind of talent, how could he bear to make his wife serve as a wet-nurse? It was a pity that she delegated the task of securing a boat to him — that's when the affair became a total disaster. (He couldn't compare with his older brother, Wu Yan, who was an excellent swordsman.) Clueless went to the riverbank and hired any old boat, not checking whether it was good or bad. Then he hired three sedan chairs and took them to the back gate of the garden where Mistress Liang was waiting with the young lady and Jiahui. They mounted the chairs and headed straight for the boat. The boatman poled the boat and off they went.

Meanwhile Jin Hui had returned in a fury to his study. Shi Jun had also returned by then and greeted Mr. Jin respectfully. But Mr.

Jin ostentatiously refused to return his greeting, which caused Shi
to wonder: "'How can he treat me so disrespectfully? It must be
that he feels my presence is an imposition. Alas, 'human emotions' are treacherous; the way of the world is superficial. I don't
have to depend on him for a living, so why should I take this
nastiness from him?" He made his decision and then spoke. "May
I inform you, sir," he said, "that I am going home to check on my
parents, whom I have not seen for some time."

"Fine. You should have gone home long ago," responded Jin.

Shi Jun found these words and this tone humiliating. Red-
faced, he summoned Jinjian to get the horses ready.

"But where are you going?" Jinjian inquired.

"I have a place to go. You just ready the horses. Who told you
to ask questions, you slave? You'd better be careful about it, too.
You're asking for a beating."

Jinjian said not a word when he realized how angry his master
was. He brought the horse over at once. Shi stood up and waved
a goodbye with his hands, saying "I take my leave." He did not
give Jin the properly respectful deep bow.

"That rude beast," muttered Jin. "He's truly abominable!"

"Abominable is it! Abominable! How can this be?" Jin heard
Shi say deliberately, but he paid him no heed, shrugging it off to
youth and bad manners. He wondered how a man like Old Mr.
Shi could have raised such a son, and this brought out a long
sigh. He then checked to make sure that all his books were as
before and opened the suitcase for a look. Aside from the poetry,
there remained only a fan, which obviously had been forgotten
by Shi.

What a pity that Shi Jun, in his rush to leave, made this blunder.
Having arrived at the Jin's empty-handed, all the books and
papers he had used since coming were those in Mr. Jin's study.
Overcome by his anger and unable to think of anything else, he
had forgotten the fan in the case of books. Had he remembered to
take it, he would have been led to ask where the pendant was,
and Jinjian would have had to tell the truth, all this in front of Mr.
Jin serving as proof. That would have cleared up this grievance
against Shi on the spot. But Shi would leave the fan in the case

and, although it was a small thing, its implications in this affair were tremendous. Had the matter been resolved then and there, the following series of disasters would never have happened.

Jin now returned to his inner chambers after watching Shi leave in a huff. There he saw his wife, dissolved in tears and quite pitiful. He said nothing, just sat down and sighed. Suddenly Mistress He was kneeling at his feet, saying over and over.

"I beg your forgiveness. I beg your forgiveness."

"What is all this about?" he asked at once.

"Sir, just pretend that our daughter is dead," she implored after telling him the whole story. "On my behalf, don't delve any further into this," after which she sobbed greatly, remaining glued to the floor. Jin stamped his foot in anger, but, out of fear that the ugly sounds would be heard by others, he desisted. He raised his wife from the floor — after all, they were long-time husband and wife and he could not bear to see her like that. "No need to go on crying. Since the situation has come to such a pass, the only thing to do is forget the whole thing."

Let us not go into detail here about Mr. Jin, for disaster was stalking the young lady. Everything that transpired was a result of the carelessness of Clueless in hiring the boat. He had engaged a bunch of thieves. The pirate boat belonged to two brothers named Weng — the Elder and the Younger — who had an assistant named Wang the Third. They took note of their passengers — an old couple with two elegant young ladies, and of the valuable parcels they carried, which incited evil intentions in their hearts. They signalled understanding to each other and, after the boat had gone only a short way, the elder Weng said: "No good — the wind is raging." He poled to a secluded spot and said to Clueless: "We must prepare some sacrifices to the gods."

"Where can we go to get incense, wax, and paper horses in this place?" asked Clueless.

"Don't worry. We have everything right here on the boat — I promise that we will have a complete spread. But, we do need your money for it."

"Well, how much do you need?"

"Not much, not much. Twelve-hundred cash will be sufficient."

"What are you sacrificing that you need so much money?" Clueless asked.

"Chicken, fish, and sheep head, for the three sacrificial beasts, on top of which there's incense, candles, and paper money — you still think it's too much? When sacrificing to the gods, you shouldn't pinch pennies."

Having no response to this, Clueless gave him the twelve-hundred cash. Before long the elder Weng invited Clueless to burn incense with them. When he came out of the boat he saw three plates on the prow. On the middle one was a sheep's head, minus the skin and brains. On the left one was a chicken missing its neck and wings. On the right was a scaly dried carp with protruding eyes, over which was hung a string of paper ingots and a few pieces of tattered sacrificial paper. Even more laughable, the hanging money was merely three totally colourless pieces of paper. But most pitiful of all was the bundle of incense, long and short sticks all uneven. And there was also one short, neither-red-nor-white candle and one long one, stuck in a pair of earthenware candlesticks.

"*This* is what you got for twelve-hundred cash?" Wu Neng blurted out angrily when he saw this pitiful showing.

"Everything's ready. We now need an additional three hundred for the wine."

"Aren't you swindling us here?" Clueless shouted anxiously.

"You are not pure of heart, and the spirits find this disturbing. You had better go into the water to insure our safety," said Weng, pushing Clueless into the water, where he fell with a great splash.

Mistress Liang, hearing this suspicious conversation, had just come out of the boat's cabin to have a look when Weng pushed her husband into the water. She could not stop herself from calling out "Help! Help!" and Wang the Third ran over and walloped her, so that she lost her balance and fell backward into the boat.

"Help! Help!" she shouted again. Mudan, hearing everything from inside the cabin, realized that things had come to a bad pass. She broke through the window and jumped into the water to escape into death. The elder Weng rushed to the cabin and, seeing that one girl had jumped into the water, grabbed the other one, Jiahui, by the hand and said: "The beautiful young lady has nothing to fear. I have something to discuss with you."

At this point Jiahui could not end her life even if she wanted to, nor could she escape. Although her illness was much improved by then, she was in terror, her body covered with sweat, a cold chill piercing her heart. Weng the Younger and Wang the Third were on the deck poling the boat away from the shore when Jiahui screamed out. "Help! Help!"

Suddenly a boat so fast that it seemed to fly appeared in the distance.

"There are people in trouble on that boat," said one of the group standing on the deck of the fast boat. "Let's go quickly and have a look in that cabin." Weng the Younger and Wang the Third saw right away that things had taken a bad turn. Using the poles to punt themselves into the water, they escaped. The Elder Weng had also overheard those people say they would search the cabin, so he escaped through the window and into the water.

"Don't be hasty," an elder man in the group said as they boarded the pirate boat. "The thieves have probably jumped into the water and escaped. Who is in the cabin?"

When they entered the cabin, Mistress Liang was hiding under the bed. She crawled out, and, with wisdom born of the emergency, said: "Please, gentlemen, save this mistress and servant. Take pity on me — my man was drowned by those thieves; our maid, in terror, escaped through the window, jumped into the water and drowned too. On top of that, my young mistress is very ill and can't be moved. Please have pity on us," she entreated them with tears streaming down her face.

"Don't cry," one of them said. "Let me go tell my master about this," and he turned and left. Mistress Liang took this opportunity to tell Jiahui in a whisper to pretend that she was the young mistress — they must not tell the truth. Jiahui nodded in agreement.

Before long four or five women servants came to help Miss Imposter. Mistress Liang was asked to help carry their parcels. In the confusion, the sacrificial items got trampled underfoot. They all reached the official boat and faced an elderly gentleman, seated in a great chair with arm rests, who asked them: "Where is the young lady from? What is your family name? Take your time and tell me."

"This humble slave is Jin Mudan," she said after properly greeting him. "I am the daughter of Jin Hui."

"Which Jin Hui is that?" asked the Old Gentleman.

"The one who was Secretary of the Military until he was retired by the emperor, who was angry that he had advised the prince of Xiangyang twice."

"So you are actually my niece," the Old Gentleman said with a laugh. "What good luck! What a marvellous coincidence."

"But I do not know who you are, Respected Sir. Why are you calling me 'niece'? Please explain everything to me."

"I am Shao Bangjie," he said with a smile, "an intimate of your honourable father. I was just transferred to the post of governor of Changsha. That's why I gathered my family in a rush to go take up my office. We just happened to anchor here for a bit; I never expected to wind up rescuing you, my niece. It truly is a lucky chance."

Miss Imposter paid respects once again and called him "Uncle." Old Mr. Shao had his maid raise her up and put her in a chair.

"Niece, what were you doing in that boat? Where were you headed?"

If you want to know how Miss Imposter answered these questions, read on.

Chapter 91

❦

Life in Death, The Young Lady Adopts Zhang Li; Joy in Misery, The Little Hero Follows Shi Yun

Now then, the young lady responded to Mr. Shao's question by telling him the entire tale of how she was taken sick and how her parents told her to go to Tang District to recuperate.

"In this," Shao said, "your honourable father was wrong. How could he order your wet-nurse and her husband to escort a delicate young lady like you, sheltered all her life."

"We usually make this trip frequently," she hastened to reply, "we never expected to run into a pirate boat this time. I think that it was a case of bad luck for me."

"I ought to see you home, Niece," Shao said, "but I have just received an urgent imperial order and I cannot delay. Rather than going to Tang District, why not come with us to Changsha — you'll have my old wife and several daughters there. You certainly won't be lonely. I'll write to your father when your illness is gone. What do you think?"

"I am in your debt and I'd best go along with your plan. But, may I inquire as to where Auntie is? Would you allow me to pay my respects?"

Mr. Shao was delighted. He had the older and younger maids escort the young lady to his wife's boat. His wife and three daughters were all quite taken with the imposter.

From that moment on, Jiahui stayed with the Shaos while she recuperated. Since she had not been seriously ill to begin with, she recovered in a few short days. Mrs. Shao had already secretly asked her if she were betrothed.

"I have been betrothed to Master Shi from childhood," the young lady had replied and Mrs. Shao had conveyed this information directly to her husband.

In time the boat arrived at the double fork in Plum Blossom Bay, where there were two routes, one southeasterly, that led to Changsha, the other northeasterly, leading to Green Duck Rapids.

Now at Green Duck Rapids were thirteen fishing families, among them one fisherman named Zhang Li, a man of over forty, extremely important among the fishermen, with an old wife called Mistress Li. This old couple, who lived by fishing, had neither son nor daughter. On one particular day, Old Zhang went out at night as usual and threw in his net. When he gave it a tug, it felt unusually heavy, and he thought that he must have caught a very big fish.

"Mother," he cried out, "come quickly. Come quickly."

"Big Brother," she asked as she ran out. "What is it?" (This old couple had always thus addressed each other, the husband calling the wife "Mother" and the wife calling the husband "Big Brother." I don't know how it came to be this way, but now they were used to it and did it by force of habit.)

"Mother, come help me! This fellow is a big one!"

Mistress Li went over and helped him pull the net up onto the boat. They opened it and looked in, only to discover the body of a woman, her hands still holding tight to a bamboo window frame.

"Bad luck! Bad luck!" Zhang Li cried in alarm. "Throw it back into the water at once!"

"Don't be so rash," his wife said, stopping him. "Haven't you heard the expression 'Better to save one life than build a seven story pagoda?' Let me see if she is still breathing."

"She is," she announced after feeling her chest beating unsteadily. "Let's get the water out of her."

Mistress Li used her palms to massage the chest and very quickly a great deal of water came out. The young lady, coming to, began to moan. Mistress Li helped her sit up and, when she seemed to be fully conscious, began calling to her and asking her what had happened.

This young woman was none other than Mudan. She was fortunate that, when she fell into the water, she held firmly to the bamboo window frame and floated along, who knows how many miles, till she reached this spot. She herself knew what had transpired, but she was unwilling to tell the true story, so she said "I am a maid in the household of a minister in Tang District. Because they had come to take away my mistress, I leaned on the bamboo window to watch her as she left on her boat. I never thought that the window would fall into the water and I would go down with it. Before I knew it, I had floated all the way here. May I inquire as to your surname, Mother?"

Mistress Li told her everything and then quietly discussed her thoughts with her husband.

"You and I have been childless our whole lives. This young lady is so lovely and speaks so intelligently, why don't we adopt her as our own? Won't we then have someone to take care of us in our old age?"

"I'll rely on you to handle this," Zhang Li said to his wife, and, when Mistress Li presented her idea to the young lady, she agreed to everything.

Mistress Li was overjoyed. Maternal feelings welled up in her heart. She refused to go on fishing and pressed her husband to return home at once so that they could get their new daughter some dry clothing. Zhang Li steered them back to the village, where Mistress Li helped Mudan into their grass hut. She found her some dry clothes and had her change into them. Her original clothes were richly ornamented; now she wore plain cloth. Mistress Li then went in search of tea leaves which she threw into the pot of boiling water. She stirred furiously with the ladle, took out a bowl, wiped it clean, blew away the froth in the pot, and ladled out a half bowl of tea. Wiping the edge of the bowl, she handed it to Mudan.

"Have some hot water, Daughter. It will drive out the chill."

Seeing how diligent she had been, Mudan could not refuse. She took the bowl and drank a few sips. She watched as Mistress Li then ladled out the leaves, washed the pot, put in another ladleful of water, got out some millet flour and made a hot and steaming bowl of knotted dumplings, which she placed before the young lady with a pair of shiny lacquered chopsticks and a white earthenware plate of salted turnip strips.

Obligingly, Mudan lifted the bowl and drank, tasting only a pleasant sweetness. There was no other flavour to it. She drank all of it and also took a few bites of the turnip strips, which were terribly salty. The hot soup drove away the chill, and her face was covered with sweet drops of perspiration. Mistress Li immediately picked up the corner of her shirt and wiped Mudan's face to reveal that extreme beauty she was born with. The old woman loved her more with each gaze and, loving her more, could not stop gazing upon her as though she were the most precious of jewels.

"Is our daughter a little better?" Zhang asked as he came into the hut.

"Please don't worry, Father," Mudan answered.

Zhang noticed at once that her voice had changed — it was no longer weak. Moreover, although he was almost fifty-years old, he had never heard anyone call him "Father" before. When he heard her say this word, he felt as if he had gone to heaven, as if someone had annointed him with rich wines. A heavenly joy penetrated to the inner reaches of his heart, and he said with a big smile: "Mother, what a fine daughter we have."

"Just so, just so," Mistress Li agreed and the two of them went on smiling broadly.

"Our daughter was a member of a minister's household," Mistress Li reminded her husband as dawn broke. "She is used to a refined and delicate lifestyle. We must not make her feel uncomfortable. When you come back from selling your fish, you must bring back some goodies for her."

"OK, then, I'll weigh a little extra ground pork and get some bean curd and cabbage. What do you think?"

"Very good. That will do it," Mistress Li responded.

Rustic folk really do not understand what "delicacies" are. All they know is that ground pork is a good thing and, if you add bean curd and cabbage, then you have the best, because, in fact, these three items are not all that easy to get hold of. In actual fact, how much do these things cost? Zhang had his own way of calculating the cost. Once you had good dishes, you would eat more and that meant that, in addition to the cost of the dishes, you would eat more rice too. So, when you figured it out carefully, it just wasn't worth it to buy good food. But now he and his wife had inadvertently acquired a daughter. On the one hand, they feared making her suffer; on the other, they feared her ridicule and condescension. So, he made up his mind to spend the money and buy the meat and vegetables, which he brought home. But Mudan just picked at it and left most of it over. So, with one thing and another, people began to suspect that Old Mr. and Mrs. Zhang had finally resigned themselves to being childless and had begun to treat themselves to good food. Some of them decided to go over and have a look at the delicacies; if they were lucky, maybe even taste them. They never expected to find, when they entered the hut, an exquisite young woman, as lovely as a Fairy Immortal. They were shocked and then curious, but thoroughly delighted to learn that the old couple had acquired a virtuous daughter. They spread the news all over town and each of the twelve fisher families came to congratulate them.

Among the villagers was a man skilled in the martial arts and unusually fearless. He was one who dared to do righteous deeds and, because of this, his fellow villagers revered him. Whenever some important matter arose, they either asked him to represent them or they desired his opinion, and, once he reached a decision on any matter, everyone went along with him. On the day the villagers learned that the Zhangs had acquired a daughter — good reason for celebration — each and every one of them went to him to tell him the good news.

"Old Mr. Zhang is a genuine and sincere person, generous to a fault," Shi Yun said, clapping his hand with joy at the news. "This new daughter will certainly bring him good fortune, and their luck is a result of their sincerity in all things. So, why have you come to see me?"

"We want to congratulate him, so we came to ask your help in planning the celebration."

"Fine. We *should* celebrate when our village has such good fortune. But, there's just one thing — we are poor folk with enough food and grain for today only — who among us has a surplus? If we all go to congratulate him at the same time, that adds up to a lot of people and might put Old Zhang in an embarrassing situation. So, I have an idea. We all earn our living by fishing — it is the way of life here. Let's give ourselves three days to work hard and fish well. Bring all the catches here to me. We'll keep what we need to eat and sell the rest, and, with that money, we'll buy food and wine. Leave everything to me! And you, Respected Little Brother," he said, turning to a man surnamed Li, "you must come often, since you can read and write a little. You'll help me write down what I need to remember."

"I'll be here every day, early."

"One other, even more important matter," added Shi. "You must all bring your own tables and stools on the day we visit Old Zhang. He certainly does not have enough furniture to seat all of us. When we get there, we'll all help — we cannot allow Old Zhang to do the work. We will insist that they relax and enjoy themselves the whole day. We will just be getting together to have a great time eating and drinking. As for giving gifts, that's all phony stuff and we don't want any false promises. What do you think of the plan?"

"Marvellous," they all replied. "Marvellous. That's exactly what we'll do. But, wait — there are some families with more people than others. How will we work that out?"

"I'll take care of it all. I guarantee it will be fair. No one will be cheated and no one will be favoured. Surely among our families, no one cares about such things anyway. Everyone go to work now. I'll go to Old Zhang's to tell him the plan.

The crowd dispersed and Shi Yun went straight to Old Zhang's place to tell him about the plan. There he saw Mudan, who was truly as beautiful as a flower, as lovely as jade. Shi was delighted. Zhang was anxious to begin preparations, but Shi told him that he had taken care of eveything.

"You, Old Brother, need only prepare the firewood. You needn't worry about any other thing."

"My respected younger brother, that's not easy to believe. How can it be that all I have to do is prepare firewood?"

"I have planned it all out for you. Everything is taken care of — we lack only the firewood. We have all else. I would never lie to you!" Although Old Zhang had his doubts, he thanked Shi deeply, and Shi bid him goodbye.

The villagers truly were united in their efforts, and everything was easily accomplished. It was a case of each one trying to outdo the others. There were those who went out twenty or thirty miles to fish, those who took their wives and children along to help, and others who took their younger family members. By only the second day no small amount of fish and shrimp were handed over to Shi Yun. Shi had planned that each family should give equal amounts, so he told those who had brought more that they needn't bring any the next day and those who had brought less should supplement it on the morrow. He went straight to the fish merchant and sold them at a fair price. He took the money and purchased food and wine and took it all to Old Zhang's place. Old Zhang was both delighted and worried when he saw the great abundance. He was overjoyed that he had gained a daughter who was so lovely, but he was worried about how to arrange everything.

"What's so difficult about that," Shi said to him with a smile. "Just tell me, have you prepared the firewood?"

"Yes. Look! It's those two piles up against the fence there. Will that be enough?"

"Quite enough," Shi said. "We probably won't even need that much. Now that we have the wood, you needn't worry about a thing. Tonight all of us will come here at the fifth watch. We will do everything ourselves. You don't need to do a thing. Just prepare to drink and be merry!"

"You have taken care of everything, dear brother. How can I allow that?"

"What's the problem?" Shi said with a smile. "We can celebrate your good fortune while letting everyone have fun and be merry at the same time. After all, it's our good fortune too."

As they spoke, a group of people approached, some carrying tables and stools, others carrying cooking utensils, others with pots on their backs. Then there were those alternating carrying things, and others carrying bundles of vegetables. They came in disorderly droves, and Old Zhang greeted them until the entire courtyard was full. Only in Green Duck Rapids could this happen. In no other place would you find such a wealth of warm human feeling and caring — all orchestrated by Shi Yun. Brother Li arrived just then and began recording each and every item. Old Zhang, fearing an error, made his own secret marks to help him remember. To each one who came, Shi Yun entreated, "Neighbour, come early tomorrow morning — don't be late, under any circumstances."

By dusk everything was complete and Shi went home with Li. But, by four the next morning, these two had already returned. And, by five, the entire village was there. Old Zhang welcomed and thanked everyone. Shi delegated all the tasks: he appointed some to get the fires going, some to make the vegetables, some to arrange the seating, some to carry the water and wood. Old Zhang did not have to give any of these tasks a thought. He was beside himself with joy, running here for a look, there for a glance, just like a monkey jumping through hoops. At one point he dashed into the hut and asked his wife, "Has our daughter eaten anything?"

"Big brother, no need for you to worry. I will take care of our daughter." He looked suddenly at his wife and laughed. "Aiya, Mother is happy today too. You finally washed your face and combed your hair."

"What are you saying?" she said, laughing too. "All our neighbours have come to celebrate. How could I greet them with a dirty face? Look at my hair — our daughter did it for me!"

"It's obvious that now that you have a daughter you are making her do your hair for you; soon you'll have her feeding you too!"

"Humph," she snorted. "Listen to your nonsense!" Giggling to himself, Old Zhang left.

Dawn came quickly, and gradually the married women and young girls of the village arrived. Mistress Li welcomed them all and there were congratulations and thanks back and forth. When they saw Mudan, they were stunned. They smacked their lips and sucked in their breath. Mudan had no choice but to do her best to charm them. Indeed, she succeeded so well they were all beside themselves with pleasure.

By the time the food was ready, the seating arrangements were also complete. The women ate inside, where there were tables, chairs, and the finer utensils. The men were outside, where there were tall tables and lower seats, big plates, and small bowls. This was all set up by Shi Yun — it truly was no easy job. No one bothered about the closeness of family relations — all was arranged by age. I took a stool, you took a utensil, and we sat there laughing and talking, sitting close all around, happy and carefree. Before long the plates and cups were everywhere. These weren't the elegant delicacies of the rich, but everything was there: fresh fish and shrimp, meats, and vegetables. Empty plates were filled and exchanged for new ones; abundance was the word. Everybody started out slowly, but soon, in their cups, they began playing guess fingers.

Shi Yun was playing with Zhang Li, who said "Seven Qiao." Shi responded with, "All have come." Suddenly from outside a voice spoke: "It's lucky I've come then?" Shi cocked his head and listened.

"Don't listen to him. Let's play guess fingers," urged Zhang.

"One moment, Old Brother. You and I and all thirteen of our neighbours are here — so who has dared interrupt us just now? Let me go out and have a look." He got up, looked through the slats of the door, and saw it was a young man with a pack on his back looking inside the hut.

"You young rascal, you," Shi cried out. "Why are you spying on us? Was that you who interrupted our game?"

"I wouldn't dare deny it," the young man responded. "It was I. I saw you all drinking and making merry. My mouth started watering, and I wanted to buy a few cups of wine to drink."

"This is no wineshop — why do you use the word 'buy?' You're talking wildly, but I'll overlook that. Just go at once!"

Shi turned to leave and was surprised to feel the young man's hand stopping him.

"You say it's not a wineshop, so how come there are so many people here drinking? Are you trying to take advantage of an outsider?"

"Why, you rude thing you," shouted Shi. "I let you go and you turn around and attack me! You say I'm taking advantage of you — well, what are you going to do about it?" He raised his hand as if to hit him, but the young fellow merely smiled, grabbed the hand, pressed it to his chest and then pushed it away. There was a cracking sound, and Shi landed backwards on the floor.

"What strength!" he thought. "I'd better be careful," he thought as he gathered himself together and stood up for a comeback.

"Don't do this!" Zhang urged as he came out of the hut and saw them. "Just say whatever you have to say." He asked the reason for the fight, then addressed the young man.

"You, young fellow, must understand. This really is not a wineshop. All of these folks are here to celebrate with me. If you want to drink, please come on in — I'll join you in a few cups."

"May I ask your name?" the young man said, delighted now that he was soon to have a drink.

Zhang told him his name, after which he inquired about Shi, who said, "I am Shi Yun. What's it to you?"

"Big Brother Shi, please forgive my rash behaviour. Don't think badly of me." And with these words, he bowed to the ground.

If you want to know what happened, read on.

Chapter 92

❦

Little Hero Scatters Gold and Drinks Himself Drunk; Old Ge Steals Chickens and Brings Himself Disaster

"What is your honourable name, sir?" Shi asked, embarrassed about the fuss, now that the young man had become so polite.

"I am Ai Hu. I was passing through here on my way to Sleeping Tiger Ditch. I couldn't help getting thirsty when I saw all of you drinking and making merry. Since you have offered me some drink, I'll take up your kind offer. Shall we?" and he stepped right in.

Do you know how Ai Hu wound up in this place? After he swore brotherhood with Shi Jun, he set out on the journey — every day he did five miles, ten miles was considered a stop. But if he happened on some good drink, he might stay three days or even five. He'd get drunk, then sleep, wake up, and drink again, all this with the silver that Jiang Ping so unstintingly gave him and that he spent so whimsically. When the villagers saw Zhang Li and Shi Yun come in with this stranger, they merely greeted him and went on with their business. Shi gave Ai Hu his own seat. Zhang Li took the jug, poured out a full cup, and gave it to Ai Hu who, without the usual polite phrases, downed it in one gulp. Shi poured him another, which Ai Hu also downed. Ai Hu then poured each of them a cup, refilled his own, and asked: "Just now, you, old sir, told me that you were celebrating — may I ask what it is that you're celebrating?"

Hearing the reason, Ai Hu laughed loudly saying, "So *that's* what it is!" He offered Zhang some silver that he took out of his pocket, entreating him to accept the small gift. "It is indeed a matter for celebration," he said.

But how could Zhang Li accept such a gift. Ai Hu wrangled

with him and managed to stuff the silver in his shirt. Zhang Li had no choice but to accept. He went back inside and called out to his wife. "Mother, here is a gift that young man gave us for our daughter. Put it away safely."

"Oh my," she cried, seeing the two ingots of five ounces of silver each. "How can we accept such a weighty gift?"

"Mother, what is it?" asked Mudan, walking over.

After Zhang had explained the origin of the silver, Mudan inquired, "Does father know this person?"

"Actually not."

"So you don't know him. This is an 'unexpected meeting among strangers.' Yet you have accepted this generous gift. That's hard to fathom. How do we know this man is not an evil person or a thief? I think we ought not to accept it."

"Our daughter is right," agreed Mistress Li. "Big Brother, take it back right away."

"Our daughter knows the proper thing here. I'll go return it," he said and took the silver back from his house to return it to Ai Hu.

By this time, the group of neighbours sitting around were in a stupor — each and every pair of intense black eyes was glued to that pile of shiny white silver and their hearts were pounding furiously. They were getting red in the face from thinking, "What good luck for this old couple — first they get a daughter and now their fortune is made. Who can keep up with them?"

Then they heard what Mudan had said to her parents and how they both agreed with her, and how Old Zhang returned that huge pile of round and shiny, wonderful silver. They all said it was a great pity. Some asked how you could turn away the gifts of well-intentioned guests. Some said that this daughter the Old Zhangs had acquired was headstrong. They tittered and fussed about this matter without end.

When Old Zhang reached Ai Hu, this is how he explained the situation to him.

"Just now I told my wife and daughter of your generous gift. But they felt that you are a guest who has come from far away and we ought to extend our hospitality to you as a matter of course. The food and drink is all ready-made here. How could we possibly accept such a weighty gift? Please do not be offended if I return to you the gift untouched."

"What's the big deal here? Have you not had huge expenses preparing this celebration? Take this silver temporarily as a token of thanks for your hospitality."

"Sir, my fellow villagers paid for this entire celebration. If you don't believe me, ask Mr. Shi."

"What he's said is absolutely true," Shi interjected. "We would never fool you."

"My silver is out of my pocket — how can I put it back? Well, never mind. I'll just ask you, Big Brother, to take this silver and arrange another celebration exactly like this one for tomorrow. Today you treated me, tomorrow it's my treat. I won't go along if you don't bring each and every one of these folks back."

"It looks as though our guest Ai Hu, here, is truly a generous and carefree person. Old Zhang, I think you'd best just accept the gift, lest we offend him," whereupon Zhang again thanked Ai Hu.

Shi Yun then kept Ai Hu entertained in earnest. They drank one bowl of wine after another, until Shi was really plastered.

"Such a very young fellow," he thought, "with such a huge capacity for liquor!" Others came to watch the performance. After drinking non-stop for some time, Ai Hu gradually became drunk. His head rolled back and forth, his body swayed and, finally, he just closed his eyes and fell asleep leaning against the table. Shi Yun let him sleep, knowing how much he had had to drink. Before long, Ai Hu sank into a dream world and began snoring thunderously. Seeing him like this encouraged the villagers to drink themselves into a stupor — all but Shi Yun, who had been sparing with his cups because of his responsibility in managing Zhang's celebration. Zhang himself was not a big drinker, so he just went about keeping things in order.

Suddenly someone called from outside, "Is Old Zhang at home?"

Alarmed, Old Zhang ran out to greet the callers. "Please come in, Gentlemen." he said. "On what business have you come?"

"How is it that you are asking us?" was the reply. "Whose turn of duty is it today?'

Who were these two men? They were, in fact, Louluo aborigines from Black Wolf Mountain. When Lan Xiao had occupied this mountain and found out about the thirteen fisher families of Green Duck Rapids, he had set up a system whereby a different fisherman was on duty every day and was responsible for providing all the fish and shrimp that they needed on the mountain. That day it was Zhang Li's turn, but, because of his celebration, he had totally forgotten about it, recalling it only when he saw these two men. So he apologized at once, saying: "This old man forgot for the moment — please convey my regrets to your leader. Tomorrow I will prepare extra fish and shrimp for you all."

"What nonsense!" they said. "Make it up tomorrow? You expect our leader to go hungry today? Never mind what you say. Come with us right now to see our boss. You tell him yourself whatever it is you have to say."

"Please don't be like this, sirs," Shi Yun interjected as he came out of the hut. "Mr. Zhang really does have a pressing matter today. Please make allowances," he added, and then told them all about Zhang's good luck in gaining a daughter.

"So, then, let's go have a look at this young lady," they said. "That'll make it easier to explain things to our boss." They forced their way in, regardless of Zhang's objections, and took a look at Mudan, whose beauty they secretly praised. As they were leaving, they spotted Ai Hu who had been sitting at the table unmoving during the whole thing. Actually when these two Louluo had first arrived, the villagers knew that something was up. The brave among them stood their ground and listened; the cowardly slipped out, afraid to get involved. Ai Hu alone just sat there, doing nothing, so how could those Louluo know that he was sleeping the sweet sleep of the intoxicated.

"Who is *he?*" they shouted. "How *dare* he not greet us! Despicable! Tie him up for us — we'll take him up the mountain."

"He's not from here and he's drunk. I beg you, gentlemen, please forgive him," Zhang intercepted. Shi Yun also came over to help explain, until finally the two Louluo left in a huff.

The villagers only then started up a loud and confusing chattering. Shi decided that they had better wake Ai Hu up and send him on his way, lest he be implicated in their affairs. Zhang woke him and explained the situation. Had Ai Hu not known about any of this, everything would have been fine, but, upon hearing the story, he cried out: "Aiyaya! Mountain bandits and cruel robbers! *I* was looking for *you* and, instead, you have come to pull this tiger's beard. When he returns, I'll take care of him."

Worried, Zhang Li tried to persuade Ai Hu to leave. But, suddenly the sounds of horses and shouting were heard, and one of the villagers came running in to report to Zhang: "Bad, bad. Boss Ge has entered our village with men and horses." Terrified by this news Zhang shook from head to foot.

"Don't be afraid, Old Man. I am here!" declared Ai Hu, giving his pack to Zhang and calling Shi over. "Come with me, Big Brother."

Ai Hu went out of the hut to face twenty or thirty Louluo surrounding an old man riding a horse.

"Old Mr. Zhang," said the old man. "We hear that you have a lovely flowerlike gem of a daughter, just for me. I've come today to propose marriage."

"Who are *you*?" Ai Hu shouted threateningly. "Speak up, you rogue!"

"Who doesn't know me — Ge Yaoming, nicknamed 'The Clam'? Who are you that you dare come here and make trouble?"

"I thought it was that rogue Lan Xiao, but instead it's a nameless squirt. I am Grandfather Ai Hu, here. What are you going to do about it?"

"You brat! What rubbish!" shouted Ge Yaoming, ordering his men to seize Ai Hu and tie him up.

Four or five responded to the order, but Ai Hu, with no rush and no fuss, turning first his left then his right shoulder, knocked two down and then kicked a third to the ground. The Louluo, seeing how formidable Ai Hu was and thinking to succeed with numbers, sent along ten more men. How could they anticipate that the Little Hero could fight in all directions at once, like a tiger killing a herd of sheep? In no time, the Louluo had all been beaten to the ground.

Watching Ai Hu's extraordinary heroism, Shi Yun praised him

silently. He himself had grabbed a five-pronged fish spear and, with a loud shout, rushed at Ge Yaoming. The Louluo had thought these fishermen would be easy to cheat, and they had come empty-handed, totally unprepared for a fight. Ge Yaoming was the only one bearing a weapon — a dagger — which he took out when he realized that his men were no match for Ai Hu. He was about to go to their aid, when Shi Yun greeted him with the fish spear. The spear had hooks on it and caught hold of Ge's dagger with great force, bringing down the shaky and feeblehanded Ge along with it.

With a cry of "Bad!" Ge ran off into the village, leaving his horse behind. The Louluo, seeing their leader fleeing, hung their heads and skulked off. But Ai Hu had gotten into the fighting. Unwilling to let them off, he seized Ge's dagger and rushed off in pursuit. "Follow them!" called out Shi Yun, shooting off after Ai Hu, fish spear in hand.

Ai Hu chased him outside the village. He let loose and closed in tightly behind them when he saw them running off. The saying has it: "Don't pursue a desperate enemy." Now our Little Hero was just like a new born calf who knows no fear of the tiger. Knowing his own talents, how could he possibly be at all concerned about these mountain brigands. That Shi Yun was also a brave young man. He followed close behind and saw how suddenly, within the circle of mountains, Ai Hu fell to the ground for no apparent reason. Louluos came out from all around him and tied him up. Shi Yun witnessed this unfortunate event, turned and ran straight back to the village to report it.

Do you know what caused Ai Hu to fall down? That rascal Ge was on horseback and reached the circle much earlier. He had the Louluo guards set up a hidden rope to trip Ai Hu. How could Ai Hu have anticipated this? Having let loose, he ran furiously — how could he not be tripped up? The Louluo grabbed Ai Hu and, under Ge's direction, fifteen of them were to take him up to Ge's mountain retreat and the other fifteen were to return to the village to steal Old Zhang's daughter. That rascal Ge was delighted with him. He had Ai Hu put on a horse and they went together up the mountain.

As they went along, a wild chicken suddenly fell from the sky. Ge Yaoming went ahead to pick it up and saw that the chest area was bloody. He realized that someone had shot it down. He went a little farther ahead and heard someone shout: "Put that chicken down right now! I shot it."

Taking a close look, Ge saw an extremely ugly young woman of about fifteen or sixteen.

"So this chicken is yours, is it?" Ge asked.

"It is," she answered.

"Don't try to fool me. You have no weapon in your hands — how did you shoot it down?"

"It was my older sister who did it. If you don't believe me, just take a look and see if she isn't standing there under that tree."

Ge looked over and saw an exceptionally beautiful young woman standing there holding a pellet cross bow.

"I am really under auspicious stars for marriage today. Old Zhang's got one beauty for me in the village and now I've run into another. Double happiness has truly arrived at my door," Ge thought.

"You say your sister shot it," Ge then said to the ugly young girl. "I don't believe it. Have your sister come along with me — we have chickens on the other side of the mountain — and show me how she shoots them." As he spoke, his sneaky eyes fixed themselves on the beautiful one in the distance.

"If you don't give it back, I fear that this young lady will not allow you to pass," she said angrily, and got herself into a fighting position. But, suddenly, Ge let out an "Aiya" and fell to the ground. He tried to get up, but there was blood flowing from the space between his eyes and the ugly young woman knew that her sister had shot him with an iron pellet. She would not let him stand up and gave him a kick with the heel of her foot. With a plop, Ge, his mouth full of dirt, fell prostrate, knowing that he had been taught a lesson. The Louluo rushed to surround the young woman who, with a sardonic laugh and raised fists, brought them all down. Her feet flying, she had them baring their teeth in anger.

By now Ge fully grasped this young woman's ferocity. Not daring to fight her, he pulled himself up and fled. The Louluo, seeing their leader take off, also dared not linger. In one great hubub, they followed behind. The young woman, busy attacking them, suddenly heard someone call out "Great work!"

If you want to know what happened, read on.

Chapter 93

Leaving Green Duck Rapids, the Fishers and Hunters Band Together; Returning to Sleeping Tiger Ditch, the Sisters Speak Their Hearts

After this young woman beat off the entire band of Louluos, only one person was left — Ai Hu — who was tied on the back of a horse, high up and able to see everything. He had watched as the ugly young woman fought those men as easily as if she were catching butterflies or chasing bees. She was skilful in the extreme. Watching, he had involuntarily cried out words of praise. Now he let out his voice and, laughing loudly, called, "Great fight. You fought well!"

"Who are you?" the woman asked him in the midst of his delight.

"My name is Ai Hu," he said, controlling his laughter. "I was ambushed by them."

"There is a Black Demon Fox and Northern Hero — do you know them?" asked the ugly one.

"Black Demon Fox, Zhi Hua, is my teacher, and Northern Hero, Ouyang Chun, is my godfather."

"Then you must be Brother Ai Hu!" She hurried to undo his bonds. Ai Hu dismounted and made a very low bow, with deep respect.

"May I inquire about elder sister's honourable name?"

"My name is Qiukui. Sha Long is my godfather."

"Who was that who shot those thieves with pellets just now?" Ai Hu asked.

"That was my elder sister Fengxian. She is the blood daughter of my godfather," Qiukui answered, waving to her sister. "Sister," she called, "come here!"

"My sister is naive," Fengxian had thought watching Qiukui

untie Ai Hu. "Women must not have any contact with men —
what *is* she doing?" When her sister called to her, she went over
slowly and asked: "What is it?"

"It's Brother Ai Hu — he's here!"

Hearing the name Ai Hu, Fengxian involuntarily looked him
over. She was delighted with him, greeted him, and received his
greeting in return.

"You two shameless slaves!" shouted someone from within the
mountain. "How dare you greet a male person!"

Fengxian and Qiukui raised their heads and saw three men halfway up the hill. It was none other than Steel-Face Budda-Warrior
Sha Long and his two sworn brothers, Meng Jie and Jiao Chi.

"Father, uncles," Qiukui called out loudly. "Come here. Brother
Ai Hu has come."

"Aiya!" Jiao Chi cried upon hearing this. "Our nephew Ai Hu!
Big Brother, hurry, come down quick!" With these words and a
tu, tu, tu, tu, he leaped down the mountain calling out all the way,
"Which one is our nephew Ai Hu? I have been dying with anti-
cipation to see him."

Do you know why Jiao Chi said these words?

When Northern Hero, Zhi Hua, and the Ding brothers arrived
in Sleeping Tiger Ditch, they told the story of how, when the
imperial crown was stolen, Ma Chaoxian was captured and how
all this was thanks to Ai Hu; they told how young and brave he
was, how extraordinary was his courage, how he went to Kaifeng
to inform on the villains and braved the guillotine; how there was
a joint investigation and how he saved the loyal and virtuous
ministers; how from that time forth he was given the title of "Little
Hero." Just listening to the tale of the heroic little Ai Hu delighted
Meng Jie and Jiao Chi, who jumped about for joy. But Jiao Chi was
an impatient man and could hardly wait to meet Ai Hu. From the
moment he heard the tale of his bravery, he thought about him
constantly. And now, when he heard Qiukui say that Ai Hu had
arrived, he flew down the mountain, screaming wildly, "I'm dying
to meet him."

"Who *is* this person?" Ai Hu wondered. "I've never met him.
Why is he dying to meet *me*?"

Jiao Chi threw down his pitchfork when he reached Ai Hu and embraced him tightly with both arms. He looked him up and down, down and up. Ai Hu had no idea what was going on — he stood there very straight and still, not moving the least little bit.

"Great!" he heard Jiao Chi say with a loud laugh. "He is, indeed, not bad. The betrothal is settled then." Sha Long and Meng Jie finally arrived and Jiao Chi called out to them.

"Big Brother, take a look at him — he's a person of good character. Don't ruin your plan. Let's settle the betrothal now."

"You are too impetuous, Honourable Little Brother," Sha Long tried to quiet him. "Is this matter something to be shouted about wildly?"

Northern Hero had, in fact, asked Second Ding to propose marriage to Sha Long for Ai Hu as soon as he heard of the talented daughter Fengxian, who was skilled in the martial arts, particularly in shooting iron pellets, which never missed their targets. Sha Long was quite interested, assuming that this fellow, who was Zhi Hua's disciple and Northern Hero's godson, must be pretty good.

"Since Brother Ouyang and Honourable Little Brother Zhi are willing to enter into this marriage arrangement," Sha Long said to Ding, "I have no objection whatsoever. But, I do have one wish — I adopted Quikui when she was young and I dote on her even more than on Fengxian. This is partly because she was orphaned and alone so early in life and partly because she has the capacity to lift five or six-hundred catties on her shoulders. It's just that she's a bit ugly. But I cannot settle Fengxian's marriage until after Qiukui has been taken care of. Please, Younger Brother, explain this to Brothers Ouyang and Zhi Hua for me."

Second Brother Ding found the opportunity to tell the two in private and they were moved deeply with a feeling of great respect for Sha Long. "We should also behave like this in handling matters," was their response. "Since Ai Hu is still quite young, it won't matter if he waits a few years," and with this they agreed wholeheartedly.

Who could have guessed that Meng and Jiao, hearing about the betrothal, constantly pressured Sha Long with great urgency: "Why do you delay with such a weighty matter?"

"I have never met Ai Hu," Sha responded, not wishing to go into detail with these two rustic men, "and I don't know what his character is like. Can there be parents who handle their daughter's most important life event in such a careless way?"

Meng and Jiao had nothing to say to this, so they simply dropped the matter. That is why, however, when Jiao Chi spied Ai Hu that day, after looking him over, he shouted out "Well, then, the betrothal is settled!" He paid no heed to Fengxian who, hearing his remark, rushed off embarrassed and blushing.

"This is my father," Qiukui finally said to Ai Hu. "And these are my uncles, Meng and Jiao."

Ai Hu greeted each of them and Sha Long, observing his youth and heroic air, was delighted.

"Why have you come here, Honourable Nephew?" Sha inquired.

"If they send yet another person to plunder Old Zhang's daughter," Ai Hu said, after explaining how he had wound up there "I will have to go back to save her."

"Great," said Jiao Chi, sticking up his thumb in admiration. "That is as it should be, and I'll go with you too," he added, picking up the pitchfork.

Ai Hu was empty-handed, so Sha Long gave him his own club and the two of them turned and went on their way.

They had just reached the mountain when they spied the Louluo who had kidnapped Mudan. They were carrying a square sort of thing, wrapped around with a cloth. On top was a sort of red, yet not-red covering. (I dare say it was a topless carriage!) They could hear the indistinct sound of crying from within. Ai Hu, swinging his big club, shouted at them, and ran in hot pursuit. Jiao Chi grabbed the pitchfork firmly and swished it round and round to make a resounding hum. This was too much for the Louluo who, scared to death, dropped the carriage and ran for their lives. Ai Hu, removing the red cloth, discovered that the "carriage" was an overturned table, the four legs facing up. A second glance showed him that there was a young woman inside already unconscious. As Ai Hu was wondering what to do, a sobbing woman came from the mountain, crying out, "Heaven help us! Please return my daughter. Otherwise I will die too. Let me exchange my old self for her!" It was, of course, Mistress Li, to whom Ai Hu responded: "Mother, don't cry. I have already rescued your daughter."

Zhang Li then rushed out and hurried over to Ai Hu. They were delighted to see each other.

Mistress Li loosened Mudan's fetters, and gradually she came to. Just then Sha Long and his daughters arrived with Meng Jie. They had been very uneasy when Ai Hu left and had all followed to the spot. They saw that the young girl was untied and the Louluo had run away. Ai Hu took Zhang Li to meet Sha Long and Mistress Li took Mudan to meet Fengxian and Qiukui. They were all quite taken with each other.

"Elder Sister, why don't you come with us to Sleeping Tiger Ditch? Those mountain brigands won't give up on you, and what will happen if they come again?" Fengxian said to Mudan, who was terrified at the thought. Qiukui, straightforward and quick-tongued, turned straight to Sha Long and told him about the idea.

"I, too, am worrying over that matter," he replied. "I have heard," he said to Zhang Li, "that you have thirteen fisher families here in Green Duck Rapids. How many people are there all together?"

"Probably all together — men, women, young, and old — fifty or sixty," answered Zhang Li.

"If that's the case, old sir, hurry back and inform your villagers about the seriousness of this affair. Tell them to pack up all their things at once and prepare to move to Sleeping Tiger Ditch," instructed Sha Long.

"I will go with Old Mr. Zhang," Ai Hu volunteered. "I left an important bundle there."

"I'll go too," Meng Jie said, and Jiao Chi also expressed the desire to go with Ai Hu, but they were stopped by Sha Long.

"Little Brother, you come with me back home. We must arrange living space for all the villagers." Sha Long then instructed Qiukui: "I entrust the mother and daughter to you two. We will return home first."

No one could have known that Mudan, who had been terrified as well as tied up, would not be able to move.

"No problem," Qiukui said. "I'll carry Sister on my back."

"Sister, how can you carry her such a long distance?" Fengxian asked.

"You've forgotten, Sister, about that horse tied to the tree up ahead, the horse that carried brother-in-law here," Qiukui said with a guffaw. Fengxian, embarrassed, turned red and made not a sound. Quikui picked up Mudan, and before long had reached the place where the horse was tied. But Mudan did not know how to ride a horse. Fengxian brought the horse over and got on the saddle herself. She walked it a little ways and, deciding that it had no eccentricities, said, "Sister, you just sit up here — I will guide the horse. I guarantee there will be no problem." It was Qiukui who put Mudan on the horse and Fengxian, holding the bit, led it along slowly. Mudan was extremely uneasy.

"Mother, you can't walk all that way. Let me carry you part of the way," Qiukui said.

"How dare I accept your offer? Let me tell you, young lady, not a day goes by that I don't walk ten or twenty miles. It's only because of that infernal chaos and confusion just now, I was anxious and angry and my feet got all weak from running. I'll be better after walking a bit. Don't you worry, young lady, I can make it." So, chatting all the way, they eventually arrived at Sleeping Tiger Ditch.

Do you know why Sha Long of Sleeping Tiger Ditch was not afraid of Lan Xiao from Black Wolf Mountain? There's a good reason for it. Originally Sleeping Tiger Ditch had eleven hunter families. Of them all, Sha Long was the oldest, the most talented in the martial arts, was an honest and an upright person, and all eleven families listened to him in everything. After Lan Xiao began his occupation of Black Wolf Mountain, Sha Long called a meeting of the families and taught them some martial arts to prepare them for untoward circumstances. Later on, he swore brotherhood with Meng Jie and Jiao Chi, so he had even more helpers. He had made discreet inquiries and learned that the fisher families of Green Duck Rapids were already going in turns up the mountain to supply the brigands with fish and shrimp.

"How do we know that those thieves won't come here

demanding game from us?" Sha Long pointed out: "We have *me*, Sha Long, here in Sleeping Tiger Ditch, and we definitely will not set such a precedent. Neighbours, please be careful when you go into the mountain."

Everyone obeyed Sha Long's instructions. None of them was willing to offer their game to the brigands. Unexpectedly, Lan Xiao somehow had heard of Steel Face Budda Warrior Sha Long, so he personally made a visit to Sleeping Tiger Ditch. Ostensibly he was there to force them into making a regular practice of providing game, but he really went just to meet Sha Long, whom he scolded for not supplying them. Sha Long let out a stream of abuse and said that he was speaking for all eleven hunting families. Lan Xiao was enraged. They glared at each other and raised their hands to fight. One on horseback, one on foot, they wrangled a few rounds and then, with a snap, Sha Long cut the stirrups of Lan's saddle.

"I am being lenient with you; you'd better understand this, Mountain Brigand."

"I've heard about your talents," Lan Xiao said to Sha Long, turning his horse and returning to the mountain. He wrote secretly to the prince of Xiangyang, telling him about his extraordinary prowess and how he would be a leader in the future. Lan had gone deliberately to make Sha Long's acquaintance, because, whenever the name Sleeping Tiger Ditch was mentioned by any of the hunters in the mountain, the Louluo did not dare to provoke them. Sha Long's heroic name resounded far and wide. Now the thirteen fisher families of Green Duck Rapids had moved to Sleeping Tiger Ditch, and the practice of sending fish and shrimp daily to the brigands in the mountain ceased.

To get back to Sha Long, he and Jiao Chi arrived home and cleared out some rooms in the west courtyard for the men and some rooms in the inner quarters for the women as temporary residences. Next, he gathered together workmen to build homes in their village. When the houses were done, the fisher families each would be given a place to live. Mudan, her mother, and the two sisters arrived shortly and they were delighted.

"That's a great arrangement! What fun we'll have." Qiukui said.

"But when the houses are ready, everyone else can move into them, except for Miss Zhang. She and her folks must remain here in the inner quarters of our home. The Zhangs are elderly and we sisters don't like being lonesome. What do you say?"

"I am worried that we will be an imposition." responded Mudan.

"Sister," Fengxian said, "please never again say such formal, polite words. Please let us take care of everything for you."

"Just listen to you two going at it — it makes me quite sick," said Qiukui. "Let's go. We'll first see Dad." They all headed for the main hall to see Sha Long.

Sha Long was there giving instructions for the slaughtering of pigs and sheep in preparation for the meal. The two sisters led the way, with Mudan and Mistress Li following behind. Appropriate greetings were made all around, while Sha Long looked Mudan over. He saw that she was extremely poised and well-mannered and, compared to Fengxian, she was even more beautiful.

"Just looking at her poise and demeanor," Sha Long contemplated, "One can see that she is definitely not a fisherman's daughter. She must be a young lady from a good family."

"Please, dear niece," said Sha Long beaming, "you have come to our home, and you must, on no account, treat us as strangers. Please tell my younger daughter whatever you need. You mustn't feel constrained." Sha Long then approved of Qiukui's suggestion that the Zhangs remain living with them, even after the houses were completed. Mistress Li went forward to thank Sha Long, after which Fengxian took them to the rear. Sha Long had no wife, so the two daughters lived together. At that point, they decided that Mudan would not go to the inner chambers, but remain there with the two sisters to chat.

If you want to know what happened, please read on.

Chapter 94

❦

The Young Fellow Determines to Seek Godfather and Master; the Petty Man Decides to Cut off Righteousness and End All Ties

Now Ai Hu returned to the village with Zhang Li and Meng Jie. Shi Yun, just then discussing the situation with everyone, saw Ai Hu come back with his two companions and asked for news. Zhang Li told him what had transpired and Ai Hu repeated how they all had to move to Sleeping Tiger Ditch to evade the mountain brigands. Who among those listening would not desire to avoid trouble? They all therefore busied themselves with packing their clothing and jewels. The bulkier, heavy items were discarded. The men were led, the women helped, the elderly carried, and the young supported along the way. They assembled in front of Zhang's home. Zhang himself had already packed everything. Ai Hu, carrying his bundle and club, led the way. Meng Jie and Shi Yun were the rearguard, protecting the entire group of fisher families as they headed to Sleeping Tiger Ditch. What a pity that the clamourous joyful celebration of the fisher families had now turned into a cold and quiet Green Duck Rapids. But now we've come full circle. Otherwise where would the fisher soldiers have come from later on?

Noisy and confused the whole way, it was quite a job to get all these people to Sleeping Tiger Ditch. Sha was waiting there to welcome them at the village gate, with Jiao Chi accompanying. Ai Hu rushed forward to pay his respects and returned the borrowed club. Sha had his servant put it away and then said to the fisher families, "The rooms are all small, so we can't put families together. We must inconvenience you temporarily. The men can stay in the western courtyard and the women in the rear with my younger daughter. We will allocate the houses when construction is finished." Sha was thanked by all and then he asked Ai Hu, Zhang Li, Shi Yun, and Meng Jiao to go to the main hall. "Where are my master, godfather, and Uncle Ding?" inquired Ai Hu.

"You're a little late. The three of them left for Xiangyang three days ago."

"How can that be?" said Ai Hu, stamping his foot without thinking. He picked up his bundle and was about to rush away when Sha Long stopped him.

"Don't do this, dear nephew. They've already been on the road three days. You'll never catch up with them. What's your rush?"

There was nothing for it but to stay, so Ai Hu put his bundle down again. He had come in high spirits; now he hung his head with sorrow. It was all the fault of his lust for drinking. If he hadn't delayed to satisfy his thirst, he would have arrived here long ago. He was filled with remorse.

Everyone sat down and tea was brought. Before long, the table was set and places laid. Hosted by Sha, Ai Hu sat in the seat of honour, with Zhang Li next. Shi Yun, Meng, and Jiao sat on either side of him. They drank and chatted, first answering Jiao Chi's question about the crown theft affair. Ai Hu told them the story and Jiao shouted with delight.

"Dear nephew," Sha Long asked, "how did you wind up here?" to which Ai Hu replied that he had come in search of his master and godfather. Ai Hu also told how he had met Jiang Ping during his journey, and how they had lost each other along the way.

"Ai Hu," Shi Yun queried, "why are you just talking and not drinking?"

"Indeed," added Sha. "Why don't you have something to drink, dear nephew?"

"I'm not much of a drinker," Ai Hu answered. "Please forgive me."

"But you drank so happily yesterday in the village. Why can't you have any today?" Shi asked.

"The effect of wine lasts one whole day. I had too much yesterday, and I'm reluctant to drink today." This silenced Shi Yun and showed how Ai Hu could, in a few words, cleverly handle an issue.

The first reason Ai Hu stopped drinking was because that moment of self-awareness, about having ruined everything because of his drinking, was upon him. The second reason was what Jiao Chi had said about the betrothal's being settled. He feared that, if the same thing happened again and he got drunk, he would become an object of ridicule. Therefore, he bore it, steeling himself and gritting his teeth, thinking that he would quit it for a couple of days and then figure out what to do.

The meal ended and Sha Long summoned the hunter families together to instruct them.

"You must all go into the mountain and discreetly find out what's going on at Lan Xiao's. Hurry back and report to me." He had the village leader prepare defence weapons lest the mountain thieves, learning that the entire fisher population of Green Duck Rapids was all now in Sleeping Tiger Ditch, come for a fight. The hunters returned the next day.

"Nothing's going on at Lan Xiao's," they reported. "We made comprehensive inquiries and learned that it was actually Ge Yaoming who engineered the kidnapping of the young woman. Lan knew nothing about it. Ge Yaoming himself was the one to report to Lan that all the families of Green Duck Rapids had run off. This did not faze Lan Xiao." So Sha Long relaxed his defence preparations.

Ai Hu alone suffered. He did not drink for two days running and then made up his mind to go to Xiangyang. Sha Long could do nothing to stop him, so he arranged a send-off meal for the next day. Ai Hu packed his bag, gave the imperial document to Sha Long, and said: "It's not convenient for me to take this with me to Xiangyang — I might lose it. It's Uncle Jiang's. It was given by the emperor to permit him to come looking for my godfather. If Uncle Jiang comes after I've left, please give this back to him." Sha accepted it and had someone take it to his daughter Fengxian, in the rear chambers, to put away safely.

The farewell feast started then. Ai Hu decided to be bold that day and have something to drink. Starting with Sha Long, each and every one toasted Ai Hu, and each time it was bottoms up.

"No wonder neighbour Shi said that our dear nephew was

quite a drinker!" said Jiao Chi, laughing aloud and clapping his hands with delight. "It is true. It's really true. Come, come. Let's us two — uncle and nephew — down three cups!"

"I'll join you," Meng Jie said. He picked up the jug and filled everyone's cup. They brought the cups to their lips, and, with a toast of "Bottoms up," they downed the wine noisily. Sha could not stop them, and, after three cups, Ai Hu picked up his bundle, gave a goodbye salute, and departed. Everyone saw him off to the edge of the village. Shi Yun and Zhang Li wished to accompany him even farther, but Ai Hu stopped them. They all clasped hands, and Shi Yun and Zhang Li watched Ai Hu disappear into the distance before they returned to the village.

You might say that I have covered the whole episode of Ai Hu's visit to Xiangyang, but, if you think about it carefully, you will discover that a detail has been left out. Which detail is that? When Jiao Chi first laid eyes on Ai Hu, he called out that the betrothal was now settled; so why, during Ai Hu's three days in the village, did Jiao Chi say not one word about it? In a story, there are details that are explicit, spelled out, and those that are not explained. Please reread the earlier section, and you will understand. Remember when Ai Hu returned to the village with Zhang Li to get his bundle and Meng Jie went along? Sha Long kept only Jiao Chi behind, saying: "Brother, you come back with me." Sha Long did this intentionally, knowing that Jiao Chi was an impetuous young man. Sha was afraid that he would mention the betrothal again, so he took him back with him and told him, along the way, that the betrothal was settled, but that they had to wait for Northern Hero's return so that they could finalize it face to face. That is why Jiao Chi never raised the issue again. It is not the case that I, the storyteller, forgot the detail!

Enough about that! Since I've said that I don't forget things, why do I never mention Jiang Ping any more? There's a different explanation for that. A story has slow-paced parts and fast-paced parts; it has things that come first and things that come second. Narrating is difficult, but it's even tougher to explain all the ins and outs. The entire story must make sense from beginning to end, one thing must follow from another. You can't be off by the slightest bit; if you are even a tiny bit careless, the donkey's lips won't match the horse's mouth — incongruous. Of what interest would that kind of story be? Storytellers truly wrack their brains to create a tale. Though their hands are writing about one topic, their eyes are already looking toward what will happen later. Not only have I not mentioned Jiang Ping recently, but have you heard me say anything about Yan Chasan, Governor of Xiangyang? I can only go one step at a time, telling it all slowly, until it naturally reaches its conclusion.

Let's talk about Jiang Ping for a bit. After Jiang rescued Lei Chen, he took him to Ling District. Old Mr. Lei was infinitely grateful and had a suit of clothes made for Jiang. He also presented him with twenty ounces of silver for road expenses. Jiang thanked him and departed, first leaving his regards for Lei Ying.

"We will meet again," Jiang said, grasping Lei's hands. "Please go in." Then off he went, making time on the main roads.

It was already late in the day. Suddenly it began to rain and, since there were no inns or villages, Jiang could only brave the rain and continue on his way. It was no easy thing finally to come upon a beat-up old temple on the roadside. He rushed up, but it was already dark and he could not make out which sacred beings were represented nor did he have time to worry about paying his sincere respects — he merely wanted a refuge from the rain. Who would have expected that you could see the sky from the decayed roof of the temple — the rain was leaking in everywhere. He looked around behind the statue and found that there was room for him to sit down. He rested and caught his breath. By the first watch the rain had stopped and the sky cleared. A bright moon lit up the sky like daylight. Jiang was about to go around to see which god the statue represented when he heard footsteps and then voices: "We can hide from the rain in here and talk," one said.

"Why should we brothers stand on ceremony? But, really, his words were too heartless."

"Number Two, that is precisely your mistake. The old saying says it well: 'A long-time gambler has no winnings.' You still won't listen to your older brother, but you use his words against him. He was worried and said those cruel things. How can you blame him for that?"

"I guess he said those things in anger. What's Third Brother's plan now? We'll do what we have to. I'll always do what you want."

"Big Brother agreed to a profitable business, so he had me come get you to ask you to go see him. It will all be settled with a little stroking and laughing, needless to say. It's doing the business that counts."

"What kind of business can be so important," someone asked.

"The old Daoist priest from the Eastern Mystic Moon Temple came looking for Big Brother and told him that there is a man staying at the temple by the name of Li Pingshan, who wants to go to Nine Immortals' Bridge in Xiangyin District. He asked the old Daoist to hire him a boat and a companion to take care of him along the way. Big Brother not only agreed to get him the boat, he also agreed to find the companion."

"Well, Big Brother really doesn't know what he's doing. We'll just show up with our own boat — who has the time to go looking for one to hire for him?"

"Second Brother, you really are a useless fellow, nowhere near as organized as Big Brother. He thought of everything long ago. Tomorrow, I will become the companion, and the old Daoist will take me to him. If Li is taken in, then that's that. The three of us will do it together, and that's even better. If he doesn't go along with it, surely Big Brother and I can take care of that man. That's why Big Brother had me come here to get you. 'It takes blood brothers to fight and overcome a tiger.' Don't be silly now," he said, laughing loudly.

Do you know who these two people were? Those two who kidnapped Mudan — Weng the Second and Wang the Third. The "Big Brother" they kept mentioning was Big Brother Weng. On the day that they killed the wet-nurse's husband and couldn't get their way, both had escaped into the water. But their evil hearts did not reform, and they continued to plot vile deeds. Who could have known that Uncle Jiang would have the good fortune to overhear the conversation!

Jiang left the beat-up shelter at dawn and went to Mystic Moon Temple.

"Is Big Brother Pingshan here?" he called out. "Is he here?"

"Who is calling me?" answered Mr. Li, coming out of the temple. "Who's there?"

He saw a small man, thin as a matchstick, not more than forty, who greeted him and asked, "May I inquire your honourable surname and ask for your instructions?"

Jiang recognized a Zhejiang accent, which he himself took up to talk to Mr. Li.

"I'm Jiang, and I wouldn't bother you needlessly. May I speak with you?"

Mr. Li led him inside to have a seat.

"I've heard that Elder Brother is heading for Nine Immortals' Bridge on business. I am going to Nine Immortals' Bridge to see a friend and it's the very same route. I came so that we could go together. I beg you to take me with you. What do you think?"

"Fine," responded Mr. Li. "I was just feeling lonely here. How lucky that you've come. It would be marvellous for us to be together on the boat."

As they spoke, the old Daoist priest arrived with the boathand, who told them the price — it was cheap.

"I know someone extremely competent and honest. He could really look after you, sir," the priest said to Mr. Li.

"Bring him to me," said Mr. Li.

"Brother Li," Jiang interjected, "why do you and I need someone else for the boatride? Can we lack friends when we arrive in Xiangyin District?"

"Okay then. We can help each other along the way. We'll make do. Once we get there, we can always find someone if we have to," said Li, explaining to the priest that they need not hire anyone to help them. Jiang, delighted by this, said: "With one fewer, I'll make a greater effort."

They decided that they would set out by boat the next day. Jiang stayed overnight at Mr. Li's place, where he helped him tie up the luggage. Mr. Li was delighted by Jiang's thoroughness and felt he was lucky to have run into him. At dawn the next day, Jiang was responsible for moving all the luggage to the boat, for which Mr. Li uneasily thanked him many times. When everything was readied for departure, the brothers Weng started the boat and they went forward. During the boat ride, Jiang regaled Mr. Li with conversation and good humour, so that Mr. Li rocked back and forth with laughter, praising Jiang to the skies. He shook his head uncontrollably, smacked his lips, kicked his feet around, and generally could not control his high spirits.

Suddenly a series of whooshing noises resounded.

"The wind is up," Weng the Elder cried out. "The wind is up! Let's find a place to hide from it."

Thinking that they were lying about the wind, Jiang got up for a look out the cabin door, but there was, indeed, a strong wind blowing. The Weng brothers quickly got the boat over to a sheltered spot at the foot of the mountain, extremely secluded.

"Brother Jiang," Mr. Li whispered, terrified by this situation, "this place is really scary!"

"It's the strong wind. There's nothing for it. We can only leave it to the Heavens."

From outside came the sudden ringing of bells. Li took quite a fright and went out of the cabin to have a look. He saw some official boats trying to pass through but having difficulty because of the strong wind. They also anchored in the cove.

"Great," Jiang said, "with these official boats here, we have nothing to fear." And, indeed, the two thievous Wengs, not daring to do evil because of the other boats, retired to the rear.

Li Pingshan and Jiang stood there watching as someone emerged from one of the official boats.

"The master has instructed," he said, "that you anchor us here securely — don't let the boat float around," to which all the boathands called out agreement.

"Is that Mr. Jin there?" Li called out loudly, delighted that he had recognized this man.

"Is that Mr. Li over there?" that man answered, after he raised his head and recognized Li.

"It is, indeed. It is, indeed. Please move a little closer. May I ask who that Old Gentlement is?"

"Do you mean, sir, that you don't know? It's our master, and he has been appointed Governor of Xiangyang."

"Aiya," Li exclaimed "that such a thing could happen! Wonderful, just wonderful. May I ask you, sir, to inform the master that I am here and request to see him."

"In that case," he said, and then had the boathand lay out the gangplank and help Li over to his boat. Jiang was puzzled by this, not knowing what relationship this official had to Li.

In fact, this official was none other than Jin Hui, selfless and upright former Secretary of the Military, who had been dismissed from that position. This was a result of Magistrate Bao's memorials to the emperor advising him first to cut off the prince of Xiangyang's wings — in this, the position of Governor of Xiangyang was critical and had to be filled by someone pure of heart and loyal. Bao had made this recommendation because Jin Hui had several times memorialized the emperor about the prince of Xiangyang and urged him to have him impeached. Emperor Renzong, seeing that Jin was upright and honest, promoted him to be Governor of Xiangyang.

Jiang was really confused as he watched Li come back over the gangplank, head held high, cheeks all puffed up, shoulders thrust out. He turned his back on Jiang and, ignoring him totally, went straight into the cabin.

"What kind of trash is this rascal! How can he be such a toady?" Jiang thought as he followed him into the cabin.

"Do you know that official over there, Brother Li?"

"Of course I know him," said Li, fluttering his eyes for some time before answering. "He is a good friend of mine."

"What a phony!" Jiang thought. "Who is he?" Jiang asked Li.

"He is Jin Hui, Master Jin, former Secretary of the Military, now Governor of Xiangyang. Everyone knows that! I'm going with him to take up his office, so I won't be going to Nine Immortals' Bridge with you. Tomorrow I will transfer my bags to his boat. You'll just have to go to Xiangyin by yourself."

"When the petty man gets his way, he at once becomes a

different person." Mr. Li had dropped the polite "Elder Brother/ Younger Brother" form of address and now used the less respectful "you" and "I."

"If that's the case," Jiang said, "what about the cost of this boat ride?"

"Since you are going by this boat, naturally you must pay. Why on earth are you asking *me* about it?"

"We originally said we were helping each other and would divide the cost evenly. How can you now expect me to pay for the whole thing?"

"It's useless to discuss this with me. I don't care a bit."

"So be it. What else can I do. Lend me a few ounces of silver then."

"We met entirely by accident," Li said with a flutter of his eyes. "What do you think we are to each other that I should lend you several ounces of silver? Don't be crazy, OK? The governor is right here. I can have you investigated and punished for such ideas and then it will be too late to be sorry!"

"What a rogue," Jiang thought. "He turns on a person ruthlessly. He is really abominable."

Suddenly they heard someone crossing the plank. Li went out to greet him, while Jiang hid himself beside the screen in the cabin, cocking his ears to listen.

If you want to know what was said, please read on.

❦

Chapter 100

An Assassin Exiled; Fast Travelling,
a Search for a Scholar

Little Hero Ai Hu headed straight for Xiangyang when he left Sleeping Tiger Ditch. He had had no wine during his three days at the village. On the first day of his trip he drank too much and put up for the night after only half a day of walking. The second day was also like this. On the third day, he came to his senses.

"This won't do," he said to himself. "If I go on like this, it will be the same as what happened on my way to Sleeping Tiger Ditch. If I do it again, then I'll blow the whole thing. I will have to behave myself." It was thus that he exhorted himself. Anxious about getting on, he rose early and went forward on the first likely road he found. By dawn, he inquired the way of someone and discovered he had taken the wrong road. He was fifty or sixty miles northeast of where he should have been. Fortunately the person he asked was responsible and told him precisely from which place, to what town, from what town to which fort, and how many miles it was from the fort to Xiangyang Avenue. Ai Hu thanked him with a bow and grasped his hand in taking leave.

"I get up at the fifth watch," he muttered to himself, "and I rush through several watches of the night — all for nothing. Half a night's effort wasted. This all happened because of my greed for wine two nights ago. If I hadn't gotten drunk those two days, I would never have been in such a rush today, and I would never have made such a blunder as this. The disastrous effects of liquor are by no means small." He was infinitely vexed with himself.

He did not expect that, because of this mistake, he would miss meeting up with Northern Hero and the others, and not see them until he arrived in Xiangyang. And it was no easy thing to find

Xiangyang! He asked at every store and residence, but no one knew where it was. He didn't realize that Northern Hero and the others would not be staying at an inn, but rather in rustic temples and primitive shrines, in order not to arouse suspicion. Little Hero searched for a long and anxious time before finding lodgings for himself.

The next day he went everywhere making inquiries, being careful not to drink too much. In all places he was told that a new governor, named Yan, had just been appointed to the district. He was a disciple of Minister Bao. He was clever and upright. Surely everyone would air their grievances before him. Also, there were some things said about him in secret, but Ai Hu felt that they didn't ring true. Little Hero decided to sit in the inn and pretend to doze off, with his ears cocked. He let his head nod and his eyes close and he listened carefully to everything that was said. They seemed to be analysing how to establish a treaty agreement, how secretly to construct Skyscraper Hall, and how to design the Brass Net Trap. Little Hero spied on them for three days running, and they talked of nothing else.

He knew the danger of the Brass Net Trap, so he dared not act on his own. Instead, he kept careful watch on the prince of Xiangyang's residence every day from across the road in the inn. One day he was upstairs in the restaurant drinking, staring expectantly across the road watching people going in and out of the residence. Suddenly two people on horseback approached and dismounted in front of the residence. They tied the horses to the railing and went in. After an hour, they came out again. Each loosened the reigns. One climbed into the saddle; the other had just stuck his foot in the stirrup when someone rushed out waving at them and, with every appearance of being upset, whispered something in the unmounted man's ear. Suspicious, Little Hero hurried downstairs and followed the horsemen. At the crossroad, he heard one say, "Let's settle it. We will meet up at Ten-mile Ward outside of Changsha Pass. Let's go then." All the time they were chatting on horseback. Then each gave his horse a taste of the whip, one trotting off to the east and one to the west. Ai Hu was watching and thought, "It's them!"

Do you know who these two were? They were old acquaintances from the Hall of Recruiting Worthies. One was Fang Diao, who had suddenly come up with the evil idea. Ever since his sword had been overcome by Northern Hero in Pinched Ditch, he had been on the run. He dared not return to the Hall of Recruiting Worthies, so he had headed for Xiangyang, where he hoped to hide out with that imposter prince.

The other one was Little Zhuge, Secret Hero of myriad plots, Shen Zhongyuan. Shen Zhongyuan, pretending to be sick, had not shown himself when Ma Qiang was siezed. Afterwards, he realized that they had been plotting to rob him, and he laughed to himself about how evil these people were. They were capable of anything.

Then he heard everyone planning to go to Xiangyang. "Zhao Jue has long been disloyal," he thought, "In the future he will not be forgiven by national law. These birds of a feather will never be able to pull it off. Why don't I meet their plot with my own and go along to the prince of Xiangyang's residence and see what's happening. If it's serious, I will try to manipulate the situation from within. I will be doing my part for the emperor — and ridding the people of evil and treachery. Won't that be marvellous?"

But, the conduct of each hero and righteous man is different. In the case of Shen Zhongyuan, it was particularly difficult. He had taken on the reputation of one engaged in treachery and evil; moreover, in front of the prince, he had to play the sycophant at all times, ingratiating himself and submitting to the decisions of others. How then can we interpret what he does as heroic? He relies entirely on his intelligence and wit. He can see right through any matter, and, as though reading a script, can act out the drama. To produce heroism from farce takes a true hero — such as Southern Hero, Northern Hero, Twin Heroes, and even Little Hero, who rescue those in danger and help the needy everywhere. This is heroism for all to see — easily. But Shen Zhongyuan cannot be compared with those. He operates secretly, without revealing the tiniest hint of it. He adapts himself to the circumstances, feigning artfully in myriad ways, but, in the end, he winds up among the heroes. Is that not extremely difficult? His wisdom and cleverness truly do no shame to those three words Little Zhuge, Young Zhuge Liang, Supreme Strategist.

It was because of an important affair that Little Zhuge came along with Fang Diao. After Lan Xiao had been kidnapped and the army was dispersed, mumbling among them there were some incorrigibly evil ones who rushed to Xiangyang to report to the imposter prince. The imposter thought about what they told him, saying to himself, "I have lost a strong arm even before anything has begun." He called a meeting at the Hall of Gathering Worthies and said, using the royal *we*, "We originally wrote a letter to Lan Xiao asking him to intercept Jin Hui as he came up the mountain and convince him to ally himself with us. If Jin Hui refused, he was to be killed at once, lest he come here to Xiangyang where it would be difficult to get rid of him. I never expected that Lan Xiao would be captured by Northern Hero. What ideas can you gentlemen come up with?"

A venerable gentleman replied, "Jin Hui's coming to harm may not matter. The emperor has just appointed Yan Chasan as Governor of Xiangyang. Moreover, Changsha has now been newly transferred to the jurisdiction of Shao Bangjie. These people intend to watch us like hawks, and we must get rid of them all. Only then will we be secure. There is, in fact, a strategy to kill the 'Three Worthies.'"

The imposter prince was delighted. "What is the so-called 'Kill-Three-Worthies Strategy?'" he asked. "Please tell me the details."

"Jin Hui," the gentleman said "must pass through Changsha. In Ten-mile Ward outside of Changsha Pass is a hostel for officials. We need only send a capable person there to assassinate Jin Hui in the night. If he succeeds, then Shao Bangjie will not be able to continue as Prefect. Jin Hui would have been killed while staying at his place — so how could he, as local prefect, not be held responsible? We will hide the assassin in your palace where we prepare a document welcoming Governor Yan to look into the murder. As Governor of Xiangyang, how can he not handle the assassination of Prefect of Xiangyang? But he will not be able to find the assassin anywhere. The emperor will find it strange and say that he is not a good administrator. By then, even Magistrate Bao himself, not to mention his mere disciple, would find it hard to recover."

The imposter prince laughed loudly. "Marvellous!" he cried, "Marvellous! Send Fang Diao there at once!"

The venerable gentleman — Shen Zhongyuan — was amused and alarmed. The others smuggly recounted his plan, totally unconcerned with its feasibility, and he couldn't help laughing to himself. He feared only the chance that, if the plan actually succeeded, a loyal and good person would be killed. "I'd better go along myself," he thought, and then went forward.

"I beg to inform Your Highness," he said, "that this matter is extremely important. Fang Diao cannot accomplish it on his own. May this humble subject go along to help?"

The imposter prince was even more delighted.

"Time is short," said Fang Diao. "We must mount our horses and go at once or we'll fail."

"Go to our stables," ordered the rebel, "and pick out your own horses."

When the two had finished all their preparations, they returned to the hall to take leave of the imposter prince, who gave them many instructions. They were about to mount up after taking leave when an intimate of the imposter prince came out to tell them, "You must come back soon, whether or not your mission is successful."

Nodding assent, the two mounted their horses and headed off to pack their things — which is how they came to be at the crossroad, their meeting place. Then they split up — one heading east, one heading west, and each went his own way.

Ai Hu, of course, heard it all clearly and saw it all vividly. He rushed back to the inn, paid his bill, and headed straight for Ten-mile Ward outside of Changsha Pass. He touched not a drop of wine the whole way and was sorry only that he couldn't get to Changsha in one great stride.

"*They* are on *horseback*," he thought, "and *I* am *walking*. How can I beat the horse?"

And then he thought, "They have split up going east and west, and they certainly will be taking luggage. Everyone looks for the chance to be lazy, and they will surely sleep at night and go on only during the day. I will walk both night and day — and just as surely I will catch up with them."

"Where there's a will, there's a way" — and, in fact, Ai Hu arrived first. He rested one night, and on the second day went to inquire about the the two assassins. He left the inn and walked around the streets and markets until he came upon a market that was very noisy. On the far side was an official Reception Hall, festooned with flowers. He learned upon inquiry that the local prefect, Old Mr. Shao, was a very good friend of Prefect of Xiangyang, Old Mr. Jin. Since Prefect Jin was to pass this spot on his way to Xiangyang, Mr. Shao had naturally prepared an elaborate welcome. This information cleared Ai Hu's mind and put him at ease. "Yes," he thought, "probably those two are planning some commotion. I will wait in hiding early the day after tomorrow."

"Where did the two of them go?" someone whispered just then, startling Ai Hu.

Ai Hu turned to look at the whisperer, recognized him but could not, for the moment, remember his name: "Who are you?" he asked.

"Second Master doesn't recognize me? I am Jin Jian. You swore brotherhood with my master. You even rewarded me with two ingots of silver."

"You're right," Ai Hu said. "You are right. I forgot about it for the moment. Why are you here today?"

"Oh," answered Jin Jian, "it's a long story. If you have nothing better to do, come into this restaurant and I can tell you the whole thing."

So Ai Hu went with Jinjian to the restaurant on the west side of the road. They picked a secluded table and Ai Hu sat down. Jinjian, himself, refused to sit. Ai Hu urged him to sit, saying, "What need is there for such formality in a restaurant? Sit, so we can chat," Jinjian announced, then sat politely on the edge of the seat. The waiter came by and they ordered wine and food. Ai Hu asked after Master Shi.

"He's fine," replied Jinjian, "he is now with the local prefect, Old Mr. Shao."

"Weren't you two supposed to go to Old Mr. Jin's at Nine Immortals' Bridge? Why have you come here instead."

"I said it was a long story," answered Jinjian, who went on to tell from beginning to end how they had headed for Nine Immortals' Bridge and how the master had gotten sick at You District. "If it hadn't been for the two ingots you gave me, how could we have paid for my master's doctoring?"

"Don't mention these small matters. Please, rather, what happened next?"

Jinjian mentioned the gift of two ingots right away because he was deeply grateful for it and thought about how it had saved him all along the way. "Better to give the hungry one mouthful," goes the saying, "than the rich a bushel."

Next they had run into a lawsuit, continued Jinjian, and his master had wanted to kill himself over it. Fortunately they met up with a Mr. Jiang, who also gave them two ingots of silver, which got them to Changsha.

"What does Mr. Jiang look like?" interrupted Ai Hu.

Jinjian described him, and Ai Hu was overjoyed, recognizing, from the description, his Uncle Jiang.

Jinjian told also how Old Mr. Shao wanted to formalize the betrothal of his daughter to master, so he sent Ding Xiong with a letter to Old Mr. Jin. "The young lady was an imposter," he recounted, "and the betrothal best cancelled — but it was too late. Yesterday Ding Xiong had returned with a letter from Old Mr. Jin, which said that his daughter had taken ill and gone to Tang District to be treated. She was enjoying the moon on a boat when she fell into the water. It was she who was the imposter."

"Which one?" said Ai Hu, surprised, "what is this all about?"

Jinjian then told him about the things he had done with Jiahui. "When Old Mr. Shao saw the letter," he said, "he called for my master and showed it to him. There was also a package. My master called Jiahui and showed her the package, which made her sob uncontrollably."

"What made her cry?" asked Ai Hu.

"The hibiscus handkerchief, the goldfish, and the jade hairclasp. My master, seeing the characters on the handkerchief, asked who had written them. Jiahui said that those on the front were written by her."

"How did Jiahui impersonate the young lady?" Ai Hu asked.

Jinjian told how they exchanged clothes. "So *that's* it!" cried Ai Hu, "And then?"

"Jiahui said, 'The characters on the front were written by this unworthy person. Was it not the master who wrote the ones on the other side?'"

Jinjian explained how this question had prodded the memory of his master, who then recognized Jinjian's hand. "He summoned me at once and questioned me. Then the whole story came out — my secret relationship with Jiahui, about which my master and the young lady knew nothing. He scolded me and then reported everything to Old Mr. Shao, who was delighted and said that Jiahui and I were young and naive, but well-intentioned, and that we had done everything in an effort to help our masters.

"But the young lady was unfortunate and unlucky. From the day she disappeared into the water, Jiahui, grief-stricken, would touch neither food nor drink.

"My master was also grieved. That's why he had me prepare these sacrifices to take advantage of tomorrow when Mr. Shao goes to meet Mr. Jin. The two of them will go to the river's edge to sacrifice into the expanse."

Ai Hu heaved a sigh when he heard this story. What he did not know was that Mr. Zhang's newly-acquired daughter, the one being celebrated in Green Duck Rapids, was precisely Mudan, the young lady they all thought drowned.

Jinjian asked the Little Hero where he was headed, but Ai Hu was reluctant to tell him the truth. He said, instead, that he was headed for Sleeping Tiger Ditch, and then changed the subject.

"I would like to see your master," he said. "Why don't you go and prepare the sacrifices. I'll wait here and then we can go together."

When Jinjian returned, Ai Hu paid the bill, and they headed for the yamen. It was not far, and Jinjian ran on ahead to notify Master

Shi, who was delighted and rushed out to welcome Ai Hu. He took him to the study and they chatted happily.

The next day, after Old Mr. Shao left, Master Shi met with Ai Hu. He apologized for not being able to keep him company, but Ai Hu, knowing of the sacrificial ceremony, did not inquire further. Taking a carriage and several horses, Master Shi, Jiahui, and Jinjian went to the riverside and, all unsuspecting, laid out the sacrificial offerings.

If you want to know what happened, read on.

Chapter 101

A True Beauty Told from a False One;
A Pair of Assassins, Beautiful and Ugly,
Separate Themselves

Master Shi and Jinjian rode on horseback, while Jiahui rode in the carriage. At the riverside, they arranged the sacrifice and changed into plain clothes. All three paid their respects. Jiahui sobbed bitterly, Master Shi wept streaming tears, while Jinjian stood by, comforting them in myriad ways. After the wailing stopped, they burned more incense, looking at the river scene while the incense turned to ash.

In the distance appeared several official boats full of people and baggage. In one boat, a maid servant was seated beside the door to the cabin, inside which was a middle-aged woman and a young girl of about fifteen. There was also a young boy. As the boat approached the shore, its occupants involuntarily looked over and saw Master Shi, with hands clasped behind his back, gazing on the river scene. They saw Jiahui still wiping tears from her eyes with her handkerchief. The young lady looked at them for some time before she said: "Brother, doesn't that woman look like Jiahui?" The madame shushed her at once, saying, "My child, speak softly. There are many look-alikes in this world. If she were Jiahui, that man would be Master Shi."

The young woman said no more, but her bright intelligent eyes stared fixedly.

These three were of the family of Prefect Jin. Madame Jin (Mistress He) was taking Mudan and Master Jin Zhang along with her. She had seen, long before they had, the people sacrificing on the shore, and recognized Master Shi and Jiahui. She had known Master Shi since he was a child, and Jiahui was even more familiar. She faced a grievous dilemma — on the one hand, should the young lady see Master Shi, she would feel very hurt and, with Shi right there, it would be awkward; on the other hand, she dared not rush to acknowledge him because of her husband's temper. That is why she shushed the child with her remark about look-alikes.

The boat went by and Ding Xiong and Lü Qing met it at its mooring. Lü Qing had already returned from Master Shi's place and, recognizing Prefect Jin's family, rushed to serve them. The maids and servants helped them out of the boat, and they took the carriage straight to the Changsha yamen. Old Mr. Jin arrived before long and Ding and Lü went to pay their respects to him. "The horses our master had readied are here. Please use them."

"Where is your master?" Jin asked, laughing.

"He is waiting for you at his residence."

Master Jin took hold of the reins and mounted while Lü Qing steadied the stirrups. Ding and Lü also mounted. Lü led the way, while Ding rode alongside Master Jin.

"When did you arrive in Changsha?" Jin asked. "What did your master say when he read the letter telling him about my daughter's accidental death?"

"I returned in a great rush after several days," answered Ding. "I don't know anything about what happened when my master saw your letter. When you, sir, meet with him, you can find out the whole story."

Master Jin nodded. Ding leaned over and urged his horse ahead. Soon they encountered a group of officials waiting outside Governor Shao's mansion. Lü dismounted, so as to be of service, while Jin and Governor Shao carried out the ritual greetings with great delight. They went together to the hall, where all the officials paid their respects again. Master Jin acknowledged each and every one with a few remarks and then had them leave. The staff dispersed, and the two governors talked a while about how they had missed each other.

When the meal and wine were laid out, the topic of the betrothal finally came up. Old Mr. Shao told the story of Jinjian and Jiahui, and Mr. Jin realized his grave error. The young lady, his daughter, and Master Shi were completely innocent of any involvement. Shao and Jin drank with gusto and chatted extravagantly. After the meal, Old Mr. Jin invited Shao to return to his office, where he kept him company for a long time before his guest took leave and returned by carriage to the yamen.

By this time Master Shi had come back to find Ai Hu missing. Worried, he asked Ai Hu's companion where he was.

"Ai Hu said nothing when he left. I don't know where he went."

Remorseful, Master Shi began to worry that his virtuous little brother had felt deserted and gone off in a huff. "Now where shall I go looking for him tomorrow?"

Suddenly he heard Old Mr. Shao returning to the yamen, and rushed to welcome him. After they greeted each other, Shao went to the East Parlor to rest, instead of returning to the yamen, and Shi sat with him there and heard the story of how Old Mr. Shao had seen Old Mr. Jin that day and learned that Mudan had been rescued and was not dead.

"Your Uncle Jin not only doesn't blame you, he feels great remorse. He wants my dear nephew to go to his place tomorrow to consummate the marriage to Mudan. Then you must return here to pay respects to me. It is only proper."

Master Shi agreed to everything, saluted Old Mr. Shao, and expressed deep gratitude.

Now Old Mr. Jin, back at his big hall, called Master Zhi to him to talk. He talked for so long that Zhi Hua began to fear that the old gentleman was exhausted, so he took his leave.

In fact Master Zhi, who had come along with Jin on this visit, had been attentive every minute of the way. Every night after the others had settled in, he had changed into his night clothes and had patrolled inside and outside several times. That night, too, by the second watch, Zhi Hua had blackened his face and stolen out of the residence to patrol. He had just reached the guard station when he raised his head and saw a human shadow walking ahead. Master Zhi crouched low and stuck his toes into the ground. With a *tu, tu, tu,* he ran along the base of the wall straight to the side room of the east-side chambers of the residence. There he bent over, steadied the point of his foot and, with a *sou!* leaped up to the side room. He looked up to see that the north side room was higher than the others. Without disturbing anyone in this room, he went to the other side to have a look. When he looked opposite him, he saw a person crouched on the roof, his hands holding tight to the rafters while his feet were hooked into the tile duct. He hung suspended, looking down.

"Strange," thought Zhi Hua. "I'll watch him."

Then appeared another, this one short and agile. As he watched, the little fellow pulled out the brick on which the other's foot was resting. As soon as the foot fell loose, the other fellow stood up, found another safe spot for his foot, and got back into his crouching position. He himself did not understand what had happened, but Zhi Hua saw clearly that, during the shift, the little fellow removed the other's sword. Zhi Hua relaxed, though he made a note to watch out for the little one. Suddenly, the crouching fellow rolled down from the main building, rushed forward, and went for his sword, only to find an empty sheath. "Bad," he said to himself and then turned, bumping straight into a flashing sword. He twisted and caught the sword, *kecha*, in his left shoulder. "Aiya," Ai Hu cried, falling to the ground, and someone else cried, "Assassin! There's somebody on the building opposite!" Ai Hu dashed up to the upper room, where he saw the person on the roof jump in one movement over the wall and into the west side room. Ai Hu did not, however, follow him over the wall. Instead, he jumped to the end of the wall, and let himself down from there. Just as he recovered his balance, he felt a gust of cold wind at his ear. He whirled and raised his sword. A *gedang* rang out, and the sparks flew as sword met sword. Someone on the other side cried, "Good! You're agile. We'll meet again. I'll take my leave." Then, with a vigorous step, hardly even touching the ground, the speaker disappeared into the forest.

Ai Hu could not let him off so easily and dashed into the forest after him. There was not a trace of him. Suddenly, a voice spoke.

"Is that you, Ai Hu? It is me, here."

"Master?" asked Ai Hu, delighted and surprised. "Yes, it is me. Where has the thief gone?"

"Caught," answered Zhi Hua.

"Big Brother Zhi," chimed in the thief, "if I, your little brother is a thief, then what about you, Big Brother?"

The thief turned out to be Shen Zhongyuan, Little Zhuge, and Zhi Hua freed him at once and inquired where he was located these days. "At the prince of Xiangyang's," replied Shen Zhongyuan.

"Who is *this* person?" Shen asked, seeing Ai Hu looking at him.

"Have you forgotten, then, Virtuous Little Brother?" Zhi Hua answered. "He is Ai Hu — the young fellow from the residence."

"Aiya!" Shen exclaimed. "Your honourable disciple? No wonder! How true is the saying 'No weak soldiers under a strong general!' How lithe and agile he is. The light and fast way he extracted that sword, the nifty way he climbed that wall — he's really got it!"

"He's good, but he tends to be a little careless. He doesn't think things through. It was lucky that I was in the forest. If someone had set up an ambush here, my little disciple would have been at some disadvantage."

Shen laughed and Ai Hu admired him in silence.

"Honourable Little Brother," asked Zhi Hua again, "What do you do at the prince of Xiangyang's?"

"All the other good spots have been occupied by your brothers. The prince of Xiangyang was the only one left. It's not just a matter of my working hard with no complaint. If I weren't there, who would inform you on the outside about his every move and every action?"

"Your diligence, honourable brother, puts ours to shame," exclaimed Zhi Hua.

"Nonsense. Why talk about superior and inferior? If we cannot reach the rulers to benefit the folk, then we must forget the words 'heroes' and 'righteous men' forever." Master Zhi nodded in agreement, requesting that Shen ask him for help if something important arose. Shen accepted this offer enthusiastically, and they took leave of each other. Little Zhuge went back to Xiangyang.

Zhi Hua returned with Ai Hu to the Jin's residence, where Fang Diao, tied up, was being questioned by Mr. Jin. Fang was relying on raw courage, telling everything fearlessly. Mr. Jin wrangled the confession out of him and then had him put under guard. Later, Zhi Hua took Ai Hu to pay his respects to Mr. Jin. Zhi Hua recounted his story to Jin, who was extremely grateful.

Next day, they called on Old Mr. Shao at the yamen, where Old Mr. Jin told Shao how Zhi Hua and Ai Hu had caught the assassin. Old Mr. Shao had Fang brought in and questioned him briefly. His answer matched his confession of the day before, so he was put under tight security and sent to the district jail to nurse his wounds. Old Mr. Shao asked to meet Zhi Hua and Ai Hu. Mr. Jin also invited Master Shi in to see Shao and he arrived shortly before the others. He greeted Jin, who was embarrassed about his error until Master Shi made a few graciously humble remarks.

When Zhi Hua and Ai Hu came in, Shao greeted them as his guests. Master Shi was thrilled to see the Little Hero and said, "Honourable Little Brother, where did you go off to? I was worried to death."

"How do you two know each other?" everyone asked.

Shi explained how he had sworn brotherhood with Ai Hu.

"I have come this time specifically to go to Sleeping Tiger Ditch to catch the assassin," announced Ai Hu.

"But how did you know that there was an assassin?" cried everyone.

"I spied on the prince's residence and overheard two people talking. That's why I rushed here. I was afraid that if I said anything beforehand, the affair would be leaked. Moreover, I didn't want you to worry, Brother, so I left you there without saying goodbye. I beg you not to blame me."

Mr. Jin felt deep gratitude and everyone was moved to admiration by what Ai Hu had said.

While they were drinking, Mr. Jin invited Master Shi to come at once to his new post and to consummate the marriage to his daughter Mudan.

"Your son-in-law has been away from home for a long time," said Master Shi. "First I must look in on my parents. As soon as I have told my parents everything, I will come to my new responsibilities. How does my father-in-law feel about this plan?" Old Mr. Jin agreed and that was that.

"Can you be planning to return alone?" asked Zhi Hua.

"I'll have Jinjian with me," Shi replied.

"I don't think that Jinjian will be a help. I'm sure you will have no trouble on your return home to report everything to your honourable mother and father. But I fear that getting to Xiangyang will require many days alone on the road, and it is that trip that I worry about."

This remark alerted Mr. Jin, who had been terrorized several times on the road, so he said, "Just so! You, my benefactor, have thought this through most carefully. So what can we do about the situation?"

"There's no difficulty here," Zhi Hua responded. "I'll have my little disciple go along with him, that's all. I guarantee that there will be no incident."

"Little Brother would like to go," Ai Hu said.

"I must trouble you again, then," Master Shi said, "and I am uneasy about this."

"What trouble?" Ai Hu said.

The plans were settled and the women started out first. Old Mr. Jin then bid goodbye to Old Mr. Shao, who insisted on seeing them off. Mr. Jin tried to stop him but finally gave up.

Jinjian had already prepared the horses. Master Shi saw his father-in-law off the first few miles and then returned. When he reached the study of the yamen's eastern courtyard, he found that Old Mr. Shao had already had Ding Xiong prepare the baggage and road expenses, which he now handed over to Shi. As he turned to go, Mr. Shao came out to bid the two of them goodbye, urging them to be careful on the road.

Master Shi and Ai Hu thanked him profusely and kowtowed as they left. They came out of the yamen to find that Jinjian had the luggage ready and Ding Xiong was there to serve them. The three left, heading for Shi Family Village in Changluo District.

Straightening out Miss Mudan's affairs for you has not been an easy job for me. Master Shi took up his post and consummated the marriage in due course — but if I were to tell you all about these unimportant things, the story proper would be delayed. What we must do now is pick up the story from the strategic juncture at which the governor, Old Mr. Jin, mentioned Prefect Yan.

When Prefect Yan started out in advance of Governor Jin, he certainly arrived there way before him. Yan had received endless petitions since he took office, all making charges against the prince of Xiangyang — charges that he usurped land, that he carried off women by force, even that he, without rhyme or reason, had young boys and sickly women hunted up and imprisoned in his home, where he had the boys put on plays and the women trained as dancing girls. That even a single common person should come to such harm would be one too many. Judge Yan handled each case in order and told all of them to return home, not to noise it abroad, and not to hand in any more petitions pressing him: "I will devise a way to capture the prince of Xiangyang and wipe out these terrible grievances for you."

The folk thanked him by kowtowing, and headed home. But, unbeknownst to anyone, the imposter prince had sent a spy with a false petition, and he had found out what Prefect Yan's response was to all the charges. Now, the spy returned to Xiangyang with a report of Yan's intentions.

Read on to find out what happened to the imposter prince.

Chapter 102

🦇

Brocade Fur Rat Visits Skyscraper Hall;
Black Demon Fox Returns to Brass Net Trap.

Now let us tell how the imposter prince, hearing the spy's report, thundered in fury, crying, "We are the uncle of the emperor! Who is Yan that he dare to talk about capturing US and wiping out the grievance of the folk? He talks too big and we are angry. He is a disciple of Blackie Bao, so he treat us with contempt. If he were one of us, this could never have gotten so out of hand. We must kill him somehow. In this way, we can both vent our great anger and also get on with our business." The imposter prince recalled a saying. "'To catch a traitor,'" he said, "'you need two people in collusion; to catch a thief, you need the loot.' It must be that our power has gotten too great and they are beginning to be aware of it at court. I'd best increase the security, and put the treaty safely away, so it doesn't fall into anyone else's hands. If there is no proof, how can we be charged?"

He ordered all the heroes and single men in the Hall of Gathering Worthies to guard Skyscraper Hall round the clock in shifts. Clues and information were to be noted. For unexpected events, the archers and spear throwers were to be called in. A gong would signal any kind of movement. Everyone must give it their all and avoid even the slightest bit of negligence. Yet the imposter prince did not know that he himself was being spied upon. Do you know who that spy was? It was precisely that seeker for first place, lover of victory, and unyielding to all — Bai Yutang — who heard and noted all the prince's precautions.

When Yan had received the seal of office and taken up his responsibilities, he and Mr. Gongsun were pressed with work, and they had had no rest at all of late. More than half of the charges they were dealing with were suits against the prince of Xiangyang. Bai Yutang had made some discreet investigations, and news of this Eight Trigam Brass Net Trap had already reached his ears. At night when all was quiet, he put on his travel clothes, left the yamen, and went straight to the prince of Xiangyang's. He looked it over generally and then leaped over the wall taking great care everywhere. He listened for a long while at the Hall of Gathering Worthies, and then, when it got quiet, he left, climbing over several walls. He finally spied a tall building, which soared up to the Milky Way.

"Imposing," he thought, "No wonder they named it Skyscraper Hall. I think I'll go have a look."

He threw out a pebble to test for solid ground and, finding a secure spot, leaped down and glided forward stealthily. When he got close, he stood up straight and was able to feel the wooden plank wall which had a stone base below and an embrasure above. The embrasure was edged with sharp points and there were three doors which he tried to open without success. He walked to another side, and, sure enough, there were three more doors, whose double leaves were also closed tightly. He walked around all four sides and confirmed that they were alike. He understood then that the name "Eight Trigam" came from the fact that there were eight sides with three doors each, every one of which was locked.

"Not a lucky day for me to have come," he thought. "I'd best go home now and come back another time to see what's what."

He turned to leave and heard the sound of a bell from the other direction. Then he heard the sound of a rattle and knew it must be the night watchman calling the watches. He hid himself quickly behind the shed, cocked his ears, and listened carefully.

Before long he heard the ringing of gongs, which stopped when he reached the shed.

"Old Wang, you ought to be on your way already. Let us all get some rest," someone said.

"Come in and rest. Nothing's happening today. Wasn't it exactly like this the last time we were on duty? Everything was locked tight, so what were you afraid of. Today's just the same. It's a vacation day, a day to be a little lazy."

"You're right," another said. "But the chief has told us to keep tight security. If the gongs don't sound, the chief is bound to make inquiries. Why look for trouble? You two aren't exactly knocking yourselves out. When you come back from the watch, we'll change the guard."

So Wang and Li went off to patrol. Bai Yutang took advantage of the sound of the gongs to get away from the shed. He slunk around the house, lept over the wall, and returned to the yamen. It was already the fifth watch, so he went quietly to his room to sleep.

The next day Yan received Governor Jin's visiting card and saw him immediately. Mr. Jin told Yan how they caught the thief Lan Xiao at Sheer Rock Cliff and that he was now under guard at Sleeping Tiger Ditch. He told also how they had captured the assassin Fang Diao at Ten-mile Ward and that he was now imprisoned in the Changsha Prefecture jail. These two men, he explained, were hard evidence against Zhao Jue and must be sent to the capital. Judge Yan ordered that the emperor be told at once. He wrote a request for the appropriate official to be sent to Changsha to collect Fang Diao and Lan Xiao, and declared that all the towns and districts along the way were to provide the escort guards. Then they were to proceed to Sleeping Tiger Ditch to take Lan Xiao into custody. Not only were the appropriate officers and guards to escort them, Ouyang Chun and Ding Zhaohui were also ordered to make secret preparations to go along. Since Second Brother Ding wanted to return home to check things out, he made a date with Northern Hero to go together to Xiangyang after all the other matters had been dealt with.

Meanwhile, Black Demon Fox Zhi Hua had been idle ever since going with Mr. Jin to take up his post. He left the yamen for a stroll with Zhang Li. They noticed a lovely spot in the northwest, where the mountains were precipitous and the trees luxuriant, so they walked leisurely in that direction. They learned from a local person that the mountain was called Square Mountain. They saw, when they got closer, that there was a temple on the mountain. It had deep red walls, green tiles, and majestic bells. Below the mountain a deep pool wound and twisted, the water crystal clear and rippling. In the pool's cove was a raised terrace, and a stone path, where the Loose Belt Pavilion stood on the spot at which Zheng Jiaofu met the immortal. There were many rooms and floors and, though now dilapidated, with a few repairs the temple could be livable. He wondered whose famous garden this marvellous spot had been.

"What a wonderful place to hide from wind and rain. I have heard that the emperor, has been unwilling to confront the imposter prince openly, but wants secretly to clip his wings. If this were to happen, village braves and righteous men would surely return. And, if the numbers are great, can they all expect to put up at the yamen? I'd better suggest to Governor Jin that this place be fixed up to prepare for the contingency. Won't that be splendid?"

With these thoughts in mind, he returned with Zhang Li and told Governor Jin about the place. Governor Jin agreed whole heartedly and reported to the Prefect, who started on the repairs immediately. Zhi Hua silently praised the straightforward and diligent way in which Governor Jin, working day and night, handled his affairs.

"The imposter prince built Skyscraper Hall and constructed Brass Net Trap," Zhi Hua suddenly remembered. "Last time, when Northern Hero, the Ding brothers, and I came, we were not able to check them out. Right now I have nothing to do, so why don't I go there on the quiet and have a look round?"

"I'm off to see a friend," he told Zhang Li. "I probably won't make it back tonight."

He took along with him his night clothes and his bag of one-hundred tricks. He left the yamen and headed straight for Xiang-yang Prefecture, where he found lodgings and slept. At the second watch he left and, using his skill in flying over eaves and climbing up roofs, he arrived at the base of the wooden wall. He looked carefully and saw that each side had three doors. The doors were opened and closed in different combinations — there were opened ones, closed ones, and ones open in the middle and closed on the sides, open on the sides and closed in the middle; two open doors with the left or right one closed, or one open door and the two on the left or right closed. It was completely different from when Bai Yutang went there investigating. Zhi Hua gave it all his attention, figured out the directions, and came to a sudden realization: "These doors are arranged according to the eight Trigrams: *qian*, the creative; *kan*, the abysmal; *gen*, the still; *zhen*, the arousing; *sun*, the gentle; *li*, the clinging; *kun*, the receptive; *dui*, the joyous.* I'll go in through the main door and see what's what."

Inside was a wooden plank wall — the planks were uneven and of different sizes — with yet more doors. The interior was winding and twisting, and left and right were all mixed up. If you tried to go east, you wound up in the west. If you wanted to go south, you, on the contrary, went north. Moreover, among the entrances, there were true ones, false ones, opened ones, closed ones, all completely different. Among the narrow pathways, throughways, blocked ways, visible ways and secret ways, one was too many.

"Impressive device. It's lucky there's no one hiding here now. If there were an ambush, how would I get out of here?"

Suddenly he heard a sound, as of slapping wooden planks — *geda* — and then something fell down, as if someone had dropped a brick. It all came from near the wooden planked wall. He looked it over carefully, but saw no one. Puzzled, he dared not stop. He continued through the maze, twisting and turning for some time, until he arrived at a door. Hearing a hissing sound, *sou*, he pulled himself out of the way. From over by the planks, came a slapping sound, followed by the sound of something falling. He bent down and discovered a small stone.

"Testing-stones are a trick used by Fifth Brother Bai Yutang. Can he be here?" Zhi Hua thought. "Let me go through this door to see."

He leaned through the door and shot to the side to protect himself from more stones. Raising his head, he saw someone looking left and right.

---

* Adapted from Richard Wilhelm, *Lectures on the I Ching: Constancy and Change* (Princeton, NJ: Princeton University Press, 1979).

"Fifth Brother, Fifth Brother," he called quietly, "it's your unworthy elder brother Zhi Hua here."

"It *is* I, Bai Yutang," was the reply. "When did you get here?"

"I've been here quite a while. I can't bear all those doors. They make my eyes blurr and my mind chaotic. I can't tell one direction from another any more. When did you get here, dear little brother?"

"I've also been here some time. These doors and twists and turns are, indeed, hard to fathom. How shall we get out of here?"

"I was clear as day when I first came in. But, now, I'm totally befuddled. I have no idea which direction to take. What are we to do?"

Then, from over there by the planks, someone addressed them. "No need to worry. I'm here!" They went over and Zhi found, to his delight, that it was Brother Shen outside the door talking to them.

"So, it's Brother Shen?"

"Yes, indeed!" he answered. "Who is this gentleman?" asked Shen.

"He's no stranger. He is our Fifth Brother, Bai Yutang."

After greeting them, Shen said, "Please follow me."

Shen Zhongyuan led the way and the two followed behind. They passed through many more doors before they finally reached Skyscraper Hall, which had tinkling pearl windows on eight sides and jade stone gates all around. In front on one side of the open space was an altar, standing all by itself.

"Let's sit here," said Shen Zhongyuan, "You can observe far off things from this spot, but not close ones." He wiped the platform clean and the three of them sat down.

"Today is my day on duty," Shen explained. "Just now when I heard sounds on the planks, I knew that you had come. That's why I came out to welcome you! It's fortunate that it's me here today. If it were someone else, it would be hard to avoid a big commotion."

"I was just a little anxious," Bai said, "That's why I threw the two stones as a test."

"Don't blame me for telling you all not to come back here

under any circumstances," Shen said. "The intelligence network in the hall is extraordinary. The imposter prince fears that someone will try to steal the treaty, so he has very tight security. Every day someone is sent to guard the stairway — that is the most strategic spot."

"Where is this stairway?" Zhi Hua asked.

"In back of the base of the tower. It looks like a horse track. There is an iron door under the stairs where only one person can fit. If someone comes, they need only set the catch of the rope and wait for the person to be caught. It's difficult to explain in a few words the details of its construction. Older Brothers, return home and warn everyone when you see them that they must not come here under any circumstances. It would be difficult to save them if they were to fall into the trap."

"It's hard to believe that he called it a day after constructing this instrument."

"He's merely waiting for the right time," said Shen. "Waiting for his chance. I have figured out the secret and devised a way to break the catch. As long as the news doesn't get out, I can handle it."

"We depend entirely on you," Zhi Hua said.

"As long as I am here," Shen said, "you've no need to worry."

If you want to know what happened, read on.

Chapter 103

**Patrolling the Residence, Bai Yutang Leaves in a
Huff; Going Against the Stream, Fifth Brother
Seeks the Golden Seal**

Now when Bai returned to his room, he simply could not rest; he
was on pins and needles.

"How come my eye is twitching and my ears ringing?" he
wondered. Tying up the soft pillow and fixing the pouch of stones
to his waist, he looked ready to kill. The whole night he spent
worrying, sleepless. Exhausted by morning and unable to eat, he
sighed long and deeply. He kept rubbing his hands together,
ready for a fight. By evening he was feeling the need to go to
sleep early, but no sooner had he lain down than a thousand cares
and ten-thousand worries pierced his heart. Anxious and ill at
ease, he tossed and turned. Finally, he forced himself to get up,
dressed, put on his sword, and went to the courtyard. Patrolling
the back and front, he walked from the western side to the
eastern. Suddenly he heard confused noises and shouts: "Bad!
The western chamber is on fire!" Bai Yutang rushed over from the
eastern side and saw the fire illuminating the main hall, where
someone was standing. He removed a stone from his pouch and
threw it. The man fell and stood up again.

"This is no good," Bai thought, as the court runners dashed
about shouting "Thief!" and trying at the same time to put out the
fire. Bai saw Yumo giving out orders, so he rushed over to him.

"Yumo, what are you doing messing around here when the
seal is not being protected?"

Yumo awoke to his error and rushed back to the main hall.
One look and he cried: "Aiya! Terrible. The seal is gone!"

Bai Yutang did not take time to inquire into the details. He
turned and rushed out of the yamen, giving chase to two fleeing

men. As he ran, he pulled out stones and threw them, hitting the
nearest man. Then he heard the sound of some kind of wooden
weapon. The man fell down because he had been running too
fast to stop suddenly. *Putong* — he was on the ground eating dirt.
Bai was there in no time and kicked him in the head. The other
fellow returned and raised his bow. Bai crouched low and kept
his eyes fixed on that fellow, who shot off what appeared to be a
secret weapon. Bai squatted and the man came closer. That clever
Bai Yutang deliberately made his hand fly up to his face, which
fooled the attacker into thinking he had wounded him. When he
rushed up, Bai threw out a stone with his right hand. The man
forgot the adage, "You hit with your hand, you protect with
your foot!" and Bai's stone hit him full in the face. With a yelp
of pain, he fled, abandoning his companion. Bai did not pursue
him but headed, instead, for the downed companion. He felt the
box containing the seal strapped to his back and was overjoyed.
From behind came the lights and torches of a whole group of
yamen runners called by Yumo, who had seen Bai go off in
pursuit of the thieves. The runners approached Bai, who was
restraining the thief. They undid the seal box from his back and
tied him up. His face was covered with blood and his cut and
kicked face was swollen badly. The runners picked up the seal
case and took the thief in custody back to the yamen, with Bai
following.

The fire in the western chamber had been beaten down by the
time they arrived. Yan and Mr. Gongsun were both waiting in the
courtroom, with Yumo standing on the side trembling violently.
The figure on the roof had turned out to be a leather doll. The
runners placed the seal case in the courtroom, and, as soon as
Yumo laid eyes on it, he stopped trembling. Then the short, fat,
bloody thief was brought into the courtroom.

"What is your name?" Yan demanded.

"My nickname," he said, speaking in a resounding voice and
not kneeling "is 'Cloud-Piercing Swallow.' But I am also known as
'Crouching Canonball' Shen Hu. That tall fellow, he's called 'Marvellous Hands, Great Sage' Deng Che."

"How is it that the two of you came together?" Gongsun asked.

"Why not? He had me carry the seal case that he stole," Shen answered, and then Gongsun had him taken away.

By this time Bai Yutang had arrived, and he told the entire tale of how he chased them, beat up Shen Hu, and scared Deng Che off with his flying stones.

"In that case," said Gongsun, shaking his head, "we must open the case and have a look before we can rest easy."

"Intellectuals are just so ridiculous," Bai thought, knitting his brows. "There were only a few minutes all together — how could that fellow possibly have removed the seal from the case? If he had actually taken the seal, why would the case still be so heavy? Being thorough doesn't require this nonsense. Well, let him open it up and see. Then I can make a fool of him again!"

"I am a crude person," he said to Gongsun. "I am not as careful or thorough as you are, sir. Let everyone have a look then," he said and had Yumo open the case.

Yumo came forward, undid the yellow wrapping cloth, and opened the cover. He began to tremble violently as everyone looked on.

"Bad, terrible! What ... what is *this*?"

Bai rushed forward to see a shiny black thing in the box. Picking it up, he noticed how heavy it was — it was, in fact, a piece of scrap iron. Anger and anxiety rose in Bai's heart. His face turned ashen, and he thought: "Bai Yutang, oh, Bai Yutang, you thought you were so smart, and now you have been tricked. Gongsun Ce is smarter than you are. How humiliating!"

"No need to feel bad at this point," Yan said, rushing forward to comfort Bai, knowing he would feel a terrible loss of face. "We'll investigate and get to the bottom of it in good time." Mr. Gongsun also tried, in vain, to cheer Bai up. Humiliated and full of rage, Bai was silent and inconsolable.

Gongsun asked Yan to return with Bai to the study while he himself interrogated Shen Hu. Yan understood his meaning and, taking Bai's hand, led him off. Instructing Yumo to put the case away, Gongsun confided in him. "Fifth Master Bai is the most important thing in this matter," he said, "you and Master Yan must keep a careful watch over him. Do not let him leave your side!" Yumo nodded and went straight to the study.

Gongsun then had the runners bring Shen Hu to him. He had the man's fetters loosened, and put on instead handcuffs and footcuffs. He had him seated and entertained him, spoke of friendship and then of proper conduct. Finally, he sympathized: "What a pity that a man like you was so deceived!"

"But I am here under orders from the prince of Xiangyang! How can you say that I have been used?"

"What an honest, straightforward fellow you are!" Gongsun said with a laugh. "Think about it — you and Deng are of the same rank. Why did he steal the seal and you only carry the case? If the seal had been in the case, it wouldn't matter. But he removed the seal without telling you, and now he has gone to take all the credit. You were left behind to get caught with a piece of scrap iron. Don't you see how you were tricked?"

"What do you mean there's no seal in the case?" demanded Shen.

"We just looked — there's only a piece of scrap iron. The seal was never in there. Deng Che removed it and that's why, when you were caught, he didn't even attempt a rescue. He was delighted to go get all the credit himself."

As the truth dawned on Shen Hu, his heart filled with hatred for Deng, and he gnashed his teeth. Gongsun ordered wine and food and dined with Shen, asking him casually all about the theft of the seal. Furious at Deng, Shen confessed everything.

"This whole thing," he said, "was planned by the prince of Xiangyang in his Hall with all of his retainers. He decided that, in order to harm Minister Yan, we had to steal his seal of office. Deng Che, bragging about his own talents, insisted on taking on this job and wanted me to do it with him," said Shen. "I felt that it concerned everyone, and so I ought to help. I never thought that Deng had evil plans. We came last night with no idea where the seal was kept — until we heard Fifth Master Bai tell Yumo to guard it. We were delighted to overhear this, but then Bai told Yumo not to rush off at once in case they had been overheard. So we made sure we could recognize Yumo, and planned to return later. That's why we weren't here until tonight. Luckily Yumo was talking to someone about guarding the seal, and we figured the seal must be hidden right there, where he was, in the inner room of Great Hall. Deng made the human figure and ordered me to set a diversionary fire in the western chamber. And it happened just as we expected — everyone was busy putting out the fire, and, when someone caught sight of the figure on the roof, they were furious! At just that moment, Deng ran in and stole the case, climbed over the wall, and, with me following, left the yamen. When I caught up with him, he handed the case over to me. It must have been when I was trying to catch up that he replaced the seal with the scrap iron. I hate him! He should have told me! If I had known I was carrying a piece of iron, I would have thrown it away and maybe not have gotten caught. He deliberately set me up! How hateful!"

"What did they plan to do with the seal?" asked Gongsun.

"The prince of Xiangyang told us that, if he could steal the seal, he would throw it into Perverse Spring."

"Where is Perverse Spring?" Gongsun asked, hiding his alarm.

"It's in the mountains surrounding Cave Hall Lake. There is one spring there whose water flows in the wrong direction, and it is unfathomably deep. Once the seal is dropped in, it can never be recovered."

The meal was over and Gongsun had found out what he needed to know. He had someone guard Shen Hu while he went to Yan's study to report. Yan was alarmed, but said there was nothing to be done. "Where has Fifth Brother gone?" asked Gongsun, looking around the room and not seeing Bai Yutang.

"He just left. He said he was going to his room to change and would come right back."

"Ai! You shouldn't have let him go by himself," Gungsun said and told Yumo to rush to Bai's room to tell him to come at once to discuss something urgent.

Yumo returned in a short time. "I spoke with Master Bai's servant," he reported. "He said that, after changing his clothes, his master left, saying he was returning to the study."

"This is bad news," Gongsun said, shaking his head. "Fifth Brother has gone, and, unless he recovers the seal, he will not return. If he doesn't get the seal, I truly fear that something terrible will happen."

"I should have had Yumo go along with him," said Yan in great anxiety.

"He was determined to go. Even had you sent Yumo with him, he would have gotten away. I originally planned to have a talk with Fifth Brother to figure out how to retrieve the seal. I didn't think he would have slipped off already. But there's no point in worrying over it now. We'll make some discreet inquiries and wait for him to come back."

From that day forward, Yan was fidgety and restless. He had no appetite, and all day long he waited anxiously for night. Once night came, he waited anxiously for dawn. Five days passed, and still no trace of Bai. Yan was beside himself, sighing and groaning and speaking incoherently. Thanks to Gongsun, who comforted and soothed him in myriad ways, he managed to take care of a little official business.

On that fifth day, the worker in the outer room came to report that five officials had presented visiting cards. Gongsun was delighted to read the names of the Southern Hero, Zhan Zhao, and Lu Fang and his three brothers. He informed Yan, who suggested inviting the visitors into the study at once. The office worker withdrew, followed by Gongsun, who went along to bid welcome and exchange commonplaces. It was Jiang Ping who noticed right away that Bai Yutang had not come out to greet them, and he began to turn this over in his mind. When they reached the study, Yan got down from his bench to greet them.

"We humble men have come here on imperial orders to do your bidding. We have come particularly to work under you," Zhan Zhao said.

"You have been commissioned by the emperor," Yan said, unwilling to accept their humility. "Moreover, you work for my own teacher in his yamen — how could I possibly treat you as subordinates? Please be seated. We'll just perform the informal greeting."

The five men thanked him for allowing them to sit. Yan was obviously distressed and flushed in the face.

"Where is Fifth Brother?" Lu Fang asked right off.

This question made Yan hang his head in silence. His face got even redder.

"It's a long story," Gongsun said, helping out, and then he told them everything that had transpired starting with Deng Che's theft of the seal five days ago. "Fifth Brother left that day without telling anyone. He still has not returned."

"Then Fifth Brother must have run into some trouble," said Lu, pale and alarmed.

"What trouble?" Jiang Ping hastened to interject. "It's just that he felt embarrassed because the seal was stolen, so he went off to be by himself somewhere. Don't worry, Big Brother! Once the seal is recovered, he'll be back. May I inquire, sir," he asked Gongsun, "do you know anything about what happened to the seal?"

"We know where it is — but it would be very difficult to retrieve."

"What do you know about it then?"

Gongsun retold Shen Hu's story, and, when he had finished, Jiang spoke. "Since we know where it is, we must go get it right away. How can any magistrate be without his seal, his credentials? There's just one thing — since the prince of Xiangyang sent some-one to steal the seal of office, he will certainly send someone to inquire about the reaction, lest it bring him trouble. We must prepare for that. Tomorrow, Big Brother, Second Brother, and I will go to Perverse Spring and retrieve the seal. Brother Zhan and Third Brother will stay here in the yamen on guard. The daytime will be no problem, but you must be on your guard at night."

Having settled on this plan, they drank and dined, but there was no way to avoid this unpleasant topic and they hardly en-joyed the meal. Afterwards they took their rest, Zhan in a room he had all to himself, Lu and his three brothers in three rooms where they and their servants slept.

Zhan, sleepless and having nothing in particular to do, went to Gongsun's room for a chat, and, when Jiang Ping showed up too, they sat down facing each other.

"As I see it," Jiang whispered, "this time Fifth Brother's expedi-tion is likely to end badly. I steered them off the subject before, because Big Brother has a big heart, but a simple way of thinking. Third Brother can be impetuous and rough around the edges. After we leave tomorrow to get the seal, Mr. Gongsun, you must give some acceptable explanation in front of Yan. By nightfall, Brother Zhan, you must keep a close watch. My Third Brother is not reliable. Moreover, don't under any circumstances say anything about Fifth Brother's chances. If Fifth Brother does come back while I'm gone, I beg you both to tie him up. Don't let him leave again. If he doesn't return, you'll just have to wait till we get back from Perverse Spring to work out another plan." Gongsun and Zhan nodded, agreeing to everything. With these last instructions, Jiang turned and went back to his room to rest.

The next morning Jiang, prepared with his underwater clothes, headed straight for Perverse Spring with Lu and Han. Jiang Ping feared that Big Brother Lu would be frightened by his underwater activities, so he left him at Gold Mountain Temple.

"Big Brother, this spot is not far from Perverse Spring. I'll just change here. You can wait here and watch my clothes and bundles." He removed his clothes, folded them neatly and put them in the bundle, then changed into his swimming gear. He and Han Zhang headed for the spring.

Brother Lu picked up the bundle and went into the temple to have a look around. It turned out to house five spirit figures. He placed the bundle on the sacrificial table and went back outside to sit on the doorsill and enjoy the scenery.

If you don't know what happened next, please read on.

Chapter 104

❦

Rescuing the Country Woman, Spilling Beans; Meeting a Brave Hero, Seeking News

Now, when Lu Fang went back outside to look at the scenery, he saw a woman running toward him and calling out "Help! Help!" She ran straight into the temple and Lu was about to question her when he saw another person in a soldier's uniform obviously chasing the woman and shouting nonsense. This enraged Lu. With a slap of his hand and a kick of his foot, he brought the soldier to the ground. Lu stepped on his chest and demanded: "What do you mean by chasing after this good woman? Explain!" He raised his hand as if to slap the soldier, who replied quickly.

"Don't be angry, old sir. I'll tell you the truth. My name is Liu Libao. I've been a small chief of the fourth rank in the stockade of Prince Zhong of Flying Fork. The other day the prince of Xiangyang sent someone with a container in which were the remains of some hero. They said the man's name was Bai Yutang. The prince feared that someone would try to steal the remains, so he gave them to my master. My master said that this Bai fellow was a good friend and righteous man, so he buried the remains under the Five Peaks of Nine Part Pine. Today he sent me again, this time with sixteen Louluo carrying sacrificial implements, so that we may pay respects at his grave. But I got left behind because I had to go relieve myself. That was how I ran into this woman. I figured that I could take advantage of her, a woman all alone in this deserted place. I just wanted to have a little fun — I didn't have any intention of harming her. That's all there is. Do you understand, sir?"

Liu watched Lu carefully as he told him the story. Lu Fang had become dazed and silent as though he had lost his mind and forgotten why he was there. He had not heard any of the last part of the explanation.

"Does this fellow have some condition? I'd better make my escape right now — what am I waiting for?" Liu thought.

He rolled out from under Lu's foot, raised himself, and ran to catch up with the Louluo. When he got there, everything was ready for the sacrifice — they were simply waiting for him to arrive. He explained nothing, but went straight to the sacrificial altar and knelt. Everyone shouted: "We have come at our master's request. We have come because we have heard that the dead man was a good fellow. Come, come, come, everyone pay respects — it is the right thing to do!"

As they all knelt and knocked their heads on the ground, Liu Libao gave a loud sob and began a great wailing.

"Paying respects is appropriate," thought everyone else. "But what's all this wailing about?"

Liu not only wailed, he cried over and over, "Master Bai, oh Master Bai! We have come to pay respects under orders from our master. I almost was destroyed in coming here. If it hadn't been for the divine manifestation of your spirit protecting me at that moment, I would have been murdered. Aiya! My dear, holy, spiritual Fifth Master Bai!"

Those who heard Liu wanted badly to laugh. They went forward to help him, barely stifling their laughter. They had all expected to have a big feast of food and drink after the sacrifice was over, but, considering Liu Libao's grief, they merely packed up the things they had brought, and got ready to leave. Some complained bitterly that they had gotten nothing nothing for such a hard day's work. Others were puzzled — who had angered Liu so badly that he came here to let it all out? No one could figure out Liu's behaviour.

Liu Libao had sharp eyes and saw, in the distance, several hunters approaching with weapons. He knew this boded ill, and he slipped away down a small pathway. The Louluo, carrying the sacrificial implements, could not stop the hunters from smashing everything and making a great noise. Two of the attackers, one carrying a club, the other a pitchfork, approached the Louluo and asked where Liu Libao was.

"Master Lu and Second Master Lu," one of the Louluo responded, since he was acquainted with the hunters. "What do you mean by this? We would not dare to do anything to offend you. Why did you smash all our things? How can we explain this to our master?"

"Never mind asking me," the one with the club said. "I'll ask you — where is Liu Libao?"

"He ran off long ago down a small pathway. What do you want with him, sir?"

"Great," the one with the club said sarcastically. "So he ran off and left you all behind to go home and ask your master if there is a custom here in Cave Hall Lake of plundering good women! Moreover, he dared to accost my wife — why?"

The Louluo now understood what Liu had done. His great sobbing must have been about that.

"Master Lu, Second Master Lu," they said entreatingly. Don't be angry. We will tell our master about this when we return, and he will deal severely with Liu. Truly, we had nothing at all to do with it."

"Dear Brother," said the man with the pitchfork to the one with the club, who still wanted to fight them, "don't hurt them, if only for the sake of our long-term relationship with Prince Zhong." Then he said to the Louluo, "It's only because of your master's position, that we don't kill you all. Go home. Tell your master all about Liu's evil doings. And make it clear to him that we don't get excited over nothing. We'll let you go for now." The Louluo started for home, heads hung in shame. The two hunters were actually brothers-in-law. The one with the club was Lu Bin; the one with the pitchfork was Lu Ying. The fleeing woman we met a moment ago was Lu Bin's wife. Lu Ying was her little brother. Expert in the martial arts, she went into the mountains often to hunt. She was doing just that when she spied this group of the mountain brigand's Louluo going up the mountain. She hid herself, fearing to be seen, and waited till they went by before she went down the mountain intending to return home. As luck would have it, she ran right into Liu Libao who was muttering nonsense. Mistress Lu pretended to be afraid and tried to mislead him so that she could hit him with her poisoned arrow to prevent this from happening again. But, unexpectedly, she saw Lu Fang sitting in front of the temple and was embarrassed to carry out her plan. She simply cried out "Help! Help!" and let Lu kick Liu to the ground. Mistress Lu then ran home and told her husband and brother, who came with sharp swords and four hunters to vent their anger on Liu Libao. Learning that he had long fled, Lu Bin and Lu Ying went in search of Lu Fang instead. They looked first in the temple and discovered only a bundle on the sacrificial table. There was no person in sight. They ordered the hunters to search the area.

"Here!" one of them called out from behind a tree. Lu and Lu rushed to the spot, where they found Lu Fang — a swarthy-face, covered with whiskers and beard, a formidable figure with a lofty air about him. They could not help admiring this imposing specimen of a man, and they rushed forward to thank him.

"Thank you so much, dear benefactor. We are eternally grateful to you for saving my wife. May I inquire as to your honourable name?"

From the minute Lu Fang heard Liu's tale about Bai Yutang, grief had pierced his heart and his senses deserted him. He had left the temple and entered the forest, all in a daze. The Lus' words suddenly awakened him and, taking a deep breath, he regained control of himself. But he refused to tell them his name.

"It was nothing," he said evading the question. "Nothing worthy of mention. Please."

The two men did not wish to press him since he was reluctant to tell them his name, so they invited him to their village for a thank-you feast. "Someone is waiting for me at the bottom of the mountain," he responded, "so I can't really stay any longer. I'll come visit another day." With these words, he waved goodbye, turned, and headed for Perverse Spring.

It was nearing evening, and, as he walked along, he saw the light of a fire up ahead. Coming nearer, he recognized Han Zhang standing there staring at the flames.

"Second Brother! What's up?"

"Fourth Brother went down twice already. He said the water was extremely deep and extremely cold, penetrating to the marrow. He cannot stay in too long, so I made this fire to warm him when he comes up and also to illuminate the water so he can see down there. Why don't you find a firm spot to stand on and look down into the water."

Lu Fang secured himself on a rock and looked into the spring. He could see the crystal clear green water swirling around, rolling waves rising up. That chilly air truly pierced flesh and bone. Lu Fang could not stop himself from shivering.

"Terrible! Terrible! How can Fourth Brother bear such icy water? His life is more important than finding the seal! Oh, how can this be? How can this work out? Fourth Brother, oh, Fourth Brother! Come out now, whether you've found it or not. I can't bear it." As he said this, his body was wracked by a violent trembling — even his teeth chattered with a loud noise. Fearing some mishap, Han rushed over to Lu and led him to the fire.

"Big Brother, you stay here by the fire. Fourth Brother will be up soon." But Lu refused to budge. He stood there, his eyes staring fixedly down into the water.

After a while there was a rippling in the water and Jiang Ping shot out for a moment, only to be sucked back under by the whirling waves. He flipped back and forth several times and finally managed to grab hold of the rock and pull his body out. Han Zhang extended his hand and pulled backwards with his full strength. Finally Jiang Ping began to rise. Han Zhang helped him over to the fire.

"Awesome," said Jiang after quite some time. "Awesome. Without the light of the fire, I would have been totally confounded down there. I'm exhausted from being thrown around by the water."

"Fourth Brother," Lu said "the seal is important, it's true — but don't go down there again."

"I won't go down again." He stuck his hand into his water gear and pulled out the seal. "Why would I go down again since I've got the item?"

"You three sirs, the deed is done — let's be happy, keep it, and celebrate."

Lu Fang looked up and saw that it was none other than the Lu brothers-in-law.

"Why have you two returned so soon after leaving?" asked Lu Fang.

"We were very uneasy," Lu Bin said, "when you told us you were coming here to Perverse Spring, so we followed you secretly. We did not know you had come on this matter. That fellow's really talented — no one else would dare go down this spring."

Han Zhang asked Lu who these two fellows were and was told the story of what happened at the temple. Jiang took his time to remove his underwater clothes and said, "Big Brother, I'm really cold. Do you know where my clothes are?"

"Aiya! I put them in the temple! What shall we do? You wear my clothes, okay?" and he started pulling off his shirt.

"Don't," Jiang stopped him. "How could I possibly take your clothes? I'd best go back to the temple to get my own."

"Please put this on, Fourth Master," said Lu Ying, handing Jiang the shirt he had already removed. "We've already had your bundle taken to the village."

"Also, it's late now," Lu Bin added. "Please, all of you, come to our humble village for a rest. You can leave tomorrow morning, okay?"

"Where is your honourable village?" asked Jiang, seeing that they could no longer refuse to go.

"It's only two miles from here, and it's called Chen Outlook — that's our home," answered Lu Bin. The five men left Perverse Spring and headed for Chen Outlook.

It really was not far. Soon they saw many lanterns and torches coming to greet them. The lights illuminated a fine village, which was very spacious and orderly and revealed quite a large population. The travellers entered the gate and went into a large reception hall, extremely spacious and bright. Lu Bin had Jiang's bundle brought out so that he could change his clothes. The table was laid in a trice, and everyone was seated and began exchanging names. The Lu brothers-in-law had known of the heroes for some time, but had had no way to become acquainted. On that day, they did not know how adequately to pay homage to these men.

"My brother and I have known of this 'seal' affair for a while. Five days ago one of the prince of Xiangyang's men came here — his name was Lei — and told us about the theft of the seal. We were shocked that he had thrown the seal into the spring before coming to see us and we reprimanded him severely. He began to regret what he had done, but, alas, what's done is done, and there was no way to undo it. After he left here, we were all terribly worried about Governor Yan. We never thought that someone, Fourth Brother Jiang, could have such a talent. We are truly in awe!"

"Please, please don't mention it," Jiang said. "May I ask, does this Lei fellow have the single-syllable name of Ying? Was he from Eight Jewel Village, about two and one half miles from the yamen?"

"That's it. He's the one. How do you know him?"

"I've just heard of him, never met him in person."

"Brother Lu, may I ask you," Lu Fang said, "is there a Five Peaks of Nine Part Pine?"

"There is. It's in the southern part of the mountain. Why do you ask?"

Hearing the place name confirmed, Lu Fang began to cry. He told them what Liu Libao had said about Bai Yutang and began a terrible sobbing. Shocked and alarmed, Jiang and Han feared that Lu Fang was unable to deal with such grief and glossed over the story. "This is probably a rumour," said Jiang, "no truth in it at all. If such a thing had really happened, how come there wasn't even a whisper of it at the governor's? I think it's all a lie. I'll look into it thoroughly when we return tomorrow."

"Don't be grieved," urged the two Lus following Jiang's lead. "We two have heard nothing about such a matter. How can you be sure it's not rumour? Fourth Brother Jiang will get to the bottom of this — then we'll know the truth."

Lu Fang accepted their words. After all, it was his first visit to the home of these new friends, and it would be inappropriate to cry his heart out there. He controlled himself while Jiang Ping changed the topic by asking the brothers what they did for a living.

"Some villagers fish and some hunt, and the two of us evaluate the catches and fix the market prices."

Han, Jiang, and Lu were delighted by what they heard. These men were clearly of a calibre with the Ding brothers.

The meal over, they all retired, but how could the three sworn brothers sleep with so much on their minds? They rose at the fifth watch and took their leave of the Lu brothers, departing from Chen Outlook to go straight to Governor Yan's yamen, not daring to dally along the way. They met with Yan and returned the seal to him. Yan and Gongsun were delighted and grateful beyond words. Needless to say, Yumo was secretly thrilled and took care of them with abundant energy.

"Have you had any word at all from Fifth Brother?" asked Lu Fang.

"Nothing at all," answered Gongsun.

"From the looks of it," Lu said, sighing deeply, "Fifth Brother must be dead!" He then told all present what Liu Libao had said, and, before he finished his story, Yan began sobbing.

"No need to upset yourself," soothed Jiang. "I am going right now to inquire and see what's what."

If you want to know what happened to Bai Yutang, please read on.

❦

Chapter 105

Third Visit to Skyscraper Hall;
Yutang Comes to Harm

Now Jiang Ping rushed straight to Eight Jewel Village to find Lei Zhen and make inquiries about Bai Yutang's whereabouts. As luck would have it, Lei Ying was at home and he and his father came right out to greet Jiang. Lei Ying first thanked Jiang for having saved his father; then Lei Zhen invited Jiang to the study for tea. After an exchange of pleasantries, Jiang asked if they knew anything about Bai Yutang.

"It is truly terrible to tell," Lei Zhen said, and then he described in detail exactly what had happened. Jiang Ping was choked with sobs as he heard the story. Even Lei Zhen dropped some tears.

This part of the story is hard to tell; I cannot bear telling it, yet I must tell it. Do you know what actually happened to Bai Yutang? From that day when he changed into travelling clothes and secretly left the yamen, he put up at a little temple. It was, in fact, little Celestial Order Temple.

"Bai Yutang," he said to himself, "your noble name has known fame for a generation — yet in the end you have fallen into someone's trap. How infuriating and shameful! Someone has dared to steal Magistrate Yan's seal, how can I not dare to steal the imposter prince's treaty of alliance? Last time Shen Zhongyuan told me about the horrors of the Brass Net Trap, but he merely spoke in general terms. He really didn't know the details. Probably it is simply a matter of making a big fuss over something that's merely a bit unusual. How can we really know anything about it? But I have my own resources. I have a body-full of martial arts — I can handle it. If I can get hold of the treaty, then I can memorialize the emperor. If I were to bring the imposter prince down, then who need worry about the seal?" The more he thought about it, the more pleased he was with himself.

By the second watch that night, he had reached the wooden wall. Since it was his third visit, he was already familiar with the gates and windows and was totally unfazed. After careful consideration, he finally decided to enter through the *kan* gate. Frustrated after trying a few doors without success, he took his all-purpose rope from his bag of tricks. Any time he was unable to gain entry somewhere, he merely had to throw up a piece of all-purpose rope, secure it firmly, and enter without even trying to find a door or a window. This happened several times in a row and he was delighted and emboldened by his success.

"What has his dubious trap to do with me, Bai Yutang?"

He jumped over several walls before he spied Skyscraper Hall. As he rested on a stone, he mused: "Last time, Shen Zhongyuan mentioned that the stairway was due north. Why don't I go have a look?"

Following the stone base, he circled around to the stairway — indeed, it resembled a horse track. But, just as he was about to go up, he heard someone call out: "Who's there? I'm Zhang Hua, Sick Elder, here," and a sword came swishing at him. Bai Yutang ducked and the sword sliced the empty air. Zhang Hua continued slashing forward, but, tripped by Bai's foot, he and his sword fell to the ground. Bai pressed on and grabbed the sword.

"This guy must be quite strong," he thought as he felt the weight of the sword. "Otherwise how could he use such a clumsy, heavy thing?"

What Bai Yutang did not know was that ever since Northern Hero had stripped Zhang Hua of his old sword he carried this thick-bladed, sharp one, extremely heavy. His only consideration was sturdiness; he ignored the fact that it was too heavy for him to handle. Since he had not needed to use this sword even once to confront anyone, he never realized, until just then, how tiring it was to carry the thing. Today, unexpectedly hearing someone coming up the stairs, he rushed forward, thrashing the sword about. Fortunately Bai was quick and ducked the sword, which, because of its own weight, carried Zhang Hua forward with it.

Bai tripped him and he fell, dropping the sword as you would expect.

Bai took the sword and laid it down on Zhang Hua's throat — and here you have the advantage of a heavy sword. With no effort at all, the sword, by virtue of its own weight, slit Zhang Hua's throat with a searing noise.

"The interesting thing about a heavy sword," thought Bai "is that you really can conserve your strength while murdering someone."

He did not know, however, that below him, near the iron door, was another person. It was, in fact, Little Plague Xu Bi. Having seen Zhang Hua lose his life, he stealthily went through the iron door and waited there in ambush for his man.

Bai Yutang could not know that he was there. He grasped Zhang's heavy sword and, seeing no one near the staircase, went up to Skyscraper Hall. He looked up from the railing — how very high it was! Since the stairway had no door, he searched the window sills on all eight sides for a way to enter, but found none. Suddenly impatient, he slid his sword along the seam of the window and began prying it open; he was delighted that it opened in no time at all. Holding fast to the sill with his left hand, he pushed out one of the leaves of the window with his right. Putting the leaf gently down on the ground, he could see bright lighting from inside the hall, though he had no idea from where it emanated. He dug out a small stone from his bag and threw it into the hall, cocking his ear to listen. The stone rolled along, as though on wooden planks, then stopped. Relieved by this, Bai raised himself up to the lentil, lowered his sword to test the floor — which was, indeed, wooden — then lightly jumped down.

Inside the hall now, he tiptoed stealthily toward the lit area — there were more of those octagonal windows through which he could see even brighter lighting.

"There is probably an ambush here," he thought "but, since I've already come, there's no reason not to take a look."

He again used the heavy sword to pry the window open slightly. The ease with which it opened surprised him. Bai Yutang raised his eyes and looked around. There were, in fact, a number

of lights arranged in a globe down below that were shooting rays
upward. The light shone straight onto the central roof beam. And,
tied securely with a cord, was a small embroidered case.

"So it's here after all," he thought. But these words had not
even left his mouth before he felt a movement beneath his feet.
He threw off the heavy sword and had just started to turn around
when he heard "ker plunk" and the rolling boards turned over.
"Bad!" he said, as he sank downward and felt pain everywhere to
the very marrow of his bones. By that time there were sharp
knives piercing his body from head to toe, and there was not a
piece of whole flesh anywhere.

Suddenly there was a tumultuous sounding of gongs and
voices shouting in confusion: "There's someone in the brass trap!"

Among them was one person who shouted loudly: "Shoot the
arrows!" and the arrows resounded in the ears like a host of flying
locusts, a sudden and violent rain. It looked as though a porcu-
pine had gotten caught in the brass trap and was unable to move.

"Stop the arrows!" the person ordered again.

The bows and arrows went down and rifles were raised.
The rabble lit torches and looked into the trap. They saw something soaked and dripping with blood. All four limbs, not to
mention the face, were indistinguishable. Little Plague Xi Bu was
extremely happy with himself. He ordered the arrows removed
from the body, but they were so full of blood and flesh that it was
difficult to look on. When they finished pulling the arrows out, Xu
Bi had someone raise the pulley to lift up the trap. But, when he
stepped forward to look in, that heavy sword fell straight down,
neither crooked nor slanted, but right onto Xu Bi's head, chop-
ping his skull into two equal parts, one mouth split clean into two
halves, one side saying "Ai!" the other "Ya!" and, falling over
backwards, he gave up the ghost.

Everyone rushed to the Hall of Gathering Worthies at once, not
daring to delay. By this time the imposter prince knew that someone had fallen into the trap. They were discussing it when a
runner came to report: "We don't know who it was who fell into
the trap, but a heavy sword flew out when the trap was lifted and
sliced Xu Bi in half."

"We never expected," the imposter prince said "that, in catching someone in the trap, two of our own brave men would die. Who can this person be? We shall go have a look."

When they arrived at the brass trap, the imposter prince ordered that the corpse be taken out, but it was already a bloody pancake and impossible to recognize. Someone standing nearby spied the bag of tricks and asked: "What is this thing?" He picked it up to have a look — the heavy sword had protected it from harm. Shen Zhong- yuan, recognizing the bag, was secretly overcome with horror: "Fifth Brother, oh, Fifth Brother, why didn't you listen to me? Now you have met this terrible death! Oh, how tragic for all of us!"

"Lord Prince," Deng Che said "what a great joy this is for you. This person is none other than Brocade Rat, Bai Yutang, who created that big stir in the capital. No one but he uses stones like this. He is no less than Yan Chasan's right-hand man."

The imposter prince was delighted. He had the corpse put into an earthenware container and sent the next day to Military Mountain where the burial mound was to be guarded by Zhong Xiong. What Liu Libao had said on the previous day had turned out to be true.

Jiang Ping could not help sobbing loudly upon hearing this grievously-told tale of Bai Yutang. Lei Zhen, standing by wiping his own tears, comforted him for a long time. Controlling his grief, Jiang asked: "Revered Little Brother, I beg you to tell me what is being planned now at the imposter prince's. I trust you will not hold anything back."

"Although the imposter prince plots rebellion," Lei Ying answered "he spends his days frolicking with male singers and dancing girls. He is one who loves music, women, and profit. But what he is obsessed with is the destruction of Magistrate Yan Chasan. Only that will make him happy. Please, sir, go back and tell the magistrate that he must take care day and night. Also, if you have any use for me, I guarantee that I will happily do anything you need me to do."

Jiang expressed deep thanks, took leave of Lei Ying and his son, and returned to the yamen.

"When I return this time and see Eldest Brother, I must do such and such," he thought. "I must force myself to make him purge himself all at once of his grief to prevent his dwelling on it until he becomes sick. That would be terrible! So this will be my strategy ..."

After a short while he reached the yamen. The minute he entered the main hall Yumo came out. Jiang asked him hurriedly where Magistrate Yan was and learned that he was in his study with everyone, expecting Jiang. Jiang nodded, turned into the second hall, and looked toward the study. First he let out a great and loud crying and sobbing: "Aiya! It's terrible! Someone has killed Fifth Brother! Oh, how cruel was his death!"

He entered the study still crying in this manner. He extended his hand to Lu Fang and took hold of him: "Eldest Brother, Fifth Brother is really dead."

Lu Fang passed out on the spot when he heard the news. Han Zhang and Xu Qing rushed over to support him and everyone wailed and sobbed. Zhan Zhao, standing nearby, was grieved as well, but he tried to comfort the others. Unexpectedly, Yan Chasan, on the other side of the room, opened his eyes wide, called out "Oh, dear younger brother," rolled his eyes, and fell over backward. Luckily Gongsun Ce was able to catch him. Just then Yumo rushed in and went to him at once, screaming wildly. By this time the study had become a veritable mourning shed, with people crying and shouting, all rushing about in one spot. What a task it was to make Lu Fang purge himself of his grief so that all the others could feel relief. Zhan Zhao went over to look after Chasan who, fortunately, was beginning to come to. This bout of wailing and sobbing was truly unbearable. Although Zhan Zhao and Gongsun Ce were also grieved, there was nothing they could do at this time but comfort the others in a hundred different ways.

Read on to find out what transpired.

Chapter 106

☙

Mr. Gongsun Disguises Himself as the Governor; the Master Schemer Plots and Schemes

Now when Zhao, Prince of Xiangyang, saw the seal imprinted on the document, he interrogated Deng Che.

"It must be mischief on the part of the one who disposed of the seal."

The imposter prince summoned Lei Ying and questioned him also.

"Where did you take the seal when I last entrusted you with it?"

"I went, on your secret orders, and very carefully threw it into the bottom of Perverse Spring. I observed, moreover, that water whirled madly there and was ice cold. Why do you ask, Lord Prince?"

"Since you threw the seal to the depths of the spring, why does the document we just received today have the seal's imprint on it?" Zhao threw the document to the floor so that Lei Ying had to bend down to pick it up. He saw the seal imprint bright and shiny — no doubt about it. He was scared speechless.

"Some would say," Zhao shouted angrily, "that you are doing mischief with the seal. You'd better confess it all now."

"I truly did drop the seal in the bottom of the spring! How would I dare to play tricks? May I ask the prince, who told you this?"

"It was Deng Che," the prince answered.

Lei Ying was stirred to hatred by this and conceived a marvellous plan.

"So, it was Deng Che," Lei Ying said sarcastically. "May I inform Your Excellency that I was just beginning to have my suspicions about this matter. I was thinking that the governor is a disciple of

Magistrate Bao and is exceptionally smart. Moreover, he has many talented men serving him at the yamen. How could he have so lightly let someone steal his official seal? He must have hidden the genuine seal and reproduced a false one, the one stolen by Deng Che. Deng thought he had achieved an incomparable feat of great merit. Who expected that the real seal would show itself today and not only render useless all my efforts but also bring on my head a serious grievance. How can I not be aggravated to death?"

Lei's words stunned the imposter prince and shamed Deng Che. But shame turned into anger, and Deng shouted with fury: "Aiya! The Great Yan Chasan! You dared to make a fool of me! I know now that we cannot both live on the same earth."

"Brother Deng," Lei said, "don't be in such a hurry. I was just speaking theoretically. Since you yourself were able to switch the scrap iron for the seal, why can't you believe that they could have switched the fake seal for the real one? At this point, I think we need to sit down and discuss it."

"Discuss what? What is there to discuss? The only thing for me to do is kill the governor and vent my anger. Nothing else is worthy of discussion. Those of you with courage, follow me!"

"I'll go with you happily," Shen Zhongyuan said at once. The imposter prince was delighted and called for food and wine in the Hall, where everyone celebrated.

After the first watch, Deng Che and Shen Zhongyuan changed their clothes, took leave of the imposter prince, and went straight to Yan's yamen. They decided along the way that Deng would do the killing while Shen stood guard. But, when they reached the yamen, Shen disappeared. Deng looked all over and saw no trace of him. Where had he gone?

"He was just chatting with me," he muttered to himself. "How could he have disappeared so quickly? Oh, right! He's always been a cowardly fellow. He brags at first, but he's never there for the showdown. So it all depends on my talents! After I succeed, I'll give him a good tongue lashing."

He jumped over the wall, entered the yamen, and looked around for the right room. He saw a brightly lighted study on the eastern side, so he crept stealthily and noiselessly over to the study window. He moistened the window paper and peeked in — the governor was sitting and turning the pages of his reading thoughtfully. Although dressed in everyday clothes, he was still imposing and very proper looking. But not even Yumo was there to serve him.

"From the looks of it," Deng thought, "he is a fine minister devoted to serving the country. I really shouldn't kill him, but I am very anxious to get in good with the prince by doing something for him, so I simply must."

He went over to the middle door, which had four leaves and was locked. The middle two leaves were closed tightly. He lightly shook it, but it was a vertical bar. He took out his sword and inserted it in the space between the door and the molding, meaning to break the bar with some force. He pressed the spine of his sword and ran it along with his right hand, pushing the door so that a crack appeared in the bar and it fell to the ground. Pressing the sword down again, he pulled it out and put it in his mouth while he used his hands to open the leaves of the door, pushing one in and pulling one out. It made a slight noise and then came open. He grabbed hold of the sword, sent it through the door first, and then followed, crouching. He went straight to the curtained eastern room, used his sword to part the curtain, and, with a battle cry, rushed into the room. As he raised his sword, he heard a creaking sound and knew he was in trouble. He turned and fled. There was a clamouring noise and then someone called out, "Let go, Third Brother. It's me!" Something crashed, and someone came out in pursuit.

Do you know why Deng left almost as soon as he came? While he was prying open the bar, Second Master Han was watching him carefully. He saw Deng push open the door and bring down his sword even before he had gotten his balance. Han, knowing Deng would head there, had then rushed immediately to the western room. Although Deng moved swiftly to lift the curtain with his raised sword, he was still a step behind Han, who had just lowered it. Deng, using his sword to clear the way, took a look in the lighted room, turned with a stomp, and left, sweeping the table-top candle-lamp to the ground on his way out.

At this time Third Master Xu Qing was lying in bed, barefoot and fast asleep. He felt someone bite his heel and woke with a start. He leaped to the ground and grabbed Han in a stranglehold, which was when Han called out "It's me!" and moved away, slipping in the process on the candle that Deng had thrown on the floor. He lost his balance and fell flat on his face with a loud *plunk*!

Who would have guessed that it was not Yan seated there reading cases, but Mr. Gongsun. He had slipped out before Han had entered, leaving Xu there. Han, fearing that Xu would grab him in the dark, saw his bare feet, and thought it best to bite him to wake him up. When Han got away, Xu tried to go in pursuit of Deng, but he fell almost at once. He picked himself up and ran out, making a clanking noise.

Han chased Deng. He climbed walls and followed closely, but Deng disappeared. Han looked all around, left and right, and was just wondering what to do when he heard someone shout, "Big Brother Deng, Big Brother Deng, you can't hide behind that elm tree. Go hide behind the pine."

Prompted by these words, Han looked around carefully and saw that there was, indeed, an elm tree and a pine tree.

"Who was that?" he wondered. "He was definitely trying to tell me that Deng was hiding behind the elm." Then, asking himself why he was still standing there, he went straight to the elm tree. But Deng had already run off, so Han set out in pursuit. He was practically neck to neck with him, but simply could not catch up.

"Big Brother Deng, Oh, Big Brother Deng, run, just keep running," someone called out again. "Beware of secret weapons!"

This remark was made by Shen Zhongyuan as a warning to Han to beware of Deng's metal arrows.

"Just so!" thought Han, reminded by these words of his own weapons. "I'm pretty close to him now — why don't I use a secret weapon to hit him? That friend really sees things clearly from where he stands." He loaded his crossbow, lowered his head, and shot the arrow — there was a *ceng* as he threw it, a *pa* as it hit, and the cry of "Aiya!" from the victim. Han knew that the thief had been hit, so he was even more loathe to let go.

"Bad," Deng thought, feeling a numbness in his back after his shoulder was hit by the arrow. Suddenly he felt a terrible sensation. "This must contain poison." He ran a few more miles but began to feel a fluttering of his heart, dizziness, and blurring of his vision. He collapsed on the ground. Han, knowing that the poison had already done its work, took his time walking over.

"Second Brother," Han heard a loud wailing behind him. "Second Brother, are you up ahead of me?"

"Third Brother, I am here," Han answered, recognizing Xu Qing's voice, and, before he knew it, Xu reached him.

"No wonder that fellow told me you were headed northeast in pursuit — he was right. Where is the thief?"

"He's already been downed by my poison arrow. But who was that person helping us on the sly? It was thanks to him that I was able to get the thief."

They reached Deng Che, who was lying on the ground struggling to get up.

"Brother, help him up. I'll carry him." Han lifted him off the ground and Xu carried him all the way back to the yamen. On the way, they were greeted by lights and some of the yamen runners. They helped with Deng and headed home.

Mr. Gongsun was waiting in the hall with Lu Fang and Jiang Ping. They asked Han to report on what had happened, and were delighted by his words. Soon Deng was carried in. Han prepared a powdered antidote to the poison and pulled out the arrow. He smeared half of the antidote on the wound. Mr. Gongsun called for bonds and fetters to be put on Deng while they waited for him to come to.

"You-named-Shen," he shouted angrily after quite a while. "You were supposed to be here to help me. But you did nothing but harm me. Fine! Now I'm furious!" Deng let out an "Aiya," opened his eyes, and saw four or five people seated around him. The room was lighted as bright as day. He tried to move, but he had no strength at all. He looked down and saw fetters on his wrists and feet. He thought about it and remembered that he had succumbed to a poison arrow, had become confused, and then must have been captured. At this point in his thoughts, his insides seem to turn over, and everything rose up in his throat. He opened his mouth, gave a loud sob, and threw up a great deal of green fluid and saliva. Though his heart was beating wildly, he understood clearly now what had happened. He closed his eyes and uttered not a word.

"Old Buddy Deng," he heard someone call into his ear. "Feeling better now? You and I are brave Chinese — definitely not kids. We always speak the local tongue. If you are truly brave, drink up this warm wine. If you are suspicious of us, then I won't force you."

"Who are you, may I ask?" he said, seeing the thin, weak-looking fellow kneeling beside him with a bowl of hot wine.

"I am Jiang Ping and I've come expressly to bring this drink to you — do you dare drink it?"

"So," Deng smiled, "you are 'Overturning River Rat!' You have really cut me to the quick with your words. You've caught me — since I don't fear swords and axes, why should I fear wine? I will drink it even if it's arsenic or some other poison. Do you see a trace of fear in me?"

"Good friend, you are truly up front," Jiang responded and brought the cup to his lips. Deng opened his mouth and drank it down in one swallow.

"Buddy Deng," another came over and said, "though you and I are not well-disposed to each other, we still believe in the same principle — loyalty to our leader. Why don't we have a chat?"

Deng raised his head to look and recognized none other than the man who had been impersonating the governor sitting in the study reading cases.

"I guess he's not Governor Yan," he concluded. "It looks like I've fallen into their trap."

"May I inquire who you are?" he asked.

"I am Gongsun Ce," Gongsun answered and pointed to Lu. "This is 'Penetrating Heaven Rat,' Big Brother Lu Fang. That is 'Piercing Earth Rat' Han Zhang, Second Brother. And, over there, is 'Boring Mountain Rat' Xu Qing, Third Brother; there's also 'Imperial Cat' Zhan Zhao, who is in the back room guarding Governor Yan. We've already sent someone to bring him in. He'll be here momentarily."

"I've heard of all these good friends," Deng said. "I've longed to meet them, longed to meet them. Since you are being so kind to me, I will just enjoy myself."

Jiang helped him over to the table, which he reached with a whooshing clatter. He did not pretend humility, but just sat down and watched as Zhan Zhao came into the room with hand extended.

"Deng, my good friend, I haven't seen you for a long time."

Deng Che had heard of Zhan Zhao long ago and had nothing to say in response but "Please sit down." Zhan sat after greeting his colleagues. The servants brought the wine and, at this point, there was nothing for Deng to do but raise his cup in a toast, pull back his head, and down the drink.

"Is the governor sleeping well tonight?" Gongsun asked Zhan.

"He's a little better, but he misses Fifth Brother terribly and cries himself awake from dreaming." This news brought tears to Lu Fang's eyes again and prompted Xu Qing to stand up, open wide his eyes, and rub his fists together.

"You named Deng, how did you kill my Fifth Brother? Tell us at once."

"Third Brother," Gongsun hurried to add, "that matter has nothing to do with our friend Deng. Stop blaming the wrong person!"

"Third Brother," Jiang intervened, "that whole trap was planned by the imposter prince. And, we all know that Fifth Brother was always trying to outdo everyone. He himself fell into the net, so how can you blame someone else?"

Han Zhang also tried to stop Xu. Zhan, aware that Gongsun wanted to question Deng thoroughly, feared that Xu would mess things up so that they would not get accurate information from him. He created a diversion by calling for more drink. There was nothing Xu could do about it, so he returned to his seat in a silent rage.

After Zhan poured the wine, he and Gongsun alternated questioning Deng about the prince of Xiangyang. Deng was actually a rustic person and, seeing that these men treated him as a friend, he told them everything truthfully — against his better judgment.

"The man the prince of Xiangyang relies on is his bodyguard, 'Flying Fork' Zhong Xiong. If you can capture him, then the prince will have a hard time." It was lights out by the time Gongsun had finished questioning Deng. Someone took Deng to the office and stood guard over him. The others returned to their own rooms to rest.

"I need to discuss something with the three of you," said Lu to his three younger brothers on the way to their rooms. "Fifth Brother has met with this terrible calamity — can it be that we will just leave his remains there on Five Peaks of Nine Part Pine? I would like to collect his remains and take them to his ancestral home. How do you all feel about it?"

"That's exactly what we should do," they answered in unison. "We also felt that way."

"I'll take my leave then," Xu Qing said abruptly.

"Where are *you* going?" Lu asked him.

"I'm going to steal Fifth Brother's remains."

"You can't go," Lu said, shaking his head.

"You're too impetuous," Han added. "We must discuss how to handle this."

"As I see it," Jiang said, "since the prince entrusted the remains to his bodyguard Zhong Xiong, he is clearly being extra careful. If we don't plan this out with great care, I fear that we will make a blunder of it — that would not be pretty."

"You are absolutely right," Lu said, nodding in agreement. "So, how should we go about it?"

"Big Brother, you're not in good health right now — no need for you to go. Let Second Brother go in your place. Third Brother is impetuous and rash — this job cannot be compared to the usual kind of bold attack we make — I'd better go in Third Brother's place. You won't be alone here. So, Second Brother and I will go to help each other. What do you think?"

"Fine," Lu replied. "That will do it."

Xu Qing looked at Jiang Ping, but said nothing.

The servant laid the table and they sat down to eat.

"Dear younger brothers," Lu said, "when will you start out?"

"No need to rush there," Jiang replied. "If we start the day after tomorrow, it will be time enough." Having decided on the plan, they began to eat.

In due course, the remains of Bai Yutang were successfully recovered, but not without the capture of Zhan Zhao, Southern Hero, by the imposter prince, and the clever rescue by Jiang Ping. As for details regarding the marvellous strategy used to depose the imposter prince and behead him with the dragon-head guillotine, the gathering of the heroes and gallants and their oath of brother-hood — all of these affairs are described in exciting detail in the story *Five Little Heroes.*

The lyric says it well:

Day after day, deep cups filled with wine,
Morn after Morn, garden blooms do start.
One sings and dances with joy-filled heart
Care free and unrestrained, from men apart.
How many spring dreams does history permit?
How many people on earth uncommonly smart?
Plotting and scheming, an unnecessary art.
Accept what comes at each new day's start.